Also by Stephanie Kane

Blind Spot (A Jackie Flowers Novel)
Quiet Time

EXTREME INDIFFERENCE

STEPHANIE KANE

SCRIBNER

NEW YORK LONDON TORONTO SYDNEY SINGAPORE

SCRIBNER
1230 Avenue of the Americas
New York, NY 10020

Copyright © 2003 by Stephanie Kane

SCRIBNER and design are trademarks of Macmillan Library Reference USA, Inc.,
used under license by Simon & Schuster, the publisher of this work.

For information regarding special discounts for bulk purchases,
please contact Simon & Schuster Special Sales at 1-800-456-6798
or business@simonandschuster.com

Designed by Colin Joh
Text set in Schneidler

Manufactured in the United States of America

1 3 5 7 9 10 8 6 4 2

Library of Congress Cataloging-in-Publication Data

Kane, Stephanie.
Extreme indifference/Stephanie Kane.
p. cm.
1. Women lawyers—Fiction. 2. Denver (Colo.)—Fiction.
3. Trials (Murder)—Fiction. 4. Teacher-student relationships—Fiction.
5. Women college students—Crimes against—Fiction. 6. Law teachers—Fiction.
I. Title.

PS3611.A769E98 2003
813'.6—dc21
2003045841

ISBN 0-7432-4556-3

ACKNOWLEDGMENTS

Special thanks to Jed Mattes, Susanne Kirk, Mary Ann Kane, Susan Brienza, Jill Vincent, Bob Gorski, Joe Cabrera, Carbon 42, and those members of the learning disability community who so generously shared their stories.

For Leslie

EXTREME INDIFFERENCE

A person commits the crime of murder in the first degree if . . . [u]nder circumstances evidencing an attitude of universal malice manifesting extreme indifference to the value of human life generally, he knowingly engages in conduct which creates a grave risk of death to a person, or persons, other than himself, and thereby causes the death of another.

—*Colorado Criminal Code,* §18-3-102(1)(d)

"Isn't this where they found that woman's head?"

"Relax," he told her. "You're with me."

The girl pretended to shiver, and he slipped his free arm around her waist. She snuggled closer and he smiled to himself.

Spring break had come early, but Left Hand Canyon remained untouched by the official change in season. In their shaggy winter coat the foothills held no appeal for the hikers who would dot the trails once the days lengthened and penstemons and Indian paintbrush burst into bloom. Here the grade was steep, the terrain rugged, and the snow that streamed down the gutters in Boulder clung to the walls of the canyon like cascading ice.

He glanced in the rearview mirror. They'd left the lights of the valley behind, and when the SUV in front of them finally turned, they were alone. He slid his arm from her waist and let his hand drop to her knee.

"Where are we going?" she asked.

"We're almost there."

She moved his hand to her lap and tugged her skirt across her knees.

"Isn't this where that CU girl was raped?"

"That was lower down, at a picnic spot. And they caught the guys, remember?"

"I don't *like* it here," she said. "Can't we go back?"

As he negotiated the sharp turn onto gravel, the wheels spun and he held his breath. It was his dad's car and being towed would mean a lot of explaining. Or, worse, being grounded. And if she saw that DEAD END sign . . . They gained traction and he slowly exhaled.

He'd scoped this spot in daylight, but now nothing seemed familiar. A log house under construction loomed to the left and his hands tensed on the wheel. No pickup trucks—the workers had knocked off for the day. Two hundred yards later a dirt drive led to a finished dwelling hidden in the trees. At the cul-de-sac the gravel ended. He pulled onto the berm and switched off his engine.

"You said you'd show me something neat."

He reached for her but she slapped his hands away. Just hard enough to show who was the boss. He leaned back in his seat. Plenty of time. No need to rush. After a moment, he gave her knee a conciliatory squeeze and this time she let his hand remain.

The cul-de-sac was framed by forty-foot pines and the wind carried a sharp scent. He felt the girl slide toward him on the seat. No resistance as he slipped his hand under her sweater, but when he reached behind to unhook her bra she suddenly twisted away. Before he could react she jumped out of the car.

"Is this what you wanted me to see?"

She pointed to a barbed-wire fence with a metal sign: PRIVATE LAND— NO ACCESS TO NATIONAL FOREST. But her tone was light, more teasing than bitchy. Offended that he'd read her so well—or simply prolonging the chase?

As he followed her through the shadows to the clearing at the edge of the cul-de-sac, his feet sank in soft mountain gravel. Past the fence the terrain was studded with moss-covered boulders, and towering trees shielded the ground from snow. A trail hugged the hillside beyond the barbed wire, and a small cabin across the ravine, perhaps a quarter mile away, was barely visible in the twilight. The scent of pine was strong, the only sound the wind rushing down from the Continental Divide. He looked up at the first stars emerging in the inky sky.

"They're brighter here," he said. On cue, a full moon began to rise.

"It *is* beautiful," she agreed, and gave a little shiver. Now that he was playing by the rules, she no longer had to pretend she was angry. As he came up behind her and drew her close, he knew she'd forgiven him for his busy hands and the earlier scare. Emotional contact, isn't that what they said? A little of *that* went a long way. . . . He led her through a break in the fence to a stand of trees. The branches sheltered them from the wind and the ground underneath felt warm and dry. Relaxing in his embrace, she let him pull her to the fragrant carpet of pine.

"I wish we'd brought a blanket," she murmured as he began kissing her throat. The needles were springy and it wasn't until she stiffened that her words registered. He stopped fumbling with his belt.

"There's one in the trunk." Would she make him use the backseat of the car?

"It's okay," she said. Knowing how primed he was, just wanting to see how far he would go to please her. As she reached for his fly he forgave her. He would have forgiven her *anything*.

"What's that?" she whispered.

The sound seemed to come from a long way off. From the direction of the ravine.

"Nothing," he lied. A small animal, maybe a fox, certainly not worth stopping now—

"There it is again!"

The thrashing was closer, interrupted by branches cracking underfoot. It was coming from the trail on the slope to their left. Did foxes drag their prey? The girl sat up and quickly buttoned her blouse.

"It's nothing," he said, to reassure himself more than her. Heavier than a fox, maybe—a cougar? But the gait was all wrong. As he zipped his fly, he tried to remember where the break in the fence was, how far it was to the car. He heard a dull clank, like metal across rock.

In the moonlight he saw it.

From the trees lurched a naked figure, a dark slash at its throat. Its feet were hobbled—was that a *chain*?—and steel gleamed dully at the wrists. It stumbled, landing on all fours. Now he saw the other end of the chain was threaded through a ring attached to the back of the neck. As it struggled to regain its balance it stared directly at him. From the gaping mouth came an unintelligible whimper, but the eyes issued an unmistakable plea.

Help.

Rising on bare feet, the apparition held out its hands in supplication, revealing a ghostly V from hips to pubis and pale lines from collarbone to breasts. Only then did he register the chestnut hair, matted and looped in a knot halfway down the back, and the silver rings on three slender fingers.

A girl, not much older than they were.

And now he recognized the pattern made by those ivory bands of skin. Bikini marks, he thought, she's a CU coed who just spent spring break in—

Ignoring the shrieking behind him, he moved to catch the girl as she pitched forward. He caught her and she began to jerk so violently she almost slipped from his grasp. Something rigid encircled her throat, forcing her chin up and holding it at an unnatural angle. She was so thin, so *cold*—

"Get the blanket!" he shouted.

He heard the crunch of gravel and his trunk pop open. As he eased the girl to the mat of needles, still warm from his own body, her chest fluttered frantically. The handcuffs sliced into bruised and swollen wrists. Her eyes were wild, almost feral. Jesus, where was the blanket? His gaze dropped to the band of leather at her throat.

The babbling sounds were getting fainter. He clawed at the metal studs, tried to undo the buckle, then gave up when he realized he had only succeeded in tightening it.

"Who did this to you?" he cried.

She jerked her chin in the direction of the ravine. The gesture brought fresh pain to her eyes and suddenly they were human again.

"There . . . ," she whispered.

Then she passed out.

One

Jackie Flowers's lizard pumps pinched unmercifully as she clattered up the granite steps to the office she shared with other lawyers on Denver's former Millionaire's Row. A chunk of gingerbread trim loosened by the recent snow chose that moment to dislodge itself from the porch, narrowly missing her honey-blonde head. The Gothic Victorian mansion was no refuge for the wicked, she thought sourly, and wondered whether she was thinking about the robber baron who'd built the place or her own clients. Her favorite arsonist's preliminary hearing was days away and more than the roof was coming down around her ears.

The only traces of the blizzard three days earlier were patches of slush that had evaded the relentless Colorado sun. March was notoriously fickle and the heat had been on full blast at the county jail. The richly paneled foyer was cool in comparison. Jackie ignored the unsorted mail on the hall table and began climbing the stairs to her second-floor office.

"Where do you think you're sneaking off to?"

Pilar Perez was standing at the reception desk in the ground-floor alcove, where she'd been deep in conversation with the latest temp. In black fedora, silk vest, and tailored slacks, Jackie's investigator managed to look both stylish and comfortable. The temp was already imitating the way Pilar held her cigarillo.

"The landlord's notice is waiting on your chair," Pilar said. If there were any way to make the sanctity of Jackie's office less appealing, it was to remind her that the building's lease was about to run out. "How's Ted?"

"How do you think? He's facing the big bitch." Catching the shocked look on the temp's shiny face, Jackie added, "Habitual Criminal Act: life with no chance of parole. And all because they caught him with a Stanley Wonder Bar stuffed down his pants."

"Ice cream?" the temp asked, and Pilar rolled her eyes at Jackie behind the girl's back. Had either of them ever been that young?

"No, sweetheart," Pilar said. "That's a pry bar, the savvy burglar's tool of choice. Costs you five bucks but you don't want a knockoff. The cheaper ones are too blunt to file."

"I thought Mr. Wolsky was charged with burning a warehouse," the girl said. She was interrupted by a bellow from above.

"The Xerox crapped out again!"

Cliff, the estate planner from across the hall. *No will too small to earn your trust.* Suddenly Jackie longed for the jail's controlled chaos. Taking advantage of the distraction, she slipped off her pumps and continued up the stairs. If she could just make it to her office and close the door—

Cartons stacked in the stairwell slowed her progress and Pilar caught up with her. The stocky investigator had run track in high school and had the legs to prove it.

"Thirty days before the lease is up," she said.

"Afraid we'll be out on the street?"

"We should be so lucky." Pilar's nostrils quivered faster as she stared first at the worn Oriental runner on the stairs, then jerked her chin up like a hunting dog. "What is that *stench*?"

The maroon-and-peach-striped wallpaper, a tribute to the robber baron's Victorian taste, smelled like a closet full of old sneakers. A mossy stain in the shape of the continental United States was migrating down the wall like Baja California. Jackie beat a quick retreat to her office.

"We've got to get out of this place," Pilar said after closing the door behind them.

If it's the last thing we ever do.

Jackie balled up the landlord's notice and lobbed it at her wastebasket.

Sinking in her chair, she began massaging a stockinged foot. Her aunt always said you could go anywhere in a good pair of shoes—how right that was! God knew you couldn't show up at the county jail and expect to see your client before hell froze over if you dressed *comfortably*. As the cramp in her instep slowly worked itself out, images of Cliff's ongoing war with the copier and the moldy wallpaper receded into the more soothing sight of her leather-bound treatises and immaculate desk.

"By the way," Pilar said, "you look lousy. Forget lunch again?"

"I grabbed something on the way to jail." Not true, but it would do.

"Your blood sugar looks low. You should be eating fruit."

Fruit was Pilar's latest kick. For each cigarillo, an apple; for every martini, an orange or a pear. Jackie had tried telling her fruits were carbohydrates, but Pilar swore she'd lost five pounds without sacrificing anything she cared about.

"What are those cartons?" Jackie asked.

"Phil's moving out."

Right into Pilar's trap.

Phil was the pots-and-pans lawyer across the hall, who specialized in breaking prenuptial agreements. No matter which side of the case you were on there was always money in those. Jackie was in no mood to be reminded that Phil carried the lion's share of the overhead. "Ted's prelim is Friday, and I—"

"You could have hung out your shingle years ago. There'll never be a better time to set up an office of our own, where—"

"—the ceiling doesn't drip and the walls don't stink. We'll talk about it after I pull another rabbit out of my hat for Ted."

Some clients were more equal than others.

Ted Wolsky had been shuffled to Jackie's desk her first day at the Public Defender's office. A burglar who wore Italian loafers on his elfin feet and shied from residences because he didn't want anyone to get hurt, he'd stuck with Jackie after making the transition from second-story man to the more challenging work of arsonist for hire. And the loyalty ran both ways; even in his new trade Ted only torched empty buildings. But with two felony convictions he was about to strike out and go away for good. The big bitch, as lawyers and their clients called it.

"You think Ted's good for the warehouse fire?" Pilar asked.

"Frankly, no. It's not up to his usual standards."

"Standards?"

"Whoever did it splashed gasoline on the walls. Pros don't waste their time."

Jackie's bond with Ted was more basic than loyalty. She remembered the first time she'd interviewed him. He'd skimmed the consent form, then scrawled his signature with a flair worthy of a quill pen. It was the odd flourishes that gave you away. . . .

"What were you and the temp jawing about when I came in?" she asked.

Pilar plopped into the seat across from Jackie. "Amy Lynch."

Jackie didn't really want to hear anything more about the CU coed's abduction and apparent torture. For some reason, hearing about Amy Lynch made her think of Lily, her nine-year-old neighbor. Lily still believed in her own invincibility. Amy was young enough that she had probably felt invincible too. Not now, though.

"Has she talked yet?" Jackie asked.

"Still in a coma. Combination of shock, exposure, and swelling of the brain."

"You hate to think of a guy like that loose in the foothills."

"The *News* said she had scars all over—" Seeing Jackie's expression, Pilar backed off. "It's a miracle she survived."

"What a shock to that high school kid who found her."

"Teach him to take a girl necking in Left Hand Canyon. I'd say it made him grow up pretty fast."

"Too fast," Jackie said, reminded again of Lily.

"And did you hear she was wearing a dog collar?"

"Enough!"

"Of course, with a daddy like Bryan Lynch, you never know who the real target was. . . ."

Without many hard facts, reporters had been pushing the heart-string angle. From soccer and cross-country skiing to homecoming queen and Habitat for Humanity, the Kent School grad had it all on her résumé.

"How did Lynch make his pile?"

"Real estate. Or was it securities?" Pilar shook her head, eager to move on to something more tantalizing. "Now, no one's supposed to know this, *but* . . ." Pilar's sources were never wrong. "They traced the handcuffs."

"Handcuffs?"

"They had a serial number."

"And?"

"They belong to Glenn Ballard."

"The *federal judge*?"

"How do you like them apples?" Tossing her boss a Red Delicious she had taken from her pocket and polished, Pilar was gone before Jackie could say another word.

Two

"Come on, Pete," Jackie said. "Drop the bitch."

"No can do," Deputy Assistant District Attorney Peter Parker said.

It was two days before Ted Wolsky's preliminary hearing and Jackie was in the prosecutor's office.

"What difference does it make?" Parker asked. He reached into his top drawer and popped a piece of candy into his mouth. "Sooner or later he's going up for life."

Parker's office was barely large enough for the gunmetal desk and a small bookshelf among whose sparse contents Jackie recognized the *Colorado Jury Instructions* and *Criminal Code.* His coat hung from a hook on the back of his door and the blotter on the desk did double duty as a calendar. His framed certificate of admission to the bar and a photograph of him with an owl-eyed judge administering his oath when he became a deputy DA hung on the wall behind his desk. They were flanked by photos of a hugely pregnant young woman and an older couple. Parker's wife beamed and his parents wore the same horn-rimmed glasses as the earnest young man standing with his mouth open and his hand raised.

"What have you got?" Jackie asked.

"You saw the forensic report, didn't you?"

No, she hadn't. According to Pilar, it had been lost in the maw of the temp's In basket.

"I want to hear it from you."

"They found a shoe print at the warehouse. A very small print. Prints are like pictures, Jackie. They never lie."

"Sounds flimsy to me." Jackie was under no illusion she could talk Parker out of the big bitch; the arson was the real prize. "And juries love Ted. Twelve citizens good and true just might talk themselves out of a verdict."

Parker chewed more rapidly, and Jackie followed his gaze to the brown paper lunch bag on the windowsill. It was not yet noon, but ADAs hit the courtroom at 8 A.M. on hearing days, and running through a dozen files could work up quite an appetite. The compact lump at the bottom of the sack and the rounded bulge at the side identified the probable contents as a pear and a rather ungenerous sandwich.

"Don't forget Ted's Wonder Bar," he said. His eyes dropped to her trim knees and Jackie wondered whether his wife had put him on more than one kind of diet. She was glad she'd worn sheer silk hose.

"Wait till they hear there was no burglary. . . ."

Parker sneaked another piece of candy from his desk. Chocolate, she guessed from his contented look, and caramel from the way his jaw massaged the treat. As the wadded foil pinged off his metal wastebasket's rim, Jackie politely looked away. On the wall opposite the window hung a framed copy of an abstract print with thousands of squared-off dabs in varying shades of green. Was it famous? Maybe. From the way Parker's chair was positioned, she could tell he stared at it. A lot.

"And speaking of shoes, what kind of shoe print was it?" she said.

"Didn't you read the report? Size 6AA."

What other arsonist had such elfin feet? Did men's shoes even come in that size?

"I mean the brand."

"It was a tennis shoe." Parker squinted at her—because he'd traded his horn-rims for contacts, or because he was confused? "I sent a photo with the report. Didn't you see it?"

Should she admit the package had been lost? Her eyes strayed to the art print. She tried to discern a pattern but the scheme appeared random. Then she caught a glimpse of a path through a woods with a light flickering at the end. A window? As she tried to hold the image constant, the background and foreground suddenly reversed. She had almost missed the cabin for the trees. Which did Parker see—the subject or the setting?

"Where's the video?" she asked.

"Video? What video?"

"Come on, Pete. The one the cops take after every bust to show no rough stuff occurred."

"But you didn't file—"

"Consider the demand made here and now. And I want a complete set of every photograph and police report relating to the crime on my desk by eight o'clock tomorrow morning. If it ain't there, I'll move for a continuance. We both know how Judge Mueller appreciates a hole in her docket." That should take care of whatever had been lost. "So that's all you have, a sneaker and a crowbar?"

Parker may have been frustrated, but he was nobody's fool.

"And an arson. How are you going to defend that—hire another expert?"

Touché.

He was referring, of course, to a case the previous summer that his boss had lost. But maybe he had something there. . . . Accepting the jab gracefully, Jackie shifted in her chair and treated him to another view of her gleaming legs. Maybe she should get a job on Fox News. They liked short skirts and legs on that channel.

"Why, Pete, you can't expect me to reveal *all* my secrets."

"We've expected great things from you. No one in my office thought they'd see you defend a guy who keeps a Stanley Wonder Bar in his pants and can barely light a match!"

How the mighty had fallen.

"Given your low opinion of my client's abilities, I assume you'll have no objection to his remaining out on bond. He's staying with his mother."

"Where else would he go?" Parker could afford this concession. With Ted's immediate freedom secured and a strategy for defending him beginning to emerge, Jackie wanted to distract him from second thoughts. "Did you hear about Glenn Ballard?"

"That handcuff story's all over town," he said.

"Personally, I can't imagine a federal judge—"

"And I thought you black hats were the cynics!"

"Tell me how a guy like Glenn Ballard abducts a coed from a crowded bar in Boulder—"

"—Finnegan's Wake—"

"—and nobody sees a thing."

"Ketamine."

"The dog tranquilizer?"

"And date-rape drug." Even for a DA, Parker's tone was infuriatingly smug. His gaze flitted to the art print and Jackie suddenly realized he'd hung it too close to his desk to see the cabin *or* the woods. Its appeal could only lie in a multiplicity of tiny squares that added up to nothing. How like a prosecutor to find comfort in that!

"Any evidence?" Jackie pressed.

"Of ketamine? Heard it on the grapevine."

"Bull. All traces vanish within hours. Amy Lynch wasn't found until—"

"Whoa! You're not representing him, are you?"

"Of course not. Unless they come up with more evidence, Glenn Ballard will never be charged." Why was she speaking up for a man she hadn't seen in years? Jackie wondered.

"Well, I don't know why you're so touchy," Parker said. "Didn't you go to law school up in Boulder? Ballard must have been on the faculty back then. You must know what a prick he is."

Only the brightest among you can hope to survive. I fear that you, Ms. Flowers, are not among their number.

"There's a world of difference between a prick and a pervert."

"Did you read that decision of his in January?"

"I'm a little behind on my advance sheets."

"Ballard upheld the tax on Internet porn."

"That hardly makes him a pervert," she said. "Just the opposite. His ruling must have cost pornographers millions. Besides, isn't he next in line for chief?"

"Chief judge is a function of age and seniority. In the federal system you can't be older than sixty-five when your term begins, or serve for more than seven years. When Simon Clark steps down in August, it'll be Ballard's turn."

"Exactly my point. Why would any man in his position jeopardize a lifetime appointment, much less when he's finally about to be made chief?"

Parker chuckled.

"Federal judges sit at the right hand of God, and ambition doesn't stop once they're appointed to the bench. Or become chief. That just ups the ante."

Did he truly believe Glenn Ballard was capable of torturing a coed? Or was Parker now regretting his agreement to let Ted remain on bond?

"Don't be fooled by that ruling on porn, Jackie. He who protests loudest has the most to hide."

Three

"Too good to be true, if you ask me," Pilar muttered before Cliff shushed her and turned up the volume on Jackie's TV.

The camera swept past an elementary school and up a tree-lined boulevard to a stately brick Colonial on a corner lot. The clematis covering the picket fence was not yet in bloom, but the gabled dormers were straight out of a storybook. The lawn had been well tended over the winter, with regular watering to ensure perfection when the first blades of grass began to sprout. Denver's exclusive Hilltop was green in more ways than one.

"What are you watching?" Jackie asked. She'd returned from lunch to find the entire office crowded around her twelve-inch television set.

"The Lynches' press conference," said Joel, the social security lawyer who took immigration cases on the side. "Five will get you ten, they make the arrest within seventy-two hours."

The Channel 7 camera panned to the front porch. An athletic man whose iron hair matched the color of his suit stood flanked by ornamental urns of salmon and scarlet geraniums. A half-step behind him huddled a plump woman wearing a blouse with a ruffled collar and a midcalf dirndl skirt. She was twisting something in her hands.

"Seventy-two *hours*?" Cliff said. "That DA ain't got the balls! I'll give you ten to one against Ballard ever being charged."

"I'll lay five on Ballard," Pilar agreed. "But we're talking Boulder— Lanny Greer doesn't take a crap without DNA results."

The bronzed face of Channel 7's ace reporter filled the screen.

"—four days now since Amy Lynch, that plucky little freshman from CU, was rescued after being abducted and held in the wilds of Left Hand Canyon." He turned to his associate. "What's the latest on Amy's condition, Joe?"

"Upgraded last night from serious to fair, but no one's been able to interview her. Quite an ordeal for that little gal. DA Lanny Greer's playing it close to the vest, but from what we've been able to learn, she hiked barefoot more than a mile in the snow to escape. They're still trying to find where she was held."

"Has she described her captors?"

"Not so far as we've been told. That leather apparatus around her throat"—the reporter shook his head with theatrical distaste—"apparently had some effect on her vocal cords. She was in shock when they found her, so a photo lineup was out of the question."

"When do they think—" He was interrupted. "We turn now to Bryan and Bonnie Lynch, Amy's courageous parents."

The couple on the porch came into focus.

"Let's start with you, Bonnie. What can you tell us about your daughter?"

Bonnie Lynch stared at the reporter blankly. Her eyes were puffy and her lipstick seemed to be an afterthought.

"Rode hard and put away wet," Cliff said.

"Will you shut up?" Pilar said.

"—terrible tragedy," the reporter commiserated. "If you could say anything to Amy's abductors right now, what would it be?"

"Give me my daughter's life back!"

The camera leaped to Bryan Lynch, the source of the outburst.

"He *has* his daughter," Cliff said. "It's not like she's dead. She's in the goddamn—"

"She's in a coma, for Christ's sake!" Pilar said. "That poor girl might not even live." They all leaned closer to the screen.

"Bryan, tell us your feelings right now."

"My feelings?" The patrician face mottled with rage. "You want to know how I feel about having my little girl abducted from school, dragged to the mountains, chained up and tethered with a *dog collar*—"

"Can you tell us what Amy was like as a child?"

The camera flitted to Bonnie, who made no sign of having heard. Jackie wondered if she'd been sedated. Bryan Lynch collected himself.

"Amy was a perfect child. She never did anything wrong."

"Is there anyone who might have a grudge against your daughter?"

"Grudge?" Lynch looked confused.

"Or against your family?"

"My family?" he echoed.

"Bryan's work—" Those were the first words out of Bonnie Lynch's mouth. Apparently noticing her for the first time, Bryan put his arm around her trembling shoulders and squeezed tightly.

"Did you see that?" Pilar said. "He acts like his wife has the plague, but the minute she opens her mouth he shuts her up."

"—ransom note?" the reporter said.

"Absolutely not!" Bryan said as Bonnie stood stiffly in his embrace. It was clear this interview was about to end. "Whoever took my daughter is a filthy pervert. The police said it was a random—"

"We've been informed of a rumor that the handcuffs have been traced. Are you surprised there's been no arrest?"

Bonnie raised her hands to her face and began to shake. With an angry look at the reporter, Bryan turned her away from the camera. The press conference was over.

"Jeez," Cliff said, "I'd hate to be in the Boulder DA's shoes right now. Déjà vu all over again." He turned to Joel. "Maybe I'll take you up on those odds."

"If you guys seriously think a United States District Judge is capable of the sadism—" Jackie began.

"When's the last time you appeared in federal court?" Joel said.

"Wait, it's not over. . . ." Pilar was staring at the screen. The scene had switched to a modern building of limestone, steel, and glass. The camera crossed the plaza and zoomed in on the revolving doors. As they watched, a tall figure with a leather briefcase emerged and was surrounded by reporters. One of them took the lead.

"Judge Ballard, any comment on the report that the handcuffs found on Amy Lynch are yours?"

If the reporter had hoped to catch his subject off balance, he was disappointed.

"None whatsoever," Glenn Ballard replied, nodding politely to the others. "Now, if you'll excuse me . . ."

Jackie stared at her former professor.

Receding in wings from a prominent widow's peak, Ballard's silver hair was clipped so close to his skull that it looked full rather than sparse. His face was still lean, and though his aquiline features had softened slightly with maturity, she saw no sign of the dissipation one might have expected of a man of his exalted status. But his eyes remained a piercing blue, and any sympathy she might have felt for him dissolved.

"Do you deny the handcuffs are yours?"

"No." There was no concern in Ballard's measured response, and the reporter struggled to regain his momentum.

"Why do you have handcuffs?"

"The U.S. Marshals Service gave them to me fifteen years ago when I was appointed to the bench. They're part of a standard security kit issued to all the judges."

"Has your need for protection increased since your ruling on the Internet case?"

Ballard's lips twitched. Was it because he'd derailed a sensitive line of questioning? Or because he'd been pitched a high hanging curve? In either case, he hit it out of the park.

"Fascinating as it is to watch champions of the First Amendment defend pornographers, I've received no threats lately."

"Any regrets about your ruling on Internet porn dealers having to pay tax? It's now on appeal—"

"I call shots as I see them, gentlemen, and leave the rest to my learned colleagues on the court of second conjecture." He stepped gracefully past the microphones. "Now, if you'll excuse me . . ."

"Any explanation how your cuffs ended up on Amy Lynch?"

The voice came from the rear and Ballard's eyes narrowed as he ferreted out its source. As in any good cross, he knew simply asking the question was enough to make the point. Would he bite?

"I noticed them missing from my chambers two weeks ago." He took another step.

"Did you report them stolen?" came the voice again.

The camera caught the minute widening of Ballard's eyes before he strode across the plaza and out of view.

Jackie switched off the TV.

"I'll put five bucks on your odds," she told Cliff. "Glenn Ballard will never be charged."

Four

Jackie stared at the glossy blowup.

The upper sole of a tennis shoe with distinctive nicks in its tread lay dead center in a shard of plate glass. Outlined in white powder on the tinted pane, the narrow print almost leaped out of the photograph. Although she'd never seen Ted Wolsky in sneakers, in his earlier career he'd given a new meaning to "little cat feet." Was Parker focusing too hard on the print itself? Or had Ted wanted to be caught, to embrace the big bitch with the fervor of a prodigal son?

"Pee-*yew*!" a sassy voice cried. "What's that awful stink?"

"How ladylike," Jackie said. "Is that what they teach in private school these days?"

The figure in the doorway struck a Greta Garbo pose. With one hand on her bony chest and the other flung to the winds, Lily gave an asthmatic gasp.

"At last I can *breathe*!"

"Why aren't you in class?"

"They let me off for good behavior."

"Time served," a voice behind the child said. Barely taller than Lily, a man who could have been anywhere from forty to sixty stepped into view. He was wearing a tailored leather jacket, pleated crepe trousers, and his trademark Italian loafers. He carried a copy of the *Rocky Mountain News* under one arm.

"I might have expected to find you two together," Jackie said.

"I got an eye for the dames," Ted Wolsky said.

Lily dropped her nylon backpack on a chair. Crossing the carpet heel-to-toe in pink tights and black calfskin slippers, she handed Jackie a stack of correspondence.

"It's a clerical half-day at school. Pilar gave me a dollar to sort mail."

"What happened to the temp?"

Lily shrugged. "She got in a fight with Cliff and quit. Want me to read your letters to you?"

"No, thanks." Lily was wearing a black leotard to match her ballet slippers and a choker with rhinestone studs. A scrap of Lycra no larger than a washcloth was wrapped around her thighs in a facsimile of a micro-mini skirt. It cramped her movements but not her style. She was the child Jackie would never have.

As Ted hoisted the girl onto Jackie's desk, Lily's eyes glittered with an excitement disproportionate to the pocket change she'd wangled from Pilar.

"Ain't she gorgeous?" Ted said. "Tell the boss the occasion."

"I got accepted to ballet camp!"

Lily and Jackie exchanged a high-five.

The dance camp in Steamboat Springs prided itself on an exclusivity that made Lily lust for a spot. She'd been taking ballet lessons only a year, following a self-imposed dawn-to-dusk regimen. Jackie's next-door neighbors Randy and Britt, who had adopted the gangly child at age four from an orphanage in Shanghai, had installed a full-length mirror and horizontal bar in their basement and had seized the opportunity to impose their own carrot and stick.

The result was Lily's transformation from near-truancy to A's in everything but English on two consecutive report cards, an increasingly pronounced duck-footed gait, and a chignon. But the child's obsessiveness made Jackie uneasy. Did Lily think that if she became a prima ballerina her parents would let her stay in America—or that they would allow her to return to China?

"How shall we celebrate?" Jackie's eyes strayed to the choker on Lily's slender throat. The only residue of a blessedly short-lived punk phase that ended the day Lily decided it was okay to wear pink, it made her look as vulnerable as a baby egret. "Cirque du Soleil is in town."

"Pilar and I were talking about the races," Ted said, as if he weren't facing the rest of his life behind bars. Unfurling his *News,* he peered at the telephoto shot of a log structure all but obscured by a stand of pines. "Looks like they found the cabin. Don't surprise me one bit."

"Cabin?" Jackie asked.

"Where that Lynch kid was kept."

"I'm not surprised, either." She glanced uneasily at Lily, trying to signal Ted to cool it. "They were bound to find it sooner or—"

"Glenn Ballard owns it. Don't you just love it when the shoe's on the other foot?" The cat-burglar-cum-arsonist grinned maliciously. "Some judges insist on leg irons *and* manacles. Here's a guy who really cracks the whip!"

Lily was all ears. "You mean he whips *people*?"

"No, honey," Jackie said. "That isn't what Ted meant at all. It's just a figure of speech."

"It's a funny thing about judges," Ted said. "No matter which side they come down on, someone always gets hurt. You don't have to whip people to treat them like dogs, Lily. A guy in a robe has lots of ways to cut someone down to size." He paused. "Of course, it ain't just cons Ballard treats that way, I'll give him that. I'll never forget this one case. Years ago, right after he was appointed to the bench. When I was about your age." Lily tittered. "I'd gotten into a little misunderstanding with the feds"—he'd burglarized the U.S. Marshals warehouse—"so I happened to be in his court. Young gal in a tiff with her boss, and Ballard wouldn't let her say a word. Muzzled her and threw her right out on the street. Yup, that judge is an equal-opportunity *prick.*"

Lily's mouth dropped open and Jackie belatedly clamped her hands over the girl's ears. Mumbling an embarrassed "Pardon my French," Ted retreated to his tabloid.

Ted Wolsky's choices in life might have given him a unique window on the judicial system, but it was difficult to dismiss his assessment of Ballard. Ted was anything but the average con. Why read books when he was so adept at reading people? As often as he'd been forced to face juries, that skill was as crucial for him as it was for Jackie.

She remembered their first trial together. Unlike prosecutors, who strove for consensus, when Jackie picked a jury she was looking to seat the dinner party from hell. When strangers were on their best behavior so much depended on nuance, the tiny frown, an instant's hesitation. In the time-honored passivity of DAs, the prosecutor had elicited just enough to determine that a prospective juror named Loretta Pinella loved God, apple pie, and the American flag. As Jackie rose to do the spadework, Ted had hissed in her ear, "Toss her!"

"What?"

"The broad's lying. Watch her hands."

Stepping to the lectern, Jackie fixed her quarry with a friendly smile. Loretta Pinella beamed back. Her hands were resting comfortably on the rail of the jury box. She wore a moderately priced wristwatch but no rings.

"Ms. Pinella," Jackie began, "you already said you have no relatives in law enforcement. How about friends?"

"I don't know any officers."

"And that would include people who work for the DA?"

She placed her right hand over her left. "Yes."

"And you're unmarried."

"That's right." It was amazing how many people looked straight at you and smiled as they lied.

"Are you divorced?"

"No, I live with a dog and two cats." Her smile was so engaging Jackie barely noticed her gently stroking the ring finger of her left hand. "And my parakeet, Carl. He never lets us forget him!"

That got a sympathetic laugh from the gallery. Pinella was a social lubricator, someone who put the people around her at ease and encouraged consensus. No mistrials on her watch. Jackie had already decided to excuse her but was still intrigued by Ted's observation.

"And Carl has been with you how long?"

The rubbing abruptly stopped. "Six years next week."

"Tell him happy anniversary from me," Jackie said, and moved to the next juror. When it came time to exercise challenges, she politely excused Pinella. After the jury hung for Ted and the DA decided against a retrial, Jackie had Pilar investigate the woman's background. Six years earlier Loretta Pinella had been married to a police lieutenant who was head of the burglary squad in Colorado Springs. The marriage had been annulled after less than a week. Her ex's name was Carl.

Jackie never questioned Ted's hunches again. As she reflected now on his antipathy toward Glenn Ballard, something told her there was more to it than Ballard's decisions or manners. But Ballard was not her problem.

Five

"I s Lily with you?" Pilar called up the stairs. "I need her to handle the phones."

Lily rolled her eyes and jumped off the desk. "For each call, I'm charging Cliff an extra buck!" She planted a kiss on Ted's cheek and started for the door.

"So what will we do to celebrate?" Jackie called after her.

"Veggie pizza and a horror movie?"

"You got it." Jackie sighed with relief. "We'll have time for something special later."

Not exactly Cirque du Soleil, but better than the dog track. As Lily scampered down the stairs, Ted emerged from his tabloid.

"Some you win, some you lose." Always the gentleman. "That kid sure is growing up."

"I could live without her taste in jewelry," Jackie said. Something about that rhinestone choker gave her the creeps.

"Used to be all she cared about was how to pick a lock."

"Are you telling me—"

"Now, don't get your balls in an uproar. It was just a phase."

Ballet camp couldn't start soon enough.

"That burglary at the marshals' facility. I thought Ballard tossed your case?"

"Illegal search." Ted chuckled. "He tore that U.S. Attorney a new asshole! Not that he didn't deserve it."

"So why isn't he your hero? Not every federal judge would do that to government lawyers who appear in front of him every day."

"Those guys are paid to take it. That young gal I was talking about wasn't. She walked into his court with her nickel-ass lawyer expecting justice and looked like she was hit by a cement truck."

Men who lacked chivalry ranked almost as low in Ted's book as criminals who worked without pay, but it still didn't explain his powerful antipathy toward Ballard. And now he was uncharacteristically reticent.

"That's it? The way he treated one girl?"

"There's more. He enjoys sentencing."

"Some judges do."

"Not like Ballard. Remember when he sent that bank robber up for three hundred and sixty-five years? Set a new record."

"So we'll just have to keep you out of federal court. And while we're on the subject, the cops never found the sneakers you were wearing the night of the warehouse fire, did they?"

"Nope. That's because I never wear 'em."

"What shoes were you wearing when you were busted?"

"These loafers."

How could she have doubted him? Ted was in the insurance business, or so he liked to say. Kicking in a window was not his style. Even without the gasoline splattered on the walls, the mode of entry screamed amateur. Ted reached into his jacket. Without counting them, he handed Jackie a wad of bills.

"First half of your retainer." He smiled crookedly. "Have to borrow the rest from Mom. Speaking of which, I gotta run. I promised to take her to bingo tonight."

The price of being released into his eighty-five-year-old mother's custody.

Jackie stood by the window and watched the little arsonist exit her building. He paused on the front porch, looking both ways like a dutiful child just learning to cross the street. Then he quickly descended the granite steps and disappeared around the corner. He didn't deserve to go up for life, especially since he was innocent.

Six

The sky had turned to slate and a brisk wind was bending the branches on the cottonwood outside her window. A sheet of newspaper skittered down the street like a ketch under sail. Pilar had mentioned snow tonight. Springtime in the Rockies.

Jackie returned to her desk. Glancing at the photo of the footprint on broken glass, she shook her head. Like Parker she'd allowed herself to be distracted by the print. What wasn't there was sometimes more important than what was. Since when did a pro like Ted kick in a window to break into a warehouse?

But her eyes kept straying to the tabloid.

No wonder the close-up of Glenn Ballard's cabin had been relegated to page three; the photographer must have sneaked past police lines to shoot it. The magnificent pines complemented the log walls and stone chimney. If you ignored the crime scene tape, the scene was oddly peaceful, in its isolation almost pristine. The cabin itself had a certain unassuming dignity—

"Lily's having a ball with the phones." Pilar was standing in the doorway. "She's cut off two of Cliff's clients already. I'd offer her a permanent job, but I hate to throw a bunch of incompetent temps out of work."

"Looks like we'll be scrapping that trip to Lake Powell with her this summer." Jackie handed Pilar the wad of bills Ted had given her and returned to the photo of the shoe print. "At least she'll get fresh air in Steamboat."

"Maybe it's just as well," Pilar said, and Jackie glanced up. Pilar was almost as attached to Lily as Jackie was.

"What do you mean?"

"With these nickel-and-dime cases and having to pick up Phil's share of the overhead, we'll have to tighten our belts."

"I wish this arson rap cost Ted just five to ten. And this time he's innocent." Jackie stared at the glossy of the sneaker print. "I need you to ask Lenny a favor." Lenny Kramholtz was a semi-retired insurance adjuster for Mutual State and one of Pilar's swains.

"I've been ducking his calls for weeks."

"I want him to look at a file."

"When?"

"Tonight. I need to know what's missing from that warehouse. What should have been found if Ted committed that arson."

Pilar groaned. "This is gonna cost me a hell of a lot more than a movie and dinner."

"Whatever it takes."

"Easy for you to say," she muttered as she gathered the police reports and began filing them away. "But seriously, Jackie, even Lily thinks the walls stink. I'm tired of dealing with new temps every three days who misplace retainer checks and quit because they break out in hives from the stress. This office and everyone in it are losers."

"Can we talk about this some other time?"

"As a matter of fact, no."

Jackie looked up again.

"Are you trying to say something?"

"You're hiding. From challenging cases, from clients who—"

—*might see right through me.*

Jackie let out her breath. Psychoanalysis she could handle; what she could not survive was a single day without Pilar.

"Maybe now isn't the right time," Pilar said, but her attempt to appease only darkened Jackie's mood. Glancing at the cover of the *News,* Pilar shook her head. "I knew it was Ballard all along. First the handcuffs, now the cabin . . ."

"How do they know that's the right place?"

"They found a leather blindfold with Amy Lynch's hair in the knot, but that won't be in the paper till tomorrow. They're still processing the scene." Jackie knew better than to question Pilar's sources. A full beat passed as she waited for the other shoe to drop. "The rafter has marks from a chain."

Law school isn't a charity ward, Ms. Flowers.

"Any fingerprints on the blindfold?"

"Nope."

Only the best and brightest students can be expected to compete.

"Anywhere else in the cabin?"

"Not so far."

Frankly, I'll be amazed if you pass the bar.

"Well, I'm sure he won't have any problem finding a lawyer." Jackie rolled up the newspaper and deposited it in her wastebasket. "He certainly can afford the brightest and the best."

"What would you give for a shot at the Lynch case?"

"To represent Glenn Ballard? Not one cent."

"Come on. A U.S. District Judge who's a *perv*?"

"I'm the last person he'd turn to."

"Are you saying that if Glenn Ballard walked in that door right now and asked you to defend him, you'd say no?"

"Believe me, Pilar, there's not a chance in hell—"

"What do you have against that man?"

"Some people don't deserve a defense!" Jackie said.

At the sound from the doorway, they both turned. Lily stood at the threshold, one hand frozen in midrap and the other theatrically drawn to her mouth. Behind her loomed a spare figure in an elegant suit.

"Is that a fact?" the man asked.

His eyes sliced through Jackie.

"I always wondered which lessons stuck," Glenn Ballard said. "Were those three years in law school an entire waste, or am I finally in the presence of a real lawyer?"

Seven

The man in the sharkskin suit rifled his papers to underscore his final point. It was seven in the morning, but the hearing had been in full swing for the better part of an hour.

"Your Honor, fundamental fairness compels you to disqualify every expert on the plaintiff's list. . . ."

In the windowless paneled cathedral presided over by United States District Judge Glenn Ballard, timelessness reigned. The artificial lighting made his silver hair glimmer but it was particularly cruel to the lawyer at the podium, who nervously ran his fingers through his greenish comb-over. Of the dozen lawyers seated in the well of the court, not one was a woman. Four feet above them, former professor Ballard silently waited to pounce. He had changed his title but not his job.

"Plaintiff is clearly attempting to buy credibility," continued the lead attorney for the defense. "By dangling retainers too large to refuse, they seek to make up for substance with bulk and preempt the most eminent authorities from testifying for our side. . . ."

How did federal practice differ from state court? The suits cost more.

As Jackie looked around the room, she realized there was more to that conventional wisdom than she'd thought. She'd never seen so many pinstripes in her life, empty or not. The cuff links alone would cost more than a month's rent at her office, including the special assessment the landlord was threatening to charge for a new roof.

She'd arrived at Ballard's chambers fifteen minutes earlier to pick him up for his arraignment in Boulder. His secretary had directed her to this courtroom as crisply as if crack-of-dawn discovery disputes in eighty-million-dollar patent infringement cases were a daily occurrence. Not to mention the judge being the chief suspect in a coed's abduction and torture. As she'd taken a seat in the last row, Jackie had reviewed what her newest client had told her the previous afternoon.

Discovery of the cabin combined with the Lynches' press conference had put Boulder DA Lanny Greer under tremendous pressure to make an arrest. As a courtesy to Ballard, Greer offered him an opportunity to surrender to a summons at the Boulder DA's office and be released on a personal recognizance bond. The key to the offer was speed: the arraignment had to be over and done with before the press demanded scalps.

Needing a criminal lawyer versed in the state court system and apparently confident the charges would soon be dropped, Ballard had hired Jackie to handle the bond proceedings. No trouble reading between those lines: she was fast, effective, and female. But Pilar had seen photos of Amy Lynch after her rescue. Not pretty. The authorities hadn't said whether she'd been sexually assaulted, but half a dozen Boulder detectives were taking turns at Amy's bedside waiting for her to identify her attacker. And Jackie had more than one question of her own.

Why hadn't Ballard reported his handcuffs stolen? He'd never paid attention to them, he said. When the U.S. Marshals issued them, he'd tossed them in a drawer in his chambers. He couldn't remember where he'd placed the key, to the handcuffs *or* his desk. He never locked anything.

According to Ballard, the cabin in Left Hand Canyon was little more than a falling-down shack. He'd been raised on a prosperous ranch his family still owned near Craig, past Steamboat Springs in Colorado's northwest corner. His grandfather had built the cabin for hunting back when the only access to Left Hand was pack mule and horse. When his uncle died, Ballard had inherited the cabin, but he hadn't visited the place in years. It was boarded up. Anyone could have broken in.

He'd never met Amy Lynch or her parents. He hadn't been in Boulder since a speech he gave at the law school the previous fall. He had no idea why this was happening to him. The whole thing was a ghastly mistake. . . .

As she'd listened to Ballard's story, Jackie had felt the first stirrings of sympathy. Her former professor had always played it by the book. He'd taken attendance at the beginning of every class, skewered his students with his famous "one question," which inevitably cut to the heart of any issue and thus could never be evaded, and he graded strictly on the basis of a written exam. The likelihood that he had abducted and tortured a CU coed was too preposterous to contemplate. And, to be honest, there was a certain satisfaction in being on the other end of the stick from Ballard. So long as it was a very long stick and Jackie's position there was temporary. The surrender was set for the DA's office at nine that morning. Her only commitment was to accompany Ballard.

". . . ask that you condemn this abuse of judicial process by striking every single name on plaintiff's expert witness list."

Defense counsel had run out of steam but Ballard dispassionately waited, his focus never wavering from the podium. From his neck, bifocals hung on a slender black cord, nearly invisible against his robe. The light glinting off the lenses as he shifted ever so slightly in his seat was the only sign that he was breathing. He had neither interrupted nor taken a single note throughout the proceeding. Nor had he acknowledged Jackie's presence. His court reporter wore an identical poker face. How did that woman feel about recording the fanciest lawyers in town receiving a high colonic before breakfast? And what did she think of the man administering it?

Watching from the last row of Ballard's courtroom in her silk blouse, blue pumps, and finest gabardine suit, Jackie felt she was once again in jeans and a sweatshirt on the back bench of his class. Not a pleasant memory. With Ballard, none of the techniques to which she owed her survival had worked. And Jackie was a master at survival. How else could she have made it through grade school?

The first warning that something was wrong came in kindergarten, when she was unable to memorize the alphabet. Letters blurred and vanished and numbers reversed themselves. If she was lucky Jackie could make out a word here or there, but sentences were a frustrating series of disconnected symbols whose meaning she was powerless to decode. Her chicken scratch was gibberish to her teachers, and when she began skipping whole lines in her reading, they suggested that her vision be checked. When she was unable to follow directions they said the problem was her hearing, but saying it louder, slower, or ten different ways didn't change a thing.

If Jackie wasn't stupid, she must be pigheaded or lazy. Report cards invariably said "not living up to her potential." Worst of all was feeling that she wasn't whole, that awful sense that all the other children knew things that she didn't. What would it be like to be different—to be like them? She was being punished for a crime she hadn't committed but that was nonetheless her *fault*.

And then Jackie got smart.

She learned to wait until another child caught the teacher's eye before raising her own hand, receiving credit for volunteering at no risk. Transient attacks of laryngitis saved her when it was her turn to recite, a trick elbow exempted her from catching or throwing a ball. She converted her inability to tell left from right into an endless series of pratfalls that kept her classmates laughing. Why else would they want to be friends with an idiot? Emboldened, Jackie aimed for grades so low they added to her cachet. Thirty percent on a spelling test—could she score as low as *five*? It was years before the hammer dropped. . . .

"—further to add?" Ballard's voice was deceptively soft. It carried without a microphone, perhaps because the courtroom was so quiet one could have heard a paper clip drop to the cork floor each time he opened his mouth. Jackie braced for the inevitable.

"No, Your Honor." At three hundred bucks an hour, that Seventeenth Street barrister could afford not to quaver.

"Gentlemen?" Ballard's gaze had shifted to the plaintiff's table. The fact that he was giving the other side a final bite at the apple was not enough to disguise that it probably contained a worm.

"Nothing further, Your Honor."

Ballard tilted back in his leather chair. With the nonchalance of a referee at Wimbledon, he surveyed his court. Eighty million dollars. However he ruled would cost someone dearly. The prospect of having an expert witness struck—not to mention disqualifying *every* witness on her list—would have turned Jackie's guts to juice. But as she looked from one set of attorneys to the other, she realized none of them appeared particularly anxious. Ballard was a stickler for logic and syntax; was it possible they thought clever sufficed? When a lawyer at the defense table turned and winked at his client in the front row, she knew something dreadful was about to occur.

"Then I have one question, Counselors."

A dozen chins jerked up in surprise.

Ballard clicked the arm of his bifocals contemplatively against his teeth. The fluorescent light cast daggers from the lenses, but his voice remained mild.

"Has any of these experts received anything but a retainer?"

The lead lawyer for the plaintiffs whispered to the pinstripe on his left.

"No, Your Honor," he replied. "We were waiting until—"

"No privileged material?" Ballard asked the defense. "No confidential communications?"

"None," opposing counsel confirmed.

Ballard steepled his fingers and rocked back in his chair.

"And it is undisputed that the witnesses on each of your lists are the most eminent experts in the field."

The reporter dutifully recorded their nods.

"In that case," Ballard continued, "I will allow each side to call two experts . . ."

A chair thudded against a table leg as lead counsel for the plaintiff reared back in dismay. It may have been a high-stakes hand of poker, but they'd forgotten who was holding the cards. And Ballard wasn't finished.

". . . provided each of you selects those witnesses from your opponent's list."

The courtroom was utterly silent.

"Shit," Jackie heard a defense lawyer mutter before he clamped his mouth shut.

"Court is adjourned," Ballard announced. In collective shock, they stumbled to their feet. For the first time, Jackie realized there was no gavel on the bench. Ballard rose and exited his court.

Eight

Denver's skid row glittered in the morning sun as Jackie and Ballard motored in his Lincoln Navigator through LoDo toward I-25. Backed by the snowcapped Continental Divide, Boulder's purple Flatirons lay smack ahead but the better part of an hour away. Even at 8 A.M. the traffic was bumper-to-bumper.

Jackie wasn't about to protest Ballard's insistence that he drive; as Pilar kindly put it, she was "directionally challenged." Nor would every client be charmed or amused by a twelve-year-old Corolla with five thousand miles on the odometer. As they neared the on-ramp to I-25 and she began to relax against the fine-grained leather of the luxury SUV's passenger seat, Jackie realized this was the first time she'd been alone with her client.

"Your courthouse has remarkable security," she said.

From Ballard's chambers to the judges' private elevator to the reserved parking behind a metal cage in the basement, up the ramp and past the manned guard shack where the security officer gave Jackie a hard look before waving Ballard on, she had counted five swipes of Ballard's magnetic card. And that was just to get out.

"Welcome to Fortress America," Ballard said. He drove with the same eagle-eyed impassivity with which he conducted his classroom and court. "I've suggested to the General Services Administration that we change the Pledge of Allegiance to 'one nation under guard.' If nothing else, it eliminates all those pesky First Amendment problems."

"What happens if you leave your card at home?"

"Anyone who really knows what they're doing can slip in."

What was that saying—God protected children and idiots? But Ballard was neither, and Jackie was glad she'd agreed to represent him only at his surrender and release. She didn't envy whomever he retained for the trial.

The lesson drummed into every rookie defense lawyer was simple: lie in the weeds and watch for the DA to make a mistake. Sometimes manna didn't drop until the day of trial. Jackie never forgot the case where the prosecutor's star witness was a shrink. He'd arrived in court late, apologizing that he'd just been to his analyst. Jackie had only two questions on cross. *Did you say you're seeing an analyst? For how long?* The jury acquitted her client in twenty minutes flat. You took what you could get and never looked back, but whoever represented Ballard could expect not a centimeter of slack. Not that he wasn't a damn sight more presentable than the average criminal defendant.

A light scent wafted over to the Navigator's passenger seat. At first Jackie thought it was the leather upholstery, but the aroma was faintly woody, with a sharp but agreeable note of citrus. A private blend of aftershave. As they mounted the entrance ramp to I-25, Ballard shifted. With his attention on the road, Jackie examined him more closely.

Glenn Ballard was so perfectly proportioned he might have been molded. His ears were long and flush to his aristocratic skull, the lobes perfectly aligned with his clean jaw. The hands on the leather-covered steering wheel were relaxed, the fingers tapered and nails buffed. His suit was a subtle shade, so finely spun Jackie couldn't tell whether it was blue or gray, and his silk tie was an Aztec print. Even Ballard's wristwatch was elegant, the black digital face wafer-thin with a narrow synthetic band. Catching her gaze, he smiled enigmatically.

"Looking for horns?"

"It's hard to imagine you on your ranch in a Stetson and cowboy boots."

"During weekends I actually drive an old Explorer."

Not exactly a Ford pickup truck, but for Ballard that was undoubtedly slumming.

"I still can't imagine you wading through—"

"—sheep shit? We raise Black Angus."

"But that must be quite a change from the bench."

"Not really." His lower lip was fuller than the upper one, and it quivered as if he were suppressing a laugh. "Why should rounding up cattle be any different than keeping lawyers in line? Of course, the Judicial Conference frowns on the use of electric prods. . . ."

"That isn't funny," Jackie said. But she felt her first stirring of respect. Not everyone in Ballard's position could joke. "Speaking of torture, your ruling this morning seemed to come as quite a surprise."

"When both sides walk out angry, I know I've done the right thing."

"Do you think they'll appeal?"

He shrugged. "The standard is abuse of discretion."

"What exactly does that mean?"

"Whatever the court of appeals says it does, five years from now."

So Ballard couldn't care less whether he was reversed. His indifference raised Jackie's opinion of him another notch.

"It doesn't sound like you have much use for your brethren."

"Federal district judges lead a Sartrian existence, Ms. Flowers."

"Sartrian?"

"Surely you read *No Exit* in college." Jackie wasn't about to correct him. "Do you know what hell is? Being chained to the bench for eternity with six or seven 'brethren' for whom you may feel nothing but contempt."

And she'd thought lifetime tenure meant regular meals and not having to bill clients.

"Do you think it's wise to keep hearing cases with these charges pending?"

He kept his eyes on the road. "The best defense is always a good offense, Counselor. And I won't be intimidated by anyone."

Certainly in character for the Glenn Ballard everyone knew. But was he really so unconcerned? "If your case goes to trial, you think a Boulder judge will give you a fair shot?"

"Frankly, I've never met a state judge who understands the rules of evidence or procedure. If they even read them." She bristled, then realized he had no way of knowing how close to home his remark hit. "Literate or not, the majority of my brethren on the bench are stream-of-comatose."

Jackie couldn't quarrel with that, but it raised an uncomfortable subject.

"I have to admit I was a little surprised when you showed up at my office."

"How so?"

Was it possible he'd forgotten what he'd done to her in law school? She quickly switched gears. "A humble sole practitioner like me? Any lawyer in town would jump at your case. The big firms—"

"You think I want to be ammunition for an army of jackasses?"

"There are any number of defense groups that have access to nationwide resources," she said. "On death penalty cases they bring in experts from all over the country."

Ballard's laugh was bitter.

"Every time there's a hint of Zyklon-B in the air, defense lawyers show up in a Macedonian phalanx."

So he *was* concerned about his fate. Ballard's literary references were Greek to her, but Jackie was feeling better all the time.

"Who do you think stole your handcuffs?"

"In my line of work, enemies are many."

"You'd tell me if there was anything I needed to know?"

"I've represented a client or two in my time, Counselor."

They were approaching the turnoff to the Boulder turnpike and Jackie began looking for the on-ramp. It wasn't that she didn't trust Ballard to get them there, but he was maneuvering the Navigator into what felt like the wrong lane. She tried to remember how Pilar did it. Wasn't the entrance on the passenger side? Suddenly she was completely disoriented.

"Something wrong?" Ballard said.

Jackie leaned back in her seat.

"I—isn't the turnpike coming up?"

"They redid the loop. It's on the left now, not the right."

"Of course."

Ballard looked at her quizzically.

"Not much of a driver, are you?"

"Not when I have the luxury of a chauffeur."

Some of Jackie's symptoms had improved with time and others had gotten worse. She knew that if she didn't keep exercising her brain, she'd regress. Thank God for speed dial and for Pilar to write her checks! There were good days and there were bad days. On good days she had always been able to read a few paragraphs at a time if there were no distractions, but scanning short blocks of text was become increasingly hit-or-miss. Because Pilar read for her, that wasn't so much of an issue. Driving a car was. It was a miracle she had a driver's license at all.

At her aunt's urging Jackie had taken her first driver's test fresh out of high school.

Flashing light, slow down. *Flashing light, slow* . . . Left at the corner. *Left at the*— No dear, the other left. *No dear* . . . Each time the state trooper issued a command, Jackie had unconsciously repeated it aloud.

And parallel parking—who knew which way to turn the wheel? But as he had with so many others, the examiner chalked up Jackie's eccentricities to nerves and passed her. And she'd justified his faith by putting fewer and fewer miles on her Corolla with each passing year.

Ballard was shaking his head. How like a woman, Jackie could hear him say. But what did it matter what he thought? Her association with him would be brief. Leaning back in her seat, she tried to enjoy the rest of the ride.

In the ultimate answer to gentrification, the suburbs between Denver and Boulder were being gobbled up. Monochromatic housing developments had sprouted like bindweed in the rolling pastures since Jackie's law school days but the foothills remained constant. With colors changing from mauve to gray with the play of sun and cloud, their gentle humps made her think of elephants at a watering hole. As the miles sped by, the wrinkled hide became ravines and the stubble became trees, and when they finally descended into the valley, the University of Colorado campus was the soothing color of warm sand.

Exiting the Boulder turnpike, Jackie was amazed at how little had changed in the fifteen years since she'd graduated. Late-model cars reflected an affluent student body, and out-of-state tags still outnumbered local plates. But she'd forgotten how low the sky was in the sheltered college town. And the laid-back, blissed-out expressions on everyone's faces. Was it any accident that Mork landed in Boulder and wasn't discovered for five years? Or that Boulder was the first city in the nation to substitute "guardian" for "pet owner" in its animal ordinances?

Garlanded by crab apples, maples, and lilacs, the two-story Justice Center backed onto Boulder Creek. Early tulips blazed scarlet and gold on berms artfully positioned to conceal a parking lot. But the narrow tinted windows reminded Jackie of a fortress, and the landscaping only strengthened her impression that Boulder's People's Court was deceptively user-friendly.

"I suppose it was considerate of Landon Greer to allow me to 'surrender,'" Ballard said. "Though I'm quite certain this case will never get past—"

"Keep going." Jackie didn't like the looks of a panel truck pulling into the parking lot ahead.

"But we're right at—"

"Drive!"

As they passed the front entrance to the Justice Center, she spotted vans from the major networks. Lanny Greer had tipped off the media.

"What will we do?" Ballard asked.

The balance of power had suddenly shifted.

"Don't stop!"

"But if I don't turn myself in, won't I be—"

"Relax," Jackie insisted, her heart thumping. "I know what I'm doing." Now they were on her turf.

When they came to a private lot past the building's main entrance, she told Ballard to turn. Reserved spaces ended at a gate with a card entry and an underground garage.

"Park behind that sheriff's van."

He obeyed without a peep.

Jumping down from the passenger seat, Jackie smoothed her skirt. Next came the dicey part. Squaring her shoulders and pasting a look of authority on her face, she led her client through the door marked DA'S ENTRANCE.

"This is a security door, miss." Jackie politely brushed past the female watchdog. "You're not a DA."

She kept her tone courteous. "We have an appointment with Landon Greer."

"You must have made a mistake."

Jackie glanced at the clock above their heads. The little hand was about to touch the nine.

"Looks like we're right on time."

"Who *are* you?" the woman asked. She now guarded Greer's gate with the ferocity of a three-headed mastiff.

"Lanny's expecting us," Jackie said. Identifying themselves would only buy Greer time to bring the media circus inside.

"He's tied up all morning on a very important matter. You'll have to come back."

"We're happy to wait."

Cerberus punched an extension. She muttered something into the receiver, glared at them over her shoulder when she saw they were still there, then hit a button on her speed dial. Ninety seconds later, a torpedo in a tweed sport coat barreled down the hall. Behind him was a blonde whose blunt haircut matched the severity of her suit.

"Lanny, how nice to see you!" Jackie held out her hand, but the angry man ignored it. "You did say something about a PR bond?"

Landon Greer knew he'd been outmaneuvered. With a dexterity befitting a politician of twenty-five years, he gave Jackie a saucy wink.

"I should have known you'd find the back way in." He turned to introduce his assistant. "I believe you've met my chief deputy, Phyllis Klein? She'll be handling this case."

Klein stepped smartly forward. Her robin's-egg suit made her hair very yellow, but her expression delivered the real jolt. The smile Boulder's date-rape queen shot Jackie packed more voltage than a stun gun.

"I'm looking forward to facing you in court."

In those few seconds, Jackie had learned three important things.

First, Landon Greer intended to prosecute Amy Lynch's abduction and assault as a sex crime. Or, rather, he was handing it off to his chief deputy because he was either afraid of Glenn Ballard or the evidence against him was not as strong as Greer wanted them to think.

Second, despite what Phyllis Klein wanted her boss to believe, she'd leaped at the chance to prosecute this case.

And last, but by no means least: they were in for a dogfight.

Nine

"Detective Shannon, you lifted the shoe print at the scene of the warehouse fire?" Assistant District Attorney Peter Parker asked the burly witness on the stand.

"Yes."

"What shoe made that print?"

Jackie nudged her client to keep his feet tucked beneath his chair as the court reporter craned to look under the defense table. Staring straight at Ted Wolsky, the detective flashed an evil grin.

"A size 6AA tennis shoe."

"How many arsonists do you know—"

"Objection." Jackie rose. "Detective Shannon has not been qualified as an expert with regard to the average foot size of arsonists in the Denver metropolitan area."

Monday was motions day in the seedy splendor of the Honorable Greta Mueller's courtroom at the City and County Building. A steady parade of men in chains had rotated through the jury box. First up were arraignments and plea bargains, euphemistically referred to as "dispos," so prisoners could be returned to jail in time for lunch. Judging from the expressions on their faces, a visit to court was a welcome alternative to orange Kool-Aid and boiled franks. Ted's prelim was the final matter on the morning docket.

Parker raised an eyebrow at Jackie, then turned confidently to the judge.

"If Your Honor wishes, I'm happy to qualify the detective as an expert in arson."

"Keep it short."

A fiftyish spinster who was the product of sugar beet farmers on the eastern plains, Greta Mueller had inherited more than her father's sagging jowls and cleft chin. In her court the trains ran on time. The difference between her and Mussolini was that she cared who boarded them and where they went.

With a respectful nod, Parker continued. "Detective, how long have you investigated arsons in the Denver metro area?"

"Six years."

"During that period of time, how many arsons have you investigated?"

"Oh . . . upwards of a hundred."

Parker glanced at the judge. Her stoic expression confirmed a hundred cases were enough. "And of those hundred cases," he continued, "in how many did the suspect—"

"Suspect?" Jackie interrupted.

"Just say how many who were convicted wore tiny shoes," Mueller said.

"In those cases, only one suspect who was arrested and convicted—"

"Objection!"

"What is it this time, Ms. Flowers?" Mueller asked.

"Relevancy, Your Honor."

"Relevancy?" Parker echoed. "Detective Shannon already testified a size 6AA shoe print was retrieved from the scene of the crime."

"I believe he said a 6AA *tennis* shoe," Jackie said.

"So what?" Parker said.

"Your Honor, the District Attorney's office has provided me with a videotape taken by the police when Mr. Wolsky was arrested. My client was apprehended one block from the scene of the arson, ten minutes after the alarm was called in. As Mr. Parker likes to say, pictures never lie. If he's unwilling to stipulate that Mr. Wolsky was wearing Italian loafers and not sneakers at the time of his arrest, I would be happy to play the tape for you now." She looked to Pilar, who obligingly waved a black videocassette box from her seat in the first row.

The door to the courtroom swung open and the cacophony of the hallway intruded. A couple of stragglers in the green pajamas of the county jail were led in by a deputy with no neck and biceps the size of hams.

"Mr. Parker?" the judge said.

The prosecutor wasn't panicking—not yet.

"Your Honor, this is a probable cause hearing. Who's to say Mr. Wolsky didn't change his shoes after he left the warehouse? And the shoe print isn't the only evidence we have. The defendant was carrying a Stanley Wonder Bar—"

"—which can be found in half the garages and toolsheds of the citizens of this state," Jackie smoothly finished. "If Mr. Parker was stopped walking down the street and found with a chisel, would that make him a criminal? Your Honor well knows that burglary tools are in the eyes of the beholder."

"You mean the hands of a known felon!" Parker protested. "Ms. Flowers is wasting this court's time with frivolous—"

"Mr. Wolsky is charged with arson, Your Honor. Not burglary. And there's nothing frivolous about a half-baked prosecution that may result in a man being sent to Cañon City for the rest of his life."

Mueller nodded. "Proceed."

Returning to the defense table, Jackie reached into a manila folder and extracted a document. Ted was having difficulty maintaining a straight face.

"Keep a lid on it," Jackie whispered, "you're not home yet."

She turned back to the judge.

"And speaking of experts, I have an affidavit by one Leonard Kramholtz." She handed a copy to Parker and the original to the judge.

Mueller squinted at the papers. "Who's he?"

"Mr. Kramholtz is an adjuster for Mutual State. In his thirty years of investigating arsons for the insurance company, he's analyzed more than a thousand fires. Several of which, I might add, were ultimately attributed to Mr. Wolsky." Jackie smiled apologetically at her client, who was eating it up. The jailbirds in the jury box were bug-eyed. "Mr. Kramholtz has examined the district attorney's file and visited the warehouse. In his expert opinion, Mr. Wolsky did not set that fire."

Parker flung down the affidavit without reading it.

"Your Honor, this is outrageous! First Ms. Flowers hijacks Detective Shannon and disparages his credentials, then she expects you to accept some bogus piece of—"

"Mr. Kramholtz is present in court," Jackie said. "He's prepared to take the stand and detail the dozen arsons he investigated which were attributed to Mr. Wolsky. Mr. Wolsky is a professional—albeit recovering—arsonist who has paid the price of his earlier crimes. It is Mr. Kramholtz's opinion that the warehouse fire fell below Mr. Wolsky's exacting standards, which he perfected over a career spanning some twenty years."

The prisoner at the far end of the dock was laughing so hard the deputy had to yank his chain. Turning to the front row, Jackie gestured to the rumpled man with the hound-dog face sitting beside Pilar. He shuffled to his feet.

"Sit," Mueller said. "Mr. Parker, do you have anything other than the wrong shoe and a Wonder Bar?"

"Your Honor—"

"I thought not. Case dismissed."

"But, Your Honor—"

Greta Mueller rapped her gavel once.

"Mr. Wolsky, you are free to go."

Ten

Colfax Avenue had been named after a politician who granted crooked subsidies to a railroad, and Jackie could associate almost every block of his tawdry namesake with a client she'd represented when she was at the Public Defender's office. Battling her way through the gridlock of Denver's major east-west thoroughfare ten days after Amy Lynch stumbled from the wilds of Left Hand Canyon, she was in no mood for the memories or the traffic.

With a film of grit collecting on the Corolla's windshield, she cranked down her window to see. Ahead of her a dump truck braked and began backing up, halting a line of cars with Jackie at its head. She sank back in her seat, momentarily grateful for the delay. With no court appearances or appointments scheduled, she was dressed for comfort—loose-fitting slacks, a jersey pullover, and well-worn flats. She glanced at her reflection in her rearview mirror. A bit of gray was showing through the honey blonde. Could Lalo squeeze her in that afternoon? Mondays were dead at the salon, but it had been so long since she'd been there. . . . Any place but the office. Between the bickering and the leaking roof, that was the last place she wanted to be.

Jackie was no fool. And criminal defense work wasn't for sissies.

From the first moment, clients never wanted to follow their lawyer's advice. They either didn't understand the system or they understood it too well. Clients came to you at their worst, and often brought out the worst in you. Unlike in a civil case, in a criminal matter you couldn't count on the judge to let you withdraw. Speedy trial rights, docket management—the judge could force you to stay on at trial even if neither lawyer nor client wanted it and you hadn't been paid. Ballard thought the life of a federal judge was rough? Try being chained to a client you despised!

But Jackie had taken so much flack from her officemates for not withdrawing from Ballard's case that she'd almost had second thoughts.

Joel didn't want to be associated with the defense of any federal judge, no matter what he had or hadn't done. Cliff accused Joel of wanting to see Ballard convicted to justify raising the odds against him in the betting pool. Cliff himself was opposed to Jackie staying on the case because he'd bet on an acquittal and was sure she would lose. Phil's office was still vacant so he had nothing to say. Pilar appreciated the retainer.

The time to withdraw was now, while Marlin Pitts would still let her pull out. But Jackie wasn't in such a hurry. Given her previous relationship with Ballard, wouldn't a victory for her in this case be particularly sweet?

As the truck lurched forward and tooted to signal its renewed attempt to back up to a torn stretch of pavement alarmingly close to the Corolla, Jackie wondered whether Phyllis Klein could possibly be at the truck's controls. Would Phyllis dump a load of debris through her windshield? She wouldn't put anything past the Boulder prosecutor. Although Jackie had agreed to stay on the case only until Ballard retained other counsel, the more facts she learned, the more convinced she was that she could walk him.

Ballard's arrest had been based on two coincidences: he owned a pair of stolen handcuffs that just happened to be found on Amy Lynch, and his name was on the title to a deserted cabin where she had apparently been held. No forensic evidence linked him to Amy, who was still in a coma. Ballard's personal and professional reputations were impeccable—as with all presidential appointments to the federal bench, he'd been vetted by the FBI!—and he had neither a motive nor any known connection to the victim. This was one case where the Boulder DA could afford to wait, at least until the victim woke up.

Assistant DA Phyllis Klein was the problem. She'd made her reputation prosecuting rape cases—cut her teeth on vice, as Pilar might say—and seldom ventured outside that arena. If she was handling Ballard's case, why had he been charged only with kidnapping and unlawful detention? The reason Ballard wasn't more concerned was because he knew Amy Lynch would exonerate him. Luckily, the doctors thought it was just a matter of time before she regained consciousness—

With a buck and a snort that shook the asphalt, the dump truck steadied itself and emitted an almost human whine. Slowly the rear bed tilted up and a shimmering mass of rubbish quivered in suspension. Jackie stabbed at the button for her radio. No need to fiddle with the knob—the only station that worked was AM.

"—unexpected turn of events, no longer a kidnapping—"

A shrill whistle drowned out the remaining words. She cranked her window shut and turned up the volume.

"—press conference in Boulder ten minutes from now—"

Without thinking, Jackie jerked her wheel to the left and jumped the yellow line to make a U-turn. Leaving the truck in middump, she sped to her office.

Pilar was turning on the news when Jackie arrived.

"Have you heard?" The investigator's eyes were unusually bright.

On the television screen Lanny Greer was making his way to a bank of reporters outside the Boulder Justice Center. In a navy suit instead of his country-boy tweed coat and knit tie, he strode to the microphones. Behind him marched Phyllis Klein.

"Looks like your old pal finally hooked a big one," Pilar said. "Think she can manage to keep it on the line?"

"This time she'll be more careful."

Jackie's history with Phyllis dated back five years, when Klein was appointed special prosecutor on a statewide grand jury investigation in a vice and corruption case. Jackie had negotiated immunity for one of the witnesses. When the grand jury was disbanded without issuing any indictments, Phyllis had blamed Jackie. But that was history. Wasn't it?

Against a backdrop of purple foothills and brilliant sky, in her snug little pink suit, Klein was positively Swiss. The only jarring note was her eyeliner, which gave her a look of startled outrage. Given her conviction rate, her makeup apparently played well to Boulder juries.

"How do you think she feels," Pilar asked, "having you on the other side?"

"You kidding? She's been waiting five years."

Lanny Greer was clearing his throat. Meant to focus the cameras on him, the cue sounded more nervous than authoritative.

"This morning at University Hospital—" He waited until the cameras had zoomed in. "This morning in the intensive care unit at University Hospital, Amy Lynch died."

Greer paused so long the reporters began peppering him with questions.

"Did she talk?"

"Will Bryan and Bonnie be making a statement?"

"What's the cause of death?"

He held up his hand and waited for the hubbub to subside.

"Amy died just after three A.M. as a result of complications from the exposure she suffered after escaping from her captor. She was a very courageous—"

A brash pip-squeak from Channel 4 pushed his way forward.

"Will Glenn Ballard be charged with murder?"

"No decision has yet been made," Greer said.

"As if it's someone else's call," Pilar muttered.

"Amy's parents have asked me to read something their daughter wrote one year ago," Greer continued. Withdrawing a sheet of lined notebook paper from his breast pocket, he paused to balance his spectacles on the tip of his nose. He gazed out at the crowd, waiting until he had its full attention. His voice trembled with emotion. "I am quoting to you now from an essay Amy wrote, which was printed in her high school yearbook. . . ."

Someone coughed and a voice said, "Shush."

" 'Right now I want to be everything,'" Greer read.

He paused until an anonymous voice broke the silence.

"You think it's the same guy who killed JonBenet?"

"We have no reason whatsoever—" Greer flushed as he realized that was a joke. Squaring his shoulders, he took a deep breath and continued. "Amy Lynch had her whole life ahead of her, a life of endless promise and opportunities. Whoever abducted that girl from the safety of her family and friends, whoever chained and held her naked in a freezing cabin, starving her and subjecting her to depraved acts for three days before she escaped into the wilds of Left Hand Canyon"—his voice rose to a crescendo of indignation and rage—"whatever *animal* did that, demonstrated such *universal malice and extreme indifference to the value of human life,* my office fully intends to prosecute him to the fullest extent of the law!"

Eleven

With its low ceiling, blond paneling, and artificial light, the Honorable Marlin Pitts's courtroom was as hermetic and compact as a shoe box. The podium separating the counsel tables was three paces from the witness stand. The angled bench was two steps up from the carpeted floor, and the jury box had swiveled chairs. If asked to describe his domain in ecclesiastical terms, Pitts would have likened it neither to the Gothic cathedrals of the federal judiciary nor to Greta Mueller's communion rail, but to a Unitarian Universalist church. Jackie had not, however, come to Boulder to be converted.

Lanny Greer's first order of business after filing a murder charge against Glenn Ballard was to renege on the PR bond and announce he would oppose bail. There'd been no time for Ballard to retain another lawyer. His rearraignment and bond hearing were set for the morning after Greer's press conference, and Jackie intended to use the opportunity to put the prosecution to the test. Greer may have moved too fast in order to avoid being accused of not moving at all. But his chief deputy was not about to rise to Jackie's bait. Not in the presence of representatives of all the major wire services, who were scribbling in their notebooks in the front row.

"—not one shred of evidence linking Judge Ballard to Amy Lynch," Jackie reiterated, "other than an old pair of handcuffs which he freely admitted were his, and which happened to be stolen. As for that cabin—"

"Your Honor"—Phyllis Klein shook her head wearily as she rose to cut off her adversary—"this is a bail hearing. Under no circumstances am I required to establish probable cause."

"Probable cause?" Jackie shot back. "To oppose bail in a capital case, the prosecution has to show far more: that the proof is evident and the presumption great that Amy Lynch died by criminal means and Judge Ballard is connected to the crimes charged. Kidnapping and murder."

"Death by criminal means?" The skirt of Klein's peacock blue suit was short enough to expose shapely calves, but the clownish bow on her silk blouse dispelled any notion of sexuality. Most DAs dressed conservatively, but Phyllis took dowdiness a step further. She looked like a schoolmarm who ran marathons. "If Ms. Flowers likes, I can call the intensive care nurse who was with Amy when she died as a result of the pneumonia she contracted from running barefoot through Left Hand Canyon."

Why the nurse?

"Not a bad idea, but I'd prefer to hear from her doctor." Jackie paused to let her words sink in.

Marlin Pitts was difficult to read. His decade on the bench was noteworthy for lack of event, but most judges cared more about not being reversed than being right. His avuncular look—along with his striped shirt, wire-rimmed glasses, and the graying hair that curled at the collar of his robe—didn't fool Jackie. He'd been passed over twice by senators in his own party for an appointment to the federal bench. Not an encouraging fact if your client was a United States District Judge.

"Come to think of it," Jackie continued, "where are the medical records?"

"The autopsy report isn't complete." Klein's nonchalance nudged Jackie's antennae higher. What was it about Amy's condition that Phyllis was trying to hide?

"What evidence do you have of sexual molestation?"

Bull's-eye. Klein blinked furiously in an effort to recover. She wanted to charge Ballard with a sex crime so badly Jackie could taste it.

"Not all the tests have come back."

"I want all the medical records you have, and the autopsy report as soon as it's available. That includes the results of any blood tests." Jackie hadn't forgotten the ketamine rumor. But she failed to reckon on the Solomonic wisdom of Marlin Pitts.

"If your request for records is to establish whether Amy Lynch died by criminal means, Ms. Flowers, do you have any objection to my taking judicial notice of the fact that she expired from pneumonia without emerging from a coma?"

The Boulder bench gave "hometowning" a new dimension. Pitts's harmonic trade-off made Jackie wonder if Klein was one of the local lawyers he jogged with every day at noon. Marveling at how quickly judge and prosecutor had aligned, she set out fresh bait.

"Even if we assume Ms. Lynch died of pneumonia from her journey through the woods, what connects Glenn Ballard to the crime?"

Klein sprang her own trap.

"That cabin's been in your client's name since 1995, and he was seen within two miles of it last December!"

Dead uncle, my foot.

At the defense table Glenn Ballard didn't stir. His unwillingness to level with his lawyer would soon be someone else's problem. The minute this hearing was over, Jackie was off the case. Until then she might as well earn her fee. "Is there any evidence Judge Ballard was there with Amy Lynch?"

"There were no signs of forced entry."

Under other circumstances Klein's smugness would have been a warning not to push. But Jackie had nothing to lose.

"What, *if anything,* places my client at the alleged scene of the crime?"

"There were no fingerprints, if that's what you mean. In fact, there were no fingerprints anywhere in the cabin."

"Then you have no forensic—"

"Don't you find it curious that your client owns a cabin in which none of his fingerprints were found?"

Klein's logic was inescapable. Prints remained detectable for years and one would expect to find Ballard's at a cabin that had been in his family for generations. If a stranger had broken in and used the place to imprison Amy Lynch, why wipe every surface clean? But the cabin was also a hundred years old and had been used for hunting. Rough-hewn walls were notoriously difficult to lift prints from.

Something else troubled Jackie. Sexual assault was Klein's specialty and Amy Lynch's abduction fairly reeked of it, but the prosecution was dancing around that issue. Had they run a toxicology screen for ketamine or other mood enhancers? Fingerprints or not, the case was entirely circumstantial and there was no basis for denying bond. The only question was how much. As if on cue, Pitts intervened.

"Despite the evident strength of Ms. Klein's case, I'm granting bail."

"Judge Ballard poses no flight risk," Jackie assured him before the DA could respond. "With his position on the federal court—"

"Half a million dollars," Klein said. Glowing with the upset she'd scored, she was preening for the media. But her antagonism had a personal quality and Jackie was well aware of its source.

"Two hundred and fifty thousand dollars," Pitts ruled. Ballard snorted at the predictable compromise. Aside from nodding pleasantly to the stringer from Reuters on his way into court, it was his first reaction all day.

"I'd like an order requiring immediate production of all medical records," Jackie demanded before Klein's toes touched the ground.

Pitts nodded. "Shall we set the trial?"

"Judge Ballard would like the earliest available date. These charges have been quite disruptive of his routine."

Pitts paged through his calendar. "How many days do you need?" he asked the DA.

"Two weeks, Your Honor."

"Last two weeks of July?" he offered.

Just four months to prepare. Knowing how prosecutors hated to be caught flat-footed, Jackie waited for Phyllis to say she was stacked with trials through August.

"That will be fine, Your Honor."

With a nod and a bang of his gavel, Pitts adjourned.

Jackie waited for the courtroom to empty of reporters before turning to her client.

"Shot yourself in the foot, didn't you?" Ballard began. "I knew exactly where she was going with those prints."

"You told me you'd just inherited that cabin!"

"It's an old shack."

"When's the last time you were there?"

"I may have stopped by over the winter to check—"

"May?"

"I don't punch a time clock when I visit my properties, Ms. Flowers. And I hardly see the relevance—"

"Look, *Glenn,* you're not in law school anymore." Unflinchingly she met his gaze. "Or on the bench. In case you haven't noticed, someone else is calling the shots. And as of this moment I'm off your case."

"Not afraid of her, are you?"

His mild tone threw Jackie off.

"Klein? Don't make me laugh!"

But Phyllis had something to hide, and it had to do with Amy's medical condition. And she would do anything to even old scores. Trying a case against her would drag Jackie back to a place she didn't want to go.

"Are you in or out?" he continued.

"What? I just told you—"

"One question only, Counselor. Are you in or out?"

A thousand thoughts ran through her head.

Greer was afraid to try this case. Just as badly, his chief deputy wanted it.

Ballard was a client who was easy to dislike and difficult to trust.

The evidence reeked. . . . And Jackie was being offered an easy way out.

"I'm in."

Twelve

The Amy Lynch plastered across the news had the hormonal allure of a girl on the verge of discovery. With her laughing squint and ponytail, chubby cheeks and untamed brows, the head shot might have been taken at the Denver Country Club pool or the Kent School soccer field on which she'd just led the girls' team to victory.

Right now I want to be everything.

Pilar called it the myth of unlimited opportunity.

The photo Jackie's investigator passed across the conference room table was different. As she scoured the four-by-six glossy, another girl stared back.

Amy's chestnut hair was swept in a soft wave from her face and clasped in a loose knot with the end cascading down the front of one shoulder in a luxuriant roll. Her eyebrows arched up and away from wide gray eyes whose gaze was challenging and frank. Even her bone structure seemed to have changed; the baby fat had been pared away to reveal high cheekbones set off by a trace of blush. The rest of her makeup was almost undetectable—soft eye shadow and the sheerest gloss on her unsmiling lips. Three tiny silver studs graced the rim of her left ear.

Amy Lynch had been aware of her own beauty, although she hadn't seemed to take pleasure in it. Was she sophisticated beyond her years in other ways, too?

"What I'd give for an hour with her stylist . . . ," Pilar said.

"When was this taken?" There was no date on the back.

"Don't know. It was in the file."

Between the ponytail and the glamour shots, Amy Lynch had learned all there was to know.

It was one week after Ballard's bail hearing, and Jackie and Pilar were sitting at the walnut table in the dining room of the robber baron's former digs. Ballard had posted bond and was already back at work. Although his criminal docket had been transferred to the chief judge for the duration, no one protested his continuing to handle civil cases.

Indeed, it was almost as if he'd never been arrested. But for Jackie it was time to get down to business. She reached for the autopsy photos.

The first was a close-up of Amy's head. The bruises on her throat had faded from black to maroon and her face looked almost peaceful. Indeed, there were no injuries anywhere above the neck. Skipping over the grisly full-length photographs taken on the slab, Jackie came to a series of what could only be called body parts. Several showed abrasions to Amy's palms and knees, as if she'd been dragged across a rough floor. She paused at a photo of Amy's right wrist.

The handcuff had cut almost to the bone, leaving a jagged wound and an ugly discoloration that had spread to the heel of her palm. She peered at the skin below the wrist. Six diagonal scars like chevrons, three on each side, pointed in an arrow to a tender juncture of veins. Unlike the marks on Amy's hands and knees and the abrasions from the handcuffs, these were clearly old. She slid the photograph across the table.

"Suicide attempt?" Pilar asked.

"Too many marks. And they're in the wrong place." The scar tissue was pale and smooth, the ridges as precise as a Navajo sand painting. "People who slit their wrists use horizontal strokes. If they want to die, they slice vertically up a vein."

"Do you think whoever snatched Amy did that to her?"

"My guess is she made the cuts herself," Jackie said. "They're old, and it looks like she went into the scars more than once."

She turned to another photo. This one made her wince.

Below Amy's bikini line a jagged series of marks emanated like rays from her pubis. Again they looked old. More shocking was the silver ring in her labia.

"Is this in the autopsy report?"

Pilar shuffled through the papers from Klein's office.

"Multiple premortem piercings in the labia minora and majora, and through the left nipple. Numerous marks that could have been made by safety pins." The close-up of Amy's chest revealed a small black hole in the left areola but no ring.

Jackie shuddered. "That must have hurt. What would possess a girl to do that to herself?"

Pilar took her time lighting a cigarillo.

"Ever heard of body art?"

"Body art? Jesus, Pilar, just look—"

"Maybe it was a turn-on."

"For *whom*?"

"Look, Jackie, I don't know where you've been, but kids have been tattooing themselves for years. Remember that waitress the last time we went to your transvestite coffee shop?"

"Those piercings were in her eyebrow and nose."

"And don't forget her tongue. It's a sign of rebellion—not that you could call it rebellious when ninety-five percent of your peers are doing it."

Jackie knew the driving force of young girls was to fit in. But adolescents also struggled for individualization. They wanted privacy and autonomy, to insulate themselves from the indifference of an increasingly impersonal society. Was Amy's body the canvas on which she'd marked out her territory? And if she needed to go to such extremes to insulate herself—from *what*?

"This is different." Jackie struggled to articulate why. "Amy's piercings were intimate, not meant to be seen by any Joe on the street."

"Which brings us back to the turn-on," Pilar said.

"You seem to know a lot about it."

"Maybe I do."

"Pi-*lar*!"

Pilar blew a perfect smoke ring. "Different strokes for different folks, I always say."

"Now I know why you date insurance adjusters and cops."

"Only when I'm desperate."

"Kinkiness aside, doesn't a ring . . . get in the way?"

"Never cramped *my* style." Pilar was enjoying this. "Jackie, you've got to get out more. There's a whole world beyond these moldy walls."

Jackie returned the photos to their envelope and sealed it. "Did the pathologist say whether there was penetration?"

"Inconclusive."

"What about the fact that they found only one ring?"

"The number doesn't matter. The thrill's in the pain associated with their insertion and forcing the victim to wear them. Or so they say. It's called S and M."

Maybe that ring had been applied earlier. And if Amy was tortured, why no injuries to her face? But Pilar must be right.

"So they're looking for a sadist . . ."

"Hel-*lo,* Jackie!"

"How on earth did Amy manage to get away?"

Pilar shrugged. "Whether it was through carelessness or sadism, it hardly matters. Amy was barefoot and naked when she was found. The cabin was a quarter mile away as the crow flies, but she had to get through a ravine and an icy stream, so the distance she had to go was much longer. Whoever held her must have known she would never survive naked in the snow—much less be able to run more than a mile in handcuffs over rough terrain dragging a chain behind her. It's a miracle she survived as long as she did."

"Do we have photos of the cabin?"

Pilar rooted through the file for another envelope and Jackie turned with relief to a second set of glossies. They provided her second surprise.

The cabin was hardly the broken-down shack Glenn Ballard had described.

Set in a clearing with commanding views of creek and ravine, the log dwelling was trim and spare and had a pitched roof to sluice off rain and snow. The mortared chimney rested on a stone foundation, and although poorly maintained, the private road that led to the structure certainly appeared passable. Most important, the cabin showed no signs of a break-in.

"What'd you expect?" Pilar knew exactly what Jackie was thinking. "Ballard wants to distance himself from the crime."

At least she hadn't said *his* crime.

"Whoever abducted Amy had to know where the cabin was, that it was accessible, and that they would be undisturbed," Jackie said. "I wonder how many locals knew it was there."

"What did Ballard say about being seen in Left Hand back in December?"

"He told me he stopped to check on the cabin on his way home from cross-country skiing near Brainard Lake."

"Brainard Lake? I thought he spent his weekends at his ranch up in Craig. That's the opposite side of the Continental Divide! But as you always say, it's easier to defend a guilty man than one who's truly innocent."

Thirteen

Jackie pushed back her chair and went to the sideboard to pour herself coffee. What had seemed like a slam-dunk was rapidly becoming anything but. And with a client who seemed intent on remaining an enigma . . . The coffee was cold and after one sip she pushed it away. "It certainly would be a novelty to defend someone blameless. Why do you think Ballard hired me, anyway? There are any number of lawyers in town who can name their price. They're in his court every day."

"Maybe that's the point," Pilar said. "You're one of the few who has never appeared before Ballard. You have no reason to hate him."

"Well, he's obviously forgotten law school."

"Maybe he respected you more than you thought."

"Ha! It's more likely that because I was his student, he thinks he can control me." Jackie remembered the challenge he had issued after the bond hearing. "It's like mud wrestling. He wants a woman to square off against Phyllis Klein."

"If that dame had any class, she'd be in it by herself," Pilar said. "The only broad I know who uses black liner on her eyes *and* her lips. How would you like her rooting through your drawers? It's almost enough to make me feel sorry for your client."

"To Phyllis, everything is a sex crime."

"In Boulder that's smart politics. You think she's stonewalling you on the medical reports?"

Pilar had placed three unreturned calls to the DA's office and Jackie was on the verge of dictating a motion for a forthwith order. She'd suspected the ketamine rumor was bull, but with Phyllis you never knew how much was fact and how much was personal.

"That grand jury mess with Phyllis and you," Pilar said. "Right about the time you broke up with Dennis Ross, wasn't it?"

"Jeez, do you have to bring up the worst time of my life?"

Pilar fired up another cigarillo. "I always liked him."

"That skydiver without a parachute?" It came out more bitter than Jackie intended.

"He had a way of landing on his feet," Pilar agreed, "even if he broke both legs doing it. That's what made him so sexy. Of course, I've always been a sucker for those frankly-Scarlett-I don't-give-a-damn types."

So had Jackie.

Five years her senior and the star trial lawyer in the Public Defender's office, Dennis Ross had taken Jackie under his wing the day she was hired. He'd let her second-chair her first felony case with him, but it was a year before their physical relationship began. By then she'd been winning felonies for six months on her own and Pilar had become her secretary.

"You never said why you broke up," Pilar went on. "It couldn't have been problems in the sack. As I recall, you two were going at it hot and heavy right to the end."

Pilar was correct, but Jackie wasn't about to go into it. The memories were too painful. When she ended their relationship, Dennis had resigned from the PD's office. After months of bumming around South America he'd returned to Denver and joined Kellogg & Kemp, the stuffiest firm on Seventeenth Street, to run their litigation department. Jackie had heard he'd married a paralegal.

"He certainly bounced right back."

"Yeah, they call it the rebound." Pilar was undeterred. "He would have come running if you'd called."

"Exactly why I didn't."

"In all fairness, it lasted less than a year."

"What did?"

"His marriage to Miss Fancy-pants."

So he probably had no kids. Jackie waited for Pilar to continue, but for once her investigator had lost her taste for gossip.

Stubbing out her cigarillo, Pilar began filing away the materials from the DA. "What do you think she's trying to hide?"

"Phyllis? My bet is they ran a tox screen on Amy."

"And?"

"Discovered something that fills in the blanks. Like, what she was doing before she was abducted." Jackie paused. "I wonder how she'll handle the absence of sexual assault."

"Wouldn't you love to see Klein try to prosecute a straight homicide!"

"Don't underestimate her," Jackie warned. "She's capable of anything if she gets desperate enough. . . . Speaking of blanks, what do we know about Amy's activities the day she disappeared?"

Pilar reached for another stack of reports.

"She was last seen at Finnegan's Wake, an off-campus bar. Her roommate—"

"Wasn't it a school night?"

Pilar stared. "Pardon me, Officer. That girl was eighteen!"

"When I was in college, we went to 3.2 beer joints on the Hill. And not on Tuesday nights."

"Lordy, how times have changed. As I was saying, Amy's roommate, Erin, told the DA's investigator Amy invited her along. But Erin had a paper to write."

"Did Erin report Amy missing when she didn't return?"

"Nooo . . ." Pilar shuffled through more papers. "Not until the following evening. Amy had an exam the next afternoon and Erin was sure she was at the library studying. When she didn't show up for dinner, she notified the dorm adviser, not the cops."

"Protecting her friend. Who else did the detectives interview?"

"Amy's boyfriend, Matt Fisher. He was working Tuesday night."

"Where?"

Pilar consulted another report. "Two jobs: student union cafeteria, and hashing at a sorority house."

"Both of which close at a reasonable hour. Who's the last person who saw Amy?"

"Bartender at Finnegan's Wake. He said she was with an older crowd."

"While Matt was slaving away in a kitchen," Jackie said.

Amy was an eighteen-year-old finishing her freshman year, living away from home for the first time. But judging from those piercings, she'd hardly been the stereotypical freshman glorying in her freedom to return from dates without her father waiting at the door. How experienced had she really been with men? Had she enjoyed testing their limits?

"Doesn't seem to have bothered Matt," Pilar said. "He insists they were getting along fine."

"A truly liberated man. I wonder what he thought of her rings. . . . Did the bartender know the people Amy was with?"

Pilar squinted at the DA's investigator's notes. "He called them 'dot commies.'"

"Dot commies?"

"Half the nonstudent population of Boulder lives on trust funds. Internet stocks may be worthless now, but some of these kids were savvy enough to cash out before they tanked."

"Amy had friends in that crowd?"

"The bartender said they looked pretty chummy. She was dressed to the teeth—skintight leather pants, sweater down to *there*. Never thought to card her."

Which young woman was the real Amy, Jackie wondered—the schoolgirl her roommate had described, at least for the benefit of the cops, or the siren at Finnegan's Wake? Jackie didn't believe that Amy Lynch's scars and piercings were body art. Like the cabin in Left Hand Canyon, she was willing to bet that none of the versions she'd heard so far was the truth. And that Amy's killer had known her before Amy walked into that bar.

"Was it really a dog collar around her throat?"

"I'll check next time I'm at PETsMART."

"Seriously, was it sold at a pet store?"

"That wasn't in the police reports. But if it was made for Fido, he must have been a mastiff. The leather was two inches wide and buckled at the first hole." Seeing her boss blanch Pilar added, "At least he didn't use a choke chain."

"Let's get down to business," Jackie said. Pilar pulled out her yellow pad and a pen. "I'll take Matt and Erin, and Amy's parents. Why don't you take the barflies?"

"My specialty. Think you'll get anything out of Bryan and Bonnie Lynch?"

Something was strange there. Jackie had driven past Amy's parents' house in Hilltop. There was an elementary school down the street, but not the one Amy went to. She had attended Graland Country Day, the private academy directly across the park from the Lynch home, until she transferred to Kent. The park was treeless and almost flat. From the second floor of their house they could have watched their daughter walk to class at Graland every day. But the Lynches could have afforded a much fancier spread in Cherry Hills. Was Graland the reason they chose Hilltop?

"I don't know what I'll find."

They mapped out a schedule and gathered up the files. As they were turning out the lights, Pilar said, "I almost forgot to tell you. Another temp quit."

"So what else is new?"

"This one knew her stuff—she revived the Xerox after Cliff beat the crap out of it. We were hoping she'd go permanent."

"What happened?" The lease renewal still hadn't been signed, and the landlord was counting every day of the grace period.

"Allergies. At least, that's what she said." Pilar hesitated. "Joel made a pass."

Sexual harassment time. "We're lucky she just quit."

"There's a new guy coming in who Cliff's just wild about."

"Great! Another body to soak up overhead."

"What kind of lawyer offers to rent by the week?"

"We'll talk about it tomorrow."

Pilar checked the burglar alarm and reached for her keys. "I called the Central City Opera House."

"Central City?" It took Jackie a moment to focus: Her mind was on that dog collar. But they'd been planning to take Lily to her first opera to celebrate her acceptance to ballet camp. "What's playing?"

"Two choices. *Alice* or *La Bohème*."

"*La Bohème*? Isn't that about a woman who dies?"

"Every opera has a heroine who croaks. That's why they're so much fun."

"What's *Alice* about?"

"A modern version of *Alice in Wonderland*. I vote for *Bohème*. The star runs around in something sexier than an apron and a headband."

"But I loved that book!" Jackie's aunt had read it to her when she was Lily's age. "Alice was a great role model. Curious, imaginative, strong-willed—"

"Just what Lily needs. Lewis Carroll was nothing but a closet pedophile."

"Pedophile?"

"He liked 'em young. Alice was a real child, you know. Innocence is seductive—if you can tell who's the seducer. Girls are a lot more sophisticated these days."

"Fascination with youth hardly makes someone a pedophile. And Alice was no Lolita. Don't you remember when she stepped through the looking glass? To get anywhere you had to walk in the opposite direction, and to stay in the same place you had to run as fast as you could."

Pilar locked the door and rattled the knob. "No wonder you liked her. Upside down and backward is your whole damn life!"

But Jackie wasn't listening.

"If the dog collar didn't come from PETsMART, who would have sold it?"

"The Dark Side," Pilar replied.

"Dark Side?"

"That S and M emporium on South Broadway."

Fourteen

Straining tea from cardamom pods, scarlet threads of saffron, and a stick of cinnamon that had unfurled like a bit of parchment, Jackie inhaled the comforting scents. She slowly added steamed milk to the amber fluid. The maiden aunt who'd raised her after her parents died had made a ritual of tea with milk before bed, adding the Indian spices as Jackie grew older. Padding around her kitchen in her bare feet and the royal blue robe she'd worn since college, she wished her aunt were still nearby.

Jackie arranged her ceramic teapot and mug on a lacquered tray and carried it to the study on the ground floor of her century-old brick Denver Square just east of Cheesman Park. She'd bought it five years earlier, when she'd left the Public Defender's office to hang out her shingle. Before settling in her aunt's brocaded armchair, she peeked through her blinds to see if Lily's light was on next door. Britt and Randy's house was dark. She poured herself a mug of fragrant tea.

Pilar didn't know the half of it when she'd said Jackie's life was upside down and backward. Of course she related to Alice and her contrary companions. How could you not love the nonsense of the Jabberwocky, written in a script Jackie's classmates had to hold to a mirror to read! Didn't running as fast as she could to stay where she was, and twice as fast to get anywhere else, define Jackie's life on a *good* day? How well she remembered climbing into a warm lap in this very chair and being transported by the timbre of her aunt's voice as she read aloud. And the peculiar relief that washed over her the day she learned about her father's cousin who'd left school in the eighth grade.

"He was a brilliant boy," her aunt had said. "There was nothing wrong with his brain."

"Then why couldn't he read?" Jackie asked.

"He had other strengths. He could fix anything he put his hands on."

"Did kids tease him?"

"Don't ever be ashamed because you're different, Jackie." If he had nothing to be ashamed of, why had he spent the rest of his life fixing radios? "Listen to me. The trick is to take what makes you weak and use it to make you strong. . . ."

Just what she had to do for Glenn Ballard now. Refilling her mug, Jackie drew her flannel robe close and turned to her client's defense.

Two enigmas were two too many for one case.

Clients were frequently unknown quantities: often the less you knew about them, the better. Victims, on the other hand, were frozen in their survivors' equally unreliable memories. Although Amy Lynch hadn't lived long enough to be a true enigma and Ballard's life was largely a matter of public record, Jackie was struggling to form a picture of who they really were. Did the Glenn Ballard she'd known in law school bear any resemblance to the man she was defending for murder?

Jackie had assumed law would entail fieldwork, interviewing, listening, and arguing in court. To her surprise, she not only survived but actively thrived in law school. Her tolerance for incomprehension made the ordeal less daunting than it was for her classmates; accustomed to not understanding what she read, she wasn't thrown by the archaic style of her casebooks nor the rhetorical claptrap of legal opinions. The complexity of their analytical structure did not faze her for the simple reason that she was oblivious to it.

Nor was it difficult to withstand the humiliations of the Socratic dialogue. Hadn't grade school taught her to survive being made fun of in front of a room full of strangers? Because she looked and sounded bright, teachers from high school on had assumed that despite her illegible handwriting, fantastical spelling, and nonexistent sentence structure Jackie was intelligent. Year after year they awarded her a pass.

Law school was no different. Most of her teachers wanted her to succeed. She was quick on her feet, and her memory for facts and details and her ability to joust with her tormentors were applauded. Jackie's professors gave her passing grades, but she lived in dread of being exposed for the fraud she knew she was. That moment came after the final exam in Glenn Ballard's class.

"Ms. Flowers, I thought it only courteous to tell you to your face that you have flunked Criminal Procedure." Ballard handed Jackie her blue book. The cover bore an enormous *F,* circled and underlined in red.

His cold eyes probed hers. "I have just one question: This *is* your examination, is it not?"

Not trusting her voice, Jackie nodded.

"I didn't think there was any way you could have copied it. I also thought I should inform you that never, in all my years of teaching, have I encountered a student so grossly deficient in the English language. How on earth did you finesse your way into law school?"

"I—"

He silenced her with a wave of his hand.

"I don't care to know the answer. You don't look like the sort who would cheat, so I can only assume your success reflects a long line of 'educators' who lacked the courage to flunk you. One of us has to put a stop to your charade, and that duty apparently falls to me."

"But—"

"Lest you think this is somehow personal, let me remind you that a law school has the responsibility to not graduate students who are unequipped to take the bar. An even more fundamental task is to weed out those who are unfit, morally or intellectually, to represent clients. Law school isn't a charity ward. Only the best and brightest students can be expected to compete. I fear that you, Ms. Flowers, are not among their number."

Jackie had tried to control the tremor that had begun in her knees. Shame gave way to fear. Crim Pro was a second-year course, not part of the core curriculum. Other students could graduate without passing it, but her grade point average was already so low she was at risk of flunking out. And what if she was truly unfit to practice law? What if Ballard was *right*?

"Frankly, I'll be amazed if you pass the bar."

Despite Ballard's prophesy and his F grade, Jackie had graduated from law school and taken the bar exam. On the first day she developed a bone-crushing headache that made it almost impossible to think. Two hours into the second day, the fluorescent lights sent slivers of glass into her cortex and she could barely see the page. At the end, all she could do was stumble home. When she received the letter from the bar examiners, she had to have her aunt call to confirm the news. Once again she had *passed.* . . .

No thanks to the man who'd judged her unfit to represent clients.

And now Glenn Ballard was asking to be her client. But if she turned him away because she despised him, or if she failed to do her very best, what kind of lawyer would she be? She didn't need Pilar to tell her what Dennis Ross would say.

We're all guilty. It's just a question of what.

Jackie poured herself another cup of butterscotch-colored tea. She peered through her blinds again, but the house next door was still dark. Had Britt and Randy taken Lily out to dinner? Her eyes wandered to the shelf of minerals above her desk. She reached for her favorite, a Chinese fluorite on a wavy sphalerite base. Holding the aqua and violet cube to the light, she stared into a storm-tossed sea. Pictures she understood: you either saw them or you didn't. Was the pattern that was emerging in her mind about Ballard's case a product of her feelings about him or of the fact that he obviously wasn't telling her everything? If only she had a better read on him . . . or maybe her read was too good.

What would her strategy be?

The big "so what"—that kissing cousin to reasonable doubt?

So what if Ballard owned the cabin where Amy Lynch was tortured?

So what if the handcuffs that bound her wrists were his?

So what if none of his prints were found in a cabin he not only owned but admitted visiting countless times?

So what if his self-righteousness and cruelty made it all too easy to visualize him torturing a young girl?

When in doubt, come out swinging. That's what Dennis Ross would do.

Dennis's philosophy was simple: Rules were made to be broken, go with your gut, and never be afraid to ask the question whose answer you don't know. He'd had nothing but contempt for big-firm litigators with their armies of associates. *Trying a case with all those people is like wearing six condoms.* And he was a master of spontaneity, the foolishly extravagant act. When he sent Jackie two dozen long-stem roses after her first solo acquittal, she'd complained to Pilar that he was trying to make the entire office think she'd slept with him. Pilar had said, "Are you nuts? Everyone knows you don't send two dozen roses *after* you get laid!"

A swashbuckler, yes. But Pilar had gotten it only half right.

What made Jackie's former lover so sexy wasn't that he leaped first and looked later, nor that through sheer instinct and holding nothing back he won defense verdicts no one else could. Nor even that what he gave in court didn't even approximate his performance in bed.

It was that he encouraged Jackie to take risks but he never let her take the fall.

Tappity-*tap* . . .

Jackie looked up. Still no light next door but a small face was at the window. Belting her robe, she rose to let Lily in.

"Isn't it past your bedtime?"

Lily was dressed in red leggings and a matching T, and her long, tapered toes were encased in the black calfskin slippers she'd been wearing since the day she was accepted to ballet camp. The rhinestone collar was gone, but Britt and Randy would not be happy if they knew she was running around at this hour in her jammies. If Glenn Ballard was not the man Phyllis Klein said he was, someone who liked young girls in the worst way was roaming the streets.

"I gave the sitter the slip. She's watching a movie in the basement. If she misses me she'll *know* to look for me here." Lifting the lid off the teapot, she gave a suspicious sniff. "Why's it cloudy?"

"Hemlock. Care for a cup?"

"Sure!"

Jackie went to the kitchen for another mug. When she returned, Lily was holding the fluorite to the light. Jackie poured them tea and added three teaspoons of sugar to Lily's cup.

"That ship's still there." Lily seemed almost resentful. "How come it hasn't sailed back to China?"

"Maybe it likes this port. Looking forward to camp?"

"Actually—not."

"Six weeks till school's out . . ."

Lily set down the fluorite. "I can't wait for it to be over." Taking a small sip of tea, she stared into her mug. "Is this *milk*?"

"Matter of fact, yes."

Lily pushed the tea away. "You know I don't drink milk."

"Since when?"

"It's fattening."

Jackie suppressed an urge to laugh. "First of all, it's two-percent. And second, you weigh sixty pounds soaking wet! Since when are you worried about your weight?"

"You can never be too thin."

Thinness—the ticket to success, glory, love.

"Who told you that nonsense?"

"Miss Wilson."

Lily's ballet teacher. Was that why she was having second thoughts about camp?

"There's lots to do in Steamboat besides dance. I'll bet they have horses—"

"Maybe I have better things to do here."

Lily's mother, Britt, was a realtor whose busiest season was spring. When her stockbroker husband, Randy, wasn't on the tennis court, he was playing golf. But Britt had racked up big sales this year and they'd booked a trip to Chile in July. A second honeymoon, Britt had said. Just the two of them.

"Such as?" Jackie pressed.

"Summer school." Lily's smile was as stiff as cotton candy and Jackie suddenly realized this would be the first time the little girl would be away from home since China. She'd spent the night with Jackie many times, but never had a sleep-over with children her own age. She just didn't want to, she'd said. Jackie set down her mug and pulled Lily onto her lap.

"My first night away from home, I couldn't even cry myself to sleep. They had to call my aunt to pick me up. I wasn't as brave as you, of course. But it's scary to be alone."

"It isn't *me*. . . . I mean, there's things I have to take care of."

"What things?"

Lily jumped off Jackie's lap. "Never mind."

"When's visiting day?"

"July fifteenth." Already counting the hours.

"How about if Pilar and I drive—"

"I told you, I don't want to go!"

"But, Lily, you've been looking forward—"

"No!"

This was clearly more than first-time-away-from-home jitters.

"Are you sleeping okay?" Jackie asked gently.

"Sometimes I wake up."

"What do you dream about?"

"China. But it's getting harder and harder to go back . . ."

One foot in Denver and the other in Shanghai.

Jackie remembered Britt telling her about the day she and Randy got Lily. After endless red tape and confusion, they had finally fetched the silent child from the orphanage and brought her to a hotel for the night. As the three of them lay awake on cots, Britt had feared they'd made a terrible mistake. Just then a little voice piped up in the darkness. It was Lily, singing them to sleep with a lullaby in Chinese. That was when Britt knew it would work out.

If only Lily could have been so sure.

And now she wanted to be a ballerina, the ultimate symbol of Western femininity and grace. Jackie brushed aside her own misgivings. Lily couldn't return to Shanghai and she needed a break from Denver. Ballet camp should be a rite of passage. A cause for celebration.

"How would you like to go to the opera?"

"Opera?" she said suspiciously.

"Pilar's ordering tickets for a Sunday matinee, and we thought you might like to join us."

"Where?"

"Central City." *Alice* had better not be sold out. Jackie dangled more bait. "You'd have to dress up. It might even be worth a trip to Lalo's for a manicure."

"Can we ride in the Spider?"

"We'll talk about it tomorrow, okay?" Jackie took Lily's hand. "Now let's get you to bed. Is your back door unlocked?"

Lily shook her head. "I climbed out the side window. The screen's open."

Keeping to the shadows so the sitter wouldn't see them, Jackie walked Lily across the strip of grass dividing their yards. She propped open the screen and gave Lily a boost.

"Now, lock that window," she whispered, and waited until the sash thudded shut and the girl twisted the knob securing the latch. With a wave, they parted.

Jackie reheated the last of her tea in the microwave and carried it upstairs to her bedroom. She thought she saw a pale face at the window in Lily's bedroom, but when she turned on her lamp it was gone. With a sigh, she reached for the remote to catch the ten o'clock news. Could Lily possibly be responding to Jackie's own fears for the girl's safety? Pilar would know—

"—anyone who tries to tarnish my little girl's reputation!"

Flushed with rage, Bryan Lynch's face filled the screen.

"—if any reporter so much as—"

Jackie upped the volume but the rest of his threat was lost.

"—earlier today at the home of the parents of Amy Lynch," a disembodied voice droned. "Bonnie Lynch was not available for comment, and Bryan Lynch was understandably distraught at the story released this afternoon by Boulder District Attorney Lanny Greer that his daughter was last seen at a bar."

The camera panned to the solitary figure of Amy's father slamming his front door behind him. His reaction seemed out of scale to the provocation. If he was angry, why blast the reporter? And what was the big deal about an eighteen-year-old girl spending the evening at a tavern? Jackie wondered about Bonnie Lynch.

Did her absence signal dissension?

Did her husband not want her to talk?

Fifteen

Under a delft sky and with the grape-tinged slabs of the Flatirons as a backdrop, Sewall Hall was a monument to the University of Colorado's picture-book charm. Its sandstone walls and limestone trim, its barrel-tiled roof and twin lions spouting water in a basin by the south lawn, its very image engendered confidence in the generations of parents like Bryan and Bonnie Lynch who'd entrusted their children to its care. But as Jackie passed through the colonnaded entryway of CU's first women's residence hall, she couldn't help thinking that what drew most students to CU, and this dorm in particular, was hardly the campus's physical attractiveness. Not by a long shot.

CU was a party school par excellence, and Sewall Hall had been its first coed dorm. Jackie was no stranger to the place. She'd lived there her freshman year.

Pilar had dropped Jackie off on the Hill and gone to track down the Finnegan's Wake bartender. The April downpour as they'd descended into the college town had drenched the grass but the sun had just as quickly dried it. On this verdant afternoon the trees were leafed out and the rain had unleashed the scents of lilac and forsythia.

As she crossed the west side of campus, Jackie tried to step into the frame of mind of Erin Carmichael, Amy Lynch's college roommate and best friend. What had CU meant to those girls from Graland Country Day? Was it the adventure it had been for Jackie? Or an escape from their parents, a place to spread their wings? If so, the forty miles from Graland to Boulder wasn't very far. . . . Jackie thought back to what Pilar had discovered.

Erin's father developed golf courses, and although savvy enough to retain a stake in whatever he built, he was a pauper compared with Bryan Lynch. Amy's father managed the family investments—meaning Bonnie's money, which originated in the most prosperous molybdenum mines in the state. He was also a CU booster who held season tickets for the Buffs and never missed a game. He contributed fifty thousand dollars a year to the alumni fund. When Amy and Erin wanted to room together at Sewall, Bryan Lynch had pulled the necessary strings. How had Amy ended up with an older crowd at a bar on a school night, and without her best friend? And what made Jackie think Erin Carmichael would tell her?

As a freshman, Jackie had owed her academic survival to her roommate. When it was time to study for exams, her roommate got her through Great Books by allowing Jackie to "quiz" her so Jackie could memorize the answers. Biology, on the other hand, was visual, and Jackie paid her friend back by tutoring her on the patterns of nature, whose intuitive order bore no resemblance to the rote data Jackie had come to dread. As for French—well, even English was a foreign language. Jackie and her roommate knew each other's weaknesses and would have taken those secrets to the grave. The question was, would Erin?

Watching students trickle back from classes in their stonewashed denim and monochromatic T's with designer logos made Jackie nostalgic for the self-conscious scruffiness of her own generation. How disappointed she'd been to discover that "coed" meant separate wings and the dubious privilege of sharing a dining room! Now some of the dorms had unisex baths. The sexual revolution may have come and gone, but judging from the length of its waiting list, Sewall Hall had lost none of its racy appeal.

As for the students themselves, Vibram-soled hiking boots would always be in style, but the curiously jaded expressions on the faces of the kids filing into the residence hall threw Jackie. They'd left innocence behind, but for what? As she gazed up at the wrought-iron balconies from which hip-hop blared, she knew establishing rapport with Erin would be a tougher sell than she'd imagined.

"Who's there?" came a high-pitched voice when Jackie knocked.

"I need to talk with you about Amy."

Honest but nonspecific. With a potentially unfriendly witness, it was a victory to make eye contact before the door slammed in your face.

"I've already said what I know." Erin wasn't buying—not yet. But Jackie wondered why she was reluctant to help. "Who are you?"

"A lawyer."

Not a lie, not exactly. As the door opened a crack and Jackie saw corkscrew curls and a wary eye, she thanked God for the genes that made bartenders card her well past her twenties. Jackie's narrow black jeans, V-necked white T, and leather belt with silver buckle also subtracted years from her age. The crack widened and, brushing aside the pinch of regret she always felt when a door opened by subterfuge, she crossed the threshold before Erin could change her mind.

If Amy's untamed beauty had fooled those who should have known better, Erin's round cheeks and Orphan Annie mop ensured her nothing more than a once-over from the opposite sex. Had Amy left her best friend behind in more ways than one? Erin's unyielding expression reminded Jackie that girls on the sidelines knew the score all too well. To buy time, she looked around the room.

Little in Sewall had changed in the two decades since Jackie had left the university. One window, two desks, a pair of iron-framed beds, and walls the nondescript cream color of high school cafeterias and prisons. An expensive computer on the desk by the window and the cell phone on the sill added more modern touches. But a tide of debris was spread across both sides of the room like sediment in an alluvial fan. Somewhere in this avalanche of stuff lay a clue to Amy and a window onto Erin.

"I had one of those." Jackie pointed to an oversized teddy bear sprawled across the balled-up comforter on one bed. There was nothing cuddly about the stuffed animal. It had been designed to appeal to adults, the sort of toy a high school boy might win at a carnival to impress his girl. Did they even have carnivals anymore?

"It's Amy's," Erin said. "I'm not giving it back."

A defiant brand of compliance. Did she think Jackie represented the Lynches? If the misapprehension bought Jackie time, she wasn't about to correct it. But why the defiance?

"You must miss her."

Erin shrugged and her sullenness began to fall into place. Remorse—for not being at Amy's side the night she was taken?

"How long did you know Amy?"

"Since Graland."

Graland was kindergarten through ninth grade. Kent, Denver's other elite private academy, had a middle school and a high school, but it was located in the south suburbs. If Jackie was correct about why the Lynches chose Hilltop, they would have been in no hurry for their daughter to transfer.

"And you went with her to Kent."

"Amy left Graland a year early."

Why? Erin's terseness warned Jackie not to ask.

"What was Amy like?"

"Fun to be with. But school was her priority."

Give a little, take a bigger piece back. Careful about the impression she wanted to leave. Erin must have realized by then that Jackie had no connection to the Lynches. Like most adolescents, she probably assumed she had no choice but to answer an adult's questions. Sooner or later she would wonder what Jackie was after and the balance of power would shift.

"Did Amy like school?"

"She never cut classes."

"What was her major?"

"Psych. But all she'd taken so far was 101."

A trace of what—irony? Academic rivalry didn't square with the little Jackie knew of their relationship.

"What did you do in your spare time?"

Now Erin looked away. "Campus movies, stuff like that . . ."

"Did Amy have hobbies, any special interests?"

A calculated shrug, and when Erin's eyes met Jackie's they held more than irony. They issued a dare. "With finals coming up, who has time?"

What had these girls gotten themselves into?

Glancing around the room again to ease the tension, Jackie saw a corkboard above one of the desks. A haphazard collage of snapshots. As she crossed the floor to examine them more closely, she saw one of a girl in a bikini on a white beach, standing with a boy who had his arm around her. A gangly kid with clipped hair despite the mandatory earring. Harmless enough. Jackie reached for that photograph.

"Matt Fisher?" she asked.

"They dated since Kent."

The boy was grinning but Amy's expression was curiously sad. To the right of that photograph was an empty space.

"Where was this taken?"

"Mazatlán. Spring break."

The week before Amy was abducted.

"What happened to—" She pointed to the hole in the corkboard, but was interrupted by a burst of laughter from the hallway. Soon Erin would say she had to leave for dinner. "How did Amy get along with her parents?"

"Fine." Erin's relief made Jackie wonder what she'd missed. "Her dad's pretty uptight. About grades, I mean . . . Why are you asking these questions? I told the detective before."

So Phyllis Klein had wanted to know about Amy's parents, too. In another moment Erin would be demanding to see Jackie's credentials. She'd never lied to a witness and now wasn't the time to start. But the girl's sudden belligerence seemed contrived, and Jackie made a note to return to Bryan Lynch. "Did you see Amy before she left Tuesday night?"

Erin nodded. "I came back to the room while she was getting dressed."

"Was she going out with Matt?" Another shrug, but the very fact that she was responding gave Jackie the advantage. "Didn't Amy tell you who she was going with?"

"She wasn't seeing Matt that night."

"Did they have a fight?" A stupefied look—the trademark of adolescence. Best friends since Graland and Erin didn't *know*? "Who was she seeing?"

"New friends."

"Who were they?" Erin shook her head. Protecting Amy, or had Amy stopped confiding in her? "Where did she meet them?"

"She asked me to go with her, but I said no."

Survivor's guilt. Keep pressing that button.

"Who *were* they, Erin?"

"I never met them!" Wanting to let it out, blame someone else for the rift between her and Amy? Or evading yet again? Jackie softened her tone.

"Why weren't you with her that night?"

"Everything was different since Mazatlán . . . and even before." The floodgates were loosening. "Amy changed. She had money. She started staying out all night, she was cutting classes, she was even dressing different."

Skintight pants and a sweater down to there. That meant a new man in the picture, maybe someone older. Was that why Erin hadn't reported her missing until the following night?

"Different, how?"

"New stuff. Expensive . . ."

"Did someone give Amy the clothes?"

"I assume she *bought* them." Erin was back on her high horse and Jackie blamed herself for handing her the opportunity.

"Did she have credit cards?"

"Her father cut her off at the end of last semester."

"How come?"

"She flunked two courses—including Psych." So much for never missing a class. "School was a joke."

"If it was such a joke, why did Amy bother to enroll?"

"Her father made her."

"What did Amy want?"

Erin ignored the question. "When she blew those classes, he tore up her credit cards. He said buckle down or get a job. Not that he was about to let her go out on the street . . ."

"And did she?"

"What?"

Jackie answered patiently.

"Did Amy get a job?"

"She waitressed on the Hill."

"Where?"

"A pizza place, but it didn't last. The tips were lousy." Erin looked like she wanted to say more.

"Was money so important? Surely her parents wouldn't have let—"

"Are you kidding? Amy wasn't about to be poor!"

"What did she want to be?"

"A model."

Like thousands of other girls. But with her looks, Amy might have made it.

"How did her mother feel about that?"

"Bonnie?" Erin spat the name. "You just don't get it, do you? In the Lynch family, Bryan's the only one who counts."

But something was missing. Where did Amy get the clothes?

"Did Amy's mother slip her cash?"

"As if! Bonnie wouldn't dare do anything behind his back."

Control freak for a father, a mother who needed permission to blink . . . and an angry young girl who liked beautiful clothes.

"When did Amy pierce her breast?"

"Her *breast*?" If Erin was feigning shock, the quality of her performance had drastically improved.

"And that wasn't the only thing she pierced . . ."

"That's gross. I don't believe you!"

"Would Amy leave the bar with a stranger?"

"Never!"

She'd have to remind Pilar to watch for that tox screen. Ketamine
was a long shot, but . . . "Were Amy's new friends students?"

"I told you, I—"

"Did she meet them over spring break?"

"There was one guy."

The face in the missing photograph.

"Who was he, Erin?"

"He never came to the dorm and Amy wouldn't tell me his name."

Jackie didn't believe that for a moment.

"Did he—"

There was a loud knock.

"Erin?" A girl stood in the doorway. "Aren't you coming to dinner?"

Erin's relief was apparent. She crossed the room to her friend,
silently daring Jackie to stop her. Slipping the photograph of Amy and
Matt in her pocket, Jackie smiled at the other girl.

"I'm sorry I made Erin late."

Erin stood in the doorway, waiting. For Jackie to hand her a card like
detectives always did, or because she couldn't believe she was free to go?
With a friendly nod, Jackie left.

"What was Erin like?" Pilar asked when she picked Jackie up.

"Typical eighteen-year-old. I feel like I just went five rounds with a
middleweight champ."

"Did she spill the beans?"

"If you mean pinto, yes. Amy's high school beau was history. She
was running with a stud she met in Mazatlán."

"If little Amy was screwing around on her guy, maybe we better
take a closer look at Matt."

"In due course." Jackie's head was pounding and she had never been
more grateful that Pilar was behind the wheel. It was rush hour and they

had to wait for the light on Broadway to change twice before they could make it onto the turnpike. "I'll tell you one thing. Amy's abductor was someone she knew."

"What makes you so sure?"

"Erin said Amy wouldn't have left the bar with a stranger, and I believe her." But if she didn't know about her best friend's piercings, how well did Erin really know her? "Did you find that bartender from Finnegan's Wake?"

"I showed him Ballard's picture. He says he didn't see him there that night, but the bar was crowded. And he wasn't the only guy on duty."

"Which means Phyllis Klein won't be able to place Ballard there, either. I'm feeling better and better about this case."

Pilar maneuvered the Spider into the left lane and downshifted. "Mazatlán sounds pretty good right now," she said. "You should be glad you weren't at the office this afternoon. I just spent fifteen minutes on the phone begging the latest temp not to quit."

"Don't tell me—"

"Cliff went ballistic. That new tenant pilfered his filing cabinets and split overnight, without even paying his lousy week of rent. Stole every one of Cliff's estate forms."

Jackie was tempted to laugh, but she knew what was coming.

"If we're going to stay for the duration of Ballard's case," Pilar said, "we've got to get professional help."

"I totally agree. There's a psychiatrist I could recommend for Cliff. "

"I'm serious. Unless you want to start kicking in his share of the rent, we're going to have to attract someone decent to replace Phil or start thinking about a move. And before you even consider signing another lease, you need to think about where you want to be." Lighting her afterwork cigarillo, she added, "I actually have the name of someone who could help. Okay if I call her?"

Jackie just wanted to go home and crawl into bed.

"Whatever you want," she told Pilar. "But I'd better pay a visit to Bonnie Lynch."

"Why?"

"There's a lot about Amy we don't know."

"Well, good luck. Last I heard, Bonnie was 'in seclusion.'" Down-shifting again, Pilar floored the gas and the Spider passed a late-model

SUV that was traveling five miles below the speed limit. Irritated, the driver sped up and began tailgating her. "Dimestore cowboy," she muttered. "Thinks he owns the left lane."

But Jackie was thinking about Bryan Lynch. At his last press conference a week earlier, he'd been alone. "Is Amy's father in seclusion, too?"

With a sporty salute and a roar of exhaust, Pilar pulled into the right lane and placed four cars between the Spider and the cowboy before he knew what she was doing.

"If that includes being walled up behind the fanciest mouthpieces on Seventeenth Street, the answer is yes."

Was Phyllis Klein trying to keep a lid on Amy's parents?

Or did they have something to hide?

Sixteen

The warm weather that dried the roof had kept the spread of the mold on Jackie's ceiling in check, but the lack of ventilation in her office had more than made up for that small improvement. She was greeted by ringing phones, musty air, and an acrid stench. A harried Pilar was manning the reception desk.

"You've had two calls from *Dateline* and one from *Today*."

"You know the rule," Jackie said. "No interviews. What's that smell?"

"The temp left the hot plate on while the coffeepot was empty." Jabbing a button, Pilar sang out the hodgepodge roster of attorneys and coolly transferred the call. "Cliff's meeting with his biggest client in an hour, and he needs—"

Interrupted again, she handled the next caller with the same unruffled efficiency.

"Where's the temp?" Jackie asked when Pilar was free.

"Went home in tears twenty minutes ago, and I don't intend to take her place. I don't give a damn if Cliff—"

While Pilar answered the phone once more, the postman dumped a sack of mail on the table by the door. "Looks like you gals got your hands full today!" With a wink at Pilar and a cheery salute, he retreated.

"What's with Cliff?" Jackie asked. Her mind was on yesterday's interview with Erin. She needed to dictate her notes while the impressions were fresh, but Pilar obviously needed to blow off steam.

"Got into a shouting match with the temp over the coffeepot, and she quit on the spot. Never mind she was in the middle of processing an estate plan for his client. . . . I'm not saving his ass, Jackie, not today. There's too much else—"

The interruption this time was a loud thump from the second floor, followed by a bellow of rage. The Xerox machine was obviously fighting back.

"That man should be on Zoloft!" Pilar massaged her temples with her thumbs. "Want me to run down the street for coffee?"

"Yeah." Jackie dug into her wallet. "And doughnuts. It's going to be a long morning."

"Treat's on me. And by the way, the air conditioner's broken. Again." The phone began ringing, and she punched the disconnect before sailing out the door.

At her desk, Jackie slapped a new cassette into her recorder and closed her eyes. Pilar was right: this place was a zoo, and serious decisions about the property would have to be made soon. Not now. She thought of the girl in the bikini at Mazatlán. Spring break, white sand and turquoise waves. A nice-looking boy with his arm around her. Sad eyes . . . Pressing the button, she began to record.

"Erin Carmichael, best friend and roommate of Amy Lynch. Sometime between the beginning of school last fall and spring break, Amy stopped confiding in her. . . ."

Was she reading too much into that? Close friendships were always complicated, and never more so than in adolescence. It was this damned office, it was impossible to think! The phone rang and rang, and next door it sounded as if Cliff was hurling books at the wall. Jackie rewound the tape.

"Erin Carmichael, best friend and roommate of Amy Lynch. Knows who Amy was planning to see the night she disappeared, and won't tell—"

"Jackie?"

Pilar was in her doorway with a tray of iced coffee and glazed doughnuts. Behind her stood a tall redhead in a celery pantsuit that looked crisper than the greens in Jackie's vegetable bin.

"This is Whitney Grais," Pilar said. "The PR maven I was telling you about."

As the woman stepped forward and extended a cool hand, Jackie remembered Pilar saying something about a marketing expert on the drive back from Boulder. How long had this been in the works?

"Nice to meet you, Ms. Grais," Jackie replied. With her eyes, she tried to signal Pilar not to pull up another chair. "It's a little hectic this morning—"

"I can imagine how busy you are." Intercepting the signal, the redhead remained on her feet. "I'm glad to return when it's more convenient."

Pilar's face drooped.

"I guess I have a few minutes," Jackie said.

"Whitney's specialty is marketing law practices," Pilar explained. "She wanted to meet everyone and see if she could help."

"I won't take any more of your time than I absolutely need, Ms. Flowers. Pilar said you have a number of practices flourishing under a single roof." Accepting a plastic flask of coffee, the PR woman took a ladylike sip. The emerald on the third finger of her right hand was almost as large as Jackie's shipwreck fluorite. "Your only formal tie is a common lease and certain shared expenses. One lawyer recently left, and this sounds like a good opportunity to explore where the rest of you are headed individually or as a group."

Articulate, well-groomed. Points for diplomacy and getting to the point.

"I thought we were just looking for another tenant," Jackie began.

The pounding from the end of the hallway was impossible to ignore, and as Pilar jumped up to close the door, Whitney shot Jackie a sympathetic grin. Her green eyes curved down slightly and the tiny wrinkles around them showed that she wasn't afraid to laugh. Jackie liked her despite the flashy ring.

"What we want is the right mix," Pilar said. What Pilar really wanted was for Jackie to get the hell out of here and take her with her. Jackie wondered when Whitney and Pilar had met.

"My role is simply to help the lawyers I work with identify their goals and expectations, so they can assess their opportunities." They certainly had their plays down, but how much would this cost? No one knew better than Pilar how tight— "In case you're wondering," Whitney continued, "I don't charge a penny unless you're completely satisfied with the result."

"What exactly do your efforts entail?" Jackie asked.

The morning was probably shot, but Pilar's look of gratitude as she resumed her seat and helped herself to a doughnut made up for that. Jackie would give them five minutes to make their pitch. Whitney Grais launched into her spiel.

"Not to sound bitchy, but law firm marketing is basically a war. With the shrinking pool of prospective clients and with everyone maneuvering for the high-profile cases, the competition is becoming all the more fierce." So much for Ted Wolsky and Jackie's stable of dope dealers. But the rhetoric was leavened by an impish smile and Jackie awarded Whitney two extra points. "That goes double for criminal defense lawyers."

"I always thought the fight was in the courtroom," Jackie said.

"You're already a winner in that arena. Maybe it's time to broaden your campaign." Whitney took another sip of coffee. "Out of curiosity, what percentage of your time is spent on administrative matters?"

One hundred percent more than she wanted. "Pilar is my right hand."

"Have you considered the benefits a larger firm might offer? You pay more for overhead, but they make up for it by—"

A headhunter, that was her game. Jackie was oddly disappointed; she'd wanted Whitney to be more than a Seventeenth Street shill. She started to rise.

"Ms. Grais, I—"

"You don't want to work for a downtown firm. No criminal defense lawyer with your record does."

Her candor caught Jackie off balance.

"My record?"

"You wiped the floor with the Denver DA in that case last year." Whitney smiled again. "I'm being delicate, of course. From what I hear, Duncan Pratt still has trouble sitting down."

Pilar stifled a laugh.

"Half the litigation firms in town must have been banging on your door," Whitney continued. "Why didn't you jump then?"

"Frankly, no one asked."

"That's where I come in."

In that instant, Jackie saw herself through Whitney Grais's eyes. The view wasn't entirely flattering.

One of the handful of women trial lawyers in Denver, Jackie at fifteen years out of law school was at the top of her game. She wasn't afraid to take on any DA or judge. She'd had a long string of wins dating from her days in the Public Defender's office. At this moment she was representing a federal judge accused of killing the daughter of one of Colorado's wealthiest families. Every network wanted a piece of her and her client. And here she was, hiding out with a bunch of guys who flirted with malpractice each time they took a leak. Who could blame Whitney for assuming she wanted to make a break?

"Of course, I'd need to know more about you before I made a recommendation," Whitney continued.

That was the price. Was Jackie ready to gamble?

"What sort of information?"

"What makes you tick."

Pilar wisely kept her mouth shut.

"Tick?"

Whitney leaned forward. "What makes you unique, different from your competitors?"

For starters, I can't read.

Jackie resisted the impulse to look at Pilar. "My strength is trial skills, not rainmaking or glad-handing. I guess that's why I never would have made it at a large firm."

"Why did you go to law school?"

"It was the only thing I ever wanted to do."

"Why criminal law?"

"I've always bet on the underdog."

"Was that what you wanted to do the day you graduated?"

"Frankly, I was just glad to be out of the damn place." And to have passed the bar. *I fear that you, Ms. Flowers, are not among their number. . . .* Would she ever be free of that voice?

"—first job after law school?"

"The Public Defender's office."

"How long were you there?"

"Eight years." Jackie held her breath in anticipation of the next question, but Whitney surprised her with another.

"Where were you the day you decided to open your own practice?"

"Where was I?"

"In terms of your life, your state of mind?"

"I suppose I felt constricted," Jackie said, stalling for time. Only the people at the PD's office knew about the debacle with Phyllis Klein. It had been in everyone's interest to keep the accusations quiet.

"But you were a star, one of their top trial lawyers. . . ."

Pilar, get me out of this!

"In an office like the PD's," Pilar said, "there ain't much room for advancement."

"Of course," Whitney said. "These questions sound silly, but I'm trying to identify your niche. And I know your time is precious. Maybe it would be best if you wrote out your personal history." Now Pilar was having a tough time keeping a straight face. "I know trial lawyers don't like to write, but it doesn't have to be heavy. Keep it light and crisp—"

"Jackie!" a voice bawled up the stairwell. Cliff had given up on the copy machine and his client, and had apparently been answering the phone. "Call for you!" An unintelligible mumbling was followed by a sheepish, "How the hell do I transfer it up?"

Good old Cliff.

"Duty calls," Pilar told Whitney. Reluctantly she headed for the hall. "Save the good stuff for me."

A moment later she was back.

"You'll want to take this," she told Jackie. Punching a button, she passed the phone to her boss's waiting hand.

The voice Jackie had just heard in her head spoke without preamble.

"While I was on the bench this morning they searched my home."

"Just a moment," she said. With her palm over the receiver, she turned to Whitney. "We'll have to continue this later."

Whitney withdrew a stapled form from her portfolio and handed it to Jackie. "Here's some questions about your practice. The highs and lows, what kind of clients you do and don't want to attract. We can go over it whenever it's convenient."

Jackie waited until Pilar had shown the PR woman out and closed the door before returning to her caller.

"Did they seize anything?"

"They had a warrant." He was too calm and collected. "My housekeeper let them in."

"What did they find?"

"Ketamine."

How had Phyllis Klein known?

Jackie struggled to match his offhand tone. "The date-rape drug?"

"I . . ." For the first time, her former professor seemed to be at a loss for words.

"Where did they find it?"

"The medicine cabinet."

"What the hell was ketamine doing in your medicine cabinet?"

"I have no idea."

That was it.

"You damned well better start coming up with answers," Jackie said, "or Phyllis Klein will!"

"I have every confidence in your ability to represent me."

Crumpling up Whitney Grais's questionnaire, Jackie lobbed it at her wastebasket. How sweet it had been, to have the man who'd almost derailed her career turn to her for help. But this case was spinning out of control. Defending him would be impossible unless he leveled with her. "I can't do it alone, Glenn."

"Isn't it obvious?" he softly replied.

"Nothing's obvious."

"I've been set up."

Seventeen

Ballard called again two days later.

"I suggest you get down here at your earliest convenience," he said.

"Where are you?"

"The federal courthouse."

She arrived just as they'd reached a standoff.

The rotunda of the United States District Courthouse was packed. At five minutes past noon, midday recess had just been declared but this confrontation was an unexpected treat. Lawyers, wide-eyed court staff, and ordinary citizens caught in the melee jousted with network and beat reporters as camcorders tried valiantly to capture the excitement. Elbowing her way to the front of the crowd, Jackie saw the situation was about to spin out of control.

At the security gate three gray-haired court security officers in polyester blazers faced down a trio of well-toned Boulder cops. Arrayed in silk sport coats and tailored slacks, Boulder's finest might have seemed laid-back were it not for the weapons in their fists.

Behind the CSOs stood six brawny U.S. Marshals with their hands on the holsters at their hips. Behind *them* stood the head of the Marshals Service, Glenn Ballard, and gimlet-eyed Chief Judge Simon Clark in cowboy boots. At Clark's elbow stood Judge Charlie Nesbit, who looked like he'd been caught on his way to lunch.

Not one of them blinked.

Jackie stepped past the cameras and into the pit.

"What's going on?" she demanded.

"We're here to execute a search warrant," snapped the cop nearest the metal detector without taking his eyes off the CSO manning the machine. None of the other participants moved. Jackie's authoritative tone had obviously led him to believe she was an ally. "They're ordering us to surrender our guns. I don't give up my service revolver to nobody." Much less some paunchy bailiff in a cheap coat.

One of the marshals came alive and motioned Jackie to rejoin the crowd.

"Step back, miss . . ."

"It's all right, Larry." Ballard stepped forward, waving Jackie through the cordon of CSOs. "She's with me."

As Jackie crossed to Ballard's side, the tension broke. A member of the Boulder contingent with sandy hair holstered his weapon. He reached into his jacket for his cell phone and she heard him ask for Phyllis Klein.

"What's going on?" she said to Ballard.

"Jurisdictional squabble," he replied with no trace of humor. She glanced at the chief judge, who was equally unperturbed. "No weapons are allowed in this courthouse. Unless, of course"—he chuckled ominously—"they belong to our side."

"Have you seen the warrant?"

"Not yet."

Chief Judge Simon Clark's fleshless lips twitched with amusement. At state law enforcement's expense? Or Glenn Ballard's? The sandy-haired cop spoke into his receiver in a low but agitated tone.

"Is there a quieter place to resolve this?" she asked Clark.

"That's entirely up to our guests from Boulder."

Hearing Klein's name again from the detective, Jackie reached for his phone. "May I?" she asked, and began talking into the cell without waiting for an answer. "This is Jackie Flowers. To whom am I speaking?"

"Lanny Greer. What the hell is going on over there?" the DA sputtered. "My men are trying to execute a legitimate search warrant—"

"—and are facing a battery of U.S. Marshals with Uzis. Not to mention a chief judge with balls the size of grapefruits. Why don't you let your guys quit making asses of themselves *and* you, and tell them to check their weapons at the door like everyone else?"

"How dare you—"

"Nice try with the press, though. They're getting a real kick out of watching Boulder's finest being humiliated by a bunch of bailiffs old enough to be their grandfathers."

"You—"

"I mean it, Lanny. You're outnumbered and outgunned."

"Give me Detective Frasier!"

Jackie returned the cell phone to its owner. A moment later he switched it off and briefly conferred with his colleagues. One by one, they sheepishly surrendered their guns and shuffled through the security gate. The crowd began to disperse.

"May I see your warrant, please?" Jackie asked. "And the affidavit of probable cause." Frasier reached into his inside pocket and withdrew a sheaf of papers.

Jackie handed them to Ballard. "Let's find a place to talk."

While the Boulder cops waited in the corridor under the supervision of three marshals, Jackie sat with her client in the empty jurors' assembly room behind the clerk's office. It took Ballard four minutes to review the warrant and affidavit. When he was finished, he handed the papers back to her. Jackie left them in the center of the table.

"Aren't you going to read them?" Ballard said.

"I trust you. Isn't it time you began trusting me?"

"I don't know what you mean."

"Step down from the bench until this is over, Glenn. I need you to focus on your defense."

"I won't give them the satisfaction of running scared."

Ballard wasn't the first high-powered client who tried to distance himself from reality by burying himself in his work. With judges, they even had a special name for it: hiding on the bench.

"Doesn't the chief judge have something to say about that?" she said.

"Simon Clark has every faith in my innocence. As should you."

Why hadn't she withdrawn when she still had the chance?

Jackie gestured at the search warrant.

"What are they looking for?"

He shrugged. "It's boilerplate. You've seen it all before."

"What's the basis for probable cause?"

"Same old stuff—my cabin, the handcuffs. And the ketamine."

"What don't I know, Glenn?"

"Lanny Greer's on a fishing expedition." Trying to convince her, or himself? But perhaps this was a ploy by Phyllis Klein to humiliate them. "You saw that circus! This is nothing but a—"

"Even DAs don't fish dry holes." She paused. "But why gamble? I can move to have the warrant quashed. Your chambers must be packed with confidential files that are clearly out of bounds, and Greer may back off. By the time we get a ruling—"

Ballard's smile stopped short of his eyes.

"I have nothing to hide."

"Why take the risk?"

"You obviously think I'm bluffing, Counselor."

"It doesn't matter what I think."

Ballard rose. "Maybe it's time to call more than one man's bluff."

The suite comprising Ballard's chambers was adjacent to his courtroom on the eighth floor of the federal courthouse. The compound was shaped like an E, with a library, lavatory, and kitchenette at one end and Ballard's private sanctum at the other. His law clerks' offices lay along the central corridor, which opened onto a reception area. The wrap-around desk that operated as a command post placed Ballard's secretary within eye contact of both a security camera that recorded activity in the exterior corridor and Ballard himself if he chose to open his door. The arrangement was not conducive to an ambush.

Despite the agreement Jackie had negotiated with Lanny Greer—who delegated the details to a surprisingly accommodating Phyllis Klein—that case files and grand jury materials were off-limits, Jackie steeled herself for a long wait based on the number of rooms to be searched. With her client in the lead and Simon Clark and two marshals following, the Boulder detectives entered Glenn Ballard's office.

"There you are!" Holding a handful of message slips, Ballard's secretary rose from her computer to greet her boss. Then she saw the entourage.

"I won't be taking any calls for the next twenty minutes, Betty," Ballard calmly replied. "Would you tell my bailiff to notify the parties that my one o'clock will be delayed?"

A law clerk emerged from the library carrying a coffee mug. Seeing the marshals and the chief judge, she froze with the mug halfway to her lips.

"Karen, would you mind doing me a favor? Gather up the wiretap affidavits and grand jury files from my back room and put them on the table in the library. Betty will lend you a hand."

Setting her coffee on the nearest counter, the clerk disappeared into Ballard's private office without a word. The Boulder detectives politely stood by as she and Betty emerged with stacks of files. Simon Clark glanced at his watch. The gesture said his colleague's predicament had provided a rare entertainment, but now he had better things to do. Ballard himself looked irritated at the interruption in his schedule. The anxiety Jackie had felt from the moment she'd received his call began to fade.

When Ballard's staff emerged with the last armloads of files, the cop named Frasier took the lead. Signaling to his mustachioed companion to follow while their colleague, a baby-faced man with a weight-lifter's build, began rifling through Betty's desk, he headed for Ballard's inner office. Jackie and her client followed with Simon Clark trailing behind. She tried to imitate their nonchalance.

Wasn't the inner sanctum the logical place to start?

The size of the sitting room in the presidential suite of a five-star hotel, Ballard's private office was almost stark in its simplicity. Unlike his wood-paneled courtroom, it was furnished in sleek Scandinavian style. His couch and sitting chairs were black leather with chrome frames, and his desk was chrome and glass, with a modern wall unit housing a seventeen-inch computer monitor. In lieu of the real thing, an oversized Jasper Johns print of the Stars and Stripes added a whimsical touch.

Frasier scouted the layout. From one side of the office an antechamber led to a cloakroom and private lavatory. On the other side an arched threshold opened onto a third room. From a brass bar at the top of the arch, the scales of justice hung. Ignoring the antechamber, Frasier crossed under the scales and into the third room.

Almost as spacious as the front office, Ballard's project room held a long worktable covered with neat stacks of briefs and floor-to-ceiling shelves of leather-bound encyclopedias, treatises, and casebooks. A thirteen-inch television monitor with a VCR stood on a wheeled stand at the end of the room. Yet another doorway led to a large alcove filled with banker's boxes and a half dozen vertical filing cabinets. Squatting in front of the fourth cabinet, Frasier reached for the handle to the bottom drawer.

A random check, Jackie thought as he began handing neatly labeled files to baby face. The junior detective made no show of skimming their contents, and the cop with the mustache just stood back and watched. Ballard's expression was unreadable. Her anxiety mounted. For whose benefit were they literally going through the motions?

Frasier finished with the bottom drawer and opened the next one up. As he began passing folders to his assistant, his tension seemed to grow. When he reached into the back of the drawer and pulled out an unmarked seven-by-four-inch plastic box, he didn't look at all surprised.

It was an unlabeled videocassette.

Frasier inserted the tape in the VCR and switched on the monitor. Not knowing what to expect, Jackie looked again at Ballard. The only change in his expression was a minute tightening of his lips. Puzzled, but not unduly concerned. The boredom on Chief Judge Simon Clark's face had evaporated.

The screen came to life.

At first there were waves of sleet. The static abruptly stopped and was replaced with a jumpy shot of a woodland clearing. Slowly the camera panned to a cabin with a stone chimney and angled roof.

Jackie took a deep breath.

Towering pines, patches of snow on grass still brown from winter. If not artistically inspired, the cameraman could not be faulted for lack of thoroughness in documenting the scene. The clearing itself had been meticulously stripped of trees; the stones in the chimney were so tightly packed almost no mortar was required. The camera circled the log structure, alighting on the only windows—one beside the door and another on an adjacent wall—before zeroing in on a wide plank door secured by an iron bar and latch. As the videographer mounted the two steps to the wooden porch, the camera jerked again. The door swung inward and the lens slowly traveled the periphery of the great room.

Prowling peeled-log walls with gun racks and hooks for clothing and snowshoes, lingering on an elk head with a twelve-point rack, it slid to a stone fireplace with a metal rod spanning the hearth and jumped to the stone floor on which stood a whirligig table with two rustic chairs. It returned to the hearth, where a fire danced. The scene might have been cozy were its implications not so horrific. Then up to the ceiling with its soaring rafters . . . The jerking suddenly ended.

Someone in the room gasped, but Jackie dared not take her eyes from the screen.

Arms straight above her head, a girl wearing only a white hood hung from chains attached to steel cuffs on her wrists. Her hands were a foot apart. Backlit by the fireplace, her naked body twisted obscenely as she balanced on the balls of her high-arched feet. . . .

At the second sharp intake of breath, Jackie glanced at Ballard. He was rapt, his attention riveted on the screen with the same sick fascination that was on the face of every man watching. Now the camera jumped again, panning to the girl's head.

The hood was made of a thin, silky cloth that clung to her face. It had no holes but through the fabric her eyelids fluttered and Jackie could just make out the contours of long wavy hair. As the girl twisted again, a lock worked its way free from the nape of the hood. She was conscious but not struggling. The camera moved from her throat to her chest. Her small breasts rose and fell in a regular motion. The left nipple was pierced by a silver ring.

As the camera moved still closer, the girl twisted violently and drew back. The light dancing on her upper torso caught the pulse in her throat and the quickening of her breath. She struggled against her handcuffs and her breasts became taut. A tall figure slowly moved into camera range.

Clad in black trousers and a black silk shirt, the man approached with a deliberate stride. With his back to the now stationary camera, he reached out with his left hand and brushed her right arm with his fingertips. Jackie could almost feel the girl's skin crawl. In one smooth motion, the man reached for the hood and pulled it from her head.

Chestnut hair tumbled down, half-obscuring eyes frozen in terror.

As Amy Lynch's mouth opened in a silent scream, the man turned to face the lens. With a raptor's look he tilted his chin up and to the right.

Glenn Ballard.

The screen went blank.

Eighteen

Crêpe de Chine, the French-Indochinese bistro in Cherry Creek, catered to a well-heeled crowd. At noon on the Thursday after Ballard's chambers were searched, every booth was filled. As Jackie and Pilar scanned the room, they spotted the anchorman from Channel 9, a personal injury lawyer who'd just won a verdict against the largest HMO in ten states, and a city councilman with a woman too old to be his daughter but less than half the age of his wife.

"We should be reviewing Amy Lynch's tox screen," Jackie said, "not courting ptomaine of our own."

"Relax."

"And would you tell the temp not to put any more calls from *Dateline* or *20/20* through? I want you to handle them. I don't care who it is. No interviews."

"That kid from MSNBC is cute."

"If you like them too young to shave."

The locals called themselves reporters; the national media fielded "correspondents." Reporters were rumpled but correspondents wore expensive suits or Ralph Lauren. So far, the guys from the *Globe* were the exception—polyester pants, off-brand polo shirts, and rubber-soled shoes for a quick getaway. Cliff had caught one of them rummaging in the Dumpster in the alley behind their office.

"I always wanted to try this place," Pilar said. "Complimentary valet parking, who can beat that? Besides, Whitney Grais is picking up the tab."

This lunch was payback for Lenny's testimony in Ted Wolsky's case.

"You never told me how you met her," Jackie said.

"At a paralegal seminar last year." Pilar had every credential but a law degree. If there was any justice in the world, Jackie thought, her investigator's name would be on Jackie's license instead of her own. "She knocked us dead with a pitch about realizing your potential."

"If Whitney's so hot, how come I never heard of her?"

Pilar sighed. "Ever heard of Dana Parcell?"

"That woman who owns the trucking company?"

"You only know the name because of Whitney. Five years ago Dana's husband's business was near bankruptcy and she'd never even changed a tire. Remember that flash flood in Clear Creek Canyon? Whitney made sure every truck in Dana's fleet was on the scene with medical supplies within six hours. Parcell Post is now the most successful woman-owned business west of the Mississippi."

"You're not crediting Whitney for that flash flood, are you?"

"She says you make your own luck."

"Well, where is she now?"

"Would you just relax, Jackie? You haven't been out of the office since the day that video was found." Marlin Pitts had agreed to enter a protective order keeping the videotape confidential until trial. He wanted a jury of fair-minded tofu eaters, not a lynch mob. Which was what the press threatened to become if Jackie didn't stop refusing to give statements. "One lousy hour won't make a bit of difference to his defense."

"What defense? It's a good thing they can't charge him twice."

"Come on, it ain't that bad."

"We have exactly two choices, Pilar." Jackie kept her voice low, although in this hubbub there was no risk of being overheard. "He either had nothing to do with it—the handcuffs, ketamine, and cabin were in the wrong place at the wrong time—or Glenn Ballard is completely nuts."

"There's always a third possibility."

"Which is?"

"Ballard truly was framed."

"Ever know a defendant who wasn't?" Jackie could imagine what Phyllis Klein would do with that. "And why would anyone pick such a bizarre crime to frame him for?"

Pilar shrugged. "You'll come up with something, you always do."

"That video makes it tough to argue 'he just doesn't look the type.'"

"Yeah," Pilar said, "the marvels of technology. Of course, you could resort to BDS."

"BDS?"

"Boulder Dissociative Syndrome. The press will eat it up."

"Come again?"

"You know," Pilar continued. "That's my handwriting on the note, my pen—"

"—my writing pad—"

"—but I didn't kill my daughter and the lie detector proves it!"

That sobered Jackie up fast.

BDS might not be far off the mark. If she believed her eyes and ears, Glenn Ballard had to be in pathological denial about his role in Amy Lynch's death. "Don't even joke about a lie detector," she warned. "The last thing we need is him taking a polygraph."

"You don't *believe* in your client? Why, Jackie, I'm—"

"Where the hell is Whitney? I told you this was a mistake."

Pilar sighed. "So she's a little uptown, not exactly our style. What's the harm in a free lunch?"

The aromas issuing from the opening in the exposed brick were enticing. Despite the Indochinese hook, the most popular dish seemed to be roast chicken. On a pastry cart a tray of freshly baked fruit tarts glistened. Jackie was hungry for the first time in days.

"With Lily going off to camp, your yin and yang are out of whack," Pilar said. "If a square meal won't fix it, I know a good acupuncturist."

"Lily's got nothing to do with this. Matter of fact, she's been avoiding me."

"Maybe she thinks you're disappointed in her for leaving."

"I'm disappointed in *her*?"

Just then they spotted Whitney at a booth against the back wall. When she rose to wave, her emerald linen ensemble turned every head in the room.

"That suit is to die for!" Pilar said. "How do you think I'd look as a redhead?"

"The minute she brings up Seventeenth Street, I'm out of here."

"Don't be so quick to dismiss BDS," Pilar hissed as they made their way to Whitney's booth. "Boulder's the one place you could pull that off. What other town has its own foreign policy?"

"Let's just get this over with."

Whitney wiggled her fingers at the blow-dried weatherman from

Channel 7, then turned her high beams on them. "Pilar, Jackie!" She signaled the waiter for two more glasses of Chardonnay.

"I don't—" Jackie began, but the PR woman shooed away her protest.

"Of course you drink at lunch. What's one glass of wine?" She winked at Pilar, who pretended not to notice. "You were right, we've got to loosen this gal up."

"I have a ton of work waiting for me at the office—"

"—which is why I wanted to finish our talk here."

Pilar jumped in. "Now that Whitney's interviewed the dead-end kids, she can come up with a plan that makes sense."

The wine arrived, and Whitney watched as Jackie took a sip. It tasted surprisingly good.

"Let's cut to the chase," Whitney began. "I know you hate answering personal questions. They're intrusive and dumb, and frankly, I don't give a damn whether you fill out that questionnaire."

Pilar's nose was buried in the menu.

"It does seem like a lot of effort to find a tenant for one office space," Jackie said.

"I told Pilar I don't normally work with small professional groups, especially lawyers with practices as diverse as yours. But what attracted me to this project was you."

She would *kill* Pilar.

The waiter wheeled the dessert cart past their booth. As she eyed a cherry tart, Pilar's innocent expression turned to lust. "I could go for one of those right now. Maybe we should skip—"

"Timing's everything." Whitney wagged her finger at Pilar. "It's always sweeter if you wait." She returned to Jackie. "I know all about your background. You won almost every trial you had at the Public Defender's office. Hell, your last case was that grand jury investigation where you got the indictment dismissed! No wonder Glenn Ballard wanted you. You have the moxie to attract a federal judge as a client, and if you joined a litigation boutique you could have cases like that every week. Unless that isn't what you want . . ."

Jackie handed the waiter her unopened menu and ordered the fish special.

"What's in it for you?"

"Call it a Pygmalion complex," Whitney said, "but seeing my clients recognized for their talents is what I live for. I'm here to make the world listen."

"Why me?"

Whitney's eyes blazed. "Whenever I see a woman sabotage herself by not seizing an opportunity she deserves, I feel like tearing out my hair!" She softened her comment with a smile. "Do you know how many female trial lawyers of your caliber are in this town? Honey, I get to promote a *star.*"

"Maybe when I'm through with this case—"

"Let me give you one piece of advice, Jackie, and then we can enjoy our lunch. At this moment you're hot. Every news show from New York to L.A. wants a piece of you. If you want to position yourself to jump, do it before Ballard's trial."

Maybe Pilar was right.

"If I wanted to make a leap, what more would you need to know?"

Whitney signaled for another round of drinks.

"With a record like yours, why leave the PD's office?"

Not a free lunch after all. Jackie tried to remember which story she'd used before. "Didn't we already—"

"Last time we talked, you said it was lack of opportunity." Whitney leaned forward invitingly. "I got the feeling there was more to it than that. Come on, it's just the three of us."

Jackie avoided her investigator's eyes.

"Why else? Because of a guy."

"Jackie sure can pick 'em," Pilar cut in with a sly grin. She wasn't about to let her boss blame Dennis Ross, who not only had nothing to do with the grand jury debacle but had resigned from the PD's office months before Jackie. "For a while it was experts, but they tend to shoot their wad on the stand."

"So you do have an Achilles' heel!" Whitney gave a delighted laugh and Jackie downed her Chardonnay.

"One for each of my two left feet with men," she replied.

"Guys." Pilar sighed. "Can't live with 'em or without 'em."

As chummy as Pilar and Whitney were, Jackie half-expected her investigator to refer to herself as the original "merry widow." After all, Pilar had rubbed out her ex. Jackie's successful defense of her was one bit of history Pilar obviously hadn't shared. But at least she was covering for Jackie now.

"—turned over a new leaf when I left Kansas City five years ago," Whitney was saying. "Now the only men I invest in are clients."

Their food arrived with the second round of drinks, and Jackie poked at her grilled sea bass with chili-coconut sauce. A pitfall of not being able to read a menu in a fusion joint. But whether it was the wine or relief at her close call a moment earlier, she was finally beginning to relax. "You don't seem to have done too badly."

"Don't get me wrong," Whitney said. "I attract my share of guys, and even enjoy them. Under the right circumstances."

Pilar couldn't let that pass. "Circumstances?"

"Dinner, the theater." She winked. "Recreational sex. I just try not to take them too seriously. Frankly, lawyers are the worst—except for judges. And federal judges are in a class of their own."

"Oh?" Jackie had never really thought of judges as men. When you appeared before them, the most you could hope for was that they would be fair. And that was no small thing.

"Nothing is more important to a judge than his reputation, not that he'd be caught dead with a PR woman on his arm. With power comes ambition. And that, ladies, is their Achilles' heel."

"Don't stop there," Pilar said.

Whitney cut into her steak. "You've never heard, 'When God has delusions of grandeur, he thinks he's a federal judge?'"

Delusions of grandeur were a far cry from torturing coeds.

"Even state court judges think they're God," Jackie said.

"State judges are continually reassigned whether they like it or not. Can you imagine anyone telling a federal judge what to do? 'First among equals'? I've represented Seventeenth Street firms whose futures depend on trial court rulings. We're talking *real* power, ladies."

Was that impulse so dissimilar to sexual domination? Jackie shook her head. The nature of any obsession was living on the edge. If Glenn Ballard was into S&M, what he had risked to indulge it!

"Who are state court judges?" Whitney continued. "Former deputy DAs and PDs. Who are federal judges? Law school professors, bar presidents, and senators who vie for an appointment to the federal trial bench. Hell, state supreme court justices give up their careers for it!"

"But they're still accountable for their decisions," Jackie said. "They can be reversed like anyone else."

"Who can afford to wait for an appeal? All the appellate court does is shoot the survivors. The power elite eat out of the hand of the federal judges on the trial bench."

Those lawyers in the eighty-million-dollar patent case in Ballard's court—how had they explained to their clients that they could call just two experts, and only from their opponent's list? But Whitney was raising a more intriguing possibility, one that made more sense to Jackie than her client being a sexual predator. What had Ted Wolsky said? No matter which way a judge ruled, someone was always hurt. There was no shortage of lawyers and parties who might have a motive to frame Ballard.

Whitney turned to Jackie. "One last piece of business, so I can write this off on my expense account. Do I have your permission to discreetly ask around?"

"For what?" Her mind was on her client. Maybe it was time for another trip to his chambers.

"To team you up with people who can boost your career."

Pilar gave Jackie a swift kick.

"Well . . . sure."

They took their leave of Whitney outside the restaurant and waited for the valet to fetch Pilar's Spider.

"About Whitney—" Pilar began.

"You win," Jackie said. "Once Ballard's trial is over, we're getting out of that place. Provided I still have a career."

"There *is* a God."

"And I want you to put together a new file."

"On what?"

"People with a motive to frame Ballard. Lawyers, defendants . . . and don't forget his fellow judges."

"Let me get this straight," Pilar said. "You want me to track down every Tom, Dick, and Harry who ever appeared—"

"Just the ones who have reason to hate him."

Nineteen

The Alferd Packer Grill at the hub of the CU campus was named after a nineteenth-century prospector who'd recycled five snow-bound companions into stew. In Jackie's day it had offered granola, fresh Danish, and greasy burgers and fries. The ethnic fast food, limp salads, and designer water the cafeteria now featured were as sterile as the fare at Denver International Airport. As she watched Amy Lynch's former boyfriend bus tables, Jackie wondered whether a generation raised on that diet was equally disaffected.

The police file had said Matt Fisher worked two afterschool jobs. In addition to cleaning tables at the grill, he hashed at a sorority. Odd for a boy whose family could afford to send him to Kent. Was it personal pride, or had his parents laid down the law? And how had the demands of his work—or its lowly status—affected his relationship with a high school sweetheart with eyes on bigger things?

Behind the cover of a latte, Jackie tried to get a read on Matt as he scoured tables. He'd put on muscle in the six weeks since Mazatlán and the self-conscious smile in the photo had given way to a grimness that warned others to stay back. But what caught her attention was the way he worked. Industrious, thorough, even compulsive—he attacked the Formica with a ferocity the likes of which Jackie hadn't seen since Pilar had gone on a rampage after spotting a roach in the office kitchen.

Matt nodded curtly to one student who greeted him and ignored the others. It was three minutes until the end of his shift. He carried his last load of Styrofoam cups and plates to the bin in the corridor and disappeared into the grill. When he emerged, Jackie made her move.

"You were a friend of Amy's."

"Who are you?"

"Glenn Ballard's lawyer."

Matt shouldered his backpack. "Why should I talk to you?"

"Because you know Ballard had nothing to do with Amy's death."

Hazel eyes flickered.

"I've already answered those questions."

"Then you know the DA's on the wrong track."

"Lady, I don't know what you're talking about." He started to walk away.

"You cared about Amy, that much we both know. So how about it, can we talk?"

Matt slung his backpack to the floor. "I have to be at Delta Epsilon in ten minutes. I'm hashing tonight."

"How long did you know Amy?"

"We met in junior high."

"Before or after she transferred to Kent?"

Matt's eyes hardened and Jackie moved Graland to the top of Pilar's list.

"Before, I guess. I used to see her at intramural events."

"What sport?" Time was precious but rapport was essential.

"I ran track and she liked to watch." Soccer—had that been exaggerated to make Amy seem like the all-American girl she less and less resembled? Or was it her athleticism that got her through that snowy ravine?

"How did Amy pick CU?"

"If you were Bryan Lynch's daughter, you think you would've had a choice?"

Jackie left it for now.

"What about you, was CU where you wanted to go?"

"MIT offered me a free ride."

If Matt had followed Amy to CU, it had undoubtedly been against his parents' wishes. Jackie was also willing to bet the relationship had been more serious for him than it was for her. He had yet to say Amy's name, but each time Jackie did he flinched as if she'd pressed a bruise. Had he wanted to teach his girl a lesson? And what did he think of her private jewelry?

"Was Amy worried about anything?"

"Worried?"

Whatever she was fishing for, he clearly understood. Jackie kept it vague.

"Was your relationship the same as always, or had things changed?"

"Same?" he snorted. "Even when things were good—"

"—you never knew exactly where you stood."

"Yeah." Pain and frustration, that one word said it all.

"When did Amy stop waitressing?"

"A couple months ago. Before we went to Mazatlán."

"Why'd she quit?"

"Some guy was hitting on her."

Not according to Erin. She'd said the tips were lousy.

"How did you get along with Amy's father?"

"Bryan?" The familiarity suggested mutual contempt. "He liked me as well as he could."

"As well as he could?"

"You know fathers. No one's ever good enough." But there was clearly more. "Bryan gave her anything she wanted. Checking account, credit cards, the works. And in exchange, she . . ."

"What?"

". . . was the perfect daughter."

Jackie swallowed her impatience. She knew about the canceled credit cards; why was Matt lying? "What about Amy's mother?"

"Bonnie didn't have a clue."

About what?

"Was Mazatlán where you broke up?"

"Who said we broke up?" Matt couldn't quite pull it off. But Jackie was less and less sure where Amy's high school boyfriend fit in the puzzle. He was too raw, his resentments too fresh. If he'd cared for Amy as much as Jackie believed and had any role in her death, she would be seeing remorse. Or at least release.

"You weren't with her at Finnegan's Wake, were you?"

His stricken expression was Jackie's answer.

"I know about the guy Amy was planning to meet," she continued. This time Matt didn't flinch.

"You mean Derek?" he spat. At last a name. The older man? "He didn't mean anything—"

"Where did they meet?"

"We ran into him in Mazatlán. He was with a bunch of guys we didn't know."

"Had Amy met him before?"

Matt shook his head but Jackie wasn't buying. Of course Amy had known Derek; hadn't Erin said things changed before spring break?

Maybe Matt told himself it was nothing serious because he needed to believe Amy would have come back. Or was it because Derek had been a mistake and she'd truly wanted out?

"What's his last name?"

"I don't know."

That she believed. If Matt had any way to sic Phyllis Klein on Derek, he would. "Is he a student?"

"He was in a local band, or with some kind of recording studio." No way for a hash-slinging engineering student to compete with that. At an age when she feared nothing, had Amy thought she could do what she wanted without paying the price?

Another piece suddenly fell into place.

"Amy wasn't living at the dorm, was she?"

"Erin tell you that?" Matt didn't wait for an answer. "They got a kick out of scamming her father. Bryan never knew."

"Who paid the rent?"

Matt shouldered his backpack. "It's late. I've got to go."

"Whose idea was it for Amy to get pierced?"

"You mean those studs in her ear? That was in high—"

"I'm talking about the ring in her breast."

"*What?*"

He couldn't have been faking.

"Come on, Matt, you must have seen it. Don't bullshit me."

But she was talking to his back.

On her way out of the student union, Jackie helped herself to a copy of the campus newspaper. She turned to the classifieds and scanned the apartments for rent. Lots of zeros at the end of those dollar signs . . . No way Amy Lynch was getting that much cash from her mother on the sly.

Derek had big bucks or that girl had found a way to support her own habits.

Twenty

Glenn Ballard's secretary looked up from her computer with the same unflustered competence she'd displayed the day her boss's chambers were searched.

"I'm afraid you've just missed him, Ms. Flowers." This prim woman with the flawless complexion was even wearing the same silk scarf. "He's at the weekly judges' meeting and won't be back until one-fifteen."

Jackie knew that.

"I have some papers I promised to drop off." She fished a manila envelope from her briefcase. Pilar could have mailed Ballard the returns on the warrants for his home and chambers. Or even phoned; after all, the latter listed only one item seized. "I'll just leave them on his desk. . . ."

Before Betty could stop her, Jackie entered Ballard's private office. Betty rose and nervously followed. Spending five minutes alone in a client's workplace taught Jackie more than five hours of listening to him talk. But even empty of its master, Ballard's inner sanctum said little.

The walls were covered with a natural fiber more masculine than grass cloth, complementing the sleek modernity of his couch and desk. The broadloom carpet was a neutral shade; on it the chrome and glass seemed to float. But the decor's simplicity felt calculated, and Jackie wondered whether Ballard had retained an interior designer to outfit his chambers. Wasn't that out of character for a man who prided himself on not caring what others thought?

"Quite an office," Jackie said. Her eye fell on the scales of justice in the archway leading to Ballard's workroom. Hanging from a brass bar anchored into the top of the arch with an eye hook, they were inscribed in what might have been Latin. "Where did Judge Ballard find those?"

Betty hovered nervously at her elbow.

"They belonged to Judge Symes. He was Judge Ballard's mentor."

She reached for the manila envelope in Jackie's hand. "I'll be happy to take—"

Holding on to the envelope, Jackie crossed to Ballard's desk. The glass was topped with a hand-tooled blotter and a pen-and-pencil set in a teak stand whose inscription she couldn't read. On a side table adjacent to the tall window on the west wall sat a collection of gavels. Crystal, briar, solid silver—they spanned the history of Anglo-American jurisprudence.

"These are marvelous! Shouldn't they be in a museum?"

"Judge Ballard is very proud of his collection," Betty replied stiffly.

A three-foot walnut mallet leaned against the table.

"Does he play croquet?" Jackie asked.

Ballard's secretary tittered. "Hardly!" She pointed to the brass ring on the handle. "That's the judge's 'Texas gavel.' His law clerks gave it to him on the tenth anniversary of his appointment to the bench."

Jackie found herself trying to guess Betty's age. Her expensive pumps drew attention to trim legs and she wore no jewelry except for pearl studs and a small gold band on the third finger of her right hand. Late forties, at least. The ice was beginning to thaw but Jackie didn't kid herself. The minute the phone rang Ballard's secretary would usher her out and close his door behind them. In the meantime Jackie had to find out as much as she could about her client. She scanned his walls for clues.

The Jasper Johns in lieu of a real flag was a playful touch. Did it also evidence her client's indifference to the customs and practices of his fellow judges? As if reluctant to depart too radically from the staunch traditionalism expected of a member of the federal bench, Ballard had also displayed a number of awards. The plaques from the Federalist Society, American Judicature Society, and ABA were standard fare, but there was one hand-lettered certificate Jackie didn't recognize. It bore the insignia of a medieval figure in a shoulder-length wig wearing what looked like a doily on his head.

"What's this?"

"The certificate Judge Ballard was awarded by Harvard when he was inducted into the Order of the Coif."

The very name evoked painful memories. Coif was an ancient law society whose members were restricted to the top 10 percent of a school's graduating class. With Jackie's struggle to maintain a passing average, membership in a club even more elite than Law Review was clearly out of the question. But hadn't she wondered, just for a moment, what it would be like to be among those chosen few?

"What's the doily on his head?"

"That 'doily' is his coif. Members originally wore headdresses that covered everything but the face, but when wigs came into style they substituted a piece of white cloth." Betty's interest in the arcane topic was finally loosening her up.

"You seem to know a lot about it."

"I ought to; Judge Ballard was secretary of his chapter. For centuries, members were the only ones who had the right to appear in court. Why, Chaucer even mentions them in *The Canterbury Tales!*"

Chaucer had been another low point in Jackie's academic career. She stifled a laugh as she imagined what Dennis Ross would say about grades being a qualification for appearing in court.

"—only society to which he subscribes."

That gave her an opportunity to change the subject.

"Judge Ballard doesn't belong to any clubs?"

"Heavens, no! He resigned from every one of them when he took the bench. He's ethically obligated to avoid even the appearance of impropriety, you know."

What an appearance that video would make if it was played in court!

The telephone rang. Before it could sound twice, Betty picked it up at Ballard's desk, efficiently jotting down a message before she hung up.

"How long have you worked for the judge?" Jackie asked.

"Twenty-two years."

"Long before he took the bench."

"Oh, yes. Since he was a partner at Preston and Hayes."

The second-stuffiest firm on Seventeenth Street.

"He took leave from there to teach at the law school," Betty continued. "Teaching was his true love."

A true Renaissance man. From Crim Pro to white shoes.

"What kind of practice did he have?"

"He supervised all the big oil and gas acquisitions." Betty's voice fairly trembled with pride, and Jackie began to see another side of her client. No one was a hero to his secretary. Was Ballard the exception? Or was Betty in love with his image? And maybe not just his image.

"How nice that you were able to come with him when he left."

"Why, it never occurred to me to turn Judge Ballard down. He took an enormous cut in pay when he went on the bench, but this appointment was a logical step." If Jackie had wondered what Betty thought about her boss's current predicament, she was about to be told. "Glenn Ballard is the most ethical man I've ever known. Why, he doesn't even belong to the bar association anymore!"

That hardly made him a champion of the people, but Jackie awarded Ballard two points for snubbing the good old boys. If her goal was to get a sense of the man behind the mask, she would have to be more direct.

"Being on the bench must have its own stresses. . . ."

"Judge Ballard has never worked harder than he does now. And when he becomes chief—"

The phone jangled again, but this time Betty let it ring until it was picked up by a clerk in the library down the hall.

"When will that be?"

"End of August, when Simon Clark steps down." Betty leaned forward. "But the word is, even before then he may be nominated for the Court of Appeals."

As if this ghastly mess Ballard was involved in were an inconvenience that would be straightened out in due course! Yet Betty's response was oddly reassuring. The woman was either delusional in her loyalty or she believed that Ballard really did have nothing to hide. But there had to be more to his life than work. Pilar had said he was divorced; what was the story there?

"I'm sure these past few weeks have been the most difficult of his career," Jackie said. "Too bad the judge doesn't have a family to share his ordeal." Before the words had left her mouth, Betty was shaking her head.

"His wife couldn't have handled this."

The age-old hostility between secretary and wife, or something more? The secretary usually won, and Jackie was prepared to test the limits of Betty's loyalty and discretion.

"What was Mrs. Ballard like?"

Betty glanced at the door, but she was too caught up to stop.

"Nancy liked the fancy vacations, the house and cars. But he needs intellectual stimulation, and she could never keep up. . . . The divorce was just dreadful. When she left, she even took their dog!"

"Is he seeing anyone now?"

Big mistake. Betty drew back her shoulders.

"Judge Ballard keeps his private life to himself." There was a sound from the reception area, and she led Jackie to the door. In a voice loud enough for anyone listening to hear she added, "I'll make sure he sees those papers you left."

A heavyset woman was snooping in Betty's Out box. She showed no concern at having been caught.

"I knew you hadn't left!" the woman cried, giving Jackie a friendly wink. "The day Betty Howard knocks off for lunch, I start worrying the federal government's going to fold."

"Looking for something, Norma?" Betty's tone was guarded.

"Just delivering the transcript in the Title VII case. You know, that sexual harassment thing." It had taken a minute, but Jackie recognized her as Ballard's court reporter. She was clearly trying to get a rise out of Betty. "The one where the gal had forty-inch implants and complained because the guys wanted a peek?"

Betty flushed and Norma seemed satisfied.

"Well, I think I'll step out for a smoke before hizzonor's one-thirty hearing," she continued. She kept looking at Jackie. "Tell him not to read that all in one sitting."

With a little wave, Norma sashayed out of the chambers. Jackie thanked Betty for her time and quickly followed. Ballard's reporter was surprisingly light on her feet. By the time Jackie reached the ground floor, her round figure was entering the revolving door. Jackie caught up with her at the plaza outside the courthouse, where court personnel were smoking and brown-bagging it in the warm May sun.

"Not here," Norma said out of the corner of her mouth as she waved at one of the CSOs. "Down the street."

Her destination was a courtyard in front of an office tower two blocks away. When Jackie caught up with her a second time, Norma was ready to talk.

"What's it like working for the judge?" Jackie said without pre-amble.

"I knew you were his lawyer when I saw you the other day in court." Norma lit a Salem. "Where should I start?"

"His chambers."

"He forbids his clerks from talking to the other judges' staff." Norma quickly added, "Not that there's anything wrong with that. The federal judiciary is like the Mafia. Employees are expected to keep their mouths shut."

Jackie wondered how close Norma was to retirement.

"How does he get along with his peers?"

"They resent him like hell, especially Simon Clark."

"Why?"

"Ballard's so primed to be the next chief, he can hardly stand it."

"What's the big deal? Isn't that more work?"

Norma rolled her eyes in exasperation.

"The chief gets two secretaries and three law clerks. He presides over all the investitures of his fellow judges. Jets all over the country on his pick of committee assignments." Those didn't sound like the kind of perks Ballard cared about. Or Simon Clark, for that matter. And the chief's slot was a function of seniority; each of their colleagues would have his turn. There had to be more.

"What's the real reason they resent him?"

"Judges aren't kids: they're supposed to be heard and not seen. Ballard grandstands. Everyone knows he arranged that press conference after his Internet porn case. His real problem is he's smarter than the rest of them and everyone knows it. He makes sure they do."

So *No Exit* was a two-way street.

"Is Ballard close to anyone at the court?"

"Charlie Nesbit's his best friend, if he has one. That Internet case was originally assigned to Charlie." Norma stubbed out her cigarette and Jackie sensed there was something she was missing.

"What's with that Title VII case?"

"Thought you'd never ask." Norma gave a hoarse laugh. "Ballard spends a lot more time on sexual harassment cases than they deserve. It's kind of a joke among us court reporters because he always orders a transcript."

"Anything special about this one?"

"The lawyers wanted to stipulate to the facts, but Ballard insisted on a full hearing. With witnesses, of course. Believe me, in this business I've seen worse. *Much* worse."

Jackie refused to take the bait and Norma lumbered to her feet. With judicious grace, the court reporter delivered her final verdict.

"I say, so what if Glenn Ballard has a little fun on the bench?"

*   *   *

An hour later Jackie was at her desk nibbling at a chicken tamale Pilar had brought. Pilar's cooking was as tasty as ever; it was the facts that were unappetizing.

At least Ballard's reporter believed he was harmless.

A letch, maybe. But harmless.

The phone spared her from darker thoughts. Ballard was on the line.

"Betty said you dropped by my chambers this morning," he began. "Didn't I mention I have a judges' meeting every Thursday?"

"Did you review the return on the warrant for your home?"

"They wasted their time."

Except, of course, for the ketamine.

"We need to discuss where we're going with your defense, Glenn."

"What other defense is there?" He sounded surprised. "The prosecution is politically motivated."

"How do you explain the videotape?"

"Obviously a conspiracy."

"By whom?"

"You think I don't know how the members of my own court resent me, let alone the countless defendants I've put away?"

BDS. Maybe Ballard *was* delusional.

"We have no evidence—"

"Then get some!"

Jackie kept her tone even. "We need to discuss your alternatives. I'd like to arrange a psychiatric evaluation."

"Taking the easy way out, Counselor?"

"Unless we base our defense on it, we don't have to disclose it."

"I'm not crazy. And I have the evidence to prove it."

She finally bit.

"What evidence is that, Glenn?"

"I took a polygraph."

"A *polygraph*?" On her legal pad, Jackie angrily began doodling a black box with wires. With lie detectors there was always less to gain than lose. They were notoriously unreliable, seldom persuaded prosecutors, were inadmissible in court . . . and so damned easy to beat. It was impossible to control the spin. "When?"

"Last weekend, after my chambers were searched."

"What did the examiner ask?"

"The only question that counts. 'Were you at the cabin with Amy Lynch?'"

At least it was the right one. Jackie began to feel better.

"Who else knows about this?"

"Just me and the examiner."

"Did he prepare a report?"

"No. Do you want him to?"

God, no.

"Let's keep it that way," she said.

Pilar would have to broaden her background search.

Not only the criminals he'd sentenced, but of Glenn Ballard himself.

Twenty-One

"**W**hat were those kids doing out this far?" Jackie said as the Spider hugged a curve.

"You kidding?" Pilar replied with both hands on the wheel and a cigarillo between her teeth. "A high school boy would go from here to Nome, Alaska, for a bare tit. The kid who found Amy Lynch got a little more than he bargained for."

On this trip to Ballard's cabin, Jackie and Pilar had two goals: to inspect the scene of the crime and, free from the distractions of the office, assess the strengths and weaknesses of Phyllis Klein's case.

It was a Wednesday morning two weeks after Jackie's visit to her client's chambers, and in the hiatus between finals and summer classes at the CU campus, the traffic in Boulder was light. As they'd traversed the quaint-by-the-numbers downtown dominated by old brick and faux brick, authentic Victorians and cunning knockoffs, Jackie had ticked off the evidence piece by piece.

"The handcuffs don't concern me. The basement of the federal courthouse is as tight as a vault, but if you're not carrying a gun, anyone can get upstairs. Not to mention the possibility of the thief being on the court's staff."

"Thief?"

Jackie ignored the cynicism. "Whoever stole the handcuffs. As for ownership of the cabin, that's a nonevent. Isolated as it is, anyone could have broken in. The most recently Klein's witnesses can place Ballard in the vicinity was last December, a good four months before—"

"—Amy Lynch was abducted, tortured, and *killed*."

"Nor am I surprised that none of his fingerprints were found at the cabin."

"How's that?"

"Two reasons: Ballard hasn't been there for a while. And if I kidnapped a girl and kept her in a one-room place for three days, I'd be damn sure to wipe every surface clean before I left. Especially if she escaped." Jackie paused. "Now that I think of it, there's another reason why no fingerprints helps more than it hurts. Is the same guy who's smart enough to wipe down the place going to be so stupid as to use his uncle's cabin?"

"*Very* clever." They'd passed the convenience stores on the sterile strip north of town, and Pilar made the left at the turnoff to the hills. "What's your spin on the ketamine?"

"It's a pet tranquilizer, for God's sake!" Taking a deep breath, Jackie continued in a calmer tone. "Ballard owned a dog but his wife got it in the divorce. When's the last time you checked your medicine cabinet? And the tox screen they ran on Amy came back negative."

"After three days there would have been no trace of it, anyway. Too bad we couldn't run one on Ballard."

"Hmm?"

"Maybe it's your client who was drugged. After all, U.S. District Judge Glenn Ballard couldn't possibly have been in his right mind—"

"You have a problem with the presumption of innocence, Pilar?"

"Not in the least. But I'll tell you what I do have a problem with . . ."

Jackie wasn't about to indulge her investigator's heresy by asking the expected question. When split-level houses with horses gave way to upscale developments and secluded show homes, Pilar finally picked up where she'd left off.

"You're forgetting one thing."

"Which is?"

"The elephant rotting on the living room floor. You're acting like you can win on reasonable doubt."

"Are you referring to the videotape?"

"A minor point, but still . . ."

"Don't you find it strange that Ballard kept it in his chambers?"

"Next to the other things he did, that ranks as pretty low on the list."

"Or that he wouldn't let me move to quash the warrant?" Jackie insisted.

"Maybe he wanted to be caught."

"Oh, please. The old 'Stop me before I do it again . . .'"

"Jackie, get real. We've got to look at all the alternatives, including the increasingly strong possibility that what our eyes and ears tell us just might be true."

"*If* Ballard did it, and *if* he had any consciousness of that fact, we'd be exploring a plea bargain. Which, I don't need to remind you, Lanny Greer would offer in a heartbeat. Plus, there's causation."

"Causation?" Pilar said.

"Klein has to prove Amy died as a result of what her abductor did."

"Which should be simple. She caught pneumonia from her trek through the woods."

"No matter what the formal charge, you know Phyllis. She'll do her damnedest to try this as a sexual assault." And to humiliate Jackie and Ballard both. Klein rivaled Nixon in her ability to nurse a grudge.

"When's the next time you square off in court?"

"I've requested a status conference. We still haven't received a copy of the videotape."

"She'd be nuts to think she can sit on evidence!" Pilar said.

"That tape should have been a needle in the haystack, but it took her boys five minutes to find it in Ballard's chambers. Somebody must have tipped her. And isn't it strange that, aside from the abrasions on Amy's neck and wrists, we've seen nothing that suggests molestation? Phyllis must have some plan to finesse that."

"Don't kid yourself, Jackie. Regardless of whether Amy was penetrated, the chains and dog collar play right into Phyllis's hands."

"Power *is* sex. But who abducts a girl just to chain her up and stroke her arm? Which brings us back to that videotape. If Ballard recorded it to relive his experience, it couldn't have been a very satisfying one."

The road cut through the Morrison fault, with petrified bands of red and green mud on one side and the crumbling sediment of the Flatirons on the other. Moments later they passed the gravel turnoff where the high school kids had gone to neck. As the Spider made the steep descent into the canyon, Jackie's stomach dropped. The mountains always did that, but here it wasn't just the steepness of the grade. It was the terrain.

Wind whistled down the canyon, and the sky had been reduced to a cindery patch. The brush along the creek crawled up the asphalt, and the trees were so thick you could get lost twenty yards from the road. Jackie's dizziness turned into nausea. She gripped her armrest.

"You okay there?"

Jackie silently counted to five. When she was sure she could answer without losing her lunch, she said, "Too many unanswered questions."

"Such as?" Pilar was staring straight ahead again, oblivious to the scenery.

"Matt Fisher, for one. He's too good to be true. He gave up a scholarship to MIT and followed Amy to CU. He must have been furious when she dumped him for some creep she'd just met."

"Furious enough to drag her to a deserted cabin and chain her to the rafters?"

Jackie winced. "You're the one who said a high school kid would go all the way to Nome, Alaska—"

"—for a tit, not to teach his girl a lesson."

"Well, what about Bryan Lynch?"

"What about him?" Pilar countered.

"There was something weird between him and his daughter."

"And your evidence for that is?"

"He was overprotective, almost obsessed." That sounded thin to Jackie's own ears, and she struggled to support it with facts. "Amy moved out of the dorm and was walking around in clothes she couldn't afford, but her parents didn't have a clue. And Bryan's relationship with his wife is obviously strained."

"Because they don't hold hands on network TV?"

"Well, you're forgetting the most obvious defense: Glenn Ballard's record is absolutely clean. There's not a hint of scandal in his background. He's been vetted by the FBI, his ex-wife says she'll vouch for his character. Hell, his worst vice is belonging to the goddamned Order of the Coif!"

"A hundred bucks says he spanks his monkey on weekends," Pilar replied. "And if he ain't playing spanky, he's got something going with a French poodle. Come to think of it, that ketamine's making more and more sense."

"Because he likes Title VII cases?"

"What's that saying? 'One man's meat is another guy's perversion'— or something like that." Pilar peered through the windshield. "The turnoff to his cabin must be here somewhere. . . ."

The road had bottomed out and Jackie's equilibrium was slowly restored.

"What did you dig up on Ballard's background?"

"Pretty much what we already knew." Pilar rattled off the facts. "Comes from a ranching family who owned most of the land around

Craig. No brothers or sisters. Father was a third-generation Coloradoan, close as you come to aristocracy thereabouts, and Mom was a schoolteacher who died while her son was in prep school back East. Yale undergrad and Harvard Law. His father ran the ranch almost single-handed until he died, and then the land was partitioned and sold off except for the original house, which Ballard still owns. No skeletons in any of his closets . . . This must be it."

If not for the tire tracks, Jackie would never have spotted the dirt road. The dense undergrowth at the side of the blacktop all but obscured its entrance. Little more than a hiking trail, it would have been even more difficult to find when covered with snow. Whoever brought Amy there had to have known about the cabin. And owned a four-wheel drive. As the Spider turned onto the path leading up the back of the mountain, Pilar kept a tight grip on the wheel.

The first quarter mile the ruts were deep enough to threaten the Spider's oil pan. At one point Pilar high-centered and Jackie had to get out and push. Placing her hands on the trunk and taking two steps back for leverage, she rocked the sports car. It took a mighty shove to bounce free.

As Jackie leaned over to catch her breath, the underbrush came alive and for the first time she became aware of the beauty of her surroundings. Invisible birds twittered and chirped, cobalt penstemons set Indian paintbrush aflame, and sweet peas and wild pansies sprang up wherever she looked. The air was fresh and cool and it was impossible to believe that at the end of this road a young girl had been chained. . . .

"Planning to walk?"

Jackie jumped back in the passenger's seat. "I can see why you'd build a cabin here. It's so peaceful."

"Next time we'll bring a picnic basket."

The clearing was breathtaking in its pristine isolation. As Jackie climbed out of the Spider, she was struck by the sound of rushing water and the scents of juniper and pine. Whoever had chosen this site had wanted to hear the creek below and sought to preserve as much of nature as possible.

The cabin was built on a foundation of cobblestones, chinked with smaller rocks to hold them in place. The logs had been peeled smooth and were weathered a silvery gray. There were two small windows, one beside the door, facing south, and the other facing west. The door was constructed of matched boards with sturdy strips of wood covering the seams. The only hint as to what had occurred were the trampled vegetation, a shiny new padlock on the latch, and a strip of yellow crime tape caught in the branches of a juniper.

"This must be the path Amy took!"

Jackie looked where Pilar was pointing. At the edge of the ravine a faint trail led down the slope and hugged the creek as it rounded a bend. On the opposite ridge the sun breaking through the clouds sparkled off metal or glass.

"And that must be where those kids went for help," Jackie said. How had Amy made it through the underbrush and across the creek? And in the snow . . . The sheer cruelty of the crime struck her with a physical force.

"Scratch that causation defense," Pilar muttered.

Jackie turned back to the cabin. Against the weathered door on the south side, the steel padlock gleamed. "Where's Ted when we need him?"

"We should have brought a bolt cutter," Pilar said. "How 'bout a window?"

The glass in the two windows was intact and, judging from the spiderwebs and grime around the sills, the windows hadn't been opened in a long time. The one facing west had a small gap between sash and sill.

"Give me a boost." With Pilar's help, Jackie hoisted herself onto the sill. She felt the seat of her trousers catch on something sharp. The frame was clotted with the husks of several seasons' worth of insects which had sought entrance and died in vain. She pushed at the window sash. It shuddered and gave way. Pilar passed her a wad of tissues but she wiped her hands on her thighs. She swung her legs over the sill and opened the window as far as it would go. She leaned out to Pilar. "Coming?"

Pilar boosted herself up and straddled the sill. Grasping Jackie's hand, she stumbled in.

Jackie gazed about the large square room. From the sun pouring through the windows it was apparent that they'd been placed on the west and south walls to trap the maximum light and heat. On the wall opposite the door stood a fieldstone fireplace with an iron bar across the hearth for hanging pots. The floor, too, was stone, and Jackie tried not to picture Amy being dragged across it. She looked at the walls. Like the exterior of the cabin, the face of the logs on the inside had been stripped of bark.

"Amy must have been freezing." Pilar shivered theatrically. "What this place needs is a good fire." She left it to the imagination whether the conflagration should be confined to the hearth. But Jackie was trying to imagine her client in this setting. The decor was a far cry from Swedish modern, but in an odd way the cabin suited Ballard. Was it the flawless craftsmanship—or the absence of anything personal? She stared up at the soaring rafters and quickly looked away.

"Where do you think he put the tripod?" Pilar said.

"Hmm?"

The whirligig table with its lazy Susan on a pivot stick, the bedstead of four strong posts with bark intact and wooden slats—each detail was familiar from the videotape. But something seemed off. Was it because Amy and Ballard were in the video and the cabin was empty now? Or was Jackie just clinging to that last breath of hope that her client was innocent?

"Or do you think he set up the camera here?" Pilar was pointing at a rough stool by the door.

"Too low. You're right; he must have brought a tripod." Yet another level of planning. "At least we know why there were no fingerprints."

"Yeah, rough surfaces like these are a cop's worst nightmare. Had enough?"

"Almost . . ."

Jackie could no longer avoid it. She stared up at the rafter where Amy Lynch had hung, balancing on the balls of her feet and twisting in the firelight. A man in black trousers and a silk shirt approached. He stroked the girl's arm.

When he turned this time, she had no trouble believing he was Glenn Ballard.

Twenty-Two

Phyllis Klein entered the courtroom from the judge's door behind the bench. Carrying a slim file, she sauntered to her seat by the jury box and began flipping through the manual of Colorado statutes waiting at the prosecution table.

Her rules, her table, her courtroom.

She looked up with a nonchalance that left her eyes cold.

"Pleasant drive from Denver, Counselor?"

Before Jackie could respond, a young woman entered from the same door carrying a plastic pitcher of water in each hand. From her tailored slacks, brocade vest, and poplin blouse, Jackie pegged her as a third-year law student at CU. As the bailiff deposited one of the pitchers at the prosecution table, Klein whispered something and they both laughed.

Jackie got that picture, too.

Not only was Klein on home turf, she controlled the judge's staff.

The bailiff smiled mechanically as she approached with Jackie's pitcher.

"Finals over yet?" Jackie asked.

"Excuse me?" The girl hadn't expected an out-of-towner to speak, much less discern her true status.

"They still make you write a paper for Ethics?" Klein had stopped paging through her rulebook and Jackie could feel her icy glare. "I remember when—"

"You went to CU?"

"Of course." Just as assuredly, Klein had not. And that made the queen of date rapes more of an outsider in the eyes of a soon-to-be fellow alum than a lawyer who had to travel thirty miles to court. "Is Philips teaching Water Law? I can't believe he's still standing."

"They'll have to carry him out feet first," the bailiff agreed. She opened Jackie's pitcher and sniffed its contents. "I rinsed it out this morning, but I'll be glad to get you fresh—"

"No," Jackie assured her, "that's okay." It always paid to be solicitous to the judge's staff. In addition to being barometers for the pressure in the courtroom, weren't they also their boss's eyes and ears? Jackie hazarded a glance at Klein, whose grin was stretched so tight her lips might crack, then smiled sympathetically at the bailiff. "You have better things to do."

The bailiff went to the door behind the bench and peeked into the back corridor for the judge. Klein was spreading the meager contents of her file across the prosecution table. Jackie had no trouble reading that message either.

I didn't even have to prepare.

The fluorescent light above the defense table flickered once, and Jackie reached into her jacket for her moss agate. The translucent wedge was no larger than the tip of her thumb, but in it floated a magnificent tangle of vegetation. Visualizing the lacy green inclusions and caressing its satiny surface enabled Jackie to focus. She was never without the agate in court.

"All rise!"

The Honorable Marlin Pitts took the bench and signaled for them to be seated. With a bemused look, he addressed Jackie.

"I confess I don't know why you requested a status conference, Ms. Flowers. Much less in open court."

Boulder judges preferred to handle disputes in chambers. A little horse-trading over a cup of herbal tea, without that pesky court reporter taking down what was actually said. For that matter, no Denver judge would commence a hearing by *not* taking charge. Rising, Jackie matched Pitts's affable tone.

"I like to be on the record, Your Honor."

At the opposing table she felt Klein bristle. The judge, too, frowned. Was Jackie going to make this more difficult than it had to be?

"Maybe that's the way you do things in Denver"—where the lawyers were slime—"but in Boulder, we members of the bar trust each other." That was the first time Jackie had heard a judge lump himself with the proletariat. He sounded more wounded than offended. "Not to mention having faith in the bench."

"My memory may be less perfect than most," Jackie continued mildly, "but I find a transcript tends to be the best way to avoid disagreements among even the most honorable of adversaries." How ironic for her of all people to tout the sanctity of a written record! She searched for words to make her intransigence more palatable. "Good fences make good neighbors. . . ."

The door at the rear of the courtroom opened, and Jackie saw Lanny Greer slip into the last row. Phyllis Klein was furiously scribbling on her legal pad, the nape of her neck an angry welt against her short yellow hair. She was taking this as personally as Marlin Pitts but, unlike him, she itched to go on the attack. Jackie beat her to it.

"With the trial less than two months away, I wanted to confirm the prosecution has disclosed its entire file."

Pitts directed an inquiring look at Klein, who shrugged and spread her hands as if she had no idea what Jackie meant. "The prosecution has fulfilled all statutory duties," she added for the record.

"You have the DA's word, Ms. Flowers. Isn't that enough?"

"Actually, no. I still haven't received certain items seized from my client."

Pitts raised an eyebrow at Klein. Jackie was getting his MO. The less he actually said, the less likely he was to be reversed.

"There must have been a mix-up," Klein replied. She knew Jackie was referring to the videotape. "My office sent all we had to Ms. Flowers weeks ago."

"Ms. Klein will take another look. Anything else, Ms. Flowers?"

"I'd like the DA to confirm that she's provided all materials that negate or tend to negate Judge Ballard's guilt."

Phyllis responded with a wounded look. "We've disclosed all exculpatory evidence, Your Honor."

Jackie's antennae soared. "Exculpatory" was in the eye of the discloser, and no prosecutor used that word unless she had something to hide. The question was how to ferret it out.

"There you have it, Ms. Flowers," Pitts said with the air of a girls' volleyball coach mediating a tiff. "You have Ms. Klein's word, on the record—"

"I have reason to believe she hasn't disclosed the identity of a key witness, who may have information useful to the defense."

Klein's cheeks were as scarlet as her throat.

"I don't know what she's talking about!"

"Who do you mean?" Pitts demanded.

Jackie kept it short and sweet.

"Ms. Klein has never disclosed her basis for the warrant to search Judge Ballard's chambers."

"My affidavit clearly stated probable cause! The ketamine, the handcuffs, the—"

"I signed that warrant myself," Pitts warned Jackie.

"The Boulder detectives knew exactly where to look." That was as close as Jackie could come now to suggesting Klein had relied on an undisclosed informant, whose existence the DA would have been under a statutory obligation to reveal.

"Just because my men performed their job thoroughly—"

"'Thorough' is an interesting word," Jackie said. "On the basis of a boilerplate warrant, they skipped Judge Ballard's anteroom and private office and went straight to a storeroom in the back of his chambers—"

"That was damned good police work or luck!"

"Some *luck*." Jackie wouldn't even dignify the other possibility. "It took them all of six minutes to make their way to the second-to-last drawer of one of four massive filing cabinets"—a guess as to time, but no one could contradict her—"where they just *happened* to find an unmarked videocassette, which just *happened*—"

"Enough!" Pitts was no Greta Mueller, but he was far from stupid. He knew there were only two implications to what Jackie was saying: that he was a complicitor in prosecutorial misconduct, or he'd been suckered into signing a warrant on the basis of an affidavit that failed to state the true basis for the search. Unwilling to face either prospect, he blustered his way out. "I signed that warrant myself, Ms. Flowers. If it was based on a confidential informant, his testimony was written with disappearing ink."

But Klein's defensiveness and Pitts's reproach only confirmed Jackie's suspicions. There was a tipster and Klein knew his name. The fact that Phyllis was concealing his identity meant he was either so scummy that calling him as a witness would hurt her case, or that he knew something helpful to the defense. Unless, of course, the date-rape queen was sandbagging her . . .

Phyllis Klein's eyes dared Jackie to do something about it.

"I've given Ms. Flowers the names and addresses of all witnesses currently known to me, and will continue to do so if I learn of any new ones before trial. Except, of course, those witnesses I might call on rebuttal."

That was how Jackie knew.

She didn't for one moment believe Klein had rebuttal witnesses. Phyllis was a control freak, and the only way she could call them would be if Jackie opened the door. No, Klein was sitting on the identity of a witness she planned to call in her case in chief. She would wait until the last possible moment to disclose him.

Mr. Big would show up on the prosecution's list on the eve of trial. And whatever he said would devastate Ballard's case.

Twelve faces scowled down at the hapless figure in the well of the court.

Clad in black robes whose pleats had not changed in the century and a quarter since Colorado's first federal judge had taken the bench, those eminent jurists with their balding heads, drooping jowls, and steel-rimmed spectacles graced the paneled walls of the ceremonial courtroom at the United States District Court, in the temporary custody of U.S. District Judge Charles Nesbit. The oldest portraits were in oil, with the more recently departed memorialized in larger-than-life amalgams of airbrushed photography and pigment that, though kinder to the wallets of law clerks pressed to contribute to the cause, captured neither their subjects' humanity nor the gravity of their office.

The apparent object of their liverishness was a fellow in an ill-fitting suit who stood with his right hand frozen in midair. His anxious expression made him look like he was requesting a bathroom break. Oblivious to the man's discomfort, the only living judge in the room regarded him with the vague fondness of a distant uncle who has forgotten his nephew's name but nonetheless credits himself for the boy's achievement. Shaking his perfectly round head with a mixture of admiration and regret, Charlie Nesbit turned to the man standing at the prosecution table. Now he allowed his eyes to twinkle.

"Well, Bill," he said to the United States Attorney for the District of Colorado, "I hope you don't expect to win all your motions this easily."

William Bradfield Bennett smiled sleekly. The swearing-in of an assistant U. S. Attorney was an entirely routine event. Routine, that is, to every judge but Nesbit. In his navy pinstriped suit cut to emphasize his broad shoulders and trim waist, Bennett approached the bench with a feline grace. He handed Nesbit the papers signifying the young man's commission.

"Your Honor, I come before you requesting . . ."

As the U.S. Attorney began reciting his lines, Jackie's attention wandered. The QUIET, PLEASE sign in the corridor outside the courtroom attested to the fact that Nesbit had been in trial and dismissed his jury in order to preside over this dog and pony show. The room was half-filled, and as near as she could tell, the attentive faces in the first row belonged to the lawyers and paralegals in the case he'd recessed. On this Wednesday afternoon in late May, Charlie Nesbit had felled two birds: he had sent his jury home early while making the attorneys stay to watch, and he would get to leave the bench at least an hour before the close of business. But no matter how much pomp and circumstance he rang out of it, it was still a second-string swearing-in.

"All rise while I administer the oath."

The attorneys in the front row jumped to their feet and the spectators awkwardly followed. Even if Nesbit shook every hand in the courtroom, in ten minutes the ceremony would be over. Jackie knew he showed up at every rubber chicken event to which he was invited; just because he was appointed for life didn't mean he'd stopped running for office. Having recessed his trial but not wanting his fellow judges to see the reserved slot in the basement empty of his Lexus, Nesbit would be available to talk when she dropped by his chambers.

With a flourish, Nesbit signed the document the United States Attorney had tendered. As she watched his gaze sweep from the vacant jury box to the lawyers unfortunate enough to be stuck with their case before him, and finally to the empty rows at the rear of the ceremonial courtroom, Jackie couldn't help comparing this event with the full-court press when a judge was sworn in.

Chief Judge Simon Clark would enter from the door to the robing room and ascend to the leather chair at the precise center of the bench. Flanked by his brethren in order of seniority, with bankruptcy judges, federal magistrates, and members of the Tenth Circuit Court of Appeals seated in the jury box, he would preside over a courtroom packed with bar association officials and representatives of the most prominent law firms in the state. Clark's eloquence and dry wit made the tedium of an investiture bearable while his economy of words left no doubt where he ranked these affairs in the hierarchy of the administration of justice. When he stepped down as chief in August at the end of his seven-year term, he would leave big boots to fill. With any luck, Jackie's client would fill them.

Two sharp raps of the gavel signaled the ceremony's end. As Nesbit began to circulate in the small crowd, Jackie realized he was shorter than she'd thought. Part of the function of the robe was to make its wearer look larger-than-life; gathered at the shoulders and falling in pleats from the collar, it was designed to add bulk and breadth. Nesbit's had been custom-tailored. With volume removed from the sleeves and the hem falling midway between ankle and knee, it fit more like a smock than a robe. Jackie stood in the back of the courtroom watching him make his rounds, then slipped out. When she entered his chambers down the hall from her client's, Nesbit's secretary had already left for the day. There was no sign of a law clerk. The door to Nesbit's private office stood open and Jackie looked in.

Nesbit's chambers were more traditional than Ballard's. His furniture was upholstered in green leather with brass tacks, his desk made of walnut. The American flag that stood in one corner was the real thing, and a framed facsimile of the Declaration of Independence hung on the wall beside it. The melancholy figure in the oil portrait behind Nesbit's desk looked familiar, but before she could get a better look the door to the reception area opened.

"You were at the swearing-in."

Charlie Nesbit's tone was jovial, but his eyes were small and hard. He was still wearing his robe and behind him stood a woman Jackie took to be his secretary.

"Judge Nesbit, I'm—"

"I know who you are. Is this what I think it's about?" He gave Jackie a conspiratorial nod. She wasn't sure what it meant but appreciated his discretion. "Gloria, hold my calls," he said over his shoulder. With his hand on Jackie's elbow, he ushered her to a seat at his desk and closed the door behind them.

As Nesbit removed his robe and draped it over the back of a chair, Jackie took a closer look at the painting. Honest Abe was sitting behind a desk that was a dead ringer for Charlie's, down to the tooled-leather blotter. The only thing missing from Nesbit's setup was the goose-quill pen. Her eyes turned to Abe's protégé. Gray wisps fringed his cue-ball head. Without his robe he seemed even smaller.

"Before we begin," Nesbit said, "I have to tell you there isn't a man alive for whom I have greater respect or admiration than Glenn Ballard. He's the tops."

"I'm sure he—"

"He was the best judge for that Internet case. The least I can do for him now is to take over some of his criminal docket while that matter in

Boulder is pending. I would be honored to take the stand in his defense. Tell me what I can do to help."

But Nesbit gave her no chance.

"I just wish some of that brilliance would rub off on an old country lawyer like me. Guess we can't all be Order of the Coif. Dreadful thing for Bonnie and Bryan Lynch."

"Are you a friend of the Lynches?"

"Why, I've known Amy since she was a child. A beautiful girl." Nesbit looked away. "Bonnie's family was my client for more years than I can count. Kellogg and Kemp can thank her grandfather's molybdenum interests for its natural resources department. Frank Kellogg took a lot of ribbing for naming his oldest daughter Molly! And they don't come any better than Bryan Lynch. Naturally they came to me about Amy. . . ."

Was it Nesbit who'd advised the Lynches to clam up?

"But you're here about Glenn, aren't you?" he continued.

"I—"

"Let me tell you about your client, Ms. Flowers." Nesbit leaned across the replica of Honest Abe's desk. "After practicing law for twenty years, I thought I was ready for the bench. The initiation can be pretty rough. My first day on the job, Glenn took me to lunch and gave it to me straight: never have your secretary put another judge on hold, and keep your mouth shut until the chief judge closes his."

Was he pulling her leg? Jackie found herself smiling back. "I'm sure Judge Ballard's advice was right on target," she replied. "About that Internet case—"

"How Glenn finds the time to do all he does, I'll never know. Of course, you can be a slave to a routine. Glenn is so disciplined you can set your watch by him." Charlie shook his head with self-deprecating charm. "Did you know he can bench-press his own weight? That's right. Before he gets here for those crack-of-dawn discovery disputes, he's already been to the gym. Gets in a full workout before I've had my first cup of coffee. Of course, there's lots of pretty girls there at that hour. . . ."

He rose but Jackie remained in her chair.

"I'm sure Judge Ballard is very grateful for your support. Do you know anyone who might have any reason to set him up?"

"Set him up?"

"You said it yourself, he's charged with a dreadful crime. Can you think of anyone who might have a motive to frame him?"

"I don't know what you mean."

"Take that Internet case. Could any of the parties have it in for the judge?"

"There's always someone mad at you when you make a decision," Nesbit replied. His studious frown almost masked his relief at the direction her inquiry had taken. "But feelings ran particularly high in that case. Not just the parties, the whole industry was shaken up by Glenn's decision. Of course, it's on appeal and you never know how these things will turn out. But Glenn is seldom reversed."

"Can you think of anyone who might have a motive to frame him?"

Charlie rounded the desk to help Jackie out of her chair. His feet were almost as small as Ted's, and he was surprisingly fast.

"My dear," he replied, "take your pick."

Twenty-Three

When Jackie arrived at work the following morning, her office was in chaos.

The front hall was lit by klieg lights, the temp was ignoring the phones in favor of her perm, and two of Jackie's coworkers were straightening unfamiliar ties in the mirror. As Cliff elbowed one of them aside to check his comb-over and in the process almost upended an enormous vase of long-stem roses that had sprouted like magic from the scarred credenza, Pilar rushed from the kitchen.

"Where have you been?" Jackie was wearing faded Levi's, and her sleeveless, jonquil-colored turtleneck was a homage to the warm May. Pilar eyed her boss's bare arms disapprovingly.

"I—" Jackie began, only to be interrupted by a cultured voice at the conference room door.

"Try over there. . . ."

Whitney Grais was directing a blond fellow who was dashing about with a light meter. He looked up at Jackie and smiled with a boyish intensity before bounding up the stairs to get a reading at the second-floor landing.

"What's going on?" Jackie asked.

"Don't you remember?" Pilar said. "This is the day of the photo shoot!"

Whitney had wanted a photographer to take pictures for some kind of brochure. "The place looks great. I'll just go to my office, and if you need anything you can holler."

Whitney and Pilar exchanged an amused glance.

"Not so fast, pardner," Whitney said. "You're the star of this production."

"I'm obviously not dressed for the part," Jackie replied, suddenly grateful for her jeans and turtleneck.

Whitney had been appraising her like a side of beef. Now she slipped out of her coral cardigan and draped it over Jackie's slender shoulders.

She squinted a moment and nodded to Pilar. "She'll be fine, we just have to do something with those eyes. . . ."

"Can I be a star, too?"

Jackie had never been so glad to see Ted Wolsky. Having freed him from the clutches of the big bitch, she had no compunction about using him as her ticket out of being photographed.

"We have an appointment," Jackie said, avoiding Pilar's skeptical look.

Whitney called up the stairwell to the photographer, "How's the light by the stained glass?"

He flashed her the thumbs-up and Whitney returned to them.

"The best freelancer in town." She smiled engagingly at Ted, who was clearly smitten. "We're lucky he wasn't completely booked."

"He looks so young," Jackie said.

"Never confuse age with experience, dear." Whitney winked at the old cat burglar. "Now, just a touch of liner and shadow around the eyes . . ."

"Nice to see you dolling up again," Ted told Jackie. "Reminds me of those days at the PD's office. Dennis Ross must have been good for something." Seeing her expression, he ended with a little cough.

Whitney gave Ted's arm a conspiratorial pat and returned to the conference room for her satchel. Pilar began herding the others upstairs to prepare for the group photo.

"Some help you are, Ted."

"Who's the redhead?"

"Whitney? She's out of your league." But Jackie's protest only seemed to whet Ted's interest.

"I love a gal with balls."

"How do you know she has balls?"

"This is the first time I've seen you really doll yourself up since that prick Ross. Balls or not, Red must be a good influence."

Had she been letting herself go for that long?

"You've spent too many years in the can, Ted. Whitney patted you on the arm—"

"—and I may never wash again." Reaching into his pocket for a roll of bills, he stopped joking. "I dropped by to pay the rest of what I owe."

Jackie shook her head.

"The guy you really owe is Lenny. He said his report was a professional courtesy, but if you want to pay him back, put in a good word for him with Pilar. And quit torching buildings insured by Mutual State."

"This time I'm going straight." As if she hadn't heard that before. Ted caught Jackie's eyes and held them. "I really mean it. I'm retiring the Wonder Bar."

She wanted to believe him. "What are you going to do?"

"I'm thinking about becoming a private dick."

"You're kidding!"

He looked hurt. "Who's more qualified than me? If there's one thing I know, it's crime. . . . And speaking of pricks, how's your judge client? Anything I can do to help?" It wasn't the first time Ted had volunteered his assistance, but if he was leaving the trade, the last thing Jackie wanted was to encourage him to rack up debts on her behalf.

"Afraid not."

"No tears shed if he fries."

"You think someone he sentenced could have set him up?"

Ted pretended to take offense.

"Why do you always look for a con? The average guy in the joint couldn't find his own ass if it was growing antlers, much less frame a judge. But if you want to know who really hates Ballard, ask your friend Ross."

"What does he know?"

"Didn't he represent that bank robber Ballard threw in the hole for four times as long as he could live? He could tell you a thing or two about what makes cons like that tick."

Pilar and Whitney converged on her. Taking Jackie by the arm, they marched her to the powder room behind the reception area. Ted tagged along.

While Jackie settled on the lid of the commode, Whitney began unpacking a makeup kit the size of a small suitcase. Pilar ran to the reception desk for a tensor lamp. Whitney lifted Jackie's chin and tilted back her head.

"Your skin is good." As she turned Jackie's face back and forth under the light, Jackie felt like she was about to undergo a root canal. "You've been using a decent moisturizer. . . ." She reached into her kit and emerged with the most unusual brush Jackie had ever seen. A good ten inches long, its handle was raw white wood. Instead of a ferrule, a copper coil held the albino bristles in place.

Flick, flick.

Holding the handle between her first two fingers, Whitney absently tapped the end upward with her thumbnail. Ted was mesmerized—or was it Whitney's emerald? But the gesture, like flicking ash from a cigar, only heightened Jackie's anxiety.

"What are you going to do?"

Whitney smiled reassuringly.

"Make those green eyes of yours leap right out of your skull."

Reaching for a compact, Whitney ran the brush lightly across the caked powder and flicked it again with her thumb to remove the excess. With the deftness of a pro, she began dusting Jackie's face. The bristles were soft as mink.

"That's quite a brush," Pilar said.

"It was designed for applying gold leaf," Whitney explained. "In college I was a theater major. My mentor gave me this brush when I received my BFA. I guess I use it to remind myself where I came from."

"Is that where you learned to be a makeup artist?" Jackie asked. Whitney was holding the brush at the end of the handle, but the powder seemed to be going exactly where she intended it.

"After I graduated I worked for Portia."

"Portia?" Ted said. "Who's she?"

Pilar withered him with a glance.

"Not a *she,* Ted, an *it.* Portia just happens to be the giant of the cosmetics industry. It's bigger than Revlon or Lancôme." She turned to Whitney. "What a dream job! Why'd you leave?"

Whitney stepped back and squinted at her work.

"I was just one of the little folks. Believe me, PR is far more glamorous."

Pilar peeked in Whitney's bag. "Don't you use their products?"

"I'll let you in on a secret. The only thing worth a damn is their lipstick." She finished dusting Jackie's eyelids and used a smaller brush to apply a sheer highlighter from the lash line to the crease of her eye.

"What's this for?" Jackie asked.

"A marketing brochure. You're looking for a new officemate, remember?"

"But lawyers come and go. Isn't it a waste when the same people may not be here next month?"

"The brochure will have pockets," Whitney reassured her. "If someone leaves, all you have to do is substitute cards."

"There's a couple of jokers I'd like to throw out now," Pilar muttered.

Whitney fished in her kit for a still-finer brush. Tilting Jackie's chin even farther back, she lined the length of her upper eyelid with cocoa from the outside in. With Pilar hovering like a scrub nurse, she repeated the procedure on Jackie's lower lid.

"Almost done," Whitney coaxed as Jackie began to squirm. Jackie glanced at Ted. The admiration in his eyes proclaimed the operation thus far a success. "Now for a little mascara . . ."

The wand tickled Jackie's upper lashes.

"Whitney?" The photographer was at the door. "We're waiting."

"Cool your jets!" Whitney kicked the door shut, and footsteps quickly receded.

"He's right," Jackie said. "Can't we speed this up?"

"What are we going to do with her?" Whitney asked Pilar in mock despair. "Most lawyers can't get enough of the spotlight!"

Scrounging again in her kit, Whitney found the pencil she was looking for and began lightly tracing the outline of Jackie's mouth. Out of the corner of her eye, Jackie saw her reach for a gold tube with twin strands of copper coiled around the tip. The balm Whitney applied made her lips soft and heavy. Jackie saw Ted's eyes widen. Suddenly she remembered a sixth-grade slumber party where the hostess had raided her mother's vanity with ghastly results. Was that jar of cold cream still in the bottom of Pilar's desk?

"Where's the mirror?" she demanded.

Pilar and Whitney exchanged an unreadable glance and her panic mounted.

"You're not quite done yet," Pilar reassured her.

"We're doing black-and-white as well as color shots," Whitney said. "Your makeup has to be four times as dramatic as you'd wear on the street. . . ."

"Give me the damned mirror!"

It was Ted who handed it to her.

Jackie stared at her reflection.

Greener now, her eyes smoldered with an indefinable promise. Her mouth was almost exactly its natural shade but now the rose was dusky and more lush, the lower lip fuller and gently curved. Even the arch of her brows was more alluring.

Whitney had transformed her into a knockout.

"—told him to do a couple of glamour shots," she was saying. "They may come in handy."

"Handy?" Jackie said. She grabbed the lipstick and tried to memorize the label. "What's this called?"

"'Tease,'" Whitney said. "It's Portia." She and Pilar exchanged another look. "There may be something big in the works."

"You have to keep this under your hat," Pilar said, "but Whitney represents three of the biggest names in town. And two superstars from out of state."

"Names?"

"They're thinking of leaving their firms and setting up a litigation boutique," Whitney continued. "A barrister's firm—no paperwork, strictly courtroom pyrotechnics . . ."

Jackie's heart leaped.

"And they're looking for a woman to round out their practice," Pilar said. Only Ted seemed less than thrilled.

"You mean they need a female to attract certain clients," Jackie said. "The ones who need a woman at their table."

"What's wrong with that?" Whitney demanded. "Don't you use that to your advantage every day?"

"Of course . . . But why would they be interested in me? I have no book of business, there's no way I could buy in."

"That's why you're perfect. You're totally focused on the courtroom, it's where you come alive! These guys are so well financed that carrying you is the least of their concerns."

Ted slipped out, closing the door behind him.

"Wouldn't it be great to have a quiet place to work," Pilar said, "with paralegals to take care of all the paper? You wouldn't believe the clients these guys represent."

Now Jackie understood why they were in a rush to photograph her.

"But I'm not a litigator, I'm a trial lawyer. I don't do depositions or—"

Whitney was exasperated.

"They need you to round out the group! You won't have to troll for clients, they have their pick of them already. And so would you. The last thing they want is another paper-pusher who's scared to death of setting foot in court. Can I float your name or not?"

"I guess so. . . ."

"Well, it's a damn good thing." Whitney winked at Pilar, who let out a whoop. "Because I already did. And they jumped at it!"

There was a pounding at the door.

"Jackie? Where the hell are you?"

Cliff. All dressed up and nowhere to go.

"Those guys were here before you came," Pilar said softly. "And they'll be fine when you're gone."

What would it be like to function without chaos, not to worry about evidence disappearing and retainers being lost? And it wasn't just herself she'd been holding back. Seeing the excitement in Pilar's eyes, Jackie realized how wasted she was as a glorified secretary.

"What are we waiting for? Let's shoot."

Twenty-Four

Jackie's gaze followed the photographer from the snow-covered shadow of the pines to a clearing where sun laid bare a mat of needles. The midafternoon light still glinted off the high window by the weathered door, but soon it would be dark—and cold. You could feel it in the air.

Click.

She stopped the videotape, rewound and replayed the first thirty seconds.

Shadows, trees, snow. Window, door . . .

Why those images?

She reversed until the only snow was the static on the screen.

Watching now in the privacy of her home, the video seemed more cunning than it had at Ballard's chambers. It had arrived from Klein's office that morning and Jackie had brought it home, where she could study it uninterrupted. Neither the soft breeze rustling her curtains nor the glow of her bedside lamp mitigated the chill.

Sipping tea, she tried to ground herself in her comforting, familiar surroundings. But as she gazed about her bedroom, everything brought her back to the cabin on the screen. Her gleaming oak floor recalled rough stone, her butter-yellow walls became peeled logs. Even her antique fireplace with its ceramic tile and brass grill was overlaid with a stone hearth. And her ceiling fan—

Jackie set down her cup and hit the remote.

The first frame was an eye-level view of what she now recognized as the approach to the clearing. The videographer panned to the crown of the trees, as if to establish the grandeur and remoteness of the setting, then lingered on a melting patch of snow. A transition—from heaven to earth? Winter to spring? The mat of needles teased the eye, the scent of pine seemed to waft off the screen. Then, as if impatient to reach its destination, the camera swept through the clearing to the cabin.

Jackie stopped the video when it reached the window.

Small and high, it had been placed beside the door on the south-facing wall to capture the midday sun. She leaned into the screen to see if anything was reflected in the glass, but the light on the window gave off a frustrating glimmer. In contrast to the majestic pines and tender patch of earth, the cabin seemed forbidding in its self-containment. It projected menace.

Was she seeing what wasn't there? Was she avoiding the inevitability of what *was*?

The way her brain worked she could never be quite sure.

Thinking in pictures had always been Jackie's strength. For as long as she could remember, she'd been able to store images the way Pilar backed up pleadings on a computer disk. Memorizing gobs of information at a glance had been her salvation in junior high. Hadn't she learned an entire semester of American history by reducing it to one index card of symbols, with her teacher's favorite battles and dates in colored ink? Using a private code to summon up arcane facts had bailed her out more than once, but as Jackie grew older, she discovered the survival skill was also a powerful tool.

As she rewound the tape and focused on the first thirty seconds for a fourth time, she tried to visualize what had been going on in the photographer's mind. The film was of poor quality but it was enlivened by an aesthetic sense. Artistic, even . . . The art of the tease. This time she kept the tape running.

The camera circled the interior of the cabin, spanning the walls but stopping short of the rafters. Peeled bark, whirligig table, rough-hewn chair . . . It came tantalizingly close to the ceiling but at the last moment skittered away. Cupboard, bedstead, hearth. Follow me and I'll take you there. . . . Omnipotent. Narcissistic. She turned off the VCR and settled back against her pillows.

Not only could she store pictures in her head, she could scavenge bits and pieces to form a new whole. Like the cut-and-paste function on Pilar's computer, her brain edited out the parts that didn't fit. When her mind wandered it tended to solve problems—that was one reason her best ideas came just before she drifted off to sleep. But the gift came at a price. Distraction was Jackie's enemy; on bad days, when she was under stress or fatigued, she tuned out. Anything could derail her. Eyestrain, two people speaking at once, a sudden loud noise. Bad days came in clusters and then the only sense that grounded her was touch.

But right now, in the privacy of her bedroom with nothing to distract her, she was functioning at her best. Her problem was she didn't want to go where her instincts led. She hit the play button and the VCR picked up at the next frame.

At the hearth a fire crackled. The camera zoomed to the rafters—
Ri-iiing!

Jackie pounced on the phone. Raucous music blasted her ears.

"Watching something naughty on cable?" said a familiar voice.

"A nature film to help me sleep."

"I wondered where that videotape went," Pilar said. "But you should have hung around the office longer. Five minutes after you left, the temp coughed up another delivery from Phyllis Klein. A revised witness list. Pitts must have thrown the fear of God in her." From the background came a burst of laughter.

"Are you in a bar?"

"Don't you want to know who was on Klein's list?"

"Anyone we know?"

"Even better: someone we didn't."

"And the Mystery Man is?"

"Derek King—the guy who replaced Matt Fisher. You know, the one who buys coeds leather so they'll look foxy in Pearl Street bars."

Jackie sat up straight.

"Do you have an address?"

"I've already been to his place." Pilar's being one step ahead of Jackie almost made up for their being a step behind Klein.

"What did he say?"

"He had my number before I opened my mouth." Phyllis had gotten to him. "I did manage to snap a real cute shot of him before he slammed his door. It's making the rounds at Finnegan's Wake even as we speak."

Good old Pilar.

"At the office the other day—" Jackie began.

"I know you think marketing's a load of crap."

"That boutique firm, you think it's the right step?"

Pilar hesitated two beats.

"I asked around. Those guys Whitney was talking about aren't just first-rate in court, they also know how to treat their staff. But the decision's yours."

More squeals in the background.

"Gotta run," Pilar said. "It's tough keeping up with kids!"

Jackie hung up the phone and again hit the play button on the VCR.

In the clearing the camera had jumped around. A certain amount of jerkiness could be expected with handheld equipment, but Jackie sensed the technique was more designing than crude, as if the videographer wanted to appear inexperienced while setting the scene in a very particular way. The art had been in the tease—the contrasts between shadow and sun, bare earth and snow.

But in the sequence with Amy and Ballard together, the footage was smooth. Seamless. The camera had evidently been mounted. Jackie was mesmerized by the precision with which the camera documented their obscene dance.

The hooded girl twisted in the flickering light. Her body was limp. There were no bruises on her knees; had the dragging come later? Were it not for the way she balanced on the balls of her feet, she might have been unconscious. It wasn't until the man approached that she reacted. When his shadow fell on her, she seemed to feel it. As he reached out, her flesh quivered. When he touched her arm, the hairs seemed to stand. As his fingertips caressed her, her skin visibly crawled. His touch was clearly repellent, but after her initial twisting, she made no attempt to draw away.

Did she submit because she had no choice? After those first seconds, it was almost as if she'd *welcomed* it. . . . Or was Jackie seeing what she wanted to believe?

There was no doubt the girl was Amy and the man was Ballard. Never mind her age and the horrific outcome; when you chained a girl to the rafters, could you really pretend what happened next was consensual? Jackie rewound the video and ejected it from the VCR.

As she turned out the light and closed her eyes, a scrap of silk drifted into her consciousness. It hung there, shimmering.

The cops had retraced Amy's escape route, but they'd never found the hood.

And something else. At the cabin, they'd seized a black leather blindfold with a strand of Amy's hair. Why use a hood if you had a blindfold?

It was time for a trip to the Dark Side.

Twenty-Five

Three men lugging square-sided litigation briefcases exited the elevator in the rotunda of the federal courthouse. Their urgent tones confirmed they'd just come from a hearing. Behind them, two secretaries with empty Tupperware lunch containers stuffed in their totes continued a whispered conversation. Staff leaving at the stroke of five.

Jackie punched the button for the eighth floor. She had the up elevator to herself. As vehemently as judges denied adhering to bankers' hours, the one-way traffic said otherwise. When the doors opened and she saw a CSO with tired feet herding a flock of nervous citizens into the adjoining elevator, Jackie knew one of Ballard's colleagues had just released his jury for the day. In the main corridor, another CSO was locking up Nesbit's courtroom. He peered into the window of Ballard's court to make sure nothing was amiss before pocketing his keys and then poking his head in the lavatories to confirm no one was hiding or stuck. In a few moments the cleaning crew would swab the terrazzo floor one last time.

Jackie caught Ballard's secretary just as she was locking his door.

"Is the Judge in, Betty?"

Betty jangled her key ring. Despite the five card swipes it took Ballard to exit the courthouse, you needed a key to enter his chambers. At least through the front door.

"You have an appointment?"

"He said to come at five. . . . By the way, is the back door to the corridor kept locked?"

"That's our little secret." Betty lowered her voice. "The CSOs pitch a fit if you use that door, because when you go out it's automatically left unlocked. You wouldn't believe the grief they give poor Judge Tuttle's staff for using it, when Amelia herself is the one who forgets and goes out that way all the time!"

So much for Fortress America. But if someone had stolen Ballard's handcuffs or planted the videotape, it only confirmed Jackie's impression that it had to be an insider.

"What did you need to see him about?" Betty said.

With the deadline on pretrial motions and endorsing witnesses approaching, this was a come-to-Jesus meeting. "We have a couple of matters to discuss."

Betty reluctantly unlocked the door.

"He may be in the little boys' room," she whispered when Ballard failed to emerge in response to her call. "Give him a moment and try again." With a glance at the security camera above her desk to make sure no one was lurking in the corridor, Betty let herself out. Jackie waited another minute before going to his half-opened door.

"Glenn?"

Hearing a sound from one of the back rooms, she stepped into his office and called again just as Ballard emerged from his project room in his shirtsleeves. Jackie had never seen him when he wasn't wearing a suit coat or his robe. Shorn of his armor, her client exuded a raw physicality. Jackie tried to picture him in a black silk shirt. Powerful shoulders, trim waist—how long had he been bench-pressing his own weight?

"I'm just finishing up an opinion that has to go out in the morning. Can you give me a couple of minutes?"

"No problem."

"Make yourself comfortable." Ballard gestured to the leather couch before retreating through the archway where the scales of justice hung. Jackie wandered over to his desk. Its surface was as unrevealing as it had been on her last visit. Crossing to the display of gavels, she hefted the one made of silver. With a dozen to choose from, why didn't he keep any on his bench? She glanced into the project room where Ballard was thumbing through an eighteen-inch stack of briefs. Black silk slipped over broadcloth and she blinked the image away. With a little luck the jury would never see that image.

How would she deal with that videotape?

The goal of any defense was to form a bond between jury and defendant. If all else failed, you planted enough seeds of conflict that the jurors' only recourse was to deadlock. Whatever the defense theory was, it had to be wrapped in a story that sated the hunger for fairness.

Because no matter what their prejudices, jurors wanted to do the *right thing*.

Jackie had rummaged through her arsenal of rhetoric the night before. "What-ifs" and "if-onlys" worked well, particularly if they performed double duty by hijacking the most damaging aspects of the prosecution's case. *What if* Amy Lynch hadn't gone alone to Finnegan's Wake that night? *If only* she had gone there with her friend Erin. . . . *What if* Glenn Ballard had reported his handcuffs stolen?

Or she could appeal to common sense, in the process exposing the desperation of Phyllis Klein's case. *No girl* vanishes without a trace from a bar. . . . *No federal judge* abducts a coed and chains her to the rafters of his cabin. . . . Any of those might work in a normal case. But this was anything but normal. And it didn't matter whether she believed her client was framed.

No matter how Jackie finessed it, the cabin video loomed. And it exuded a gamy stench. It was the proverbial elephant rotting on the living room floor. The gag order Pitts had issued forbidding Klein from publicly disclosing the video's existence before trial was only a temporary reprieve. Unless they succeeded in suppressing that tape, six weeks from now it would rot in the well of Marlin Pitts's court.

Jackie looked in on Ballard again. His fountain pen whipped across his legal pad, dismissing arguments with the dispassionate logic for which he was famed. His intellect had taken him from Order of the Coif to a professorship to a partnership in a prestigious law firm, all the way to a coveted seat on a powerful bench. And now that very talent could be his downfall. For Jackie had little doubt how Ballard would react when she told him they needed an expert. All he had to do was take the stand in his own defense, he would say. The jury would believe he was innocent because he would tell them so. Didn't they hang on his every word when he was on the bench?

Restless, she crossed to the anteroom where Ballard hung his coat. The smell of disinfectant from the adjoining lavatory reminded her that the janitorial crew cleaned the judges' chambers during work hours because after five, the back corridor was secured. She looked inside.

The bathroom was utilitarian, with the same mauve tile that covered the floor flowing up the walls to chest level, where it was met by white paint. Paper towel dispenser, washbasin, medicine cabinet with a mirror over the sink, a plastic soap dispenser that looked plugged. Ballard's private bath had all the amenities of a medium-security prison. The only jarring note was an item that sat on the metal shelf below the medicine cabinet.

A silver and gold flask in the shape of a gladiator's breastplate. After a grueling day on the bench, did her client enjoy a snort? Maybe he and Betty—Jackie unscrewed the cap and took a whiff. A heady scent assailed her.

Lime, with a floral end note. Jasmine?

Not Ballard's dignified aftershave.

She screwed the cap back on and opened the medicine cabinet. It held a toothbrush still in its plastic wrapper, a travel-sized bottle of generic mouthwash, and an unused double-edged razor. If Ballard dolled up for dates after Betty left, he obviously didn't bring them back to his chambers. And they were classy enough to merit sexy cologne.

As she turned to leave, something else caught her eye.

Behind the door with toes neatly aligned sat a pair of slip-ons. But these weren't just any loafers. Much dressier and far more fashionable than Ballard's oxfords, they were fine, woven leather. Closing the door behind her, Jackie stooped to pick one up. The leather felt like skin—

Hearing a sound outside the door, she quickly put down the shoe and turned on a faucet. She let the water run and then reached for a paper towel, rattling the dispenser. When she opened the door, Ballard was waiting outside.

"I hope you don't mind that I used your bathroom."

"Not at all. I'm sorry I kept you waiting."

Jackie sat on the couch and he settled on the opposite chair.

"Do you know a Derek King?" she began.

"Should I?"

"Phyllis Klein delivered her witness list on Friday. His name was on it."

"Who is he?"

"A friend of Amy Lynch's."

Ballard shrugged. "Then there's no reason why I should know him."

"She also endorsed an expert to authenticate the videotape."

"So?"

"If you've been framed, Glenn, we need an expert of our own to examine the video. The deadline for endorsing witnesses is two weeks from today. Give me the go-ahead and I'll line someone up tomorrow. He'll view the tape and—"

Ballard shook his head. "Experts are loose cannons. You only need them to bolster testimony if it's weak."

"But you'll be asking the jurors to disbelieve their own eyes. When Klein plays that tape—"

"She's not going to."

"That's her whole case!"

"Not if Marlin Pitts suppresses it."

"Why would he do that?"

Ballard rose and strode to the window. He stared down at the traffic for a long moment before turning back to her.

"You know that search was rigged. The cops were obviously tipped by an informant. Do I have to remind you what the Fourth Amendment says?"

"But Pitts already ruled the affidavit for the warrant stated probable cause," she said. "He's gone on the record that there was no informant."

"Move for an in-camera hearing to quash that search." Ballard stood directly in front of her, forcing her to meet his eyes. "Trust me, Jackie. Marlin Pitts is on thin ice with that affidavit and he knows it. In a case with national press, no matter what else he's done in his career, he'll always be known as the judge who tried the Ballard case. He'll grant that hearing to cover his ass. He has no choice."

"I'd still feel better if we line up an expert."

Ballard shook his head decisively.

"I'm not running the risk of dignifying the DA's case, or having someone on my own team detract from the force of my testimony on the stand."

"Who else can I call?"

"No one. No character witnesses."

"But—"

"Just me. A judge is nothing without his reputation. That's why I refused to step down from the bench while this matter is pending. And I'm certainly not going to open the door to every lawyer I've ruled against to say why he hates me. I want to be the only witness for the defense."

Grandiosity—or honor? Jackie chose her next words carefully.

"I admire your idealism, Glenn, but the minute you take the stand it's open season on your character. You know how prosecutors are. Phyllis Klein will call your third-grade teacher to say you stole your classmate's homework and your Cub Scout leader to say you shaved points on a merit badge. It won't matter whether any of that's true."

"She's not going to sucker me into a squirting match." Ballard smiled. "If there's one thing I've learned, it's how to stick to the facts."

"Have you ever been on the stand?"

"No. But I've sat three feet above it for fifteen years."

"You think the jury will believe you because you're a judge? In Pitts's courtroom you won't be wearing a robe."

"You know why I don't keep one of these on my bench?" He stood at his collection of gavels. "If you're in control of a courtroom, you don't need a gavel. And you don't need a robe. The jury will believe me when I tell them I was never at that cabin with Amy Lynch."

As her client turned away, the last of the sun glinted off the brass scales. Now Jackie knew why he hung them despite their dissonance with the designer decor. It wasn't just that they belonged to his mentor. Those scales represented everything in which Glenn Ballard believed.

She gave it one last try. "Wouldn't you feel better if we have a fallback?"

His voice was very soft.

"Only the guilty need a fallback."

She reached for her briefcase. "I guess I have my marching orders, then."

Ballard walked her to his door. At the threshold he stopped.

"Charlie's quite a character, isn't he?"

She made no reply.

"He's a great guy, but he likes to talk. And he loves those ceremonies."

Jackie got the message. Why did he need to deliver it?

"He would have made a good chief," he continued. "It's a pity he'll never get the chance."

"Why not?"

Ballard shrugged.

"You do the math. After Simon Clark steps down in August, I'll serve for seven years. Charlie will be sixty-six when my term is up."

Twenty-Six

Cherry Creek Mall offered the cheapest day care in Denver.

At noon on the last Wednesday in May the play area at the lower level on the fast food end was overrun with toddlers. They scrambled over the enormous sculpture of eggs sunny-side up and the six-by-six-foot plaster waffles with the molded blob of butter, cavorted on the bacon slide, and tooted as they rode the choo-choo train of sausage links. As Jackie and Lily made their way through mothers bonding over cappuccino, the scent of sugar mingled with cloying perfume from the department stores and ammonia from the tile floors. Lily's school had recessed that morning for the summer and their mission was to find her a dress to wear to the Central City Opera House.

"I'm starving," Jackie said. "How about a caramel pecan bon?"

"Ninety-eight percent fat."

"So what? You haven't had lunch."

Lily shook her head emphatically.

"I'll bet we could find sushi . . . ," Jackie tried.

"Not here. Besides, I'm not hungry."

When Britt and Randy had first brought Lily home from China, she would eat only soup, noodles, and rice. As her repertoire expanded to hot dogs, chicken tenders, and pizza, egg drop soup remained her comfort food and sushi her all-time favorite. Jackie supposed it was the boiled rice. The girl's current obsession with fat was just another phase, she told herself. She had no doubt she'd be able to tempt Lily with something before the afternoon was over.

They strolled through the lower level of the mall.

"What's *Alice* about?" Lily asked as they peered at a display of sandals whose heels were the width of a matchstick. They were lashed to the ankle by straps.

"A girl your age who follows a rabbit down a hole and enters a world where nothing is the way it seems. She meets a horrid queen and all sorts of fascinating creatures who can talk."

"Isn't that Dorothy and *The Wizard of Oz*?" Lily asked suspiciously.

"Alice is more curious than Dorothy. And the creatures she meets don't help her, they get in her way. In one of her adventures she becomes a pawn on a giant chessboard where all the pieces are alive."

One of the department stores had a display of flannel pajamas in a teddy-bear pattern with built-in slippers. Jackie thought they were kind of cute until she realized the models were supposed to be grown women. When she saw the cutoff T-shirts with cartoon characters in adult sizes in the next window, she was less fooled. They passed a cosmetics shop thronged with girls slightly older than Lily.

"Want to go in?" Jackie asked.

"Nah, that stuff's junk. They sell knockoffs of Portia."

"You used to love nail polish."

"It's okay." Lily shrugged. "I'm into lip gloss now. What's a pawn?"

"A person who's controlled by somebody else, without being aware of it. But Alice's worst enemy was the Queen of Hearts. If anyone crossed her, she'd say, 'Off with his head!' Sentence first and verdict afterwards." The ultimate prosecutrix—not unlike a certain woman in Boulder. "She even ordered Alice's head cut off."

They stopped in front of a boutique called Entrez-New. Swatches of acetate were draped across the mannequins' bony shoulders and hips. They had long necks and no mouths.

"Black is in," Lily said.

"I have news for you, honey. Black is always in."

"Look at that." Lily pointed to one in a satin pencil skirt and a leather bustier over a sleeveless T whose neck was torn. The bustier ended in stiff underwire that converted the mannequin's tiny breasts to missiles.

"Think you could breathe in that?" Jackie asked. But Lily had already moved to the next window, where the model wore hot pants and a Lycra harness. A braided length of silk lay coiled at her feet.

"Isn't that cool?" Lily said.

"You'd freeze your buns off in that. We're looking for a dress for the opera, not an outfit that will get you carted off by the ASPCA. Besides, these are for adults. Not kids."

"Wanna bet?"

Taking Jackie by the arm, Lily led her into the shop.

Inside the door was a rack of cropped tops with spaghetti straps. Lily thumbed through them until she came to a scarlet number the texture and weight of a Kleenex. She brought it to the counter, where a waif with sooty eye makeup lounged. Like the mannequins, she was either an emaciated adult or fifteen years old. Would Alice's creator have been fooled?

"Is this my size?" Lily asked.

"It stretches," the clerk replied. "Try it with the vinyl mini."

"Where are the kids' clothes?" Jackie said.

The clerk stared at her blankly.

"Do you have one of these in her size?" Lily asked.

"They're all the same." The clerk pointed to another rack where the tops were two inches longer but the price tags ended in the same number of zeroes.

"Whatever happened to that pop star you girls worship?" Jackie grumbled. "The one with the hip huggers and the glitter?"

"She's into tube tops now. And she's no longer a virgin. Can I buy one?" Lily's crafty look made Jackie wonder whether this was a preteen bait-and-switch. At least Lily wasn't pressing for a harness. "All the kids at school are wearing them."

"We're shopping for a dress. Maybe after lunch."

They left Entrez-New and took the escalator to the mall's upper level.

"Speaking of school—" Jackie began.

"I'm not going back."

"You don't have to till September."

"Not *ever.*"

"I thought you were getting along better with your teachers."

The smell of popcorn from the multiplex above the food court must have made Lily hungry, because Jackie caught her eyeing the custard stand.

"'One-hundred-percent natural frozen dessert,'" Lily read. The treat that dared not call itself yogurt. "'Nine calories—fat free.'"

At least Pilar wasn't there to tell them how infrequently the machines were washed. Jackie pulled out her wallet.

"Get whatever you want. And make it a double."

Lily returned with two cups of custard and they found an empty bench. Digging carefully into her treat with a plastic spoon, the girl began eating it in tiny bites. "What happened to Alice?"

"Hmm?"

"After the Queen of Hearts said off with her head."

"She realized the Queen was nothing but a playing card and blew her away. Looking forward to camp?"

"Can't I stay with you this summer?"

"Honey, you were so excited—"

"The only thing I hate worse than camp is school!"

"Did something happen?"

Lily jumped to her feet and tossed what was left of her custard in the trash bin. When she turned back to Jackie, her expression was as synthetic as the fat-free dessert. "Weren't we looking for a dress?"

They made another circuit of the shops and finally ended up in front of Neiman's. A copper coil suspended from the ceiling above one of the makeup counters reminded Jackie of something.

"Mind if we go in?" she said.

The aesthetician had that natural look that took hours to achieve. Her dress was a wine-colored jersey with a cowl neck and a Portia pin— copper threads rising like twin asps from a ring of coils. She gazed at them impassively.

"I'm looking for lipstick," Jackie said. "Do you have 'Tease'?"

The aesthetician nodded. Smiles caused wrinkles. She stooped to look through a drawer, and when she rose she held the gold tube at arm's length to read the label without squinting.

"Would you like to test it?"

"No, just let me see it." It was the same shade Whitney had used, a dusky pink with a bronze undertone. "And now a lip gloss for my friend."

"Jackie!" Lily cried.

"What do you think?" Jackie said, boosting her onto the stool.

The aesthetician examined the girl's face under the light.

"Gorgeous eyes," she murmured. "I have just the thing. . . ." Fishing in her drawer again, she emerged with a tester tube. "'Tea Petals.' It has mica for shimmer and a touch of watercress. Let's see how it looks." Using a small brush, she applied the rose-colored gloss to Lily's mouth and brought her the mirror.

Lily's lips curved with delight. "I told you Portia's the best!"

The aesthetician dipped her chin in acknowledgment.

Jackie whipped out her credit card and the sale was completed. They left Neiman's with Lily clutching the copper-colored Portia bag.

"So what happened at school?" Jackie said.

"What makes you think something happened?"

It was midafternoon and the play area was deserted. Jackie settled on a carpet-covered bench facing the plaster tub of shredded wheat. Lily sat beside her.

"You've come so far, Lily." Such a short while ago Lily had refused to read. According to Britt, her spelling and punctuation were still a problem, but once the child set her mind to it, she learned at a phenomenal rate. "Tell me."

"It doesn't matter how well I do, nobody believes my work is mine."

Jackie turned to face her. "What are you talking about?"

"My teacher accused me of stealing."

"What?"

"She told us to write a story about a feeling, so I wrote about a rock."

"What kind of rock?"

"Gray, what most people see when they look at rocks. My rock got pounded by the wind and the rain and the snow. And what went on inside." Lily paused. "But if you held it up to the light, you could see a picture."

"Like the Chinese fluorite?"

"Yeah. Except instead of an ocean with a ship, it was a spring. Blue water."

"How wonderful! Why did she think you stole it?"

Lily's eyes blazed.

"Because I'm not good enough to come up with it myself!"

"Lily, that's crazy—"

"That's what she said. 'This sounds too good to be yours. Did you find it in a book about China?'"

Lily began shaking, and all of a sudden she started to cry. At first her tears were silent and then she let go in great, heaving gasps. In them Jackie heard not just rage, but humiliation and despair. What could be more devastating than being denied praise for a job well done—and being forever damned by your weakness?

"It was m-*my* idea, Jackie!"

Impotence and righteousness—the cry of a child who'd bared her soul only to be told her contribution was too good to be hers. Above all, the *injustice* . . . Jackie drew Lily to her chest and prayed for the wisdom of her aunt.

"I di-*didn't* steal it!"

"I know, I know . . ."

"Jackie, that story was *mine!*"

"Did you tell her about the fluorite?"

"She wouldn't let me talk." Sentence first and verdict afterward. Lily's next words were choked by shame and frustration. "—saying it wasn't mine. I can't go back!"

Jackie rocked her until the sobs finally began to subside.

"I want you to listen carefully. Right this minute it feels like this is the worst thing that could ever happen to you, and that the pain will never go away. But the trick is to use it to make yourself strong."

"I want to punish her so she can see how it feels!"

"Remember Alice and the Queen of Hearts?"

"Off with her head?"

"That's the one. Remember what Alice did?"

"She pictured her as a playing card."

"That's exactly what you're going to do. Each time you see that teacher, you're going to imagine her as the queen in a deck of playing cards."

"Which one?"

"An ugly one, with yellow hair." Like Phyllis Klein. "And when you have that image fixed clearly in your mind, you're going to close your eyes, take a deep breath, and blow it out as hard as you can."

Lily put her palm over her mouth and blew. "Like that?"

"Softly, so no one hears. What's important is that as you breathe out, you picture the card with her face on it blowing away in the wind."

"What if I never see her again?"

"Will she be at school next year?"

"Yes."

"Then you'll see her. In the meantime, every time you think about her, you can practice. By September you'll be a pro."

Lily disengaged herself from Jackie's arms. "I can hardly wait."

Together they rose.

"Now, let's find you a dress," Jackie said. "We're going to the opera."

Twenty-Seven

The fluorescent light above the defense table flickered and the paneling in Marlin Pitts's courtroom seemed to pulse.

"—other matters you wish to explore, Ms. Flowers?"

The insincerity of Pitts's solicitude would never show up in a transcript. But no judge appreciated the unexpected, and Jackie had been too quiet during this final pretrial hearing. She, in turn, was trying to figure out how to use her last chance to goad Phyllis Klein into revealing as much as possible about her case.

"As a matter of fact, yes. I'm at a total loss as to the theory behind this prosecution." Blinking to inoculate herself against the shimmering walls, Jackie stepped to the podium. She reached into the pocket of her suit jacket and her fingers closed around her moss agate. "A key witness for the state has refused to be interviewed. I don't know whether he's acting on the DA's advice, or—"

"Good Lord, must I spell it out?" Klein addressed her rhetorical question to the media representatives in the front row. Bolstered by the MSNBC man's nod, she ticked off the evidence in an aggrieved tone. "Cabin, ketamine, handcuffs—"

"Nothing in the DA's disclosures even hints at a motive," Jackie interrupted. Not that a lurid sex crime needed one. "All I can conclude is that the prosecution is politically inspired. Is that why Lanny Greer only talks on TV?"

"You're the expert at manipulating public opinion!"

Jackie felt the heat rise to her face. Did anyone else know what Phyllis meant? Thank God, Ballard wasn't there. The chaos in Pitts's courtroom was a reminder that at this trial it would be all the more imperative to ground herself in orderly routines. Laying out her makeup and clothing the night before, her cereal to remind herself to eat . . . The reporters were scribbling in their notebooks. They smelled blood but didn't know the source. Jackie couldn't afford to retreat.

"I certainly appreciate Ms. Klein's desire to treat Amy Lynch's abduction as a sex crime, but there's absolutely no evidence of assault." Most of Amy's injuries were old. "Ms. Lynch died from exposure."

"You—" Sputtering, Klein drew back. "My office has provided the defense with every item to which it's entitled, as Ms. Flowers is well aware. We'll let the jury decide Glenn Ballard's guilt."

"Anything further?" Pitts said.

Jackie slipped her talisman back in her pocket and withdrew a sheaf of papers from her briefcase. "May we approach?"

Klein opened her mouth. Mindful of the reporters and not knowing what to expect, she closed it. Pitts beckoned them forward.

"What is it now, Ms. Flowers?"

Jackie handed them copies of her brief.

"A motion for an in-camera hearing," she replied in a low voice. To be conducted in chambers. "I'd like it filed under seal. Given Ms. Klein's sensitivity to publicity, I'm sure she'll have no objection."

"A hearing on what?" Pitts demanded.

"The search of Judge Ballard's chambers. We believe it was conducted in violation of his constitutional rights."

"Your Honor—" The courtroom was silent and Klein, too, lowered her voice. The last thing she wanted was the integrity of her search hashed out in the presence of the national press. "You've already ruled—"

"I want to examine Detective Frasier under oath. And I want to do it before the deadline for endorsing witnesses."

"Hedging your bets?" Klein asked.

Jackie ignored her. "The cutoff is two weeks away and the hearing will take no more than an hour. My client deserves a chance to make his record." A not-so-subtle reminder that Pitts, too, had a record to protect.

"Very well, Ms. Flowers," he said. "Next Friday at two o'clock. That will leave you three hours to decide whether you wish to endorse an expert."

Court adjourned and the reporters clamored by the swinging gate. When Jackie paid them no heed they reluctantly filed out. As she finished packing her briefcase, hot breath caressed her ear.

"Lanny Greer wasn't afraid to try this case. I begged him for it."

Her instincts warned her to walk away.

"Publicity, my ass!" Klein's eyes glowed. "I know who leaked that grand jury transcript."

"Phyllis, look. That was a long time ago."

"Not for me. You think I don't know—"

"But I never even"—*read the damn thing!* Jackie stopped just in time.

"—why they booted you out of the PD's office? That stunt of yours crossed the line even for them, didn't it?"

The accusation would have been laughable if Jackie could have defended herself. But there was nothing more dangerous than a gun primed to misfire, and she wasn't about to give the woman who blamed her for destroying her reputation the ammunition to load it.

"This is one case I intend to win, Flowers."

They returned to Denver in near silence.

"You knew it would come up sooner or later," Pilar said.

"If Phyllis goes public with that accusation, my career is over."

"Come on, Jackie, no one will believe her now. It's been years. . . ."

When the governor had appointed Phyllis Klein special prosecutor five years earlier in an investigation of vice cops shaking down hookers for favors, Phyllis's star had been on the rise. Soon the investigation was broadened to encompass the entire state. There had even been talk of her running for attorney general. Still at the PD's office, Jackie had negotiated immunity for one of the girls.

But behind the closed doors of the grand jury room, Klein had tried to coerce the girl into testifying that the vice cops had all been in it together as in a fraternity initiation. When Jackie's client balked at having lies placed in her mouth in addition to everything else, Klein threatened to yank the girl's immunity. Grand jury proceedings were top secret and only the prosecutor and defense attorneys had access to the record. But the transcript of Klein's unethical behavior ended up on the front page of the *Post* and she had slunk back to Boulder. The toughest sex-crime prosecutor in the state was reduced to handling date rapes. And that wasn't the end of the story.

The grand jury was disbanded and the vice investigation dropped. To deflect attention from his special prosecutor's misconduct, the governor launched a private investigation into the leak's source. The reporter refused to talk and attention shifted to the PD. A witch-hunt began. Jackie had never seen the transcript, but because it was her client who'd been threatened, she was the logical fall guy. Although it put out a press release touting Jackie's victory in derailing a politically motivated investigation, the PD's office demanded her resignation. Pilar had grabbed her purse and joined Jackie as she headed out the door.

"Phyllis can't prove a thing," Pilar said. "If she had any evidence, she would have gone public with it back then. And there's no evidence for her to have. You're innocent. Anything she says now will look like she's slinging mud because you're opposite her on this case."

To a criminal defense attorney, integrity was everything. Defense lawyers were a tight collegial bar. Referrals were routinely made and you often ended up representing codefendants. Phyllis Klein's mud didn't have to stick; just the accusation would be enough to make Jackie a pariah. And it didn't stop there.

In the courtroom, nine out of ten rulings were discretionary. That meant a judge could go either way without accountability or fear of being reversed. Phyllis's mud would destroy Jackie's credibility with any judge before whom she would appear. Her effectiveness would be reduced to zero because her clients would never get an even break. Including Ballard.

Five years ago Phyllis's mutterings could be written off as sour grapes because the indictment was dismissed and the focus was on political corruption. But they just might find an audience now, with the spotlight on Jackie because of Ballard's trial. And what about the lawyers at Whitney's litigation boutique? If the rumors caused reputable local lawyers to shun her, what about out-of-towners who'd never heard them before and would have no reason to dismiss them?

"Try telling Ballard it's mud," Jackie said. "Even if he believed me, he'd be nuts not to retain another lawyer."

Pilar drove the length of the Boulder turnpike without replying. As they turned onto I-25, she finally spoke.

"What are you going to do?"

Skip the tea and hit the scotch.

"What else can I do? Win the damned case."

"Where was Ballard this afternoon, anyway?" Pilar asked.

"Betty said he was in Chicago."

"Chicago?"

"Giving a speech to the ABA. 'The American Jury Trial.'"

"Better the ABA than *20/20*," Pilar said. "Maybe it's time for another come-to-Jesus with your pal Glenn."

"The speech was scheduled months ago. You know Ballard, he's a control freak. He's hell-bent on acting like none of this is happening. And he got it cleared with the chief judge. At least he isn't talking about the case."

The tom-tom that had begun in Jackie's skull when Pitts's fluorescent tube went bad was pounding like a snare drum. She closed her eyes and pictured herself crawling into bed with her comforter over her head. No. She had an appointment. She pulled down the passenger-seat visor and stared into the mirror. She looked every bit as crappy as she felt. Maybe Pilar—

She could hardly ask Pilar to cancel a date Pilar knew nothing about. If Jackie told her about it, she would never hear the end of it. Could she blame a no-show on traffic? The man she was going to meet would never believe that.

What had possessed her to ask Dennis Ross to join her for a drink?

Given their history, Pilar wasn't the only one who should have had doubts.

On Jackie's first day at the PD's office Dennis had appeared at her door and told her to grab her coat. He'd been one of the lawyers who interviewed her for the job, but the word was he had no time for rookies.

"Where are we going?" she'd asked.

"To try your first misdemeanor."

Dennis said he liked to fly solo because if he crashed and burned, he didn't want to take anyone with him. But he and Jackie never lost a case they tried together, and he always made sure she got more than her share of the credit. And none of the blame. How green she'd been! The first felony she drew was a rape. She had wanted to put their client on the stand.

"You're nuts," Dennis had said.

"Why? Don't you believe his story?"

"You obviously do."

"As a matter of fact—"

"Have you talked to him, Jackie?"

"Of course I have! I just spent three hours with him at the county jail."

"Did you look at him?"

"Look at him? I told you—"

"No, I mean really *look* at him."

She didn't know what to say.

"Because whether you believe him or not, Jackie, no jury will. Whether he's telling the truth or not, he looks and sounds like a thug. That's what the jurors will see."

"Well, thank God you're not sitting in judgment," she'd said. "With an attitude like that, the poor guy doesn't stand a chance."

Dennis had taken no offense. "If he wants to testify and you think he belongs on the stand, we'll put him up."

On the stand the client had changed his story twice and couldn't make eye contact with his own lawyers. The jury had hung and the DA had declined to retry the case. Afterward, Dennis took her out for a drink.

"I guess I have a lot to learn," she'd said.

"Forget it. In this business, a mistrial is a win."

"I should have listened to you."

"That was a legitimate judgment call, Jackie. It's no sin to go with your instincts."

"But I'm so stupid!"

"Stupid? Whoever said that?"

She looked into her glass. "I flunked Criminal Procedure."

Dennis had laughed so hard the couple at the next table turned and stared.

"I know," he'd said after wiping his eyes. "That's why I talked the boss into hiring you. It takes a hell of a lot of guts to apply to the Public Defender's office after racking up an F in Crim Pro. . . ."

As Pilar headed up skid row toward Broadway, Jackie peered in the mirror again. Parboiled eyes, hair like snakes, skin the color of oatmeal. Call him tomorrow and say you were sick . . . or don't call at all. Even in a city the size of Denver, if you wanted to avoid someone your paths never seemed to cross. But the minute you set things in motion—say, called a former lover strictly for professional advice—and then changed your mind, you couldn't turn around without bumping into each other. And did she really want to be alone on this of all nights?

"Let me out."

"Here?"

They were eight blocks from the office but Pilar pulled to the curb.

"I need to walk," Jackie lied.

"But it's getting dark. And you left your car at home, remember?"

It was two miles to Jackie's house.

"If I have to, I'll grab a cab."

Dennis Ross's office was in a fifty-story tower shaped like a ship's prow. The bar off the lobby catered to the moneyed crowd, lawyers who took their clients out for a drink before returning to the office to supervise associates pulling all-nighters on megadeals. The only plus was the tinted glass and intimate lamps that made every hour twilight. Running a hand through her hair, Jackie knew she should walk another block to the Brown Palace Hotel and hail a cab. Instead, she ducked into the ladies' lounge off the entrance to the bar.

She raked her comb through her curls and twisted them into a knot. Why had she canceled her appointment at Lalo's? She needed a touch-up and a trim. . . . She hadn't seen Dennis in more than four years. They'd run into each other at a continuing legal education seminar after he returned to Denver. He'd been wearing a wedding band. They'd chatted awkwardly at the coffee machine during the break, then took new seats on opposite sides of the room.

She whisked "Tease" across her lips and dug into her bag for mascara.

Why couldn't he have been there when she really needed him, when the shit hit the fan with Phyllis Klein?

Angrily, she flicked her lashes with the wand. What did she care what Dennis Ross thought? She'd called him because Ted Wolsky suggested it, not to get him into the sack. She stared at her reflection in the mirror. This wasn't her at all. She yanked her hair free and let it fall to her shoulders. Before she could change her mind, she zipped her briefcase shut and pushed open the door.

Peering into the bar's dim interior, Jackie felt light-headed—an improvement over that pounding in her skull. She'd forgotten to eat lunch and refused the granola bar Pilar had tried to force down her. It was past six and every table was filled. She ignored the admiring glances from a trio in three-piece suits. What a fool she'd been. . . . An athletic figure rose from the last booth and waved. She slowed her step.

His cautious smile gave way to an off-kilter grin that brought Jackie back to the moment they met. That knowing, insolent look she'd felt to her toes. As he bent to kiss her cheek, she noticed his dark hair was flecked with gray.

"It was great to get your call." He still drank his scotch neat. "I meant to congratulate you after that big win of yours last summer."

"I got lucky."

"You always did have a way with experts."

A veiled reference to the shrink in that case, or the DNA expert from Quantico she'd had a fling with right after she and Dennis broke up? He signaled the barmaid without asking what she wanted. How she used to love that gesture and its proprietary implications!

"Like old times," Dennis continued, "watching you mop up the floor with Duncan Pratt. And now you've landed the hottest case in the country. What's it like having a federal judge at your mercy?"

The barmaid brought Jackie's whisky sour. From the way Dennis was nursing his scotch, she knew it was his first.

"You haven't done too badly yourself," she said. After leaving the PD's office he'd walked the head of the region's largest savings and loan from mail fraud charges it took the FBI half a decade to bring.

"Pilar still with you?"

"Cigarillos and all."

"Best investigator the PD had. If she ever wants a change, there will be twenty firms waiting to snatch her up. And I'll be at the head of the line."

What was Charlie Nesbit's firm paying him, a few hundred grand a year?

"I never figured you for the Seventeenth Street type."

"Dad always said there's no money in responding to calls from the bus station. But the sexy cases are long past." Dennis's dark eyes lingered on hers a moment too long, and he took a sip of scotch to cover it. "Now I'm just another mouse in a suit."

"That's a hell of a suit." The charcoal wool fit so beautifully it must have been custom-made. And his silk tie was a bold Italian print, the kind a woman would pick. His ex or someone new? "You obviously landed on your feet."

After you threw me out on my ass.

Jackie braced for the words, but Dennis contented himself with an ironic smile.

"A step up from con artists and pimps, but the same devious minds are at work. Still representing Ted Wolsky?"

Jackie had never understood why Ted and Dennis clashed. "For a recovering burglar he ain't doing too bad."

"Talk about a squirrel out of his cage . . . But you can't fault Ted for his taste in lawyers." Dennis lifted his glass to her. This time he didn't look away.

"Miss the old days?" she said.

"Not the politics. That place was so incestuous, I woke up every morning feeling like I'd just had sex with my sister."

What did *that* mean—they were too much alike for it to have worked? Taking a large sip of her drink, Jackie reminded herself why she'd called him. That bank robber he'd represented. As Dennis set down his glass, she glanced at his left hand. When she looked up he seemed amused.

"It lasted six months," he said.

"So I heard."

"Why didn't you—"

"My luck with guys ran out years ago." She was only half-kidding.

"Luck? That's a funny choice of words. Are you going out much?"

"I do have a date for the opera."

His eyes narrowed. "Finally a man with class."

"A nine-year-old girl. We're celebrating her departure for ballet camp. Maybe one day I'll—"

The barmaid interrupted with another round of drinks. As Jackie's second whisky sour slid down her throat, she wondered if she was leading Dennis on. But wasn't he the one who liked to lead? She had to get this on track before she forgot why she'd called him. "The reason I called—"

"You wanted advice about a client. Glenn Ballard has all the charm of a puff adder."

"That doesn't mean he abducted Amy Lynch."

"Don't tell me you plan to put him on the stand?" Dennis smiled when she flushed. But they were no longer mentor and protégée.

"We're all guilty, Dennis, don't you remember? It's just a question of what."

He winced. "I must have been awfully young to have said something as dumb—"

"Why do you dislike Ballard? Other judges have handed down stiff sentences."

"You talking about Austin Lee? I guess three hundred and sixty-five years isn't so out of line for abducting a bank teller. Another judge might have settled for something less than four times the defendant's natural life. But with Ballard it's more than grandstanding. The worst parts of his job are the ones he really enjoys." Hadn't Ted said that too? "When he sentenced Lee, I remember saying, 'But my client can't do three hundred and sixty-five years, Your Honor. That's physically impossible!' You know what Ballard said? 'Just tell him to take it one day at a time.'"

"You think a defendant he sentenced could be setting Ballard up now?"

"Can Austin Lee reach out from his maximum-security cell and touch a federal judge?"

"He was angry enough to make threats after the sentencing." Pilar had found that out. "We both know contacts don't end at prison walls."

"Threats make a nice movie-of-the-week, but it takes a lot more clout than the average bank robber has to deliver on them. This is one time Lee is innocent."

"But maybe he knows someone. You could nose around."

"You're asking me to tap into sources, maybe implicate a client?"

"I just want to know if someone might bear Ballard a particularly nasty grudge. I'm not thinking it's Lee. Maybe you know someone else."

Dennis tossed back his drink and signaled the barmaid for the tab.

"Try the phone book."

"Phone book?"

"Look, I told you." Dennis was pissed. Because she'd asked him to compromise a client, or invited him for a drink with nothing more in mind? "Ballard goes way beyond where he should. You know that Internet porn ruling? He didn't have to hold the tax constitutional, he could have decided the case on narrower grounds."

"Since when do you give a shit about that kind of Con law?"

"I happen to have represented three of those defendants."

"Is that why Charlie Nesbit recused himself? Because Kellogg and Kemp was in the case?"

"He called the head of the firm to pressure me into withdrawing so he could keep it." So much for Nesbit's claim that he'd been delighted when the case was reassigned to his good friend Ballard. "Case like that comes along once in a career—for a lawyer *or* a judge. If I ever appear in front of Charlie I'll expect to be reamed. Not that your precious client cut me any slack. Ballard's ruling probably put my guys out of business."

"One less porn shop . . ."

"They're not tying up coeds and torturing them to death."

Dennis threw two twenty-dollar bills on the table.

"We may all be guilty, Jackie. The difference between you and me is, I no longer have to defend whoever walks through my door."

He left without looking back.

Twenty-Eight

Bonnie Lynch perched at the edge of a blue couch in the living room of a hotel suite in the Denver Tech Center. The freshly barbered man beside her was not her husband, but her lawyer. He'd been talking for five minutes straight and revealed nothing Jackie didn't know except the fact that he had absolutely no experience in criminal law. As his client stared at Jackie without expression, Jackie wondered why Amy's mother had so readily agreed to this meeting.

The couch was too deep to be comfortable and the coffee table that separated them was too low for anything but bumping your shin. A floral arrangement too lush to be anything but silk sat on a highboy that had no other apparent function. More than its physical discomfort, the artificiality of the setting imposed an additional barrier to winning Amy's mother's trust.

"—appreciate the fact that neither Mr. nor Mrs. Lynch is under any obligation whatsoever to confer with any representative of the defense—"

Why *had* Bonnie Lynch agreed to meet?

"—but wanted to tell you certain things regarding her daughter, to enable you to understand how precious to her Amy was."

So Jackie would think twice about putting the victim on trial, if she were stupid or insensitive enough to be so inclined. Bonnie's lawyer was from one of the other Seventeenth Street firms, not Kellogg & Kemp. Had Charlie Nesbit's antipathy toward Dennis cost his firm its biggest client?

"I'm grateful for Mrs. Lynch's willingness to talk," Jackie replied. "Where is—"

"Mr. Lynch was unable to join us. He had a prior commitment."

That didn't explain why Bonnie chose to meet with Jackie at a hotel. Jackie was willing to bet her husband either had no idea this interview was taking place or strongly disapproved of it. Which was the case?

"And your client, Bryan Lynch—" Jackie began.

Bonnie's lawyer had small, sharp teeth. With no choice but to set the record straight, he flashed every one of them at Jackie.

"I represent Mrs. Lynch, not her husband. Mr. Lynch has corporate counsel."

"I see."

So Bryan Lynch had been advised not to attend. Was it because he had something to hide? And why did Amy's parents need separate lawyers? In a criminal case, that usually meant one spouse feared he was about to be named a suspect and the other was considering a deal to protect her own derriere. Although Jackie would have given much to have the two Lynches in the same room together, she might learn more talking to Bonnie alone.

"This has been a dreadful ordeal for your family, and I'll try not to take too much of your time. Why don't you tell me about your daughter?"

"Amy was a normal, happy, loving child who never gave my husband and I a moment's worry." Bonnie's voice was flat, but this time her lipstick was on straight. In her powder blue suit and smart pumps, she seemed a great deal more composed than when she'd last appeared in public. At the interview before her daughter died. "The rumors that surfaced in the last two months have been so hurtful."

"Rumors?"

"That she was headstrong. Amy had her share of teenage episodes"—Bonnie gave a tinny laugh—"but my husband was no stricter than any other father."

Did she have any idea what her daughter had been into? And what was with that "my husband" bit? Wouldn't it be more natural to refer to him as "Bryan" and the two of them as "we"?

"What sorts of episodes?"

"You know, *girl* stuff." Bonnie looked at Jackie as if she should understand. Jackie waited. "That incident at Neiman's in Cherry Creek. She did it on a dare."

"Dare?"

"Do you honestly think a fourteen-year-old girl has any use for a peignoir? Of course they didn't press charges. Her friends were a bad influence."

So that was why Amy left Graland a year early: she'd been caught boosting a nightie. What a blow that must have been to Bryan! And

Bonnie's willingness to talk was beginning to make sense. Damage control. No matter what strings Bryan had been able to pull, she was afraid that story would come out. But didn't she realize her daughter's juvenile record was sealed?

As Bonnie gazed at her coolly, Jackie wondered what had motivated Amy to pull such a stupid stunt. Her parents could have bought her any nightgown she wanted. Was shoplifting at the ritziest store in Cherry Creek a sign of adolescent rebellion? Or did she do it to embarrass Daddy?

"Peer pressure can be a potent force at any age," Jackie said. "Kids will do anything to be hip. Crazy hairdos, tattoos. Just the other day I saw a girl at the mall who had a stud in her nose and three hoops in one ear. . . ."

Bonnie didn't blink.

Erin Carmichael and Matt Fisher had described the mother as clueless. If Amy's boyfriend and roommate were unaware of the girl's body armor, why would her mother know about it?

"Was Amy into that, too?"

"You mean her body art? Amy was so proud of it. When she was fifteen she did the one on her wrist." The chevron-shaped scar below the ball of her thumb. Why hadn't Amy stopped there? "Naturally I was appalled when I first saw it, but it seemed harmless. It was actually quite pretty."

"What came next?"

Bonnie shrugged. "She had a friend pierce her left ear for silver studs. All the girls were doing it."

"What did Bryan think of it?"

"My husband didn't understand."

Jackie wasn't sure she did, either. Again that distancing reference to the man she should have been referring to in more intimate terms. Was he the one who'd wanted to live literally within sight of his daughter's school? Maybe that's why Amy felt the need to slip the leash. But Bonnie's apparent lack of concern over her daughter's self-inflicted scars was even more intriguing. It was almost as if she'd been cheering Amy on. Was she indeed indifferent? Or had she gotten a vicarious thrill from her daughter's need to shock?

"What else did Amy do?"

Bonnie Lynch's lawyer shifted uneasily on the couch. He was bright enough to sense he was out of his league, but not to see where this was going.

"My daughter's jewelry was removable, if that's what you mean."

So she knew about those piercings too.

"Did your husband—"

"My client has been under enormous stress." Bonnie's lawyer had finally awoken. He might not be representing Bryan Lynch, but even he could tell heavy metal was not the image of Amy this interview was designed to project. "She's been more than generous with her time and I think it's best to wrap this up."

"One last question, Mrs. Lynch. Have you ever heard the name Derek King?"

Bonnie looked confused. "I thought she was dating Matt."

Jackie hadn't said anything about Derek being a boyfriend.

"Do you know where Amy got her money after your husband canceled her credit cards?"

"Bonnie, don't say another word!" the lawyer warned.

But his client's expression said it all.

Amy Lynch might not have confided everything to her mother, but Bonnie had a damned good idea what her daughter had been up to.

And she'd done nothing to stop it.

Twenty-Nine

The shop on South Broadway was Victoria's Secret with a twist.

The blonde in the window wore black fishnet stockings and vinyl boots with her red merry widow. Her male companion was in heavy leathers and a hood. The bulge in his pants made Jackie wonder whether they also sold codpieces.

"I know what I'm getting you next Christmas," she told Pilar.

"Biker Bob or that adorable teddy?"

Welcome to the Dark Side.

The store was open from 8 A.M. until midnight, but to avoid other customers they had chosen ten-thirty on the Thursday morning after Jackie met with Bonnie Lynch. Gazing at the leather and lace on this seedy block of South Broadway, Jackie wondered why they'd bothered to be so discreet. Not only was the merchandise benign, but judging from the lack of traffic, the Dark Side was in no danger of a raise in rent. Next door was Kitty's, a twenty-four-hour video arcade whose windows were painted black. As they watched, one man exited the arcade and two others went in.

"Not bad for this hour of the day," Pilar said.

"We're here for dog collars and chains. You can come back for the peep show later."

Pilar squinted at the mannequins. "Phyllis looks pretty good in drag. I'd say the guy in the hood was Marlin Pitts, but he ain't got the balls. . . ."

Jackie's antagonists had pulled a fast one.

Pitts and Klein had called that morning to inform her that the in-camera hearing set for the following day was postponed because the DA had fallen off her bicycle. Limp to Pitts's chambers or send an underling? No way. Furious, Jackie had demanded that Ballard's deadline for endorsing an expert also be postponed. Not unless they were willing to continue the trial until after Labor Day, the next two-week block on Pitts's calendar. She'd been had.

Pilar pointed at the Dark Side's door. "Well, what are you waiting for?"

"Not a thing."

"Might as well go in."

"So, come on . . ."

Both reached for the door at the same moment, but stopped short of the knob.

It was Pilar who finally grabbed it and gave it a decisive twist. Once inside, Jackie saw her reach into her purse for her handkerchief and surreptitiously wipe her palm.

At first glance, the Dark Side could have been any other lingerie shop. The front room was filled with brassieres, corsets, and bikini bottoms, in everything from satin and silk to vinyl and other synthetics Jackie couldn't identify. Hand-lettered signs above the racks warned customers not to touch the merchandise.

Pilar nodded her approval. "Hygienic."

A doorway opened into a second, narrower room with a glass display case and a cash register, where a teenaged clerk chatted with a fellow his own age. A much older man had quickly left when Jackie and Pilar entered, and the only other customer was a man in his forties by the lingerie. From the quality of his suit, he could have been a lawyer or an investment banker. Why would a man like that risk patronizing such a place? Not that he was likely to run into anyone who knew him, at that hour of the morning. Pilar nudged her.

"Look up."

From the ceiling a six-foot mummy bag hung.

"Keep that in mind for your next party," Pilar said. "Available in calfskin *and* nylon, like any other high-quality luggage."

The man in the suit glanced up from the vinyl bikini he'd been fingering.

"Will you keep your voice down?" Jackie whispered.

"Little hot for the beach, don't you think?" Pilar boomed. "But at least they're waterproof." The man sidled away, feigning interest in a lace corset. In another moment he slipped out the door.

"I can't take you anywhere," Jackie said. "You just cost this place a sale."

"It's his own fault; the sign says not to touch. And he probably went next door to Kitty's. Unless he finds something more interesting, he'll come back when we leave."

The salesclerk and his friend were watching.

"I don't know what's worse," Pilar muttered, "being here at all, or being waited on by an eighteen-year-old with pimples." Hanky still balled in her hand, she smiled brightly and sauntered into the next room.

With a hasty "Catch you later" to the clerk, the only other customer left. The clerk returned to his magazine and Jackie followed her investigator.

The back room housed hard-core paraphernalia—what Pilar would have called the good stuff. On the wall opposite the cash register hung an impressive array of blindfolds and whips. The whips were braided silk and leather, in all lengths, colors, and sizes. One was knotted like a cat-o'-nine-tails, another was reminiscent of a medieval flail. The blindfolds ranged from utilitarian strips of cloth to confections suitable for a costume ball.

"All the rage . . . ," Pilar quipped, and abruptly stopped.

Cut from a single piece of hide, the black swatch could only be described as elegant. Its fine-grained leather was butter soft, the twin hexagons supple enough to cover the eye sockets without slipping. It tied in the back.

Amy's blindfold.

"Well, at least he has taste," Pilar continued. "And you can get it right at your neighborhood S and M shop. You don't even have to mail-order it from one of those sticky catalogs."

"I doubt it was bought here. Why risk being seen?"

But Jackie was thinking about the well-dressed man who'd just slunk off. If he hadn't been afraid to come here in the first place, why should Glenn Ballard be? And if living on the edge was a turn-on, wasn't risk what it was all about?

Next to the blindfolds were the dog collars. The most popular design was a two-inch-wide leather belt with riveted studs. The display model had been buckled at the first of five holes, but even the last would have choked any mastiff that could have worn that wide a collar. The steel ring attached to a five-foot chain. Jackie turned, and her breath caught in her throat.

The heads wore leather masks that gripped the face like cellophane.

There were no holes for eyes and the opening where the mouth should have been was zippered shut.

"Discipline masks," a voice behind her said.

The clerk was leaning over the counter.

"They sell real well," he continued.

Jackie found her voice. "How about hoods?"

"Hoods?"

"Sell many of those?"

"The leather one in the window, yeah."

But she was thinking about the one Amy had worn.

"I'm looking for something white, in silk. More like a cowl."

The clerk shook his head.

"Never seen nothing like that," he said in a tone that left no doubt as to his authority. "Silk's okay for whips, but in a hood you want leather. Silk is too soft. It breathes and the wearer can see out. Course, you could have anything made. . . ."

Pilar joined them at the counter. The display case held handcuffs, leg irons, and chains. In one corner an assortment of brass and silver bands nestled in a velvet-lined case. Jackie pointed to one of them.

"Do you do body piercings here?"

The clerk exchanged a glance with Pilar.

"That's a cock ring, lady."

Pilar came to Jackie's rescue. "Tell us about your handcuffs."

Reaching down to unlock the case, he withdrew two models. The cuffs in each set were separated by a two-and-a-half-inch length of chain. "These are top of the line."

"What's the difference?" Pilar asked.

"One's a double lock, the other a single. Resistance makes a single lock tighten." Seeing Jackie's confusion, he pulled out a pair of ankle cuffs. Wider in circumference than the handcuffs, they were connected by a fifteen-inch chain. "Kickproof, pickproof, and runproof—manufacturer guaranteed. Double lock keeps 'em from tightening if you stumble or play around." He winked at Pilar. "That is, if you care about your partner."

Why would Ballard use his own cuffs and risk having them traced?

"—good deal going on these." The clerk was reaching for a pair of candles made from flesh-colored plastic. One of them had a cord attached.

Pilar grabbed Jackie's arm.

"Not interested," she said, and pulled Jackie out the door.

Back on the street, Pilar tossed her hanky in the garbage can. As if on cue, the man in the suit exited Kitty's and returned to the Dark Side.

"Know what bothers me?" Pilar said. "What makes that kid think *I'm* the dominatrix?"

What bothered Jackie was the hood.

Amy's abductor could have been anyone. The dog collar and blindfold were standard issue, and handcuffs indistinguishable from the ones the U.S. Marshals used were available right in that store. The hood— now that was a different story. Not only was it unnecessary if a blindfold was used, but silk was hardly the material of choice.

Amy's abductor had gone to the trouble of having it custom-made.

Thirty

"**F**ree parking!"

Lily pointed to a lot behind one of the casinos.

"It's only free if you're willing to dump your piggy bank into their slots," Pilar explained as she continued hunting for a spot for the Spider on the narrow streets of Central City, the mining-cum-gambling mecca. It was the last Saturday in June and Lily was leaving the following morning for ballet camp. With Ballard's trial beginning in two weeks, Jackie could ill afford time away from planning his defense. But sending Lily off in style was more important.

"You mean we can gamble?" Lily asked.

"Not today, sport," Jackie said. "We're going to the opera, remember?"

The ride through Clear Creek Canyon with the top down had brightened Lily's cheeks and unleashed her hair. Jackie thought the off-the-shoulder red jersey they'd bought at the mall a trifle sophisticated for a nine-year-old, but having seen the alternatives she had no complaints. And it showed off the necklace she'd given to Lily for an early birthday present. The midday sun set the opal on the black velvet ribbon aflame.

Pilar finally pulled up to the scraped edge of a promontory overlooking the town, where the parking had no strings and scant structural support. What had been "the richest square mile on earth" had undergone a century of decline, only to be reborn to prosperity in a second gold rush.

Because the hotel restaurant near the opera house didn't take reservations, they'd arrived well in advance of curtain time. As the hostess led them to a table in a courtyard more suited to a Roman villa than a Colorado mining town, Jackie finally relaxed. The hotel featured the casino town's gargantuan portions at cafeteria prices. While Pilar chose between prime rib and porterhouse steak, Jackie watched Lily disinterestedly scan the menu. What the girl was really starved for was normal fare, like encounters with March hares and white rabbits.

"Prime rib," Pilar decided. "What'll it be for you, pet?"

"Salad." When she added, "I never eat anything with a face," Jackie and Pilar exchanged a look of relief. The old Lily!

"You know what *Alice* is about?" Pilar asked Lily after the waitress left.

"A girl who falls down a rabbit hole and meets an awful queen." She turned to Jackie. "I know what happens to the queen, but you never told me how it ends."

"Alice wakes up and realizes it was all a dream. It's an adventure, Lily, like camp."

"If I wake up, do I get to go home?"

The arrival of the food spared Jackie the necessity of a reply.

They passed the next hour in the garden adjoining the opera house. As curtain time drew near, a crier in a frock coat strode up and down Eureka Street, ringing his bell every fifteen minutes to herald the coming event. His enthusiasm was contagious, and Lily began timing him on Pilar's watch. Finally a band of chorines came marching up the street, arms linked and singing a lusty song.

"Shades of the beer hall putsch," Pilar muttered, but Jackie could see that she, too, was caught up in the excitement. Pilar retrieved their tickets from her purse and led the way in.

Built at the height of the mining town's first boom, the opera house was more than a century old. It had been constructed of granite after a fire destroyed much of Central City, but had fallen into disrepair and been renovated through the sale of memorial chairs. As Jackie climbed the steep steps to the balcony behind Lily and Pilar, she tried not to look down at the carpet, whose fleur-de-lis pattern seemed to swarm under the artificial light.

With Lily sandwiched between them, they squeezed into their red velvet seats in the front row of the balcony. The stage seemed very close and the balcony almost touched the ceiling. The curtain was flanked with six-foot winged-horse friezes that could have been wallpaper if not for the shadows. Then Jackie realized even the shadows were painted on. Taking a deep breath, she looked down at the orchestra section. The well-heeled couples represented the cream of Colorado society, and every woman had an escort.

Why had she let her meeting with Dennis end so badly?

Lily fingered the brass fittings of her chair. "Is this real gold?"

Pilar paged through the program book for a description of the performance. "'A Freudian take on the beloved children's tale,'" she read, groaning. "I knew I should have held out for *Bohème*."

The gallery was rapidly filling. The heat in the balcony rose and Jackie suddenly felt assailed by every sound, from the subhuman strains of violins tuning up to the crackle of a candy wrapper five rows behind her to snatches of conversation in the orchestra pit. The chandelier flickered and dimmed, signaling the usher to close the balcony door. Jackie squeezed her eyes shut. Everyone began clapping.

"Why are they clapping?" Lily whispered.

"So they'll hurry up and start," Pilar said.

The curtain majestically rose.

A white rabbit the size of Jackie Gleason bounded across the stage.

"I'm late, I'm late. . . ."

He disappeared down a black hole to the left of the orchestra pit.

"Ain't *this* a hoot?" Pilar muttered over Lily's head.

And so the opera began.

When the lights came on for the first intermission, Lily was at the edge of her seat, staring at the empty stage. Blinking to adjust to the sudden brightness, Jackie looked down at the sea of opera lovers. In the third row from the stage, one bright head stood out.

"Give me your glasses." Pilar handed Jackie the binoculars.

She focused on the front of the orchestra section. The statuesque redhead in the sea-green pantsuit was impossible to miss.

"That's Whitney!" The PR woman was making her way up the aisle on the arm of a dapper man Jackie thought she should recognize. She passed the glasses back to Pilar. "Who's she with?"

Pilar gave a low whistle.

"Jimmy Phipps. Don't you love that swagger?"

"Phipps?"

"One of the guys in Whitney's litigation boutique. He can afford to strut. He moved here from Plano, Texas, because he likes the mountains. Hell, after whipping that tobacco company six months ago, he can *buy* a mountain. Let's say hello."

But the sight of Whitney on the arm of one of the hottest trial lawyers in the country brought home an unpleasant reality. All Phyllis Klein had to do was open her yap about that grand jury and Jackie's future was over. True or not, would Jimmy Phipps want his reputation tarnished by associating with a lawyer accused of leaking a sealed transcript? The only way to defuse the charge was by converting it to sour grapes. Glenn Ballard's freedom wasn't the only thing at stake in his case.

"What are you waiting for?" Pilar said.

"They're obviously on a date."

"Don't be silly. Remember what Whitney said about investing in clients? They're here to be seen, not to neck."

Lily was already halfway up the aisle, and Jackie followed. By the time they reached the lobby, the crowd had spilled onto the street. While Pilar searched for Whitney, Lily clutched Jackie's hand.

"I have to go to the bathroom."

"Okay, honey. I'll wait with you in line."

"Why, Jackie!" Whitney was right in front of them. To Jackie's relief, she was alone. "And who's this?"

Jackie made the introductions.

"Is this your first opera?" Whitney asked Lily.

Lily stood a little taller.

"Lily's off to ballet camp tomorrow," Jackie explained as the queue for the rest room snaked forward. "In Steamboat Springs."

"Lucky you!" Whitney said. "I always wanted to be a ballerina. I even took lessons."

"Why did you stop?" Lily asked.

"I just wasn't good enough. But I found other things I was good at. . . . Are you enjoying the opera?"

Lily thought for a moment.

"I haven't seen the Queen of Hearts yet, so the Mad Hatter and the March Hare are my favorites. They're so rude!" Jackie wasn't surprised; there was a certain freedom in dirtying your dishes and simply moving down the table. "But the best scene was where Alice shrank when she took the drink and stretched when she ate cake. I wish I could do that."

As Whitney leaned forward, the jeweled clip in her hair caught the sun.

"Don't you like the way you look?"

"Well . . ."

"You should have seen me when I was your age. Coke-bottle glasses, hair like wild carrots, it was a wonder I had any friends at all!"

By now Pilar had joined them, but Lily was focusing too intently on Whitney to notice. "How did you make friends?"

"By making the other girls pretty." Whitney smiled at Lily's skeptical frown. "It's true; I got ahold of my mother's makeup and practiced on them."

"But—"

"Of course, looks are only skin-deep. Makeup is just the way it sounds: make-believe. You can be whatever you want, so long as you don't lose sight of where you came from and who you really are." She winked at Jackie and Pilar. "That's what I tap into for my clients. What makes them special all along. The mistake most people make is trying to be something they're not."

The line had brought them to the rest room door. Impulsively, Whitney reached up and unclasped the clip from her hair. She handed it to Lily.

"For you, on the eve of ballet camp. To an adventure more exciting than Alice's!"

Thirty-One

Streaming through the vaulted atrium, the afternoon sun warmed the granite floors and gave the soaring ficus and planters of kalanchoe and Peruvian lilies a jungle glow. A swallow enticed by the green and trapped by the glass swooped and lit on a branch to watch the exodus of investment bankers and lawyers from the priciest square footage in Denver.

As Jackie waited in the doorway of the lobby's convenience store, a tall man in a tan suit exited the nearest elevator. She counted to three and stepped from her hiding place just as he crossed her path.

"Dennis!"

His eyes lit for an instant, then went flat.

"What are you doing here?" he said.

"Hoping I'd run into you."

Jackie was jostled from behind and Dennis pulled her out of the flow of traffic. His hand lingered on her arm until he self-consciously dropped it.

"I thought you were only interested in Glenn Ballard's enemies."

From this angle she could see the scar at the bridge of his nose, and it brought back a flood of unexpected memories. Jackie had been in court the day a client took a swing at Dennis from the stand. A broken nose was a cheap price for an acquittal, he'd said, though he never much liked the insanity defense after that. They'd been planning to spend the weekend camping at Bear Lake, and once the verdict was in and Dennis was discharged from the ER, they took off for the mountains in his SUV.

Sleeping in a tent was not Jackie's idea of a good time, but Dennis wanted to go fishing for trout and skinny-dipping in mountain water. The broken nose might have been an omen, because the trip had all the makings of a disaster. The lake was cold enough to chill a martini, it poured for three days straight, the tent had holes, and his nose hurt like hell. The only place that was warm and dry was their sleeping bag. Rain or not, it was the most erotic weekend Jackie ever spent. . . . What was it she wanted from him now?

"I'm sorry about the other day," she began. "I shouldn't have asked you to do my dirty work."

"Once a client, always a client. You know that." Wincing at the priggish sound of his own words, Dennis started over. "Hell, I overreacted. Behind bars or not, Austin Lee will never change. Not that I would have done you a favor by turning over that particular rock. Or any other rock my old clients might be hiding under."

"Because there's no possibility that Ballard was framed?"

"Because you should be watching your step. Glenn Ballard has powerful enemies. And while we're on the subject—"

"Like who?"

"—tell Ted Wolsky to quit asking around. It won't do him or you any good."

Jealousy, or something more?

"This isn't about Ted."

"You're right, that Polish answer to the Keystone Kops is way out of his league."

"Has he been stepping on the wrong toes?"

Dennis's smile was strained.

"You never give up, do you?"

"*You* never did. . . ." A man with a briefcase gave Jackie the once-over, then winked. When had this turned into a quarrel? She took a deep breath and began again. "Can I buy you a drink?"

"Is that a peace offering, or do you think you'll get what you want by getting me bombed?"

She flushed. "Does everything have to mean something else?"

"You tell me." His face darkened with anger. "But what can I expect? It's not every guy who gets dumped on his ass after five fucking years without being told why!"

The mistake most people make is trying to be something they're not.

"I wasn't ready for marriage," she said. "I told you that."

"What was my crime, wanting us to have a future?"

"It wasn't just us, it was—"

Kids. He'd wanted them to have kids.

Dennis glanced at his watch.

"I've got to run. A meeting with a client . . ."

As he stared into her eyes, she knew he was lying. Before she could reply, he was gone.

Ted Wolsky answered on the first ring.

"I told you I didn't need any help," Jackie said.

"Who said anything about help? I wouldn't offer a hand to that prick Ballard—"

So Dennis had been right.

"Who have you been talking to?"

Ted was all innocence. "An old friend."

"You promised me you'd go straight."

"I have no intention of breaking any laws."

"That includes staying away from known—"

"You think I consort with criminals?" He laughed. "Why, Jackie, I'm wounded. You've cut me to the quick!"

"This isn't a joke, Ted. If you're onto something, I need to know it now. And if you aren't, I want you to lay off before you get us both in trouble."

"You have my word. And now, if you'll excuse me, I need to see a *person* about a dog." He hung up.

Ted and Dennis—what did either of them know?

And they'd had the gall to patronize her.

But she was the one who'd allowed herself to be whipsawed by Klein and her client. She should never have allowed Ballard to talk her out of endorsing an expert, should have foreseen Klein's trick knee and a postponement of the in-camera hearing, should have known she was being set up with that early trial date. . . .

Too agitated to sleep, Jackie hit her remote to catch the ten o'clock news.

"—earlier today on the *Morning Show*."

Her client's face filled the screen.

"The only problem with our jury system is we don't have enough faith in it," Glenn Ballard was saying. The camera moved to the earnest young coanchor.

"Judge, does that mean you don't hesitate to place your own fate in the hands of a Boulder jury ten days from now?"

"None whatsoever. I have every confidence a jury will vindicate—"

Punching the off button, Jackie grabbed her phone. She was so furious it took her three times to dial the number right.

"Glenn? What the hell do you think you're doing?"

"I take it you caught the *Morning Show.*"

"A little warning would have been nice! Better still, why don't you just keep your mouth shut?"

"Do you have any idea how much I have riding on this case?"

She silently counted to five.

"I know this has been a nightmare for you. I can only imagine—"

"No, you can't. Win or lose, my reputation's at stake. I have to take every chance I get to tell the public I'm not afraid to fight in court. If I don't, what kind of judge am I?"

"Glenn, you owe the public nothing. And to the media you're just a story. If you live by the press, you die by the press. Do I really have to—"

"You think I'm a loose cannon, don't you?"

Jackie hesitated.

"Actually, I think you're wound too tight."

It took him even longer to respond.

"I grew up on a ranch, Jackie. There's not much childhood to it. You think it's fun to rope and brand a calf? The first time I did that, I was eight. On a ranch, every day is life and death."

"Is that what this feels like? Life or death?"

"My reputation *is* my life."

"Look, you're not alone in this. There are a lot of people who believe in you."

"Believe?" Ballard snorted. "You think a courtroom is a place for sentiment?"

"Is that why you judge with your head instead of your heart?"

When he answered, it was with none of the hubris Jackie had come to expect.

"You learn the hard way that the heart is more fallible. When I was first on the bench, I listened to a defendant instead of paying attention to his record. Two weeks after I let him out on probation, he robbed another bank. Both he and the guard were killed."

"And that's why you sentenced Austin Lee to three hundred and sixty-five years."

"I knew he would kill and I wanted to make damn sure it wasn't on my watch."

"Will you trust me to handle my watch?" she asked softly.

"I—"

"And stay away from the press until the trial is over?"

"Okay."

For the first time, Jackie felt she understood her client.

If she was falsely accused of a crime, wouldn't she want to tell her side? And if she was not only innocent but a judge, wouldn't it be imperative to be heard? As a lawyer, her reputation meant everything to her. How much more did it mean to a man whose profession depended upon not just the reality but the appearance of incorruptibility?

She padded to her VCR and shoved the cabin tape into the slot. The three minutes sped by in a blur. She rewound the tape.

A shot of the clearing, the jump to a pitched roof. Back to eye level as the videographer mounted the steps. The door swung inward and the camera slowly circled the room. Lingering on the elk, flirting with the fireplace, dropping to the floor.

Trying to document something that wasn't there—*to be something it was not*?

Sweeping up to the rafters for a tantalizing glimpse . . . The jerking stopped as it zeroed in on the girl. Moving closer, lingering on her face, Amy struggling as she sensed its approach.

And then the man.

The instant Ballard entered the screen, Jackie froze the frame. Then she fast-forwarded it to the moment he turned to face the camera just before he reached for Amy.

What was it about that gesture that so antagonized her? Its smugness, the tease of the first ninety seconds for such an infinitesimal payoff? The omnipotence with which he revealed himself to the viewer before claiming his prize? For there was no doubt the man in black was Ballard. That arrogant tilt to his chin, the raptor's look—how well Jackie knew it!

She rewound, hoping to spot something in the fast reverse—anything. Frustrated, she played it again. No blips or signs of splicing. Even the jerks and jumps made sense. It was all so seamless. . . . And just wishful thinking to try to imagine that some tiny detail was not right. She flung down the remote.

She should be relieved, shouldn't she? Ten days before trial was a hell of a time to start believing your client was telling the truth—and having to prove it!

She hit the play button once more and accidentally fast-forwarded.

The images flew by in a cartoonish frenzy.

Damn.

She tried to hit stop but the tape kept playing. Ten seconds from the end something caught her eye. When the action stopped she carefully rewound and took it from the top. When the man in black first appeared, she had her finger on the stop button.

Had she seen that correctly? She backed up a couple of frames to make sure.

Glenn Ballard slowly turned toward the camera, cocking his chin.

But not in Amy's direction.

The gesture was out of context. He appeared to be responding to something outside the frame. Jackie rewound and ran the tape one last time.

Even given the poor quality of the video, the gesture was unmistakable. Ballard wasn't turning away from Amy. He was looking past the camera and at a forty-five-degree angle to its right.

Was someone else there?

Thirty-Two

"**B**ut we have no proof!" Pilar protested.

It was Friday afternoon and Jackie's desk was littered with coffee cups and the remains of the sandwiches Pilar had brought from the takeout place on Colfax hours earlier. They'd gone over the tape so many times she was ready to throw it and her boss out the window.

"Even if a third person was there," she continued, "it doesn't let Ballard off the hook. What's his story?"

"He's sticking to what he told the polygraph examiner," Jackie said. "What he's said from day one: 'I was not in that cabin with Amy Lynch.'"

"At least he's consistent." Pilar's tone left no doubt how far that went.

"If I can't crack Detective Frasier at the in-camera hearing, that video comes in. I have to have a fallback. That means some other way of identifying who's behind this."

"What do you want me to do?"

"Go back over every witness statement regarding the victim. Her last day, what the people at Finnegan's Wake said. There's something we've missed, and it has to do with how Amy got to that cabin. If you have to, interview them all again. And start with the boyfriend, Derek King."

"Whoa!" This wasn't the first time Jackie had gotten a wild hair on the eve of trial. "Jury selection is a week from Monday. Derek King won't talk, remember?"

Jackie ignored her.

"I don't care what Dennis Ross says, we can't overlook the possibility of a conspiracy. The presence of a second man at that cabin—"

Pilar held up her hand like a traffic cop.

"How'd we get from a two-second gesture on a jerky videotape to a third person at the cabin, to a second man at the scene of the crime?"

She waited for that to sink in. "Let's go over this again. What exactly makes you think Glenn Ballard is the victim of a conspiracy?"

"Four things." Waving away the stale doughnut Pilar held out, Jackie began pacing her office as she rehearsed her arguments. "First, no motive. Why would a federal judge with an impeccable reputation abduct a young girl and chain her in his uncle's cabin? Second, no connection between him and the victim—"

"—that we know of."

"Third, no reason for someone as cautious as Glenn Ballard to leave ketamine and an incriminating video lying around, waiting to be seized."

"There's no evidence Amy was drugged," Pilar said, "and the bottom of a filing cabinet in the back room of his chambers is hardly—"

Jackie whirled triumphantly.

"Exactly my point! Fourth, there's no way Phyllis Klein could have known about the existence—much less the location—of the video without an informant. That spells conspiracy."

"Accomplice, maybe. But conspiracy to do *what*?"

"There was a third person at that cabin," Jackie insisted. "Something made Ballard look away from Amy and past the camera to the right."

"He still turned in the direction of the camera. If he recorded it to get his rocks off, why wouldn't he want his face to show? 'Look, Ma—no hands.'"

Jackie reached for the remote. "You want to see it again? He's not just looking, he's listening!"

"So now you *do* think he was there. . . . Forget Ballard's insistence he was never at the cabin with Amy; what makes you think we can get to the bottom of it in a week?"

"Maybe we're still missing the point. What if Ballard isn't the target, but a fall guy?"

"Now you've really lost me."

"What if the target is Amy's father?"

"But there were no threats or demands."

"That we know of. Bryan Lynch fits into this somewhere. Dig deep enough—"

"—and at the bottom of the hole we still have the videotape. Even if there were fifty other people in the cabin, the only thing that counts is Glenn Ballard was there."

"There's something funky about that tape."

Pilar began gathering up the coffee cups and waxed paper.

"Phyllis Klein doesn't think so. She's so confident she's endorsed one of the top honchos at the CBI to vouch for its authenticity."

"It's not just Ballard looking in the wrong direction, something else is off."

Pilar had heard enough.

"Of course it's off! How many bondage flicks have you seen where a federal judge chains a girl to his own goddamned rafter? You'd better hope Glenn Ballard was framed."

"Let me worry about that. You find Derek King."

It was almost midnight when Jackie gave up on sleep.

She started for the window to see if Lily's night-light was on, only to remember that she was tucked away in her bunk in Steamboat. Should she fix a pot of tea or call Pilar? No, tea would only ensure wakefulness, and Pilar would have been in touch if she'd learned anything new. Finally she reached for her phone. This number was hard-wired into her brain; after five years her fingers still knew which buttons to push.

As soon as the line rang she regretted her decision. Friday night. It rang again. Either he was out or a woman would answer—

"Dennis?" Before he could react she said, "Don't hang up."

"Do you know what time it is?" But he sounded wide-awake.

"What did you mean about your client Austin Lee being the wrong rock?"

"Jesus, Jackie." In his irritation he didn't even pretend. He knew exactly what she meant. "Can't this wait for tomorrow?"

"If Lee didn't frame Ballard, someone else did. I think you know who."

"And I warned you to stay out of it!"

Anger—or fear? Ballard had one last shot to suppress that videotape.

"Dennis, if what we had meant anything—"

"You'll use it, won't you?"

"—you'll tell me what you know. This isn't personal, I owe it to my client. If you were in my position, you'd do the same."

"Just for once can't you accept that your client did it? Or are you so in love with your role as defender of the downtrodden that you've become your own victim?"

Fury overcame her.

"I've had enough of your sanctimonious shit! You're the one who stormed out of the PD's office, who wasn't there when—"

"And you're paying me back now by invading the privacy of my home. Look at the clock. It's goddamned—"

"Is that what Seventeenth Street taught you—to roll over on a client?"

When Dennis replied, it was with the cool professionalism of a stranger.

"That's exactly what you're asking me to do."

So it *was* a client who was behind this.

"You told me Austin Lee was innocent."

"Do you really think any of us are?"

The receiver clicked in her ear.

Thirty-Three

"Judge Ballard, I'm sure you understand I take no pleasure in this matter."

Marlin Pitts rocked back in his burgundy leather chair. Befitting a Boulder jurist at work in his chambers on a Friday afternoon, the cuffs of his striped shirt were turned back twice. To underscore his sympathy for a fellow judge, he'd even loosened his knit tie.

"I can only guess what this case has done to you," he continued. "The reassignment of your docket, the awkwardness in your dealings with your peers on the bench, not to mention the public's—"

"I appreciate your concern." Ballard was attired in a dark gray worsted tropical-weight suit, a white shirt, and a paisley silk tie. "I know you'd like to get this over with as quickly as I would. Why don't we get on with it?"

Pitts straightened in his seat.

"Very well." He gestured to his court reporter to begin transcribing the proceedings. "On the record, I'd like to inquire as to Ms. Klein's health. Have you fully recovered from that accident with your bicycle, Phyllis? Those canyon roads are treacherous and knee injuries can be so debilitating."

Klein smiled prettily and Jackie kept her expression cool. They all knew what this was about.

"Tendon damage, Your Honor." Phyllis gingerly extended her leg. An elastic bandage was wrapped around her knee but it didn't look swollen. "I'll be quite ready to proceed with the trial on Monday."

"When I continued the date of this in-camera hearing as the result of the prosecutor's inability to participate through no fault of her own, I gave the defense the opportunity to postpone the trial. Isn't that right, Ms. Flowers?"

"Yes. And we objected to any continuance that would result in a ruling after the deadline on endorsing witnesses." Ballard's chair creaked. Jackie hadn't told him she'd hedged their bet, but from his small nod of approval she concluded he assumed she'd made the objection for tactical purposes.

"And I ruled that what was sauce for the goose was sauce for the gander. Pushing the witness deadline without postponing the trial would have prejudiced the prosecution." Pitts looked to Klein.

"That's correct, Your Honor. At the bond hearing Ms. Flowers demanded your earliest trial date. Pushing the deadline for endorsing witnesses after she refused to postpone the trial would have made it impossible for the People to adequately prepare."

Now that they had that straight, the real shaft job could begin.

"Bring in Detective Frasier," Pitts told his bailiff.

Pitts's chambers overlooked Boulder Creek. Through his open window came the sound of rushing water, and the breeze smelled of summer. A baseball bat leaned against the golden oak credenza that matched his desk, and the usual certificates and diplomas were interspersed with photographs of a paunchy and winded Pitts embracing every marathoner who'd trained in the foothills in the past twenty years. The decor was meant to disarm. It failed.

They all knew the DA held the cards. The burden was on the defense to prove the search of Ballard's chambers was a setup. What Jackie had going for her was the improbability that the Boulder detectives would have been able to locate a veritable smoking gun so quickly without having been told exactly what to look for and where to find it. What Phyllis had going for her was a judge who was loath to concede he'd been had, and witnesses who weren't about to admit hitting the jackpot through anything but their own genius and extraordinary luck. Was that why she was feeling no pain?

As Frasier took his seat to one side of Pitts's desk and raised his hand to be sworn, Jackie thought he, too, looked a little relaxed for the occasion. He wore the same sports coat as the day he'd executed the warrant, but his sideburns had been trimmed and his sandy hair was freshly cut. Stating his name and occupation for the record, he fixed Jackie with a clear gaze. Either he was about to lie through his teeth or he had nothing to hide.

Jackie questioned him from her seat.

"Detective Frasier, walk us through the search you conducted of Judge Ballard's chambers on April twenty-sixth."

"We arrived at the courthouse at a little before noon. . . ." In minute but accurate detail, Frasier described each step leading to his arrival at the door to Ballard's private office. There he stopped.

"What precisely were you looking for?"

"That's in the warrant," Klein interrupted. "Surely the judge can take judicial notice of the list. 'Photographs, recordings, negatives, documents, *videotapes* . . .'"

Had Phyllis known from the moment she drafted the affidavit?

Jackie kept her eyes on the prize.

"If you were looking for photographs, negatives, and documents, why didn't you begin your search in Judge Ballard's desk?"

"In my experience, if someone wants to conceal something, they don't put it in their desk. That's the first place you'd think to look."

"And if you were planting evidence, you wouldn't put it in the suspect's desk either, because he himself would be likely to find it."

Frasier looked like a puppy who'd been slapped.

"If *I* were planting evidence?"

"There's no evidence anything was planted!" Klein said.

"That's exactly why we're here," Jackie said. "Detective Frasier, do you always start in the place where you're least likely to find what you're looking for?"

Frasier looked to Klein, who was staring at her legal pad.

"From the suspect's point of view, I guess that's correct."

"Why the filing cabinet?"

"It had to be a place big enough—" He stopped.

"—for a videotape? That's what you were looking for all along, isn't it?"

"I—"

"Once you found it, you stopped looking. Right?"

"We—" He raised his eyes again to Phyllis, who was doodling in mechanical strokes. "When we found the tape, we knew it was important. We wanted to get it to Ms. Klein right away."

"So there was no reason to keep looking. Heaven knows you wouldn't expect lightning to strike twice, right?" No need for an answer, either; the question had to register with Pitts. "How did you know it was a video you were looking for?"

Frasier appealed to the prosecutor for the last time for help. This time she responded with a nod. As the Boulder detective raised his hands in mock surrender, Jackie had the sinking feeling this hearing was choreographed.

"We *were* looking for a video," he said. "But not that one."

She dreaded his next answer.

"What video were you looking for?"

"We had reason to believe your client downloaded certain material from the Internet."

"The Internet?"

"A bondage site, to be exact." When Frasier paused this time it wasn't to consult Phyllis Klein. Relishing the moment, he leaned forward in his chair. "We traced the site to the computer in your client's chambers."

"Did you have a warrant?"

"Didn't need one. That's one of the beauties of the Internet—you can track things from either end. Sort of like reverse engineering." He couldn't resist a sly glance at Ballard. "The feds do it all the time. How else do you think they crack those porno rings? Lucky for us, these creeps are never as smart as they think they are. And this was a very special site."

"Detective—"

Jackie ignored Klein's attempt to cut him off.

"What's so special about that site?"

"Amy Lynch was on it."

The hole in Klein's case—the missing link between Ballard and the victim.

"It contained a video produced by her friend," Frasier said.

"What friend?"

"Derek King. It was his website."

Would Ballard have been that careless? And what else had Phyllis been hiding?

Turning to Pitts, Jackie thought fast. "There was no statement by Derek King in the material Ms. Klein produced. At this time, I move to dismiss all charges against Glenn Ballard on the basis of the prosecution's flagrant disregard of its constitutional obligation to—"

"Derek King made no formal statement," Klein cut in. "There was nothing to disclose. My notes of his interview are protected under the work product doctrine."

"When were you planning to turn over that video of Amy Lynch? The trial starts Monday!"

"If you want a postponement, I have no objection."

Ballard would never agree to a continuance and Phyllis knew it. Once again they'd been royally screwed. Jackie's only hope was to stay on plan. Get Pitts to see that the search of Ballard's chambers had been nothing but a sham from the start. If she wanted him to toss the cabin tape, she had to deal with Derek King's flick here and now.

"When was the King video first posted on the Web?"

"January, when your client accessed it. From his chambers," Frasier added with a smirk.

Jackie didn't trust herself to look at her client. She shot in the dark.

"In January of this year, Judge Ballard issued a landmark ruling on the taxation of Internet porn. That decision is currently on appeal to the Tenth Circuit. In preparation for its issuance, my client extensively researched all the issues—including the prevalence of pornographic material on the Web. Naturally he could have logged on to Derek King's website. If he had anything to hide, why access it from his chambers?"

The bullet ricocheted.

"Your client must have done a hell of a lot of reseach," Frasier said.

Jackie braced herself.

"Because he visited that site two dozen times."

Thirty-Four

The bar was straight ahead, the johns to his left. Through the doorway to the kitchen a night-light flickered. Stepping onto the dining floor of this chichi LoDo nightspot, he caught his toe on the edge of the carpet and banged his knee on a table. He bit back the expletive.

The eyes weren't what they used to be. But he was in no rush.

In the dark Ted Wolsky came alive.

In addition to the bistro, the converted saddle factory housed a brewpub and a photo gallery. The joint had been jumping when he'd eaten there two nights earlier, but restaurants were a risky venture.

A little problem with the landlord?

Ted specialized in breaking leases.

But he wasn't there to break a lease; he'd left all that behind. Tonight Ted was embarking on a new career.

Over the cleaning solvent left by the night crew floated the rich scents of stock and roast lamb. The other evening he'd ordered the lamb. Garlic and rosemary potatoes, topped off with Burgundy and crème brûlée. Priced a bit steep—and they called *him* a thief!—but what the hell. He'd feasted on his new friend's dime.

In the kitchen a fifteen-gallon stockpot simmered on an eight-burner stove. Chicken, veal and pork bones, carrots, onions and celery. He was glad he wasn't here on a job; what a pity it would be to snuff out that delectable aroma with the acrid odor of gas! He gave the walk-in freezer the once-over and peered into the pizza oven built into the brick wall. A gleaming steel contraption with a digital display and an aluminum hood caught his eye. The digital display showed a chef's hat, a red-bulbed thermometer, and a clock. Self-starting oven, he decided. One of those foreign dealies you preset to turn on by itself . . .

A creature of habit, Ted had cased the building. At 3 A.M. the bakers would arrive to start the dough for the following day's bread. By then he would be long gone. But the thrill of being alone in the dark had seized him and he allowed his mind to wander. If Ted had one regret, it was that he'd never torched a restaurant.

How would he do this one?

Leave the gas cans by the stand for the maître d', locate the telephones and unplug them from the walls. In the kitchen find the hot-water heaters and extinguish the pilot. Then twist the flexible hose behind the stove until it cracked. There was no such thing as too much gas, no sweeter sight than an insurance investigator shaking his head sadly and muttering, "It's a total."

Ted had pulled his first arson at age eighteen. All it took was balls and a Bic lighter. When the guy who hired him refused to pay, he took a Mason jar full of gas and splashed it in his face. He was immediately paid—and the price had gone up. He'd started out burglarizing cigarette machines; he had a thing for smokes. You could always tell a smoker by the way he held a pencil or a pen. Some had a special grip, like a signature. Ted never missed a gesture and he never forgot a face.

He'd done plenty of time. He'd never bitched because it was his choice. Talk about taking the heat. When you're standing in a building that's blowing up around you, *that's* taking the heat. And the only thing that saved you was keeping a cool head. You couldn't panic or get excited. You just headed for the door. . . . If he were torching this place, what would he do next?

Plug his timer in the socket by the stove to test the juice, repeat the ritual with his electric hot plate. He bought them at Sears and Ace Hardware—reliability was key. He got his five-gallon plastic cans at Kmart, the gasoline from half a dozen self-serves throughout the metro area. No flirting with the checkout clerks, keep a low profile at the service station, always pay cash. You'd be surprised how unobservant people were, but still . . . Ted paid without a word. How he missed being in the game!

His next step would be to cover the drain in the kitchen floor with a dishrag. Wouldn't do to have the gasoline run off. A pint equaled eight sticks of dynamite, but the fumes had to build. This was LoDo. The walls were brick, a hundred years old. This building had to be *leveled*.

In the dining room he would line up the gas cans ten feet apart. Tie one end of a nylon cord through the handle of the first can and unscrew the lid, string it through the next handle. The last can he would set in the center of the kitchen floor. Pull the cord and the cans would topple like dominoes. The gas would soak into the carpet and within minutes the restaurant would be permeated with fumes.

Timer in the wall, wired to the hot plate. Five books of matches arranged around the coils—it never paid to be cheap—red and blue tips splayed. Before they were bad for your health, he'd used cigarettes. But who wanted to die of cancer? When the timer went off, the coils would heat and the matches would light. By then even the smallest spark would ignite the fumes. When the fumes began to rise, the pungent odor would fill his mouth, robbing him of the ability to smell or taste anything else for the next hour. As the gas ignited it would devour oxygen with a low rumble, a sound that would turn into a freight train driving up your ass.

Over the hill?

Hardly.

He was at the top of his game.

Amateurs—for them Ted had nothing but contempt. The mutts who used booze instead of gasoline because it had a lower flash point, or started three or four fires to make sure they took. They even used metal gas cans, for Christ's sake! Not to mention the weenie-whackers who jerked off to the sight of a flame. In and out—that was Ted's motto. Clean and fast. Like he always said, it was the little things, the tiny errors in judgment that fried you. Damn right he was too much of a pro to splash accelerant on walls!

He laughed when he thought about the last time Jackie got him off. An insurance adjustor swearing he was too good to set that warehouse fire? Priceless! Go straight? He had every intention of keeping his promise. But who said anything about retirement?

Tonight marked a new beginning.

Ted Wolsky—private dick. Not to be confused with *prick*. That was the province of Glenn Ballard and Dennis Ross. Which of the two did he despise more? The judge who had everybody fooled, or the great pretender? If Jackie knew what that bastard Ross did it would break her heart. There was very little Ted didn't know, and nothing he forgot. Not a face and not a gesture. In a few moments he would learn even more. Enough to crack the Ballard case and hand Jackie the win she so badly needed. Talk about old times—how ironic that his source had come to *him*!

For a moment he was back in Ballard's courtroom the day after he was busted for burglarizing the U.S. Marshals' warehouse. How was he to know it was federal property? As he sat in the dock waiting to be arraigned, he'd watched Ballard in action. Funny how things had a way of coming full circle. Now the shoe was on the other foot and the hangman was getting what he deserved. If Jackie wasn't holding the bag, Ted would have let Ballard fry. For an instant he wondered why he'd been contacted instead of Jackie, but what difference did that make? After tonight every lawyer in town would be knocking on *his* door. . . .

Ted raised his nose and sniffed. He'd given his imagination quite a workout, planning how he'd torch this place. So good he could almost smell gas! At the rate he was going, the next thing he'd hear was the click of a spark.

The entrance to the photo gallery was by the stove, just as he'd been told. Like the door through which he'd entered the bistro, it had been left unlocked. In another moment he would cross the threshold and join his friend with all the answers.

"You may not like what I show you, but you'll know how it went down. . . ."

That's why he was there.

The steel contraption again caught his eye. Its heavy door was adorned with dials calibrated for temperature and, what—humidity? The name of the manufacturer might have been in Kraut. He peered through the glass window. Just a peek . . .

Click.

In one step he was at the side door.

Whoosh.

He twisted the knob. It wouldn't turn.

Rrrrrm . . .

Hair and clothes in flames, he flung himself at the door.

In the instant before that freight train thundered up his ass, Ted Wolsky had time for one last thought.

I've been fucked.

Thirty-Five

The girl squinted in the tropical sun.

Her hair was so shiny its color could have been any shade from flax to chestnut, and its soft waves ended just below her shoulders. Cut high on the thigh and with a slash of cloth across the breasts suspended by narrow straps, her bikini showed off a toned body with a baby-oil tan. Blue sky, turquoise ocean, arched feet planted firmly in white sand.

Jackie had thought Amy's eyes were sad; now her expression was blank. The girl rose on the balls of her feet. Her arms lifted as if they were attached to strings. She began twitching like a marionette. . . .

Ri-inng!

She jerked awake.

Riiii-nnng!

She groped for the phone.

"Jackie?"

It was Pilar.

"Yeah?"

"Sorry to wake you. This couldn't wait."

She fumbled for her bedside lamp. The numerals on her digital alarm swarmed. "Jesus, Pilar . . ."

"What do you want first—the bad news or worse?"

"Shit."

"I'll start with the bad. Ted Wolsky died tonight."

"What?"

"He torched a building in LoDo and went up with it. Just got the call from one of my buddies on the force."

Not Ted.

"Everyone's luck runs out." Pilar's voice was unnaturally soft. "What did he always say? 'It's the little things.' Remember?"

Maybe she was still dreaming.

"When did it happen?"

"Two hours ago."

"Too soon to know it was arson . . ."

"They thought it was a gas leak because the place blew right when the oven was set to go off. A spark could have ignited the fumes. But Public Service was just in to inspect the hoses, and the guys on the scene could smell gasoline."

"How could they possibly have identified—"

"The body of a sixty-year-old male was blown out the back door. Ted's motorcycle was parked in front."

"But he promised . . ." Realizing how ridiculous that must sound, Jackie searched for another reason. "Ted never would have driven to the scene."

"We all slip."

"Maybe the building blew accidentally." Why was it so hard to accept? "What kind of business was it?"

"A bistro. That new place on Market Street—the one between the photo gallery and the brewpub. We drove by a couple weeks ago, remember?"

Ted only torched buildings for money. And all sorts of accidents occurred in restaurants. Gas leaks, faulty ovens . . . "Was the owner in financial trouble?"

"Too soon to know. One outfit owned all three places and they were totaled."

Jackie fumbled in her nightstand for a tissue. She pressed it to her eyes.

"Has anyone told his mother?"

"Jackie . . ."

"I'll do it. I'll go there right now."

"Wait."

"She's eighty-five years old, Pilar."

Jackie swung her legs over the side of the bed. A quick shower, get dressed, grab some coffee, and she could be at Ted's house in Globeville before the morning paper hit his mother's doorstep.

"There's more." Pilar hesitated. "I had two pieces of news, remember?"

Taking the cordless phone with her, Jackie headed for her closet. Had

Ted mentioned any other relatives? She grabbed the first article of cloth-ing she touched. The next few days would be dreadful, his mother shouldn't have to be alone. . . .

"I was in Boulder tonight," Pilar continued. "With the trial on Mon-day, Derek King finally spilled. Phyllis Klein has another little surprise."

"So Ballard logged on to the website. That still doesn't show he knew Amy, it was probably one of dozens he accessed in researching his opinion. At least he did it from chambers."

Pilar's fatigue finally registered in her voice. "He also logged on from home."

"So? He—"

"—was particularly smitten with Amy. Like clockwork. From January till she was abducted at the end of March, Glenn Ballard hit that site every Saturday night."

The last hole in Klein's case had just been plugged.

Thirty-Six

The crystal vase on Marlin Pitts's bench sparkled under a new fluorescent bulb. The empty seats in the jury box were swiveled expectantly in his direction. Pitts himself had undergone an upgrade. He'd traded his wire rims for contact lenses and was wearing a silk bow tie. At the prosecution table Phyllis Klein was lining up her files. Her navy blue dress and bib collar evoked Plymouth Rock.

Glenn Ballard's trial was about to begin.

In the white suit and simple gold chain she reserved for opening day, Jackie knew she looked the picture of confidence. As her eyes swept the gallery she spotted reporters from all the local outlets and commentators from Court TV and MSNBC. Pilar had stood over her that morning until Jackie's cereal bowl was clean. Under the stress of trial she took nothing for granted. Still, she had a mild buzzing in her ears. This was no time for a bad day. The revelation that her client had stalked Amy Lynch on the Web had brought her back to where she'd begun.

Flying not just solo—but blind.

The prospective jurors began filing in. Jackie turned in her chair to watch while Ballard stared stiffly ahead. In his elegantly dotted tie and double-breasted suit, he sat so erect she could have dropped a plumb line from the crown of his aristocratic head to the seat of his impeccably tailored trousers. But their last meeting had seriously strained the attorney-client relationship. Ballard still insisted he'd never been at the cabin with Amy; in his mind, that was the only question that counted. Oh, he might have stumbled across the website while researching his opinion, but he certainly didn't access it two dozen times—much less from home. Their confrontation the night before rang in Jackie's ears.

"I've said it all along: I've been framed."

"By *whom*, Glenn?"

"By any one of the thousands of litigants whose cases I've presided over and who didn't like the result. And that goes double for their lawyers."

"Any of them have a key to your private office or condo? Name a single person with the means, motive, and opportunity—"

"That's your job!"

If a little knowledge was dangerous, a lot was more so in the hands of a client like Glenn Ballard. He reminded Jackie of a con man whom Dennis Ross had advised on the eve of trial to "lose the tan." But if you were representing a federal judge accustomed to being addressed from a lectern by attorneys looking up at him, how did you tell him that the impression he gave of status and authority was likely to be his ruin? Jackie's greatest challenge would be reducing the god to a man. Her success would depend on the people entering this room.

Watching the prospective jurors, she wondered just how "average" they were. Was it any wonder most citizens believed that "businessman" was synonymous with "thief," or that the mere filing of a sexual harassment suit meant the plaintiff had a legitimate claim? In this day when an award of millions was considered chump change, Jackie didn't envy her counterparts in the civil arena. But how big was the leap from corporate executive to federal judge? And if most jurors had no qualms about ignoring the instructions a judge gave from the bench, would they also ignore the testimony of a judge who took the stand?

Boulderites prided themselves on being anything but average, she reminded herself as the last of the jurors took their seats. Their reputation as a horde of xenophobic liberals who rated sex crimes on a par with murder was borne out by the fact that the affluent college town had more crisis counselors per capita than SUVs. Nor was their physical appearance a comfort.

Ballard's jury pool came straight out of a faculty meeting of the sociology department at CU, with a smattering of superannuated ornithologists and buzz-cut computer engineers from Boulder's Silicon Valley thrown in for diversity's sake. Natural-fiber sweaters and open-collared oxford shirts under tweed coats predominated, and Teva sandals mingled with brogans. A couple of Levi's-clad college students looked like they'd wandered into the wrong library. Jackie remembered the last time she'd defended a Denver client in Boulder—the sea of white faces was no less daunting now. What scared her this time was not their color, but their homogeneity.

To calm her nerves, she smiled at the bailiff, who couldn't help reciprocating. Jurors distrusted lawyers but identified with the judge. The last thing Jackie wanted was for them to sense she was an outsider. Her job was twofold: to make inroads in their prejudices, and to establish herself as both a member of Marlin Pitts's charmed circle and as a renegade who had complete confidence in her client's innocence. Which meant peeling away enough of each juror's facade to identify the rogues. She couldn't depend on Phyllis Klein to do her spadework.

Klein rose and, with a nod from Pitts, wheeled the lectern to a position directly in front of the jury box. The bailiff called twelve names and a like number of men and women shuffled to the dock. Blinking rapidly, the prosecutor favored each candidate with a broad smile before embarking on her voir dire.

"Miss Massie—I do have that right, don't I? It's not Mrs. or *Ms.* . . ." Klein waited for the elderly woman to nod. Pilar had reviewed the jurors' questionnaires and—like Phyllis Klein—Jackie knew this seventy-year-old woman relished her unmarried status. Score one for her opponent.

But Jackie had certain prejudices of her own. At the top of her reject list were women over the age of sixty and any kind of teacher. Both groups tended to respect authority. Elderly women were death on female lawyers, and teachers were a little too accustomed to judging their pupils and meting out punishment. That was another reason not to represent clients who committed crimes in genteel college towns.

With a simpering grin, Klein continued.

"I see that before you retired, you taught at Chatfield School."

Edna Massie's cardigan swelled with pride. She would have no difficulty identifying with Bryan Lynch, or the travails of his spirited daughter.

"And you founded a women's poetry group . . ."

That did it. The cabin video would replay every night in Edna Massie's dreams, and she would never forgive Glenn Ballard. Even as Jackie sketched a short stack of books in the blank box that represented Massie's chair on her seating chart, she'd decided the retired teacher would be the defense's third strike. Throw a senior citizen off too early and the others would never forgive *her.*

Klein moved down the jury box. She made short work of a graduate student who moonlighted as a cabdriver, and a fry cook at the only local restaurant that admitted to using lard. She skittered past a Naropa instructor as if the very act of posing questions brought bad karma. The next juror seemed a safer bet.

"Dr. Hamil, how long have you been a psychologist?"

"Twenty-five years." The fellow in the tweed coat eyed Ballard with undisguised interest. "I have a family-oriented practice."

"Would serving on this jury inconvenience your patients?"

"To the contrary—it would enrich my experience in dealing with them. And I have colleagues who pinch-hit in an emergency."

"I see. So you treat both men and women?"

"Especially men."

Klein had asked one question too many; Hamil's response screamed abuse counselor. Which could explain why the good doctor was so eager to serve. Of course, shrinks always wanted to be jurors. Jackie glanced at Ballard's copy of the seating chart and saw he'd placed a decisive X over Hamil's box. For once she and her client were in agreement.

As she watched her adversary cultivate her constituents with just the right blend of solicitude and awe, Jackie knew Klein was weeding out kooks and trying to ensure that whoever remained liked her. That was not as simple as it sounded. Like all creatures confined to small spaces, it was easier for jurors to form antipathies than affections. And when you were forbidden to discuss the evidence until the case is over, what else could you talk about but the lawyers? Worst of all, the simpering seemed to be paying off. Watching the jurors warm to the DA in her Puritan garb, Jackie realized that what she had assumed was a lack of flair in Klein's ensemble was being turned to devastating advantage. If nothing else, Phyllis Klein knew Boulder juries.

As a defense lawyer, Jackie had to be more ambitious. Her instincts said to go for skeptical males, but walk a fine line: avoid men whose status and upbringing would cause overidentification with Amy's father, while retaining those savvy enough to reject the obvious. That meant staking a bet on an engineer, which Jackie was loath to do. And she had drastically underestimated the ratio of females to males in the Boulder jury pool. It was weighted heavily in favor of retirees, and women lived longer. The fact that she herself was a woman only compounded her challenge. She had to project sympathy for Amy, while at the same time demonstrating competence at the earliest moment. That meant taking more than the usual risks with her opening statement.

"Professor Holland," Klein addressed a balding man at the end of the second row, "you're a member of the Philosophy Department at CU?"

"Mmm . . ."

Jackie sketched a windmill in the professor's box. From the way Holland folded his arms over his paunch, she could see he was comfortable with himself. That alone posed a threat to a prosecutor. And he was the only person in the room wearing shorts. Klein wouldn't waste a moment on him—but Jackie was wrong.

"As a philosopher, do you have any problem believing what you see and hear?"

"Heavens, no!"

"Even if your perceptions are at odds with preconceived notions?"

There went *no federal judge abducts a coed* and *no girl vanishes without a trace from a bar.*

"Preconceived notions?" Holland echoed.

Klein's rabbitty eyes darted to the defense table.

"About how a person of a certain status, power, and prestige might be expected to behave?"

"My dear woman, a man *is* what he does!"

Klein smiled at Holland as if the two of them shared a secret. Ballard shifted in his chair. He didn't like what had just occurred but knew better than to show it. But Jackie was reevaluating her strategy. There was something about Holland that she liked. Had she found her Don Quixote?

Other prospects were a feng shui consultant who tapped into the psychic energy of office furniture, a graduate student whose monosyllabic answers marked him a dry sponge, and a geophysicist from the National Center for Atmospheric Research. By the time Klein had tossed her last softball to a woman who baked pet treats for a living, it was clear she'd been a hit despite her painted smile.

Marlin Pitts was looking down at Jackie from the bench.

"Ms. Flowers, are you ready to proceed?"

Jackie slowly rose.

It was ten minutes before noon and, unlike the new light over the judge's bench, the fluorescent tube above the defense table had been flickering all morning. She could have used the time to consult with Pilar, but when she scanned the packed courtroom her investigator was nowhere to be found. In the second row of the gallery sat Dennis Ross. Their eyes locked and Jackie blanked.

"Or would you prefer to begin your voir dire after a recess?"

She stepped to the lectern. Slipping her hand in the pocket of her suit jacket, she felt for the sliver of agate. The foliage in the quartz never failed to bring her back.

"I—uh . . ."

Forget Dennis and focus on this jury. The guy with the paunch—something about what he'd said . . .

"—almost noon and I would prefer to remain on schedule," Pitts continued.

Her fingers slid across the silky surface. Focus, focus. Was it coming?

"Your Honor, I would like to proceed." What the hell was that juror's name? Jackie turned back to the defense table. For an instant she met Ballard's eyes. What is the matter with you? they said. She reached for her copy of the seating chart. As she searched for the box for the man with the paunch, she saw the windmill and everything clicked into place.

"Professor Holland, you said a moment ago a man is what he does. If the act doesn't fit the man, which do you believe?"

His eyes narrowed. "Are you posing a false dichotomy, Counselor?"

"I only went to law school, I don't know what that means!"

The laugh she received was at both their expenses, and Holland joined in.

"I suppose I'd reserve judgment on the man *and* your question."

It didn't get better than that.

She turned to the scientist from NCAR. Rail-thin, he had the pin-point stare of a zealot—in his box, she'd drawn a lightbulb. Klein planned to call an expert from the CBI lab to vouch for the authenticity of the cabin tape. To muddy the waters, Jackie needed Tom Swift in her corner.

"Dr. Jasick, I assume you've spent at least part of your career in the lab."

A dry chuckle.

"More hours than not."

"Do you ever find that A, B, and C are not necessarily followed by D?"

"Only when I abandon the alphabet."

Jackie acknowledged her clumsiness with a self-deprecating smile. Humor won allies. If she allowed Jasick to remain, points he scored now would be credited to Ballard's account later. Now was the time to bury a couple of land mines.

"Let me start again. Have you ever conducted an experiment where the end result wasn't what you expected?"

"Why experiment if you already know the answer?"

"So it's important to keep an open mind?"

"Science is all about discovery," he agreed. "What you think you see is not necessarily what you get."

Break out the Bunsen burners. Jackie had another live one—unless Klein threw Jasick off. But men of science were like men of the cloth and prosecutors were notoriously conservative. Fingers crossed that Klein would keep him, Jackie returned to Edna Massie. Women of any age—and particularly her vintage—were fatal to lawyers of their own sex, but there was no way to eliminate them all. And for once the prosecutor shared Jackie's disadvantage.

"Miss Massie, how long did you teach at Chatfield?"

"Thirty years. I gave my life to those girls."

"That must have been rewarding."

The blue eyes were unexpectedly shrewd. "They weren't all angels."

A closet misogynist? Mindful of a trap, Jackie proceeded with caution.

"I'll bet some of them were a handful."

"Girls today . . ." Massie shook her head. "I wouldn't put anything past them. Of course, they're very influenced by boys. In that sense nothing's really changed."

Jackie could hear Phyllis whispering to her assistant. Massie's flip-flop had made her a wild card, anathema to the forces of law and order. Enough to throw Klein off her stride—or make her squander one of her precious strikes? Regardless of whether Massie remained on the jury, Jackie had one more point to make.

"In your years of teaching, you must have come across students who surprised you."

"In what way?"

"My aunt always said, 'You only have one chance to make a first impression.' But isn't it true that first impressions can be a hundred and eighty degrees wrong? That someone who seems cold and distant may be painfully shy?"

"The more private a person is, the harder it is to know her"—Massie looked pointedly at Ballard—"or him."

No dumb chromosomes had slipped into Edna Massie's gene pool. The point had been made: even muckety-mucks could be misjudged, especially those who would never be finalists in a personality contest. Jackie turned to the man in the band-collared shirt. In his box she'd sketched a yin and yang.

"Mr. Carlin, could you tell us a bit about feng shui?"

"We attempt to create harmony with the universe."

Pilar had gone through a phase where she'd tried to apply feng shui to the office, with predictably disastrous results. But Jackie could affect a charming helplessness as well as the next. "Do you favor—I don't know, certain colors or shapes?"

Carlin was only too happy to explain.

"We tend to prefer soft curves over sharp angles and straight lines. White draws on mental energy. Green stimulates the liver and calms people down. Flame colors represent fire." He smiled somewhat patronizingly. "I wouldn't wear them unless I wanted to provoke the people around me."

"I'll leave my red suit home!" Jackie promised, and waited for the laughter to die. With the jurors warmed up, it was time to strike her first blow against the linear logic Klein and her ilk held so dear. "Harmony through curves . . . To mix metaphors, would it be fair to say the path to cosmic order is not necessarily a straight line?"

Receiving no quarrel, Jackie moved on.

It was close to one o'clock when Marlin Pitts called for jury challenges. Klein rejected the Naropa instructor and Jackie tossed the shrink. The prosecution's next strike was the feng shui master, who seemed to represent a grounding element. Jackie was secretly relieved. If forced to rely on a mistrial, the last thing she wanted on Ballard's jury was balance. Edna Massie survived the cuts. She would see all of Amy Lynch.

Pitts recessed for an hour for lunch and Ballard slipped out, leaving his notes on the defense table. Jackie was just stowing them in her briefcase where they would be safe from prying eyes, when a voice behind her spoke.

"Nice job with Massie. You had the old broad eating out of your hand."

The compliment was halfhearted.

"I thought we had nothing more to say," she replied without looking up.

"I heard about Ted."

Jackie turned. Dennis's eyes were hollow and he'd cut himself shaving.

"We have to talk," he said. "Can we go somewhere?"

"What's wrong with here?"

He took her arm. "The jury room."

Jackie allowed him to lead her to the empty deliberation chamber. He closed the door behind them.

"You know that bistro where Ted was killed?" he began.

Jackie's heart leaped.

Killed. Not died . . . She'd been right not to believe Ted torched that place! But could she have been to blame for his being there?

"My client owns it," Dennis said. "He also owns the photo gallery and the brewpub on either side. The gallery is a front for a porn operation. Ballard's Internet ruling pissed off a lot of powerful people."

"Why tell me now?"

"Ted was asking around about Ballard. Maybe he found the right place."

She never should have suggested to Ted that Ballard was framed. She should have stopped him from trying to help her. . . . But this was no time to mourn him, and vengeance could come later. She had another client to save.

"Why didn't you tell me before?"

"I've never ratted out a client." The look in Dennis's eyes said what that cost now.

"I need more than your suspicion. Ballard's jury is impaneled, Dennis, there's no time to screw around!"

He shook his head.

"Klein's a master at smoke and mirrors. You'll never be able to show who's behind this."

Jackie rose from the jury table and started for the door.

"Then I'll take the jury through the looking glass."

Thirty-Seven

"On the last day of her life as she knew it, Amy Lynch had everything a girl could want. . . ."

Phyllis Klein paused until the last muffled cough died.

"She'd sailed through her midterms in the second semester of her freshman year at CU, she was the apple of her parents' eye, she was at the center of a large circle of friends."

Klein's male assistant rolled out a screen from its hiding place behind the judge's bench and strode to a projector across the room. He inserted a slide.

"This is what she looked like," Klein said.

A carefree Amy, head thrown back and hair flying as invisible hands pushed her on a swing. Not the girl in Mazatlán.

And certainly not the one in the cabin in Left Hand Canyon.

"She had just declared her major. She was lining up a summer job as a lifeguard at the rec center pool"—funny how Erin and Matt had neglected to mention that!—"she'd even promised her mother she wouldn't go steady until she was a sophomore."

Klein needn't have taken the pause when she did. The jury was riveted. Even Ballard gazed at the prosecutor with the fascination a rat reserves for a snake. Jackie didn't have to worry about the jurors noticing. They were too alienated from her client to look at him at all.

"Amy Lynch woke up that morning and headed off to class. One of the last things we know she did that day was take a biology exam. Then she went out to celebrate the end of her midterms. Amy felt very safe. What was there to be afraid of? After all, she was in Boulder."

Klein's backward glance dared Jackie to object. Amy had not been able to talk before she died, and Klein had no way of knowing what was on her mind the day she was abducted. But Jackie declined the bait. Instead, she squeezed Ballard's knee, hoping to break his trance. He kept staring at the screen as Klein continued to spin the victim's silver-spoon upbringing into gold.

"Amy was a beautiful girl who liked to have fun. She invited her roommate to go out with her that night, but her friend declined. She went to a place where she was well known. She planned to make it an early night. . . ."

Klein's assistant returned to the projector.

"This is what Amy looked like three days later when she was found."

A naked child in a dog collar, eyes deadened in shock.

"One person didn't care about Amy Lynch's welfare. His *indifference* was so *extreme*—"

Shifting in her seat, Jackie jostled a file with her elbow. It wobbled an instant before flying off the edge of the defense table. Ballard sprang to life and tried in vain to catch it. Papers sailed everywhere and they both scrambled to retrieve them. The jury was no longer focused on the DA or the screen.

An old trick that always worked. But only once.

Phyllis Klein was furious.

"Your Honor, if counsel wants to object—"

"Object?" Jackie replied in confusion. "I apologize for my clumsiness."

Pitts frowned. This was his courtroom and on the most rudimentary level his job was to control it. On the other hand, Jackie was the player who'd scored the laughs in voir dire, which would redound to his credit. Slap her down or give her more rope? From his expression it was clear he expected her to hang herself.

"Ms. Klein, please proceed."

Phyllis tried to pick up where she'd left off but the spell had been broken. Not only had Jackie thrown her off her stride, she'd accomplished the near-impossible. She'd elevated her client from a stalker of nubile coeds to a man sufficiently decent to get down on hands and knees to assist his lawyer after she'd made a fool of herself. Whether he was indeed decent, or simply clever enough to pick up on her ploy, was beside the point. What was important was that the jurors were now looking at him. As her adversary fumbled for her next line, Jackie blinked helpfully.

"And—the man *responsible* for what you see is sitting"—Klein had to turn to ensure Ballard had indeed returned to his chair—"right there!"

The jurors gazed at Ballard noncommittally.

Sensing the slackening interest, Klein rushed through the evidence against Ballard. Handcuffs, ketamine, the cabin—Jackie half-expected her to play the video right then but Klein knew better than to fire her smoking gun prematurely. She ended instead with an appeal to reverse prejudice.

"Don't be swayed by the high and mighty, those who pride themselves on membership in the 'old boys' club.' No man is above the law."

And then it was Jackie's turn.

As she stepped to the lectern she passed the projector. With a decisive gesture she flicked the switch and the screen went blank. The best kind of story was one the jurors had already heard, and Klein had handed Jackie her opening.

"How many of you remember the Mad Hatter's tea party?"

The snicker from the rear of the courtroom was quickly hushed. The scientist from NCAR would be the hardest sell; Jackie looked him straight in the eye.

"Each time the folks in Wonderland dirtied a plate, they moved on down the table. But a man's reputation is not a dish. You can't soil it and walk away. Despite what Ms. Klein wants you to believe, this isn't Wonderland."

Jasik wasn't buying—not yet. He required specifics.

"And that wasn't the only strange thing Alice encountered. When she drank from a bottle she shrank, and when she ate cake she stretched. Ms. Klein's evidence is equally malleable. Notice how it stretches and shrinks to incriminate Glenn Ballard.

"Let's start with the ketamine. Ms. Klein needs to explain how Amy Lynch got from Finnegan's Wake to the cabin, and ketamine seems to fit the bill—it's a pet tranquilizer and an old bottle was found in Ballard's home. Only problem is, there's no evidence Amy Lynch ingested it. Need I tell you Glenn Ballard owned a dog?" She nodded at the woman who baked pet treats. "A remedy to keep a chow from chucking milk bones has been stretched to fit the prosecution's theory of the case."

Edna Massie was skeptic number two.

"That cabin in the woods? Does it belong to Glenn Ballard? We won't dispute that, nor that a blindfold found there contained a strand of Amy's hair. But I'm betting you won't hear any evidence from Ms.

Klein that Glenn Ballard was at that cabin at the time of the abduction, or that it couldn't have been broken into by a stranger. Has the prosecutor looked for that stranger? Of course not. It's so much simpler to shrink the cabin to fit one man."

Massie gave Klein a hard stare and Jackie downshifted. Confident that Pitts wouldn't restrict her physical movements—after her clumsiness at the defense table, would he dare?—she left the lectern and stood directly before the jurors.

"Professor Holland says who you are is inseparable from what you do. Maybe that's why Ms. Klein feels it's so important to define my client by his status and presumed power. So who is the man I represent?" She paused to flash Ballard a confident smile. "Glenn Ballard is a United States District Judge. He has been on the federal bench for fifteen years. It is a lifetime appointment by the President of the United States, with the advice and consent of the Senate. In all of his years on the bench, there hasn't been a single stain on his record."

Her gaze swept from the fry cook to the biscuit baker.

"Before Judge Ballard was appointed to the bench, he was a professor at CU Law School here in Boulder. Indeed, he was *my* professor." She smiled ruefully at Holland. "I wish I could tell you he gave me an A, but his standards were too high. Is such a man capable of the atrocity committed on Amy Lynch?"

She locked eyes with each juror.

"We learned something else this morning. An experiment is a process to determine a result. If you already know the result, why go through the process?" A nod to Jasick. "Sentence first and verdict afterward is the way they did it in Wonderland. But Wonderland wasn't the only fantasy world Alice visited. Stepping through the looking glass was even stranger. There two of anything was cheaper than one, and to stay in the same place you had to run as fast as you could. When you listen to the prosecution's case, ask yourself if Ms. Klein isn't throwing a little too much circumstantial evidence at you. If she isn't running a little *too* fast."

A grunt of outrage from the prosecution, but Jackie didn't turn.

"Aren't the ketamine and the cabin a little *too* perfect, a little *too* neat? In the realm of the absurd, two myths are always cheaper than one. At the end of this trial I hope that you—like Alice—will break free of the spell by recognizing the prosecution for what it is: as flimsy as a house of cards."

"Objection!"

But Jackie was through.

When Marlin Pitts dismissed the jury for the day, Klein stomped out, leaving the cleanup to her silent assistant. As the other reporters rushed off to file their stories, Jackie saw Ballard talking to the commentator from MSNBC. The kid nodded as he scribbled in his notebook and gave Ballard a friendly wave as he left. When the courtroom was clear, Ballard turned to Jackie.

"What kind of an opening was that?"

A damned good one.

She continued loading her briefcase with useless files and blank legal pads. Window dressing, just like her opening. And hadn't she warned him about the media?

"I used what I had."

"Fairy tales don't cut it in federal court. Why didn't you tell them I was framed?"

Now was the time to tell him what Dennis Ross had said, but Jackie hesitated.

What did it matter whether she finally believed Ballard was right? She could barely control her client now; if she shared Dennis's suspicions, Ballard would go berserk. They had a shot at winning on reasonable doubt, but if he took the stand and made accusations they had no chance of making stick, Phyllis Klein would be home free.

"Because there's not a speck of evidence to support it. I can't promise the jury what we can't deliver."

"You still don't get it, do you? It doesn't matter who framed me; all I have to do is testify. Only one question counts, Counselor. They'll believe me because I was *not* at that cabin with Amy Lynch. And didn't I tell you to stay away from character? 'Not a stain on his record'? You made me sound like I was applying for a job at the post office!"

United States District Judge Glenn Ballard was unraveling. She had to keep him off the stand and get this case to the jury fast.

"I should fire you for that performance!" he said.

Why had he hired her in the first place? He'd refused to endorse an expert in the hope that Pitts would suppress the videotape. He was willing to roll the dice on his own testimony but she was not. She could no longer afford to be sucked in by her client's grandiosity, and in that moment Jackie had never pitied or disliked a client more.

"You go right ahead, Glenn. But who would you blame if you're convicted?"

"You know damn well Marlin Pitts won't let you withdraw!"

And *he* knew how bad it would look to the jury if he canned her.

Pilar was waiting in the Spider and Jackie had one last thing to say.

"Then we're both stuck."

Thirty-Eight

"Tell the jury about your daughter, Amy. . . ."

It was Tuesday morning, and Phyllis Klein was leading off with Bryan Lynch. Recovered from Jackie's opening, she wore a mint-colored two-piece dress with navy piping. Jackie admired her crisp style and the way her voice softened whenever she mentioned the victim's name—always the first, never the last.

"Amy was a good girl," he said.

Bryan Lynch represented everything Klein held dear: God, inherited wealth, and the Republican Party. Her examination thus far had been a model for glossing over the forces that made the all-American product of an all-American family pose for a bondage flick on the Web. But as the questioning continued, Jackie sensed an unexpected roadblock.

"A little high-spirited, perhaps?"

Klein was trying to prepare the jury for Derek King's videotape, in which Amy had clearly been a willing participant. The problem was, she hadn't cued her star witness to her strategy.

"No more than any girl her age."

Behind the lectern Klein's pointed toe tapped in frustration. Juries had nothing but sympathy for a bereaved father, and she couldn't afford to challenge or provoke this one.

"Would you say your daughter was sheltered?"

"Sheltered?"

The obvious point was that, despite posing for a bondage flick, Amy was not responsible for her abduction. That there was evil in the world and the girl was overcome by forces she was not equipped to handle. But Klein was increasingly out of synch with her own witness. "What I mean to say is—"

Bryan Lynch leaned across the stand.

"I told you, my daughter was a good girl!"

Klein pulled back.

"She was doing well in school?"

Control shifted before Jackie's eyes.

"She was current with her schoolwork," he said. "And holding down a responsible job."

"A responsible job. And wasn't—"

"There was absolutely no friction between us."

"No friction . . ."

"Amy was devoted to her parents."

"Yes."

The dynamic had reversed. Phyllis Klein was Charlie McCarthy to Lynch's Edgar Bergen. But his need to control was his weakness.

"—called home every night," he was saying.

"Every night," Klein parroted. Was it possible she hadn't showed him Derek King's video?

Jackie looked at Ballard. His lip was curled in contempt. For the hapless prosecutor—or Amy's father?

"She was a good girl," Lynch said.

With that, Klein sat.

Jackie slowly rose.

It was time to lead the jury through the looking-glass world of Bryan Lynch's family life. Jackie's royal blue suit and simple white blouse reflected a purity of purpose. She had to convince them that, rather than being Saint Bernadette bringing forth the sacred waters of Lourdes, Amy had courted her destruction. But the victim's father had to do her dirty work.

"Mr. Lynch, I understand your daughter was an excellent student at Graland Country Day."

"She received top grades."

"Graland is quite a bit smaller than CU, isn't it?"

He smiled grimly. "Your point is?"

Jackie maintained her deferential tone.

"Simply that leaving home is more difficult than any of us care to remember."

"Perhaps."

"And even the most diligent parent can't possibly know everything a child is going through." Even if she went to a private school where he could watch her walk to class every day.

"There was nothing about my daughter I didn't know!"

Good. Let him bully *her.* Edna Massie was leaning forward.

"Perhaps you can tell us the first time Amy had her body pierced."

"Her ears? You'll have to ask her mother."

Did he really not know? Or was he daring Jackie to humiliate him with specifics?

"You mentioned Amy's job," she continued pleasantly. "Where did she work?"

"She was a waitress at a pizza parlor on the Hill."

"That must have been difficult, with a full load of classes."

"She didn't work the first semester."

He hadn't cut up her credit cards until she'd received two F's.

"Why did she take the job?"

"I—it was time Amy started taking responsibility."

"That have anything to do with her grades?"

"She knew the consequences of violating our rules!"

Our rules, or *his*? Prod Lynch, but don't let him lose control too soon.

"Did you have many rules?"

"I told you, Amy was a perfect child. . . ."

"Is that why you cut off her funds?"

"I was simply trying to teach my daughter the value of money!"

Every woman in the courtroom knew what that meant. And now it was time to show him and the jury that Bryan Lynch had not been in control of his daughter. Any more than he could control Jackie.

"Amy didn't tell you she'd quit her job at the pizza parlor, did she?"

"No."

"And she didn't tell you she'd moved out of the dorm?"

"She wouldn't dare—"

"Or that she was seeing a man named Derek King?"

"That son of a bitch who made her pose?"

So he *did* know what his daughter had been doing. But did he truly believe she'd been forced?

"When did you find out about Derek's video?"

"Last January—" He abruptly stopped.

The bondage flick had been on the Web for three months before Amy was abducted. Her father had known about it and done nothing to stop it. Was that when he and his wife went to their old friend and now Federal Judge Charlie Nesbit for advice? As Jackie paused to let the implications of Bryan Lynch's response register, she glanced at her client.

Ballard was leaning forward. He'd abandoned his legal pad and was making no attempt to disguise his contempt for Amy's father. Was it because the father pretended not to have known the true extent of his daughter's activities—or because he actually *had*?

Jackie had just one more question.

"Do you still think you knew your daughter?"

Thirty-Nine

"Amy Lynch was sheltered, wasn't she?"

The gallery was even more packed than it had been that morning. Over lunch word had gotten around that Phyllis Klein had stumbled with Bryan Lynch. Now she was in a rush to show evidence of motive: the bondage video that inspired Ballard's obsession with a beautiful coed. But after the outburst by Amy's father, the jury was more interested in seeing Derek King in the flesh. He, in turn, was playing to the crowd.

"Just answer the question," Klein said when he hesitated.

"Her daddy belonged to the Denver Country Club, if that's what you mean."

Klein wanted to get him off the stand fast, and Jackie could understand why. Derek King was fluid, elastic, so handsome he was almost pretty. But behind those guileless blue eyes something was missing. What could Amy have seen in him?

"Wouldn't you agree you were more experienced than Amy?"

"In what way?" He knew Klein was trying to paint him as the initiator.

"You were older, you'd worked with a rock band. . . ."

"I knew how to support myself."

"How long had the two of you been dating before you got Amy to pose?"

"Dating?"

Klein backpedaled. "When did you meet Amy?"

"Last fall."

"The video was your idea, wasn't it?"

"If that's what you want—"

"You were the one with the camera, correct?" Klein's clipped words emphasized her distaste for him.

"I paid for the film, too."

"You never met Bryan Lynch, did you?"

Derek bristled at Klein's reverent tone.

"Amy didn't—"

Klein gestured to her assistant, who'd exchanged his projector and screen for a VCR and display monitor. All eyes were on him as he assumed his position at the remote.

"Why did you make the film?"

"Kicks."

At a nod from Klein, the monitor sprang to life.

The opening shot was of an empty room with cinder-block walls and a metal bar suspended from the ceiling. The tape's quality was poor. From stage left entered a girl with brown hair, naked but for a blindfold, handcuffs, and a studded leather collar. A man in black with his back to the camera attached chains to the cuffs on her wrists. She made a show of struggling against them, thrashing about and whipping her head.

Beside her at the defense table, Glenn Ballard slowly exhaled when the video ended after ninety seconds. If he recognized the tape, he didn't show it.

"Are you the man in black?" Klein asked Derek.

"Yeah."

"And the girl was Amy Lynch."

"Um-hmm."

"Who did the filming?"

"I mounted the camera on a tripod."

"What did you do with the video?"

Derek shrugged. "Posted it on my website."

"No further questions."

As Bryan Lynch's surrogate, Klein had treated her witness like something to wipe off the bottom of her shoe. How would he respond to simple courtesy?

"Was Amy Lynch injured in any way in the filming of the video we just saw?"

Derek gave a derisive laugh. "Of course not!"

"You cared for her . . ."

"Of course I did!"

"And you were with her at Finnegan's Wake the night she disappeared."

"I left."

"Had you quarreled?"

"I guess."

"What was the quarrel about?"

"I don't remember."

But it was enough to establish that Amy might have been in a reckless mood that night. Jackie moved to the well of the court, draping one arm over the lectern as she continued in a conversational tone.

"Was Amy with anyone when you left?"

"It was crowded."

"No one in particular?"

Derek shook his head.

"Did you see Glenn Ballard at Finnegan's Wake that night?"

He hesitated but Jackie knew the answer. If it were otherwise, Klein would have brought it out on direct.

"He would have stood out?" she pressed.

"Guy that old? Sure."

The jury let out its breath.

"How did you meet Amy?"

Derek settled back in his chair. "Saw her on campus, thought she was cute."

"When was the video made?"

"Right before Christmas."

"Did Amy know you planned to post it on the Web?"

"Sure. She liked that."

Jackie moved a step closer to the witness stand. "Liked what?"

"The fact that guys would see her."

"Whose idea was it?"

"To make the video?" He hesitated just long enough to give his answer credibility. "Amy's. She had a great little body and she liked showing it off."

But Derek was holding back. Had Amy done more than pose?

"Was that the only footage of Amy on your website?"

"No," he admitted. "But she wore clothes in the stills."

"Why?"

"They were shots of her at work and on campus, doing stuff a coed normally does. It's a bigger turn-on that way."

"Weren't you concerned about her safety?"

"Safety?" Derek said. "From who?"

"Guys surfing the Web, trying to meet her in person."

"There was no way to identify her, unless you already knew her. That's why she wore the blindfold in the raw stuff."

"Did any guys ever contact her?"

"No."

So much for Klein's claim that Ballard stalked Amy after seeing her on the Web.

"Wasn't she concerned about her family finding out?"

Derek leaned forward.

"Amy would have liked it just fine if her daddy knew!"

So Klein's victim not only held the whip: she'd cracked it at her father.

Hello, reasonable doubt.

Forty

Phyllis Klein had spent half an hour identifying a single strand of Amy Lynch's hair. When Jackie rose to cross-examine the police technician, she had just one question.

"Were any of the hairs or fibers found at the cabin linked to Judge Ballard?"

"No."

"The witness may be excused."

On this third morning of trial, the prosecutor had summoned a battalion of forensics experts. Now the cabin's age and rustic setting were Jackie's ally. No matter how thorough they were, there was no way the Boulder cops could trap and catalog every bit of dust and animal hair in that hunting shack. From each expert there was only one thing she wanted to know.

"Were Judge Ballard's fingerprints found anywhere in the cabin?"

"No."

When Klein exhausted her crime-scene investigators, she started down her B list. Jackie was content to hammer her single point.

"Was Judge Ballard seen anywhere in the vicinity of the cabin in March of this year?" she asked the woman who said she saw his SUV in January.

"No."

"February?"

Edna Massie and the biscuit baker exchanged a knowing look. Anticipating Jackie's questions was becoming a sport with the jurors. The next witness was the Boulder County toxicologist who'd analyzed the dog tranquilizer seized from Ballard's medicine cabinet and run the tox screen on Amy after she stumbled from the woods.

"Any evidence Amy Lynch ingested ketamine at the time she was abducted?"

"No."

Next witness.

"Other than his failure to take the time and effort to file a five-page written report, do you have any reason to believe Judge Ballard's handcuffs did not disappear from his chambers months before Amy Lynch's abduction?"

"No."

The fry cook shook his head in disgust.

When the emergency room physician took the stand after lunch, the jury perked up. This time Jackie had two questions.

"Was there any evidence that Amy Lynch was sexually assaulted?"

"No."

"Did you recover any evidence linking Amy to her attacker?"

"No."

The postlunch torpor that beset any trial, the barrage of incontrovertible forensic testimony, and the predictability of her own cross were lulling Jackie into a dangerous complacency. By the time Klein called her last witness, she had to pinch herself to stay awake. Jerome Bettendorf's appearance did nothing to alert her. In his open-collared shirt with a plastic ink guard in the breast pocket, he looked like the kind of guy you'd go bird-watching with.

"Dr. Bettendorf, tell the jury your profession."

"The past twenty years I've been employed by the Colorado Bureau of Investigation."

Klein's timing was flawless. With the state crime lab's videographer at the trigger, she would fire her smoking gun just before court adjourned for the day. As the prosecutor ran Bettendorf through his paces, Jackie watched the jurors. Holland's paunch strained against his belt as he leaned forward in his chair, and Jasick had uncrossed his arms. She was in worse trouble than she'd thought.

"—FBI fellowship in Quantico, Virginia . . ."

Bettendorf recounted his thirty years of training in photographic interpretation in an easy drawl, glossing over his participation in a number of federal programs whose acronyms translated into even less intelligible mandates. Had any of those boondoggles won the Golden Fleece Award—or were they protected by the National Security Act? Regardless of whether he'd served his country as Casper the friendly spook, the jury was entranced by Bettendorf's aw-shucks demeanor and rock-solid CV. Even Klein seemed to have trouble refraining from calling him Jerry.

"And you've analyzed the video the jury is about to see?"

Over the noon recess, Klein's assistant had moved the TV monitor to the left of the jury box. Now he wheeled it front and center.

"I certainly have."

"And do you have an opinion as to its authenticity?"

"I certainly do."

"And what *is* your opinion?"

Bettendorf turned to the jurors with an expression of mild regret.

"The videotape you're about to see is authentic. Moreover, it is an accurate representation of the crime scene."

"And what's the basis for your opinion?"

"The absence of any evidence of tampering."

"Tampering?" Klein frowned as if that thought had never crossed her mind.

"When you analyze a photograph to see whether it's been faked, you look for a number of things. The same general principles apply to images on videotape." He leaned back comfortably in his chair. "Number one is light and shadow. Shadows have to fall in the same direction and be consistent with the source of light and the size and shape of the object. . . ."

With the TV monitor assuming the psychological dimensions of a forty-foot screen, Klein was not simply building the suspense. She was also making a shrewd trade-off. The cabin video was less than ninety seconds long and each time it was played its shock value diminished. Bettendorf was setting the stage at no sacrifice to the drama.

"—scale and depth of field. Objects closer to the camera should appear larger and focus should vary with distance. In other words, if an object in the foreground is in perfect focus and those at a distance are too, something's out of whack. Naturally we look for crop lines and inconsistent tones. Consistency between action and reaction—"

"What about the quality of the footage?" Klein was anticipating discrepancies. "If part of a tape is jerky and the remainder smooth, does that mean it was doctored?"

"Not at all. Handheld shots are always jerkier than when the camera is mounted on a tripod. The same photographer might start out holding the camera as he moves—for instance, panning to take in a larger scene—and then use a tripod for close-in shots." He paused for a meaningful look at the jury. "Perhaps even of himself."

A sharp point, and an objection would only have driven the point deeper.

Klein signaled her assistant and the video began to roll.

Long shots of the clearing, the slow pan to the cabin door . . . Holland was frowning but Jasick was fascinated—this was livelier than what went on in his lab. When Amy Lynch made her appearance, the baker's jaw dropped, and as the man in black turned to face his audience, you could have heard Edna Massie's teeth click. Only the fry cook appeared bored.

The screen went blank and a dozen pairs of eyes turned to the defense table. Ballard stared straight ahead and Jackie slowly released her breath.

"Your witness," Phyllis Klein said with a triumphant smile. She glanced at the clock, as if noticing the hour for the first time. "Your Honor, I had no idea it was so late. Perhaps we'd best adjourn."

Jackie jumped up. Screw the disadvantage of recessing in the middle of her cross; she wasn't about to let Edna Massie go home with those images seared into her brain. "Your Honor, it's not quite five. I can speed things up by starting now."

"Very well. But make it brief."

Striding to the lectern, Jackie pinned Bettendorf with her most disarming smile.

"You didn't shoot that video yourself, did you?"

"No." His grin matched hers. "Of course not."

"And you weren't present when it was shot, were you?"

"No."

"You didn't visit the cabin until—how many days after Ms. Lynch was found?"

"Five."

"Yet you're certain it accurately depicts a crime scene." Jackie hesitated. "Why, you don't even know whether the tape we just saw is a copy, do you?"

"A copy?" Spreading his hands in a gesture of confusion, Bettendorf looked to the jury. The baker's encouraging nod confirmed points were awarded for candor. "No, I suppose that's right."

Pitts glanced at the clock and Jackie cast about for another question. Eager to cement his image as an expert with no ax to grind, Bettendorf made his first blunder.

"I can't even tell you whether that tape was digitized."

"Digitized?"

Competence restored, Bettendorf settled back in the stand.

"A process of converting images into digital data. What we call pixels."

"Pixies?" Jackie had no idea what he was talking about, but the longer he kept talking, the faster the video faded.

"An abbreviation of 'picture element.' Once they're recorded digitally on a disk, they can be manipulated singly or in groups and reassembled in a different form. We call that compositing."

It sounded suspiciously like the way Jackie's own brain worked.

"The resulting image is seamless." Bettendorf was proud as a new parent.

Klein interrupted their love fest.

"Your Honor, this is beyond the scope of my direct."

"The witness opened the door," Jackie replied. Pitts nodded and she continued. "If it's seamless, how can you tell if compositing has occurred?"

"Let's take an example." He glanced around the courtroom and stopped at the crystal vase on Pitts's bench. "See how that bowl reflects the judge's bow tie?" Red and blue refracted off the cut glass like a kaleidoscope. "Let's say I shot footage without it and wanted to dress things up by adding it later. From the way the light falls, you'd expect to see the tie reflected in the glass. The fact that there's no reflection tells you the vase wasn't in the original scene. Of course, it's a lot trickier to composite moving figures. Every action creates an equal and opposite reaction."

"Do you mean to tell me—"

Pitts cleared his throat.

"Whatever Mr. Bettendorf means, he'll have to save it for tomorrow." Right hand fiddling with his tie, he banged his gavel with the left. "Court adjourned."

Jackie punched the stop button just as the cabin door came into view.

"God Almighty!" Pilar groaned. Searching in vain for the slightest detail that might be out of place, they'd replayed their copy of the videotape more times than she could count. "Can't you give it a rest? We have to be in court tomorrow at eight."

"How long was that?" Jackie replied, pouring herself the last of the coffee. "Forty-five seconds?"

"I'm not timing it again! What you need is a good meal, not caffeine. You're already wired tight as a—"

"Why waste half the footage on the exterior of the cabin?"

"Like in a documentary—to frame the action. Or it could be because it's his lair. And who knows? Maybe Ballard hated his uncle." Pilar shook her head. "Klein may be slow but she ain't stupid. What if her expert's setting you up?"

"I've known a hundred Jerry Bettendorfs. He works full-time for the CBI—he's volunteering to help the prosecution so he can feather his own nest as a consultant when he retires. And even a smart DA can get blindsided by a witness. Once Phyllis knew we couldn't call an expert, she had no reason to prep Bettendorf beyond the basics. She couldn't foresee him opening the door." Jackie forwarded the tape to where Ballard reached out to stroke Amy's arm. "Why so few frames of him with Amy?"

"Aren't those enough? He's pawing her, for God's sake! Look at the revulsion on the poor girl's face."

"Think about what Bettendorf said." Jackie peered at the screen. "Watch the way the shadow falls."

"Again?"

The rafter was between the camera and the fireplace, and although neither the fireplace nor the rafter was in the frame, the earlier footage showed the hearth had been lit. Although Amy was primarily lit from behind, late afternoon light also filtered through the window on the west side of the cabin. As Ballard approached Amy, it cast a shadow on the left side of his face, his left hand, and Amy's right arm. Amy flinched through the hood, her neck in shadow and jaw in sharp relief.

"The light's falling from the right direction," Pilar said. "And remember what Bettendorf said about action and reaction? Ballard reaches for Amy and she flinches." She grabbed her purse. "I'm taking you to dinner. Then we're going back to your place and pick out what you're wearing to court tomorrow. We'll set out your lipstick and shoes, dump your Grape-Nuts in a bowl, and plug in Mr. Coffee for the morning—"

"Why end the tape there?"

Pilar sighed.

"Didn't you say Ballard's a control freak? Maybe the point was capturing Amy's fear. And the camera was mounted. Maybe the angle prevented him from filming the rest."

Jackie forwarded to the frame where Ballard turned to the camera. That startled quality—where had she seen it? His quick recovery of poise . . .

"Forget dinner."

"Jackie, you know how you get when you don't—"

"I want every scrap of footage of Glenn Ballard."

"Tonight?"

"Start with your sources in the local newsrooms. Find me tape of every speech he's made, every press conference, each time he opened his mouth in public."

"But, Jackie—"

"I might not be able to identify who framed him, but maybe we can show how."

Forty-One

When Jerry Bettendorf resumed the stand the following morning, Jackie picked up precisely where she had left off. Spook or not, in his wash pants and plaid short-sleeved shirt, Klein's expert was only too happy to provide a tutorial.

"Before we adjourned, you were telling us about digitization. Could you explain how that works?"

"Digital data is the only language a computer understands. When you convert an analog to pixels—those tiny electronic units I mentioned yesterday—you're sampling based on file size—"

"Hold on." The jury room's fructose-sweetened rice cakes and herbal tea were no substitute for caffeine and greasy doughnuts. Only Edna Massie seemed awake. "What's an analog?"

"An analog device has infinite resolution." He tried to make it even simpler. "Just think of it as the original object. When the object is scanned—digitized—it's converted to computer language on your hard drive. In the process, massive amounts of information are lost. Once you digitize a file, you can never reanalog."

And once you opened the spigot, how did you shut it off? Jackie caught Pilar's eye. Her investigator drew a line across her throat to signify that the witness was boring them to death. She'd spent half the night shaking down sources for videotape and was convinced this was a wild-goose chase. On the stand, Bettendorf cast for an analogy.

"You're a lawyer, you take notes." Jackie didn't have to look to know that the snicker from the second row came from Pilar. "And when you take notes, you're not transcribing verbatim what you hear. Instead, you use a form of shorthand. You try to capture what's important but the meaning changes slightly because nuances are lost."

Klein rose to object but thought the better of it.

Jackie had placed her in a box.

The jury was registering every tenth word and objecting would only pique their interest. Klein obviously didn't know where Bettendorf was going, but one thing was sure: he was *her* expert. The longer Jackie kept him on the stand with an aimless cross, the more credibility he acquired and Jackie lost. She certainly couldn't let the jury think she'd been sand-bagged by a member of her own team. But Jackie knew it was only a matter of moments before she would catch up.

"Digitization enables you to create a composite image," Bettendorf continued. "With the right tools, you can edit an image pixel by pixel and transform it into something else entirely."

Klein sprang to her feet.

"Your Honor, I object! Ms. Flowers's questions have nothing to do with the substance of the opinion this witness offered on direct."

"Where exactly are you going?" Pitts asked Jackie.

"I'm eliciting the foundation for a second opinion I'm going to ask Dr. Bettendorf to give." Aware that she was fishing with no assurance that Pilar would be able to dig up the bait, Jackie continued before the judge could slap her down. "Transforming straw into gold—that sounds like Rumpelstiltskin. I imagine it takes pretty fancy equipment."

"Not at all! The software program is like the cut-and-paste function on a word processor. All you really need are that and a scanner."

"Scanner?"

"It looks something like a photocopier—a flat bed with glass and a long fluorescent bulb. As I said before, the digital data goes directly from the scanner to the hard drive. Any flat object will work, from a still photo to the palm of your hand. If you want to scan a video, you pipe it into your computer by means of a capture card. The scanner isn't fast enough."

Out of the corner of her eye, Jackie saw Pilar glance at her pager and scurry from the courtroom. The jurors had stopped shifting in their seats—whether from interest or having lapsed into comas was anyone's guess. Time to turn up the heat.

"We were talking about compositing images. Have you done that yourself?"

Bettendorf chuckled sheepishly.

"Actually, it's a hobby of mine."

She would never have guessed.

"Tell us what sorts of things you do."

"Well, it started with family photos. My brother-in-law has a mole on his left cheek and for his birthday two years ago, I cut it out." The biscuit baker winced and Bettendorf quickly added, "From the photograph, of course. A simple matter."

Holland suddenly woke up.

"Then I thought it would be fun to give my German shepherd green eyes. After that I changed the color of my wife's blouse." He blushed with guilty pleasure. "She *hates* magenta. Last August we had a reunion and I painted my great-aunt in—she's been dead for twenty years—and my mother-in-law out. That one didn't go over so big."

Klein cut the laughter short. "We're all fascinated by the witness's hobby—"

"Ms. Flowers, what's the relevance?" Pitts demanded.

"Mr. Bettendorf testified on direct that the prosecution's video was authentic. He based his opinion on the absence of any signs of tampering. I'm simply exploring one way in which tampering might occur."

"We've gotten the point. Move on."

Pilar was scribbling something on a legal pad. When she passed the message to Ballard, he stared at it and frowned. Jackie struggled to remember where she'd left off. Tampering . . . "Is it possible to combine images from different sources?"

"Well, sure. The problem is making them look like they belong together."

Ballard tried to pass the pad back to Pilar, but she gestured for him to show it to Jackie. With a sickening familiarity, Jackie's mind went blank for the second time in three days.

"Ms. Flowers?" Pitts asked.

She reached into her jacket for her moss agate. But in her haste that morning she'd grabbed the first thing that came to hand. A cobalt blue rayon dress with no pockets.

Think, think, *think*.

Pilar lifted her hand to her mouth and pantomimed.

Facing the lectern, Jackie launched into a coughing fit.

"Do you need water?" On the eve of retirement, the last thing Marlin Pitts wanted was a Denver lawyer having a stroke in his courtroom in full view of the national press.

Nodding gratefully, Jackie returned to the defense table and poured herself a cup from the plastic pitcher. Pilar leaned over the rail and whispered in Ballard's ear. Jackie sipped the water slowly, patting her client's arm reassuringly.

"What did Pilar say?" she asked in a low voice.

"I didn't quite understand. Something about a press conference."

"Ms. Flowers?" Pitts glanced from Jackie to the clock, and back again. Klein was suspicious but Jackie didn't care. She coughed again for good measure.

"Are you all right? Shall I call a brief recess?"

"Thank you, Your Honor."

"Haven't seen you pull that in ten years," Pilar whispered as the jury filed out.

"It's been that long since my own investigator screwed up my cross!" Pilar knew Jackie preferred wrath from a judge rather than his solicitude. "And the next time I let you talk me into buying a dress, it damn well better have pockets."

"Come on, it was a favor!" Pilar said. "Pitts was about to cut you off at the knees. Besides, I got the goods."

Jackie was in no mood for games.

"What's that about a press conference?"

"My contact at Channel Seven came through. They're compiling clips of Ballard. We'll have them tonight."

"Mr. Bettendorf," Jackie resumed five minutes later, "you said you could paint one person into a photograph and another out. Your deceased great-aunt, as I recall, stepped in for your mother-in-law at a family reunion?"

Jerry Bettendorf was enjoying his sojourn on the stand. How pliable would he remain? But Jackie's biggest concern was that she was betting the farm on footage she hadn't yet seen and that might not exist.

"The art is in making the photo look like it was really shot that way. You're trying to fool the eye."

"And you can do the same thing with video?"

"The shorter the better, of course. After thirty seconds the compositing begins to show."

"Particularly if you were trying to coordinate the movements of two people?"

"Yes."

"The process sounds quite complicated." His diffident shrug invited Jackie to go a step further. "It must require a great deal of expertise."

"Not with the technology available today. Five years ago you needed half a million dollars' worth of equipment to pull it off. Now anyone can do it on a home computer for a grand."

Klein looked like she wanted to object, but the judge's solicitude for Jackie's health was too fresh.

"There must be practical limits to what you can accomplish."

Bettendorf shook his head emphatically.

"Not with digitization. If it's skillfully done, the human eye can't tell the difference."

Edna Massie had been with Jackie all along; now the other jurors were awakening. Had the bailiff substituted coffee for herbal tea on their last break?

"Do the elements have to come from the same source?"

"You mean, can you composite film with videotape? Sure."

"How about stuff downloaded from the Web?"

"Depends on how good you want it to look." He smiled apologetically at the jury. "I don't want to get too technical here, but whenever you download or digitize, you end up with a smaller file. That means information is lost. The clarity might be fine but when you blow it up it pixilates—becomes blurrier. If you displayed it on a small screen"—his eyes wandered to the TV monitor, which was still near the jury box—"the resolution would tighten and the image would look better."

"So one way to tell whether an image has been digitized, or even composited, might be to blow it up?"

Bettendorf looked away. "Well, I don't know."

Jackie backed off.

"Let's say you wanted to combine images from a number of sources and wanted the final product to resemble a home video. What steps would you take?"

Klein was on her feet.

"What steps he might take are neither here nor there. My witness"—she was finally reclaiming Bettendorf as her own—"and this jury have indulged Ms. Flowers long enough. I ask you to put a stop to this now."

Pitts surveyed his jurors. They were not just alive, but warm. And they wanted to hear the answer. "You'll have your chance on redirect. Restate your question, Ms. Flowers, and be specific."

Jackie turned to Bettendorf.

"Let's say you wanted to make a home movie of your great-aunt and your mother-in-law. Your great-aunt has unfortunately passed on—"

"She and my mother-in-law couldn't stand each other anyway!"

"—and all that's left is a video of her on your cousin's website. Your mother-in-law, on the other hand, is memorialized in home movies, one of which was shot at a picnic. You want to heal the family rift by showing your mother-in-law passing your great-aunt the potato salad. Is that possible to do?"

Bettendorf responded without missing a beat.

"I'd download my aunt over my modem into my computer and paste her into my mother-in-law's picnic. The key to pulling it off would be the potato salad sequence. If there's already footage of my mother-in-law passing the bowl to someone else, I could edit that person out and my aunt in. Same with my aunt; if the clip from the Web shows her reaching for an object of the right size, it'd be child's play. Worst-case scenario, I could get footage of two other gals passing a bowl—assuming they were approximately the right ages—track their motions with my editing software, and paste in my aunt's and mother-in-law's heads. The key is to keep the composited sequence short. Certainly no longer than thirty seconds."

The fry cook looked confused.

"Why is that?" Jackie asked.

"No matter how lucky you are, it's almost impossible to get the heads to rotate the right way. The digitization and compositing are technologically undetectable; the giveaways are tiny details that don't jibe."

"Let's make it tougher. The final product must be not only seamless, but also look like it was recorded on an old camcorder."

"Piece of cake," Bettendorf said. "It's always easier to destroy quality than to improve it. All you have to do is blur or shake the final image to make it look fuzzy. By the time I got through with it, it might as well have been shot by my great-aunt!"

Jackie glanced at the clock. Not quite noon.

"The other day Ms. Klein asked about the quality of a tape. You said if one segment is jerky and the remainder smooth, it doesn't necessarily indicate tampering. But if you wanted to composite sequences created by different handheld cameras—"

"—they'd be almost impossible to match."

"Why?"

"Unless the camera's mounted to something stationary, like a tripod, the image wavers because your hand can't help but move. The jerkiness is random and chaotic; no two hands shake the same way."

"So if you had two pieces of tape to combine, one of which was shot by a handheld camera—"

"—you'd stage the sequence so it made sense for the camera to be stationary in the second part. At least, that's what *I* would do."

And whoever had fabricated the cabin videotape.

As Jasick locked eyes with Jackie, she knew the point had not been lost. Nor was Klein oblivious to its significance.

"There's no evidence that happened here!"

"No one said it did," Jackie replied. "Yet."

Pitts took the easy way out.

"Recess until one o'clock."

"Nice work, Counselor."

Jackie looked up.

From Klein the compliment was anything but sincere.

"He was *your* witness."

"And I'm looking forward to returning the favor with yours." Klein smiled tightly at Ballard, who was watching closely. "Have you decided to take the stand?"

"You'll be notified if and when that decision is made," Jackie said.

"Surely your client can make his own decisions." Klein's eyes were unnaturally bright as they impaled Ballard. "How about it, Judge—do you walk the walk? You could stand on your Fifth Amendment right. But if I were falsely accused, I know what *I'd* do."

Ballard was watching her with the same dispassion he showed the attorneys in his court. But there was a coiled quality to his watchfulness, and Jackie tugged at his arm.

"Ignore her, Glenn."

"And what will your buddies in the media think if you don't testify? 'The only thing wrong with our jury system is we don't have enough faith in it. . . .'"

"She's goading you," Jackie warned.

"I'm well aware of my constitutional rights, Ms. Klein." Deep in his eyes something flickered. "I fully intend to testify on my own behalf."

Jackie dug her nails into his sleeve. Things had been going too well. "That decision is still—"

"In this instance, Ms. Flowers doesn't speak for me."

Jackie dropped his arm. Phyllis was so intent on Ballard she didn't even notice.

"I'll look forward to that, Your Honor. And you can look forward to something in return."

"What might that be?" Jackie asked.

Phyllis ignored her.

"This is your life, Glenn Ballard. Tune in and find out."

Klein left the courtroom.

"What was she talking about? Come on, Glenn. Don't make me send Pilar out to beat the bushes."

He was staring after Klein.

"Are you out of your mind?" she said. "What were you doing, telling her you're taking the stand? We haven't decided—"

"*We,* Counselor?" Ballard turned to her at last. "As I recall, that's the client's decision. And I just made it."

"You didn't make it—you let the prosecutor play on your ego and your pride."

"Are you sure keeping me off isn't a matter of *your* ego and pride? Putting a client on the stand takes more than guts. It requires a level of skill—"

"If you don't respect my judgment or my abilities, why did you hire me?"

"I told you, you came highly—"

"Did you think you could dominate me?"

Ballard's lips twisted. On anyone else it might have been a smile.

"Dominate you?"

"Is that what this is about? Hire the student you flunked in law school because you think she'll jump when you crack the whip—"

"Were you even in my class?"

Could the decision that almost ended her career before it began have meant nothing to him?

"Calling balls and strikes was my responsibility as a law professor," he continued. "And it's my job as a judge."

Invisible. That's what she'd been to him.

Jackie stared at Glenn Ballard with his impeccable suit and silver hair. Ted Wolsky had paid for this man's hubris with his life.

How right Dennis Ross had been.

We're all guilty of something. It's just a matter of what.

She would settle Ted's account later.

"I can't stop you from taking the stand in your own defense. But I'll damn well do everything I can to win this case before you get that chance."

Forty-Two

Pitts adjourned in the early afternoon because the biscuit baker was expecting and "had the queasies." Jackie was grateful for the reprieve. She'd pushed Bettendorf as far as she could without solid evidence that the cabin video had been fabricated.

"What's going on between you and Ballard?" Pilar asked on the drive back to Denver. Having left the courtroom when Pitts called the recess, she'd missed the fireworks.

"Nothing." Jackie's head was pounding and she didn't have the energy to get into it.

"That gavel up his butt seemed even straighter than usual."

"When are you getting those clips?"

"I'm picking them up on the way home. Since this is your baby, I thought you might want to watch them tonight."

"Fine."

Short of a miracle that would give her another crack at Bettendorf, Jackie's cross-examination was over. In the morning Klein would rest her case and Jackie would have no choice but to move for a judgment of acquittal, which Pitts would never grant. Then she'd have to let Ballard take the stand.

"Cheer up," Pilar said. "At least the case will be over."

Jackie put off viewing Pilar's video until she'd eaten a can of soup and laid out her suit and makeup for the following day. Trials always seemed to trigger a string of bad days, when she had to force herself to eat and might show up for court in mismatched shoes or earrings if she didn't make herself stay on track. How she welcomed the weekend! Two days away from the client whose case she never should have taken. What had made her think she could defend a person she loathed?

Pilar's cassette contained five clips.

The two most recent showed Ballard being ambushed on the Lynch case. The others were interviews outside the courthouse after landmark rulings. In their own way, they revealed as much about Glenn Ballard as the cabin tape. As Jackie watched them, she wondered how such a promising jurist had allowed his life to spin so wildly out of control.

The first sequence had been taped shortly after Ballard was appointed to the federal bench. Jackie remembered rejoicing with the other Public Defenders when he'd closed Old Max. The ruling had made Ballard persona non grata at the state legislature, which was forced to appropriate tens of millions of dollars over the following decade to build a new maximum-security prison.

The second clip was recorded when he ordered the release of the head of a union who claimed he was being prosecuted in retaliation for leading his constituents in a crippling strike. It was fascinating to watch Ballard's evolution—the intellect shining through his brashness, his fearlessness in calling shots. But now it was impossible to see them as anything but the product of his own grandiosity. Was it ambition that made him so callous, so indifferent to the human values at stake? A funny thing about judges, Ted Wolsky had said. No matter which way they ruled, someone always got hurt.

The third segment had been shot six months earlier, when Ballard upheld the tax on Internet porn. Jackie watched her client's chin tilt imperiously in response to a reporter's question. He looked arrogant.

"The president just issued a statement opposing any tax on the Internet," the reporter said. "I quote, 'If pornographers also flourish, that's the price of a free society.' Are you concerned about the White House's opposition to your ruling?"

The camera zeroed in to catch the amusement on Ballard's lips.

"Not in the least. The president serves until the next election. I am appointed for life."

What was it about this particular segment that bothered her so much? Ballard's sense of his own power, a high-handedness bordering on omnipotence? No wonder he'd opposed her defending him on the basis of character. The very concept must have been unspeakably demeaning. She fast-forwarded to the most recent footage—a thirty-second clip of Ballard outside the federal courthouse after the ketamine was discovered.

"Judge Ballard, how will you defend this case?"

Tilt of the chin. Bemusement—who are you to question me?

"I was framed, it will all come out at trial. . . ."

His arrogance had cost them dearly. After that statement, Phyllis Klein had endorsed Jerry Bettendorf to authenticate the videotape.

As she brushed her teeth, Jackie stared at herself in the bathroom mirror.

You are going to lose this case.

And she was also going to lose her ticket out of the dugout she'd holed up in since she'd left the Public Defender's office. She could kiss the opportunity to join that litigation boutique good-bye. How long would it take Phyllis Klein to resurrect the grand jury leak? How long before Pilar received an offer she couldn't refuse—from the boutique or from Kellogg & Kemp?

After the hell he'd subjected her to in law school, why did Ballard have to come to *her*?

Jackie flung down her toothbrush and climbed into bed.

An hour later she was still awake. She switched on her bedside lamp and padded to the VCR. Fast-forwarding, she stopped at the press conference on Internet porn.

"Are you concerned about the White House's opposition to your ruling?"

Ballard's chin jerked in surprise, then amusement crossed his lips.

"Not in the least. The president serves until the next election. I am appointed for life. . . ."

Jackie froze the frame. He'd turned to face the camera but overshot the mark. Ballard was looking to the right of the lens, at a forty-five-degree angle. He was searching for the reporter who'd called out the question.

The bastard *had* been framed.

She reached for her phone and blindly punched the speed dial.

"I need you to go to Craig."

"Craig?" Pilar's voice was blurred. "What do we need him for?"

"Not Craig, the lawyer. The ranch where Ballard was raised."

"That's two hundred miles from here!"

"Take the weekend if you have to. Talk to the foreman, Ballard's childhood friends. . . . Turn over every rock. I'll find a way to keep him off the stand until you report back."

"How will you get to court?"

"Don't worry about me. This case ain't over yet."

Forty-Three

Piece of cake, Jackie told herself at five-thirty the following morning as she climbed into her Corolla. How much traffic could there be at that hour? She certainly wasn't going to ask her client for a lift. *Whoom.*

A sixteen-wheeler whizzed past as Jackie tried to merge onto I-25. She stomped on a pedal and the pickup truck behind her skidded as the driver slammed on his brakes. He flipped her off and passed on the right. She unclenched her hands. All she had to worry about was getting onto the Boulder turnpike. That was much more productive than thinking about what lay ahead of her in court.

Driving in the right lane at fifty miles an hour, she tried to remember the directions Pilar had given her. Something about the entrance being on the wrong side of the road. Despite her anxiety that she would miss the turnoff, now that she was actually on the highway, she began to relax. Eyes straight ahead—that much she remembered. She had plenty of time, and at the rate she was going there was no risk of catching up to the cars ahead of her. The ones that pulled up behind her moved out of her lane. She had the road virtually to herself—was that the trick?

Be-eep!

Jackie floored the accelerator and lurched into the center of I-25 as a four-wheel-drive threatened to mount the Corolla's trunk. It was a good thing she did, because straight ahead loomed a familiar overpass. The only problem was which side of the road was the exit ramp on? Right, left—directions were meaningless and signs impossible to read. Frantically trying to recall how Pilar turned, she took a chance and whipped the wheel to the left. Moments later she was on the turnpike. Just a highway after all—not like driving in the mountains.

In the slow lane once again, she patted Pilar's videocassette on the passenger seat beside her. Pilar had left her cell phone in Jackie's mailbox before setting out for Craig before dawn and would be checking in at noon. If Marlin Pitts allowed the defense a little rope, it might be just enough to keep Glenn Ballard from being hanged.

When Pitts called his court to order, Jerry Bettendorf resumed the stand. Phyllis Klein rose for redirect but before she could speak, Jackie stepped to the lectern.

"I haven't finished my cross, Your Honor."

Pitts glanced at the clock. He had hoped to wrap up the prosecution's case so he could deny the defense's traditional motion for acquittal before lunch. On the weekends he liked to give his juries an early break.

"How much more do you have?"

"This will take no time at all." Jackie gestured to the bailiff, who wheeled out a second TV monitor to join the first one in front of the jury box. "If Ms. Klein would be kind enough to lend me her assistant?"

Even more satisfying than drafting the judge's staff was appropriating her opponent's. Eager to play some role—*any* role, even the defense attorney's gofer—Klein's second-in-command jumped up before his boss could protest. Popping a tape in the second VCR, Jackie handed him the control.

"Your Honor," Klein said, "Ms. Flowers has no right to waste this court's—"

"A three-minute demonstration. Ms. Klein can time it." Jackie beckoned to Bettendorf with a friendly smile. "Why don't you join us?" He climbed down from the stand and stood by one of the monitors. Strike three for the prosecution—Klein's own expert was now on Jackie's team. With every eye in the courtroom on her, Jackie aimed her remote at the first monitor.

Trees and a small log structure went by in a blur, a door whipped open, and the camera made a mad circuit of rough-hewn walls. The moment the girl in chains appeared, Jackie froze the cabin tape.

"Watch this." Jackie nodded to Klein's assistant. "Fast-forward until I tell you to stop." The second monitor came alive.

Cinder-block walls, steel frame, chains . . . a naked girl twisted on the balls of her feet.

Derek King's porno tape. A clean sweep for Jackie—she was using Klein's key evidence against her.

Frame by frame Jackie and Klein's assistant advanced their respective tapes. Twist to the left, slack jaw, pull to the right, grimace, then a look of heartrending vulnerability as the girl sensed the approach of a figure in black. The only difference was that in Derek's tape Amy wore a blindfold instead of a hood. And now the fuzziness of the cabin video seemed contrived. When the unidentified man extended his left hand to stroke Amy's arm on both monitors, the jury flinched along with her.

Jackie ejected Derek King's video. As she retrieved a third cassette from her briefcase, Klein jumped up.

"If you think I'm going to accommodate Ms. Flowers's theatrics one moment longer . . . Your Honor, she hasn't even introduced whatever that is!"

"Network footage of Ms. Klein's favorite video star. If you like, I can have a producer from Channel Seven here to authenticate it in"—fingers crossed lest her bluff be called, Jackie pretended to consult the courtroom clock—"oh, about ninety minutes. Of course, with Friday traffic . . ."

Pitts glared at Klein. Afraid to push her rapidly diminishing luck, the prosecutor threw up her hands in exasperation. Jackie fast-forwarded to the Internet press conference. When she reached the frame where Ballard tilted his chin in response to the reporter's question, without being asked, Klein's assistant advanced the cabin tape to the precise moment where Ballard turned to face his audience. The arrogant twist to his lips was as unmistakable as the fact that in searching out his interrogator, he rotated past the camera an extra quarter turn to the right.

Jackie gave the jury a moment to catch its breath. Bettendorf's reflexive smile had long since dimmed to something even less readable. Retrieving the remote from Klein's assistant, she rewound the cabin video to the moment Amy Lynch recoiled as she sensed the man approach.

"I promised Ms. Klein we'd keep this short." Jackie turned to Bettendorf. "When the tape begins to play, would you time it to the end?"

Recoil, two steps forward, reach, draw back, touch, stroke, revulsion.

"How long was that sequence?"

"Twenty-two seconds."

"Well within the thirty seconds after which you said compositing would start to show . . . Thank you, Dr. Bettendorf. You can return to the stand."

As Klein rose to rehabilitate her fallen star, her cheeks were the color of raw meat. Her first job was to cover her own ass with the jury.

"*Dr.* Bettendorf"—no more "Jerry" for her!—"you said nothing about digitization in your report. Did you?"

"That is correct."

"You have no reason to believe the videotape of Glenn Ballard abusing Amy Lynch was fabricated, do you?"

"Well, I—"

"Much less is there any way to prove any portion of it could have been derived from either of Ms. Flowers's clips."

"Well—"

"There isn't, is there?"

"Nooo."

Was he relishing Klein's discomfort? Having been kept in the dark about Derek King's videotape, Bettendorf was not about to fall on his sword for the prosecutor. But if her star witness's equivocation was meant to cement his new role as Jackie's straight man, Klein was having none of it. She continued firing questions at him with the precision of a sniper.

"Nor that the tape of Glenn Ballard abusing Amy Lynch was composited at all?"

"No."

"Nor that parts of that tape were shot at any time or place other than they purported to be?"

"No."

"And your opinion as to the authenticity of that tape remains unchanged?"

The last question carried a clear warning. Bettendorf did the math. Seven years until retirement, followed by a second career as a consultant. Who was the more likely source of referrals—the District Attorneys Council or a ragtag bunch of criminal defense lawyers? His résumé already included an impressive list of cases in which he'd testified, but smart kids were entering the field every day.

"I have no basis for changing it."

"And whether the tape could have been fabricated is sheer speculation?"

Bettendorf fixed his persecutor with a defiant stare. That he was going along with her didn't mean he had to like it.

"That is correct."

Klein turned to the judge. "Your Honor, I ask you to instruct the jury to disregard Dr. Bettendorf's earlier testimony as to potential fabrication of the tape."

What did it matter which way Pitts ruled? If a picture was worth a thousand words, the similarities among the three videos were worth ten thousand backpedaling opinions. But the judge had a nasty surprise of his own.

"I'll do more than that, Ms. Klein. Unless Ms. Flowers identifies the individual responsible or proves that the video could not have been made at the time of Ms. Lynch's abduction, I will forbid her from arguing even the possibility of fabrication to the jury."

He banged his gavel.

"Court adjourned until one P.M."

Forty-Four

As soon as Pitts left the bench, Ballard exited the courtroom by the back door. He was furious—that much was clear. Jackie couldn't entirely blame him. Despite his insistence that he'd been framed, juxtaposing the cabin tape, a bondage flick featuring Amy Lynch, and footage of his press conference must have been excruciating. Every second his face was on the monitor was a fresh blow to his dignity. And Pitts's ruling had been the last straw. As Jackie sat in the empty jury room awaiting Pilar's call, she fully expected a motion demanding her removal from the case by the time court reconvened. Not that that wouldn't be preferable to putting Ballard on the stand.

"Jackie?" Pilar's voice was tinny. "How'd it go?"

"I got to the end of my limb and Phyllis sawed it off." She briefly recounted the morning's events. "Any luck in Craig?"

"That depends . . . Like you suggested, I've been turning over rocks. This being the Western Slope, there's the usual stories about things you can do with sheep—"

"Cut the crap. Does anybody remember him?"

"A federal judge?" Pilar laughed. "Oh, yeah."

"When he was a boy?"

"Luckily for us, Glenn Ballard stood out. There's at least one girl who remembers him real well."

"Did you speak to her directly?"

"Next best thing—her dad. Who just happens to be the brother of the foreman at Ballard's father's ranch. The *former* foreman, I should say. He no longer works—"

"Get to the point!"

"You're not going to like this."

What Pilar could discover in a matter of hours, Phyllis Klein had undoubtedly known for months. Jackie counted silently to three.

"There's nothing about this case to like. Just give it to me straight."

"When Ballard was twelve, he got into a thing with this girl."

"What sort of *thing*?"

"It was more like he was caught with her."

Jackie bit back a giggle. "All kids that age experiment. What were they doing, playing doctor?"

"More like pediatrician. The girl was eight."

"A ranch is an isolated environment." Jackie was already trying to find a way to deal with this. "I don't suppose there were too many girls his age—"

"Not ones small enough to tie up."

"Tie up?"

"Ballard trussed her like a hog. He lured her to a shed where no one could see them. Luckily they found her before he could do anything else."

He'd roped his first calf at eight. At least he hadn't branded her.

"Kids who grow up on a ranch are exposed to that stuff from the time they're born," Jackie tried. It sounded weak to her own ears. "They act out what they see. I'm sure it was just a game."

"Nobody thought so back then. The girl was terrified and Ballard's father hushed it up by paying big and sending the boy east." Pilar hesitated. "I got the distinct impression it wasn't Ballard's first time."

Shit.

"Why didn't the FBI tumble to it when they vetted him?"

"Country folk look after their own. The matter was settled and they weren't about to air their dirty laundry to the feds."

"Then how did Klein find out?"

"She has her sources, I guess. . . . Want me to keep digging?"

"If there's anything worse, I'd rather not hear it. You might as well come home."

"I'll stay the night and drive back in the morning. Were you okay this morning on I-25?"

"Piece of cake."

Jackie already knew what Ballard would say. He'd deny the incident and accuse her of trying to bully him into staying off the stand. He'd be dead meat when Phyllis Klein opened her cross. No wonder Jackie's worst enemy had wanted this case!

"It's Friday afternoon," Pilar said. "The press have to file wrap-ups, and if I know Marlin Pitts, he'll find some way to recess early. Just hang in there till I get back."

What difference did a weekend make? Once Ballard took the stand and Klein hit him with his boyhood exploits, even the unlikely chance of a mistrial went out the window.

"Don't get too cocky on the Boulder turnpike, hear?" Pilar was saying. "It's the weekend. There's all kinds of jackasses on the road."

When court reconvened, the prosecution rested and Pitts sent the jury out. Jackie argued a futile motion for judgment of acquittal and Pitts made short work of denying it. By then it was late enough to dismiss the jurors for the weekend. Ballard left without saying good-bye, and Jackie dispiritedly packed up her files and the videocassette of her client's news clips.

The parking lot was almost empty. In this town of soy milk and unfiltered honey, justice operated on bankers' hours. Pitts and Klein could probably fit in an afternoon jog. Too bad it was clouding up . . .

"Miss Flowers?"

She was unlocking her car when Pitts's bailiff cornered her.

"I've been looking all over for you." The girl stopped to catch her breath. "The court reporter thought she saw you go into the jury room but it was empty."

"Did I forget something?"

"You have a message." She handed Jackie a yellow slip covered with chicken scratch. Jackie didn't even try to decipher it.

"What's wrong?"

"Do you know a Lily Myers?"

Jackie's heart stopped.

"Judge Pitts received a phone call from a camp in Steamboat Springs. They think it's meningitis."

"Meningitis?"

"It was apparently quite sudden. Is she a relative?"

More than family. Much more.

"I—have her parents been notified?"

Even as she asked, Jackie knew the answer. There was no way to reach Britt and Randy. They were in Chile, skiing or hiking a volcano.

"They said she asked for you."

The bailiff's words caromed in Jackie's head. Pilar had offered to drive her to visit Lily last weekend—why hadn't Jackie gone?

"What's the fastest route to Steamboat?"

"Well, you could go through Lyons to Estes Park," the bailiff said, "or back to Denver and I-70. But it's Friday afternoon, and the traffic—"

"Is there a quicker way?"

The bailiff thought a moment. "Left Hand Canyon."

"Left Hand?"

"It gets you to the Peak-to-Peak Highway, then into Estes Park. After that you take Trail Ridge Road through Rocky Mountain National Park to Grand Lake. Lyons would normally be faster, but—"

Left Hand was familiar.

"Peak-to-Peak to Estes Park, Trail Ridge Road." Jackie climbed behind the wheel of the Corolla. "Thanks for the advice."

"Want a map? The judge's secretary has an atlas at her desk."

What use was a map to her? Besides, she'd memorized the route. Left Hand, Estes Park, Trail Ridge Road. After that, stop and ask.

"You'll be fine," the bailiff assured her. "Just follow the signs."

Forty-Five

As Jackie left the Justice Center parking lot, the sun peeking through the clouds set the marigolds and zinnias aflame. At the cusp of the monsoon season, cool moisture riding off the Gulf Stream collided with the hot, dry air of the plains and caused mood swings as wild as the barometric fluctuations. Looking up, she saw a squadron of storm clouds converge on the last patch of blue. Large drops of rain began pelting her windshield.

Stopping to fill her gas tank, she replayed her last conversation with Lily. Jackie had phoned the ballet camp exactly one week ago.

"Homesick?" she'd asked.

"Nah. We have two hours of dance in the morning, and swimming and more ballet in the afternoon. The lake has canoes." Lily's voice had been curiously flat.

"Having fun?"

"I guess."

"What are the other girls like?" Not, have you made *friends*. That word was a hot button with Lily.

"Most of them know each other . . ."

Or if they didn't, they'd acted like they did from day one.

"How 'bout if I drive up tomorrow?"

"Parents' Day was Sunday." No reproach; in its place, a listlessness far more troubling. Why hadn't Jackie responded to the need in that small voice?

Think of something else, she told herself. Anything else. As she sped up Broadway, Ted's face came to her, but Jackie pushed him away. Time to pay him back later, once this trial was over . . . Glenn Ballard in the cabin tape. Maybe he hadn't been framed. We're all guilty, it's just a matter of . . . She tried to superimpose Ballard's head over the man in Derek King's videotape but saw Amy Lynch instead. Not in the cabin video, but the way she looked when she was found. The leather dog collar . . . That brought her back to a studded choker. And Lily.

Randy and Britt had driven to Steamboat on the eve of their departure for Chile; should Jackie have gone on Parents' Day instead? But *they*
were Lily's parents—her only real status was a friend. And what was it
the school psychologist had said? The child needed to *bond* and *separate*.
To and from whom wasn't clear. No wonder the kid was exhausted.

"What'll they do if Pilar and I show up," Jackie had growled into the
phone, "call the Routt County sheriff? Maybe we'll kidnap you. At least
for an ice cream cone."

Even Lily's giggle was halfhearted. She should have *gone*.

"I'm serious. Say the word and we'll be at your tent tomorrow."

"No! I don't want you to come."

"Why not, baby?"

"It's just—" She'd sounded like she was about to cry.

"What's wrong?"

"I have to do this myself!"

"Okay."

Jackie had thought she was putting Lily's needs ahead of her own.
But had she, really? With Ballard's trial approaching it had been all too
easy to defer the trip. And now she wondered if she'd misinterpreted
Lily's reluctance. Was that the first sign something was physically
wrong?

Passing the shoppette north of town, Jackie decided that overlooking the early symptoms of meningitis wasn't the only thing she'd
missed. Why hadn't she paid more attention when Pilar drove to Ballard's cabin? With relief she spotted a wide intersection that seemed
familiar. Left turn to Left Hand? She spun the steering wheel in the
direction of the mountains. The road began a gentle ascent.

It would be *okay*.

Within a half mile of Broadway, Jackie was in the country. In generous loops the blacktop wound past horses and stables. Expensive homes
perched on the hillside, a small valley opening below.

The guardrail sprang up out of nowhere.

Then a warning sign for a curve—a writhing snake that made her
stomach flip. Had that been there when Pilar drove? Aspen, pines, and
firs began to replace cottonwoods and the asphalt flattened out. A
sign displayed a leaping deer. How simple life would be if all signs
were pictures!

Like a flock of exotic birds, a band of cyclists in gaily colored jerseys came flying down the road. Lycra shorts and plastic helmets gleamed just before the clouds let loose. The downpour made the blacktop slick but they didn't seem to mind. Just as suddenly the asphalt was dry. Behind the wheel in the mountains, and in the rain—Pilar would never believe it. And Lily—

A black arrow leaped off a yellow sign.

With each twist and turn Jackie's briefcase in the passenger seat lurched and it was all she could do to keep the Corolla on the road. Queasiness overtook her as the rain once again returned. This vehicle is going nowhere without me, she thought, and that reminded her of Pilar's cardinal advice if—God forbid!—Jackie should ever find herself behind the wheel on an unfamiliar road.

Keep your eyes on the car ahead. You may not end up where you want to go, but at least you'll stay on the road.

What if there were no other cars?

Hugging the shoulder, Jackie eased off the gas.

Think of this as an adventure—like Lily going to ballet camp. Was that the turnoff to the cul-de-sac where those kids found Amy? And then she plunged down a roller coaster.

Steep gully on the driver's side, solid rock to her right. No shoulder, dense underbrush. The narrow two-lane at the bottom of the canyon was dark and winding and she could see only a hundred yards ahead.

Eyes on the poles at the edge of the road, stay between them and the double yellow line . . . Breathe deeply.

Suddenly the welcoming flash of taillights as the vehicle ahead of her braked for a curve. An older-model SUV with a flickering bulb in one of its brakelights. Rounding another bend, Jackie emerged in late-day sun. As the valley opened the SUV picked up speed and she accelerated to stay with its driver.

For the first time she was glad she'd chosen this route rather than driving through Lyons or returning to Denver to catch I-70. A road with no lettered signs, just a beginning and an end. And with the SUV to lead her, how could she get lost? The sun made the scrub oak glisten and the grass was tawny and seeded like ripening wheat. As Indian paintbrush and the red bark of chokecherries sprang up around isolated mailboxes, she finally loosened her grip on the wheel. When she came to the junk-yard that was the old mining town of Ward, she slowed to a crawl behind the SUV and her thoughts returned to Ballard's case.

Pitts had imposed an impossible burden: if the cabin videotape was fabricated, prove who did it or Phyllis Klein could rest her case. Had pinning the entire defense on deconstructing the video been a mistake? But what were the alternatives—counting on Ballard to wow the jurors with the force of his presence, or relying on reasonable doubt? Images tumbled through her brain. The hood—why the hood? White instead of black, utterly superfluous in light of the blindfold. She shook her head. Rather than focusing on something that didn't belong, perhaps she should be seeking the opposite. Something that should have been present but *wasn't . . .*

With a start, Jackie realized she was on a new road.

The Peak-to-Peak Highway was freshly surfaced and the SUV sped off. The lanes were wider, the yellow lines newly painted. A beat-up Audi took the SUV's place and Jackie stayed a prudent three car lengths behind. If she remembered correctly, this highway would take her all the way to Estes Park. Then Trail Ridge Road and on to Steamboat . . . The landscape began to change. The rock at the side of the road was no longer soft and crumbly. Here the mountains were cold and gray, sloughing off boulders like scales.

A girl in a dog collar.

Lily's face appeared and Jackie pushed it away. *Think of something else, anything . . .* Glenn Ballard with Amy Lynch. Was she an idiot to have believed him—especially after learning he'd logged on to Amy's image every Saturday night from January to March? Or was she ultimately so in love with her own theory about the video being composited that she'd blinded herself to the obvious?

In Glenn Ballard's court, justice was not simply blind. It was indifferent.

Until now the greatest injustice Jackie had personally suffered was being judged stupid or unfit. Now she realized there was an insult much worse: mattering so little as a human being that you were invisible. Wasn't that what Lily had been to the teacher who'd accused her of stealing her own idea? And wasn't that what Jackie herself had been to the client she'd sworn to save? Maybe Ballard deserved to go down in flames. Maybe he wanted that himself.

That day the search warrant was executed at his chambers—when the detectives knew where to look—Ballard hadn't seemed surprised. Because he'd known he was being framed? If so, why hadn't he let her call their own expert? And he must realize how badly the childhood incident with the girl at the ranch would play. Why was he so intent on taking the stand?

Ballard's pride would destroy him.

Was this trial the vehicle for him to self-destruct?

A sign with a numeral and the Colorado flag confirmed that Jackie was on the right road, or at least heading to a place where other people wanted to go. The clouds were descending like a pillow of smoke and twilight would soon follow. Stuck behind a camper with a flatland plate—no mountains or green—and emboldened by the smooth asphalt, she accelerated and passed.

Pretty gutsy.

Watching the camper shrink in her rearview mirror pumped her up and Jackie stayed in the left lane until the unbroken yellow line warned her the passing zone had ended. She caught up to a four-wheel-drive that sped up and left her in the dust. The abrupt changes in speed revived her nausea. She tried to summon Lily but saw instead a girl with arms held over her head by chains. When she blinked Amy Lynch away a barrage of images took her place.

Mix and match a lion's head with a monkey's torso and talons for feet—the deck of cards her aunt had given her when she was a child. What should have been in the cabin video but wasn't?

Be-eep . . .

Jackie swerved to the shoulder. She shook her head to clear it, knowing answers never came if they were forced. But she kept returning to Amy. She was the key. Not the bondage video or the cabin tape. Something else.

Amy on the beach with Matt at Mazatlán. Lost, when she should have been on top of the world. White sand, blue sky, bikini . . .

The road was descending into Estes Park. A car approaching from the opposite direction flashed its brights to remind her it was almost dusk, and Jackie looked away. Traffic crawled through the tourist town, a pack of four-wheel-drives trying to maneuver through a herd of Winnebagos.

She was exhausted, hyped, and more than a little proud. This was the longest she'd ever been behind the wheel of a car, her first trip to the mountains—and after being in trial all week! No breakfast or lunch, running on adrenaline. Without Pilar to nag her, she had forgotten to eat. But with independence came an unaccustomed sense of power. That poky old SUV that escorted her through Left Hand Canyon? Who needed it? Jackie caught up with and passed the beat-up Audi she'd first seen in Ward. How had she let it get ahead?

Power . . . Control.

How ironic that her client felt such contempt for Bryan Lynch, when the same need drove them both. But if Ballard abducted Amy, the girl had proved more than a match for both men. The piercings and carvings Bonnie Lynch called "body art"—what had they meant to a teenage girl? Symbols of submission, enslavement? Or a means of exercising control? And not just over her own body, but over the men who oppressed her? Maybe they were Amy's own way of ensuring she would never be invisible. . . . And maybe the fact that *she* wielded the whip was what attracted *them.*

How arrogant to think she could dissect a girl she'd never met! Jackie reminded herself that she would never know what ran through Amy Lynch's head, any more than she could be sure what drove Glenn Ballard.

The herd of Winnebagos had thinned as Jackie left the tourist town of Estes Park. Four-wheel-drives once again ruled the road. The black-top widened and she was grateful for the last hint of remaining daylight. Trail Ridge Road began at the mouth of Rocky Mountain National Park. Could she possibly make it to Steamboat before it was pitch-dark?

At the gate to the national park Jackie fished in her briefcase for the entrance fee. Handing a bill to a ranger in a black-banded Smokey the Bear hat, she accepted her change without counting it.

"A little snow up ahead," he warned.

"Snow? At the end of July?"

"Not enough to close the road." He meant to reassure her. "Probably won't see it below eleven thousand feet."

"Eleven thousand *feet*?"

"Just stay away from the edge. . . ."

Trail Ridge Road started out with gentle loops and rolling vistas. The first hairpin came before Jackie expected it. Then began a much steeper climb.

Ba-*room*!

She rolled up her window just in time. The thunder was followed by an intense cloudburst. The four-wheel-drive in front of her flung a sheet of water onto her windshield, blinding her.

You've entered a tunnel, with one way in and one way out. No, not a tunnel, a—

Gripping the wheel, Jackie drove straight. The downpour abruptly stopped and the last rays of sun broke through the clouds.

Eyes on the yellow line, stay between it and the white.

The road climbed through high, rolling terrain. With evergreens on both sides she could pretend she was on flat ground. The mountains were lumpy and domed, massive ridges of granite sweeping down to a broad valley with rocks strewn across its floor. The SUV ahead of her proceeded at a comfortable clip and she kept pace. Suddenly it slowed. A taillight flickered and brightened.

Her friend from Left Hand Canyon?

Unlikely, but the notion was a relief. Her aunt always said help came when you least expected it. What was the harm in believing someone was looking out for her? The SUV passed a slower car with enough room for Jackie to follow, and she sped up to repeat the maneuver.

The higher she climbed, the more rapid the changes in terrain. Large outcrops of stone began to replace patches of spruce and pine. The trees themselves were stunted and sparse. The wind whistled. Her fingers curled around the steering wheel.

Eyes on the SUV.

Now the trees had branches only on the downwind side. A mountain in the distance looked like something had taken an enormous bite out of it, leaving a hole the size of an amphitheater. The light was almost gone and the road couldn't climb forever. Her hands were cramping and she was forgetting to breathe. Each thousand feet there was less oxygen in the air. But that was the least of her concerns. What would the way down—

Jackie had to get off this road right now.

What was the risk of pulling to a nonexistent shoulder at ten thousand feet? As she spotted a place ahead where the asphalt seemed to widen, she tapped her brakes. But instead of refuge, what she saw was Lily. A child who'd been terrified to leave home but had nonetheless gone because she didn't want to be ruled by fear. She was at a sickbed in Steamboat, waiting for Jackie. . . .

If you pull over now, nothing will ever change. You will always be afraid to drive and you will be of no use to the people you love, who are depending on you.

Forcing her eyes back to the road, she saw the comforting flicker of a taillight.

Place yourself in the hands of the driver of the SUV.

It threaded its way around slower vehicles, negotiating curves and timing each burst of speed with enviable control. Not even Pilar was that good. Jackie tried to catch a glimpse of the driver, but he was two feet higher off the pavement and all she could see was a Stetson. It had to be a guy; his confidence and economy of motion said male. Did he know she was depending on him?

The SUV's driver not only made good use of his ability to see at a greater distance, he extended the benefit of his vantage point to Jackie. He passed only where it was wide enough to do so safely, leaving room each time for her to follow, and soon they were the only vehicles in the westbound lane. The hat said rancher and the license plate was splattered with mud. Did he have a spread near Ballard's in Craig? Steamboat was on the way to Craig. Could she count on him to lead her there?

Jackie's thoughts returned to Ballard. Or rather, to Amy Lynch. A fragment of an image hovered like a mote of soot. Not from the cabin tape, nor Derek King's footage. The studio portrait? Not that either. Mix and match, cut and paste—pin the face of the girl in Mazatlán to the body of the quivering creature in the dog collar. . . . And then Jackie had it. What was missing from the cabin video was—

The Corolla caught a sudden gust and swayed. For the first time in many minutes Jackie looked out the passenger window. Broad terraces flowed from the roadbed to a canyon whose bottom she couldn't see. Just as she was about to panic, the taillight winked again.

If Stetson can do this, I can.

All at once the asphalt was white. On one side of the road dwarf bushes clung to bare rubble and the other dropped thousands of feet. There were no trees, just twenty-foot-tall stakes jutting out of the snow. Guides for plows—the only way to tell where the road ended and—

The blacktop narrowed and the Corolla was rocked by a huge blast of wind.

Eyes on the winking taillight, Jackie clung to the wheel. The road cut through sheer rock and she was momentarily plunged into blackness. On the other side of the cut the pavement widened and as it began to descend, there was a pull-off. She slowly unclenched her fingers.

She should have taken I-70.

Lightning shattered the inky sky and Jackie was shaking so badly she could hardly breathe. If it wasn't for that blessed SUV, she would have gone off the road. Now that there was an honest-to-God shoulder, the impulse to pull over was overwhelming. She could not spend another instant behind the wheel. Maybe she could flag someone and hitch the rest of the way. What lay at the bottom of this roller coaster? Grand Lake. A resort; there would be a bus to Steamboat. But what if no one stopped? A small van passed in the other direction, flashing its brights to remind Jackie to stay on her side of the road. A Volvo wagon was close behind. All the traffic was headed in the wrong direction.

She had to get to Lily.

The SUV had slowed. Would Stetson give her a ride? They'd traveled this far together. The wind was blowing so hard and the landscape was so barren they might have been on the moon. As if sensing her dilemma, the driver was pulling to the shoulder. Trembling with relief, Jackie began to follow.

Suddenly she was furious at herself.

Maybe Stetson could afford to stop, but she couldn't.

A split-rail fence separated the shoulder from a wasteland of rubble heaved to the surface in a violent peristalsis, and the SUV idled in the gravel by the fence. On the opposite side of the road lay a sheer drop of a thousand feet. The SUV's headlights illuminated a sharp curve just beyond the shoulder. There were no other cars. Stetson rolled down his window and leaned out.

The brim obscured his face, but there was something about the clean jaw that seemed familiar. Certainly there was nothing threatening in the way he craned his head. If anything, Stetson seemed bemused. Did he think she needed directions?

Jackie jerked on her emergency brake and shifted into park. She rolled down her window. Mindful of the snow-packed gravel beneath her wheels, she kept the engine running. Pellets of ice stung her cheeks and the wind was so loud she couldn't have heard Stetson if he'd shouted. He ducked his head back in. A graceful motion—was that familiar, too?

Stetson's lights were still on and the plume from his exhaust pipe told her the SUV's engine was running. The driver drummed his fingers on his door. He flicked the outside of the handle, as if contemplating opening it. What was he waiting for?

He raised his hand and signaled to Jackie.

Suggesting that she park? No—motioning her forward. Stetson didn't want her to wait for him. As she watched he leaned out his window again and turned to face her. Another wave, reassuring. A hint of impatience?

Come on, that gesture said.

I've been watching. You don't need me anymore.

You can do this.

Stetson leaned out farther and waved more insistently. He wanted her to pass him. Jackie released her emergency brake and shifted out of park. She tapped her accelerator and turned her wheel in the direction he pointed. Confident now, she kept her foot on the gas so the engine wouldn't stall as she traded gravel for asphalt. With her savior urging her on, she trod on the accelerator.

Just then an oversized truck hauling a camper hurtled around the curve straight at them. Without thinking, Jackie floored the gas and jerked her wheel in the opposite direction. As the truck thundered past, she heard the SUV's engine gun and its tires catch in the gravel.

The Corolla slammed through the fence and didn't stop until it smashed into a boulder three feet in circumference. Jackie went head-first into the steering wheel. Had she not been wearing her seat belt she would have gone through the windshield. In what felt like slow motion, she turned.

Behind her the SUV was skidding across the blacktop. As she watched in horror, it teetered at the edge. Oblivious to the freezing wind and the blood pouring down her face, she unfastened her seat belt and leaped from her car. At the last moment, Stetson righted his vehicle and hurtled back down Trail Ridge Road in the direction from which they had come.

Forty-Six

"What happened to your face?" Ballard asked.

It was Monday morning and they were waiting for Marlin Pitts to take the bench. The gash in Jackie's forehead had taken twelve stitches to close. From now on, she would be wearing bangs.

"Where were you Friday night?"

He didn't seem surprised at the question.

"Having dinner with Charlie Nesbit."

"All rise!"

Pitts called the court to order. Before instructing the bailiff to summon the jurors, he swept his courtroom for irregularities. Two easels were propped in front of the jury box. Mounted on each was a four-by-six-foot blowup of a girl.

"What are those?" he asked.

"Photographs of Amy Lynch," Jackie said.

The explanation was hardly necessary. One was the picture Phyllis Klein had used in her opening statement. Taken the night Amy was found, it showed the victim bruised and comatose, with the dog collar still around her throat. The other had been printed from a slide Pilar made from the cabin video over the weekend. Blurrier than its counterpart, it showed Amy twisting on the balls of her feet in the uncertain light.

"Hasn't that poor girl suffered enough?" Klein strode to the lectern. "I demand that Ms. Flowers take those down before the jury returns. She's obviously trying to prejudice the jurors."

"They're the same photos the prosecution has already placed into evidence," Jackie said from her seat at the defense table. "But I agree we should hold off on bringing the jury in. I have a motion for acquittal—"

"That's been denied!" Klein said.

"—on grounds there was no proof the video of Ms. Lynch and Judge Ballard was faked." Rising, Jackie walked to the center of the courtroom. "But according to the prosecution's expert, pictures can and do lie."

"I've already ruled," Pitts warned. "Unless you can establish the video couldn't have been made at the time of the abduction, I'm instructing the jury to disregard Dr. Bettendorf's testimony regarding compositing and digitization."

"Ms. Klein's own evidence proves the video was fabricated." Retrieving the pointer that had been leaning against one of the easels, Jackie directed the court's attention to the picture of Amy in the dog collar. "Ms. Lynch spent spring break in Mazatlán. She returned to Boulder just days before she was abducted. On the beach she wore a bikini." She traced the white lines that snaked from Amy's golden shoulders to a band across her breasts, and then the pale V of her pubis.

Jackie turned to the blowup of the slide taken from the video. Despite the graininess of the image and the weak lighting under which it had been shot, Amy's skin was uniformly pale.

"No bikini marks. The video had to have been composited from footage taken of Amy before she was abducted at the end of March. On that ground, I move that all charges against Judge Ballard be—"

"You can't do that!" Klein shouted. "None of this has been placed into evidence!"

"Are you denying that these came from your own photograph and videotape?" Jackie said.

"No—but the weight they should be given is for the jurors to decide." Klein turned to Pitts. A moment earlier she'd claimed the pictures were too prejudicial for the jurors to see; now she was advocating that the same people be the sole arbiters of their worth. "You can't take this case away from them!"

Marlin Pitts stared at the images of Amy Lynch.

Jackie didn't envy his dilemma. On Friday he'd said on the record that unless she could prove the video had *not* been made at the time Amy was abducted, Jackie couldn't argue it was fabricated. He'd reiterated his ruling not five minutes earlier. He also knew that once the jurors saw those photos side by side, Glenn Ballard would likely walk. Edna Massie alone was enough to hang them. And rather than ending his own career having brought low the high and mighty, he would be the butt of every joke at the state judicial conference for years to come.

Phyllis Klein tried again.

"I have a rebuttal witness."

"Rebuttal?" Jackie replied. "I haven't called any witnesses."

Pitts saw a way out. "Do you intend to put on a case?"

Jackie didn't blink.

"No, Your Honor. The defense rests."

Ballard pushed back his chair but Klein spoke before he could act.

"Then we'll reopen our case!"

"You said you had a rebuttal witness," Jackie said. "Unless we put on a case, there's nothing to rebut."

In desperation, Klein scanned the gallery. Jackie knew she was looking for Lanny Greer. The DA had slithered out of the courtroom when Jackie picked up the pointer. In the last row Jimmy Phipps sat with Whitney Grais. He probably wanted to see Jackie in action before asking her to join his boutique. Catching Jackie's eye, Whitney shot her a thumbs-up.

Klein threw down her ace.

"If Amy Lynch's abduction and murder were part of a massive—and incredible!—scheme to frame a federal judge, who's behind it? Ms. Flowers has offered not one shred of proof as to the identity—"

"It's not the defense's burden to solve the case for the prosecution," Jackie said. "But since Ms. Klein asked, I'll be happy to provide her with any leads my investigator has worked."

Phyllis was apoplectic. The last thing she wanted was the opportunity to prove she'd prosecuted an innocent man. Pitts spared her that burden.

"That won't be necessary, Ms. Flowers. Rather than taking your motion under advisement, I'm prepared to rule now."

Marlin Pitts was no shill for the prosecution. Gazing out over his courtroom, he milked the moment for all it was worth. Given no alternative, he had the guts to do what was *right*.

"I'm granting the motion for acquittal."

He banged his gavel twice.

"All charges against Glenn Ballard are dismissed."

Jackie's last thought before pandemonium broke out was that her future was at last secure. There was no way Phyllis Klein could hurt her now.

"Splendid job, Counselor."

Her client's words meant more to Jackie than she'd imagined.

They were standing in the back corridor of the Boulder Justice Center, waiting for the crush of reporters and well-wishers to dissipate. Whitney had given her an exultant hug and Jimmy Phipps said she'd be hearing from him and his partners the next morning. A jubilant Pilar had left to bring the Spider to the back entrance so she and Jackie could make a getaway.

"Doing anything to celebrate?" Jackie realized how little she knew about Glenn Ballard's personal life.

"I'm going back to my chambers."

She smiled as she remembered the fancy cologne. Maybe he did have a toots on the side.

"Do you have any idea what this trial has done to my docket?" he continued.

"Your docket?"

"This will be the first time in three months that I've entered the United States District Courthouse a free man," he said softly. "I'm rather looking forward to it."

So his ordeal *had* meant something to Ballard. Maybe it would affect how he handled his court. "There's something we need to talk about."

"If you're referring to the rather testy manner in which I—"

She brushed his apology away. He'd gotten his justice.

But what about Trail Ridge Road?

"You were framed, Glenn. Don't you want to know by whom?"

"The only thing that matters is it's over. I just want to get back on the bench."

It was late afternoon by the time Jackie and Pilar left Boulder. The media had staked out every exit, and even after they got tired of waiting for Jackie to show her face, she had other matters to attend to. Ballard wanted her to ensure everything seized from his home and chambers would be returned, and the clerks at the DA's office had no incentive to hurry. It wasn't until she settled back in the passenger seat of the Spider that she realized how exhausted she really was.

"How's your head feel?" Pilar asked.

"Like someone's stabbing it with a thousand needles."

"Can they do anything with the Corolla?"

Jackie shook her head.

"Totaled."

"I can't believe you drove on Trail Ridge Road. . . . Did you talk to Lily?"

"She's fine. Her headmistress in Steamboat was really upset that someone called Pitts's chambers with a phony claim that Lily had meningitis."

"Can you believe someone would use your affection for a little girl like that?" Pilar paused. The weekend had been so hectic that they hadn't really discussed what had happened. "Who do you think the driver was?"

"I gave the Rocky Mountain Park police a description of the SUV, but I'm useless when it comes to cars. The license plate was covered with mud. Not that it would've mattered."

Knowing how impossible it was for her to keep a sequence of numbers straight, they both laughed. But the reminder that an attempt had been made on her life forced Jackie to face what she could no longer put off.

Whoever tried to send her into the path of that truck must have killed Ted.

Pilar read her mind.

"It's over now. You said it yourself, there's no way to identify the mastermind. And you have no proof that the person who framed Ballard had anything to do with Ted's death."

"What about the porn king Dennis represents?"

"What about him? Just because he owned that restaurant doesn't mean he lured Ted there and killed him. And even if he did, do you really think someone as sophisticated as that would've done it himself?"

"So what should I do? I can't just—"

"Drop it."

"I can't do that. I owe it to Ted!"

"What you owe Ted is to have a fancy dinner, go home, and get a good night's sleep. Tomorrow is a new day. You want to be fresh when Jimmy Phipps calls about the new job."

"I'm not sure I'm ready."

Pilar turned with sudden anger.

"You want to pay your debt? Use this win to get the hell out of that rat hole where you've been hiding since you left the PD's office. Ted would have wanted you to dance with the stars!" Her voice softened. "Don't kid yourself, Jackie. You may never get another chance."

The Seventeenth Street skyline loomed.

"You're right . . . about everything. Including that dinner."

"It's only six. I can still get us a reservation at—"

"I need to be alone." Jackie saw the hurt on her friend's face. "You know how I am after a trial."

She waited until the Spider turned onto Seventeenth.

"Pull over."

Dennis Ross's office was half a block away.

"I know something else to do after a trial," Pilar guessed shrewdly.

Jackie reached for the door.

"I'm going to treat myself to a steak and a cab home."

"Um-hmm . . . Want me to call later and make sure you're safely in bed?"

"Don't wait up, Mom."

Forty-Seven

Greenery and glass muffled the sound of accountants and lawyers jumping ship at the end of the first day of the workweek. As Jackie punched the button for the elevators that led to the upper decks of this office tower luxury liner, the steel doors swished open and discharged a horde of men in pinstriped suits and their female counterparts in rayon and crepe.

Suddenly conscious of the surgical tape on her brow, Jackie tugged at her hair to cover it. Stepping into the now-empty elevator, with its pink marble walls striated with crystal and the strains of Vivaldi emanating from invisible speakers, she hit the button for the thirtieth floor. The doors whispered shut and she caught her reflection in their polished surface.

Over the weekend her forehead had hatched an egg, and Mercurochrome bled past the corners of the tape. She'd been instructed not to shower until the stitches were removed. Her hair was a rat's nest and her linen suit was a mess from the ride in the Spider. . . .

The doors opened into the lobby of Kellogg & Kemp.

At six o'clock the receptionist was as fresh as the bouquet of long-stemmed roses on her granite desk. A far cry from the temps at the dead-end club, Jackie thought, but as of tomorrow they would no longer be her concern. As the door pinged shut the girl glanced up with a professional smile. When she saw the bandage on Jackie's forehead, her expression froze.

"Is Dennis Ross in?" Jackie asked.

The receptionist looked at her dubiously.

"Tell him Jackie Flowers is here."

The girl murmured into her headset.

"You can go straight back."

The offices were identified by brass nameplates and Jackie caught glimpses of men in shirtsleeves at glossy desks, staring out floor-to-ceiling windows as they talked on the phone. Furnished with leather sofas and expensive artwork, the corner offices opened onto private conference rooms. At the PD's office seniority meant your cubicle was that much more crammed with paper and exhibits. No wonder Dennis had left. But was Kellogg & Kemp where he belonged?

Through a crack in the door at the second corner office, she saw a pair of wing tips propped on a mahogany desk in front of a vibrant oil painting. She rapped lightly.

Dennis straightened in his chair.

"Come in."

The first thing Jackie registered was how happy he was to see her. The second how glad she was that she'd come.

"Close the door behind you."

As she did, she saw the metal sign hanging on the reverse side. It was shot through with bullet holes.

NO BEAR HUNTING IN THIS DUMP.

They'd stolen it on the way home from the camping trip they took after Dennis's client broke his nose. Five lifetimes ago.

"That used to hang on the outside of your door."

He reached into his bottom drawer and pulled out a bottle of scotch.

"At the PD's my office *was* a dump."

Dennis tilted the bottle at her and Jackie nodded.

God, she needed it!

He poured them each two fingers of whisky. Jackie raised her glass in a toast.

"To the old days."

Dennis met her eyes. Memories flashed before her.

They hadn't spent the entire three days in that musty sleeping bag. Jackie remembered waking up entangled with him, smelling the sex they'd had the night before, hungry for it again. And jumping naked in the freezing lake while Dennis tried to catch a fish. They'd stopped at a landfill on the way home and Jackie had scrambled down the slope to steal the sign.

"What the hell happened?" he asked.

To them—or her forehead?

Jackie chose the easy way out. "I had an accident."

"It obviously didn't cramp your style." Dennis saluted her with his glass. "Your win was on the news."

"Would you have called?"

Dennis loosened his tie. "I hope to God not."

"Why?"

"A lot has changed, Jackie. Not all for the worse." His gesture encompassed his lavish digs, then he smiled sardonically. "I forgot you're a hard woman to impress."

"You said I was a sucker to believe in my client. Why come through for me in the end?"

"It was *you* who broke up."

And there it was. Their last fight.

She had refused to marry him because she knew he wanted kids.

"But you still helped me."

Dennis refilled their drinks and brought the bottle with him to the couch. He leaned back with his hands behind his head. She settled beside him and slipped off her pumps. The painting behind his desk suited him. Not a print, an original. Slashes of crimson and swirls of cobalt. The trial lawyer's slash-and-burn.

"Not much," he said.

"If you hadn't told me what you suspected, I might have given up on Ballard's defense. Do you really think your client was behind it?"

Dennis slipped his arm around her. "Too big a coincidence. When I heard about Ted . . ."

"I never could understand why you hated each other."

"I didn't hate him. I guess I was . . . jealous. He meant more to you than other clients." He pulled her closer and their bodies molded in a familiar way. "If I'd gone to you sooner, maybe Ted—"

"Shh." Jackie touched his lips. "Let's not talk about it."

And then his lips were touching hers. Softly at first, then more insistently. How could she have waited this long?

It was Dennis who finally disengaged.

"That must hurt like hell." He gently brushed the hair from her brow and she knew he was remembering Bear Lake. "My nose, your forehead—we make quite a pair. You think I'm some kind of hero, don't you?"

"You believe in your oath."

Dennis rose from the couch. "You don't know me at all."

"Dennis, you don't owe me—"

"You're wrong, Jackie. I owe you big." He poured them both another shot. After tossing his back, he leaned against his desk. "I've got to say this, and for once you're going to shut up and listen."

The scotch burned Jackie's throat. Did she know what was coming?

"I gave that transcript to the *News*," he said.

"What?"

Dennis repeated it slowly and distinctly.

"I'm the one who gave the transcript of your grand jury hearing to that reporter."

"Why?"

"I thought it would help you. Phyllis Klein was rabid, she was savaging your reputation. The press was eating it up. The only way to protect you was to leak what was really happening behind that grand jury room door."

"Bullshit!" Jackie cried. "You did it because you were pissed off!"

"You know how much it hurt when you ended it? The *way* you ended it? You never even told me why!"

Jackie was on her feet.

"You bastard. You went to South America and left me holding the bag!"

"I never thought you'd be accused—"

"Who did you think would be blamed? Why didn't you protect me?"

"When I left, you were the toast of the town for getting that grand jury dismissed." Dennis was angry too. "I didn't know the shit hit the fan until I got back. By then it was too late."

"Too late for what?" Jackie pulled on her shoes. "A call to the PD to set the record straight?"

"You'd already left. I tried to call *you,* if you remember. But Pilar said you didn't want to talk."

"That's all my reputation was worth? A couple of lousy calls?"

He reached for her. "If you want, I'll go public with it right now."

Jerking her arm free, Jackie flung it at the painting on his wall.

"And lose all *this*?"

"Didn't our relationship mean anything to you?"

She grabbed her briefcase and threw open his door.

"It's always a pleasure to be fucked by a *friend*."

Forty-Eight

Jackie was so furious she could barely see. She punched the button for the elevator three times and when it arrived, she entered and turned her back to the door. How dare Dennis blame her for his betrayal? She'd been crazy to think they could recover what they'd lost.

And now she knew even that was a sham.

Ping.

The elevator signaled its arrival at another floor and Jackie was forced to face forward. A laughing couple entered, the man with his arm around the woman's waist. They wore suits and carried briefcases but it was after hours and they were finally free. With barely a glance in Jackie's direction they began kissing. How she wished she could erase the taste of Dennis's lips! Staring stiffly at the door, she had no choice but to confront her own reflection.

And what about *you*? she thought.

Whether Dennis had acted out of love or anger, hadn't she played some role in the outcome? What if she'd told him how afraid she was to have children? That they would have to fight the same battles she confronted every day—or spend their lives fixing radios? Would he still have wanted to marry her? At least he would have understood *why*.

The elevator opened onto the main lobby and Jackie quickly wiped her eyes. As she waited for the light on Seventeenth Street, the air cooled her burning cheeks.

What was it Pilar had said about a new beginning?

Night had fallen and taxis accounted for most of the traffic. Denver's answer to Wall Street was a dead zone after work. Should she make good on her promise and treat herself to a steak? But even the thought of food was repellent. Bed, then, and the call in the morning from Jimmy Phipps. She smiled ruefully. Well, she could thank Ballard for *that*.

As she waited for a cab to cruise by, Jackie wondered what her former client was doing. Sorting through the accumulation of files on his desk, she imagined. His reward for the acquittal.

Odd that Ballard wasn't more concerned about who'd set him up.

He hadn't even wanted to know who Jackie thought it might be.

She waved at a taxi, only to realize there was a passenger in the backseat.

If the mastermind was a pornographer, the method by which Ballard had been framed made sense. What would be more ironic—and more humiliating to Ballard!—than revealing that the judge who'd brought that industry to its knees was himself into kinky sex? And with a girl he'd seen in chains on the Web?

Of course, if it was Dennis's porn client who had shot at the king and missed, he would be in no rush to repeat the attempt. With all charges against Ballard dismissed and the prosecution so soundly discredited, the next person who thought about framing a federal judge would have to think twice.

But what if it wasn't Dennis's client?

And what if humiliating Ballard wasn't the goal—but destroying him was?

No matter how angry at her father she'd been, Amy Lynch was no gullible child. It had taken ingenuity to lure her from a crowded bar. The cabin, the cuffs, the videotape . . . It had taken even more ingenuity to fabricate and plant the evidence that would ensure Ballard's arrest and conviction. Whoever did it must have planned it for a long time. Would someone who hated him enough to do that give up so easily?

If Dennis was right, Ballard's antagonist had also been desperate enough to trick Ted into meeting him, and then to torch his own restaurant to prevent Ted from revealing what he knew. She tried to remember what Ted had said when she warned him to stop. He'd been talking to an old friend, something about a dog. Dog collar? That would make sense; Ted's informant would have used his knowledge about Amy's abduction as the carrot to lure Ted to the restaurant. But an old friend? Was it someone Ted knew—or recognized?

Whoever the killer was, he'd also been desperate enough that when Jackie came close to exposing the frame in court, he'd tried to kill her on that mountain. And he'd done it in a clever way. She had no idea what the killer had said to convince Ted to meet him at the bistro, but she did know how Stetson had lured her to Trail Ridge Road.

He'd used a little girl who was precious to Jackie.

Did that sound like the actions of a porno king?

And what about the evidence the killer had planted in Ballard's chambers?

Getting into the federal courthouse after hours couldn't have been easy. The parking garage was heavily secured, but Ballard himself had said anyone who really knew what he was doing could get in. How many people knew that the back door to a judge's chambers remained automatically unlocked if the judge used it as his private exit? That would explain how the killer had gotten hold of the handcuffs, particularly if Ballard left them in an unlocked drawer. But the killer must have had an accomplice . . . And it had to be someone close to Ballard himself. Not just a student of the judge's habits, but someone physically close enough to use Ballard's computer to access Derek King's website at home and in his chambers, and to plant the fabricated video.

At night, downtown Denver was a canyon of steel and glass. Jackie peered up Seventeenth in the direction of the federal courthouse. The empty skyscrapers towering above her evoked the same disquiet she'd experienced driving through Left Hand with Pilar.

She had to warn Ballard.

Forty-Nine

The federal courthouse rotunda was almost deserted when Jackie arrived. She handed her briefcase to the sleepy court security officer by the X-ray machine.

"Who are you here to see, miss?"

"Judge Ballard. I'm his lawyer."

The CSO ambled to his telephone. With the receiver at his ear, he watched her while he waited for Ballard's chambers to answer.

"No one there."

Jackie stepped through the gate and grabbed her briefcase before the CSO could think the better of it. "He told me to meet him in his courtroom."

"Want me to go with you?"

"No, that's okay. I know where it is."

"Well, all right then . . ."

So much for Fortress America.

He stood by while she waited for the elevator. Jackie's eyes went to his polyester blazer. No gun. How could she have forgotten? Only the U.S. Marshals were allowed to carry weapons inside the federal courthouse. She pressed the button for the eighth floor.

The elevator opened onto a deserted hallway. The smell of ammonia said the night crew had come and left. She peered through the glass in the door to Ballard's courtroom. It was dark except for a night-light over the bench. She pulled the handle. The door was unlocked. All that security left in the hands of a single cleaning woman!

To the right of Ballard's bench was a door to the judges' private corridor. The artificial light in the hallway made the carpet look like linoleum, and the scent of floral air freshener tickled Jackie's nose. Suppressing a sneeze, she crossed the hall to Ballard's chambers and rattled the knob. It turned in her hand.

Betty would never have left without locking up. Ballard must be there.

Why worry about the back door when you left the front one unlocked?

The wraparound desk where Ballard's secretary sat was covered with neat stacks of paper. While Ballard was fighting for his liberty, his staff had been keeping the home fires burning. The security camera on the wall behind Betty's chair monitored the corridor from which Jackie had just come; glancing at the screen, she saw the hall was empty. In the library at the opposite end of the chambers, a light burned.

"Anybody here?"

It was empty.

She returned to the reception area, checking the clerks' offices on her way. The door to Ballard's private office was ajar and a light seemed to be coming from a back room. She hesitated. Maybe he was in the john.

"Glenn?"

Nothing.

She pushed open the door.

Ballard's inner sanctum was even more austere and cavernous at night than by day. A floor lamp between the display of gavels and the window on the west wall cast a glow on the scales at the threshold to the project room. The rest of the office was in shadows.

"Glenn?"

No answer.

Suspended by chains from their brass bar, in the dim light the scales were a cross between miniature flying saucers and a baptismal font. An apt symbol for a man who prided himself on calling shots as he saw them. Next to the scales hung his Order of the Coif certificate. The knight with the doily on his wig had epitomized to Jackie all she'd been denied, but now she thought him oddly fitting. The Coif and scales defined the two irreconcilable sides of Glenn Ballard: elitism and impartiality.

"Jackie?"

The cultured voice made her turn.

Whitney Grais stood at the threshold to Ballard's private office. The PR woman was still dressed in the silk suit she'd worn that morning in Boulder but had let down her hair. As it fell to her shoulders in luxuriant waves, her jade jacket made it flame.

"What are you doing here?" Jackie asked.

Whitney's eyes were very bright.

"Glenn and I stopped by on our way to dinner." Sensing Jackie's confusion, she added, "Didn't he tell you we were seeing each other?"

The sexy cologne.

"How long has that been going on?"

"About a year." She smiled. "Remember what I said about dating clients? The more discreet ones don't like to be seen with a PR woman on their arm. And no one is more discreet than a federal judge. You know that."

Glenn Ballard had been living on the edge in more ways than one.

For a federal judge, avoiding contact with public relations people was more than a matter of discretion. An open display of ambition could destroy the prospect of nomination to a higher bench faster than a 100 percent reversal rate. The lengths to which he must have gone to conceal his relationship with Whitney were amusing, particularly under the recent glare of the national spotlight.

"Where is he now?"

"He stepped out." Whitney was the last person Jackie had expected to encounter here, but she showed no curiosity as to why Jackie was there. She stepped past Jackie into the office proper with a proprietary gesture. As if she'd been there many times. "Speaking of clients, have you heard from Jimmy Phipps?"

"He's calling in the morning."

"They're quite excited at the prospect of you joining the boutique. But to give you a heads up, they have one question."

"What's that?"

"Why you left the Public Defender's office." She smiled again. "I'm afraid I may have been the one who put that bug in their ear. My weakness is I allow myself to get so involved with my clients that I can never leave well enough alone." She paused. "Did you know there's a nasty story floating around about the circumstances under which you departed? Something about a grand jury transcript."

"I had nothing to do with that."

Whitney wandered over to Ballard's desk. Where was he?

"You don't have to convince me, dear. The question is, will Jimmy and his partners believe you?" She reached for the silver pen in the teak stand and turned it over to admire its inscription. "Trial lawyers are so careful about their reputations. Of course, whatever I tell them will probably suffice."

"Where did you hear about the transcript?"

"After those dreadful charges against Glenn were dismissed, I had the most interesting conversation with Phyllis Klein." Reading Jackie's expression, she reflexively tapped the pen against the glass top of the desk. "Yes, yes, I know. Sour grapes and all that. But there is a certain logic to her suspicions, you'll grant her that?"

"I told you, I had nothing—"

"Jackie, you're talking to a friend. Who do you think recommended you to Glenn Ballard?"

So that was why he'd hired her. But it didn't explain what was in it for Whitney.

"Don't you see, Jackie? There's only one way to clear your name. If you didn't leak the transcript, who did? One name and it all goes away. Not even Glenn needs to know."

If Whitney didn't believe Jackie was the leak, why would she think Jackie knew who was? If she expected her to betray Dennis, she had another think coming. . . . But why was Whitney bargaining with her at all? Was there something Jackie had that Whitney wanted? Or was she just playing with her?

Flick, flick went Whitney's thumbnail. Like tapping ash from a cigar.

Where had Jackie seen that gesture before?

"You've been orchestrating his campaign," Jackie said. "Those interviews and speeches—were they all part of a plan to advance his career?"

Whitney shrugged.

"Today the Court of Appeals, tomorrow—"

"—the Supreme Court."

"With a judge as talented as Glenn, the sky's the limit. There's always been something larger than his acquittal at stake."

"You haven't told me how the two of you met."

"Funny you should ask. It was in court. . . ."

Flick, flick.

Whitney holding the makeup brush while she prepared Jackie for that photo shoot. Ted Wolsky had been entranced. . . . At a sound behind her, Jackie turned.

Glenn Ballard stood in the back doorway. How long had he been there?

"We've just been talking about you," Whitney said. "Your counselor wishes you luck on the Court of Appeals."

Ballard smiled but Jackie sensed his predicament.

"My relationship with Whitney could be very embarrassing for me," he told her. "My reputation is my future. You're an attorney, you know what loyalty means. You wouldn't do anything to harm me."

"But I'm not the only one who knows about your ambitions." Jackie looked from Ballard to Whitney. "Are you sure you can trust her?"

"Whitney? You must be joking!"

Flick, flick . . .

"—knows everything about me," Ballard was saying. Crossing to the desk, he put his arm around the PR woman's shoulders. As his hand tightened on her silken sleeve, Jackie saw the power in his grip. So different from the tentative touch of the man in black. "We're a team. Once the Tenth Circuit nomination is made, we plan to announce our engagement."

"How long have you known each other?"

"A little over a year." He gave Whitney's shoulder another squeeze. "One of her clients introduced us."

"I thought you met in court."

"Court?" Ballard shook his head. "No, it was—"

"That's what Whitney said."

He looked at Jackie in confusion.

"Isn't that right, Whitney?" Jackie continued.

"Fifteen years is such a long time," she demurred, "I hardly expected Glenn to remember."

Ted's old friend.

"What kind of a case was it?" Jackie asked.

"Just a small matter, so insignificant no one would remember. . . ."

"Try us."

"Fresh out of college with a BFA in theater, I was hired by a small cosmetics company to develop face powder." Whitney's eyes flashed and her voice rose. "I had an idea for a new line of lipstick and gloss and they said whatever I did on my own time belonged to me. When Portia bought that company a year later, Portia said my work belonged to them. It was so unjust. They were *my* ideas."

Jackie, that story was mine!

The humiliation and rage of a child denied credit for her achievement. The need to punish for an injustice that went to the core of her identity. To make her persecutor pay. . . . Whitney was the girl Ted had seen so long ago in Ballard's court. But it must have been more than the way she clicked her pen to make him remember.

Flick, flick . . .

And not just recognize her when he ran into her at Jackie's office years later, but be willing to meet her at a LoDo bistro after closing hours.

Ballard was looking at Whitney as if he'd never seen her before.

Flick . . .

Fingers drumming a metal door. Just before they waved Jackie into the path of a truck on that mountain road. Whitney was Stetson. But why?

"What about your lawyer?" Jackie asked. "Didn't he defend you?"

"Against a giant like Portia? Glenn was my last hope." Whitney's green eyes blazed at Ballard. "But you don't remember that, darling, do you?"

Ballard shook his head.

"I honestly don't." Just as he'd forgotten Jackie as a student.

"Do you know how many questions you asked, before you let them take everything I had? Exactly one." Whitney's voice deepened in imitation of his. "'Just one question for your client, Counselor. Did you sign that contract, Ms. Grais?' When I said yes, you wouldn't let me say another word. I was worthless, defenseless. You—you stripped me bare. You muzzled me like a dog."

A naked girl in a studded collar.

"You ordered me to complete my work on that lipstick and turn it over to Portia. For two years I was *in bondage. . . .*"

"A year for each day you kept Amy strung up in chains before she escaped."

"I made her crawl on her hands and knees. Just like Glenn did to me. She didn't want to talk. Too scared, I guess . . ." Whitney laughed. "You think I'm heartless? Glenn likes fine things, and Amy was beautiful. I left her face alone."

There was more than one kind of torture, wasn't there? Each insult to that girl's spirit had been a reenactment of what Whitney felt she'd suffered. And she'd tried to inflict that degradation on Ballard.

"Look at him now, he still doesn't remember! Snuffing out my future was all in a day's work, because as a human being I meant nothing to him."

Law school isn't a charity ward, Ms. Flowers. . . . Frankly, I'll be amazed if you pass the bar.

But no matter how unfeeling Ballard had been, he'd only done what he believed was right. Whitney wasn't righteous—she was insane. By killing two innocent people she'd defiled the very justice she claimed she was denied. And her plans were hardly over. The ultimate revenge would be to reveal her persecutor's ambitions to the world on the eve of his nomination to the Court of Appeals.

But Ballard was mesmerized.

He was staring at Whitney with the same bemused fascination he'd displayed when the Boulder detectives discovered the videotape. The same look he'd given Phyllis Klein when she goaded him about taking the stand. Revulsion and—admiration?

Jackie had to break the spell.

"How did you get Amy to leave Finnegan's Wake?"

Whitney didn't blink.

"She wanted to be a model, didn't she? Anything but like that pathetic excuse of a mother." What she tapped into for her clients—their vulnerabilities. What made them special. How she'd recognized Lily's isolation and bonded so effortlessly with her at the opera house. What had she played on with Ted, his chance to finally be a hero? And Jackie's own ambition to break out of her dead-end practice. "If there's one thing I know, it's girls. And it had to be Amy. She was the only one it could be."

And Jackie was the only lawyer Ballard could have hired.

Whitney had thought she could control Jackie; she'd been Phyllis Klein's "anonymous source" from the very start. Even if she hadn't stacked the odds, just having Jackie on the defense side would have goaded Phyllis into doing whatever it took to win.

Until Jackie tumbled to the compositing of the video, the defense could only have lost. When things began to change, Whitney used Lily to lure Jackie onto Trail Ridge Road. How well she'd read Jackie on that score!

And when that failed she'd hoped just now to blackmail Jackie into keeping her mouth shut by threatening to destroy her future at the litigation boutique. Did Whitney have any idea it was Dennis who leaked that transcript? The one thing she'd misjudged was Jackie's willingness to betray a man she'd loved in order to dance with the stars. . . . But Whitney's words echoed in Jackie's head.

"Why did it have to be Amy?"

"I'll let Glenn answer that," Whitney said. "But that would mean kissing the Court of Appeals good-bye."

Ballard was silent. Bemused detachment, his trademark on the bench? Now Jackie felt the tension in his coiled physique. His watchfulness masked not dispassion but *arousal*.

"She never meant for you to have that promotion," Jackie warned. "Not after killing two people to destroy you!"

Whitney pointed at his prized certificate.

"Look at that, Jackie. Do you know what the coif used to be?"

Ballard's secretary had told her the history of that cap. Before they wore wigs, it had been some kind of headdress, covering all but the—

"—hood," Whitney was saying. "It was a white hood."

Amy's hood.

Whitney stood at the arched threshold to the project room. Above her head the brass crosspiece to the scales of justice gleamed. "Think about that video, Jackie, when Amy was in chains. Ever wonder why the rafter doesn't show? Maybe that's because that sequence wasn't shot at the cabin at all."

"It was composited," Jackie said. "We proved that!"

"You thought the footage with Amy and Glenn was faked. Did it occur to you those were the only parts that were *real*?"

What Whitney was saying was impossible—wasn't it?

In Jackie's mind's eye, subject and setting abruptly reversed. The frame was the cabin and not the players. Could Ballard have shot the sequence with Amy as a willing participant before she went to Mazatlán, never dreaming it could be combined with independent footage of his uncle's cabin to engineer a fraud? No wonder Amy's roommate said everything after Mazatlán had changed. . . . And if Ballard had taped Amy hanging from the brass bar, even the lighting would have been right—weak sun from the west, backlit by the project room . . . no abrasions on her hands and knees. Those had come later. Much later.

No wonder he'd passed the polygraph. And no wonder he wanted to pin his defense on the only question whose answer he didn't fear.

If Whitney was telling the truth, he and Amy had never been *at the cabin.*

"He would have to have known her," Jackie protested.

But hadn't Derek King testified he'd posted other pictures of Amy on the Web? They'd been taken at work and on campus, with Amy playing out her life as a normal coed. Maybe Ballard had targeted her. . . . Every Saturday night on his home computer. But who had logged on—Ballard or Whitney?

This was crazy.

"You never give up, do you?" Jackie told Whitney. "What comes after the Court of Appeals, the final kill?"

Whitney reached over her head and grabbed one of the scales. It slipped off the rod into her hands. Holding it by its chain, she swung it at Jackie like a mace.

"Whitney—"

She let loose and five pounds of brass hurtled straight at Jackie's head. Jackie tried to turn but the scale struck her shoulder and knocked her to the floor. Through her pain she looked up and saw Whitney coming at her with her fingers outstretched. Green fire flashed and Jackie put her hands over her face.

Whump.

Wood on bone. A splitting sound.

A crushing weight collapsed onto Jackie. She heard something crack and for one horrible instant, she couldn't breathe. She tried to fill her lungs. A cloying perfume engulfed her. A sticky wetness touched her face.

"Jackie?"

The Texas gavel Ballard was holding was shiny with blood.

He was trembling. With rage—or *exultation*? As Jackie stared into his eyes, she did not know which. His next words rang in her head.

"She'll never hurt us again."

Fifty

"When does Lily arrive?"

"The bus from Steamboat gets in at three," Jackie said. "She goes back to school in another week."

Pilar plopped the *Post* on her boss's desk.

"Want a lift to the station?"

"I can manage it myself." Under Pilar's guidance she'd had more than a month to get used to a rental car, but this would be Jackie's first solo voyage since Trail Ridge Road.

The wall trembled as something the size of a body crashed into it and slid to the floor. Pilar shook her head in disgust.

"I refuse to broker another deal between Cliff and that Xerox machine. I don't care whether he's petitioning social security for death benefits for Ted's mother or not, you'll have to call in a professional."

"Remember what happened the last time we did that?"

"Okay, okay!" Pilar threw up her hands. "For the time being, you've earned your peace. So to speak." She cast a dirty look in the direction of the office next door, then brightened. "Did you hear who fired Kellogg and Kemp?"

"I couldn't care less."

"Bryan and Bonnie Lynch! And they're selling their house in Hilltop and moving to a fancy spread out in Cherry Hills."

Still together, but with more room to be apart.

"You know what else?" Pilar reached for the *Post* and without waiting for Jackie's assent began to read.

"'The President of the United States today announced his nomination of United States District Judge Glenn Ballard to the vacant seat on the Tenth Circuit Court of Appeals. With the retirement of Chief Judge Simon Clark, District Judge Charles Nesbit was sworn in as the new Chief Judge of the United States District Court. . . . Judge Ballard was acquitted six weeks ago of all charges in a case in which a former defendant in his court, Ms. Whitney Grais, had attempted to frame him for the heinous abduction, torture, and murder of Boulder coed Amy Lynch. Ballard demonstrated his unwavering faith in the judicial system by mounting a vigorous and successful defense to the charges. Just hours after his acquittal, his attorney, Jackie Flowers, was brutally attacked in Judge Ballard's chambers at the United States Courthouse. Judge Ballard saved Ms. Flowers's life by striking her attacker on the head, a blow which proved fatal—'"

"I've heard enough," Jackie said.

Ballard's courageous act had been almost universally hailed.

Only one person had her doubts.

"Whitney certainly was good for our business," Pilar said. She folded the newspaper and stuffed it in the wastebasket. Jackie had turned down the litigation boutique; not only had Whitney's association made the move unappetizing, but leaving this place felt disloyal. Didn't she owe more to Ted's memory than social security benefits? "Phone's been ringing off the hook. Speaking of which, how long do you intend to keep Dennis Ross in the doghouse?"

"What makes you think he's anywhere on these premises?"

"A temp may be manning the phones, but I keep track of the messages." Reaching into her vest pocket, Pilar produced a wad of pink slips. "Twice a day for six goddamn weeks. Is he trying for some kind of record?"

"Dennis always did have more guts than sense."

"Well, are you gonna call him back?"

Jackie allowed herself the luxury of a shrug. It was a little difficult with a dislocated shoulder and three broken ribs. "I'm in no rush."

"What're you doing tonight?"

"Lily's sleeping over. She wants to tell me about a friend she made at camp."

"Is three a crowd?"

"With you? Never."

Pilar rose. "I'll pick up the veggie pizza."

On her way out, she tossed the message slips in the trash.

Jackie had his number.

ABOUT THE AUTHOR

Stephanie Kane, born and raised in Brooklyn, has clerked for the Colorado Supreme Court and been both a partner in a top Denver law firm and a criminal defense attorney. The author of *Quiet Time* and *Blind Spot,* she is married to a federal judge and lives in Denver, Colorado.